Had the roaring decreased? She wasn't sure.

"How you doing?" he asked.

She could hear him now. He wasn't shouting.

"I don't want to die," she whispered. The words came as a surprise to her. Yesterday there was nothing she wanted to do. Nowhere she wanted to go. And now she just wanted to see the sky again. Dive into cold water. Inhale the scent of peonies.

"We're both going to live." He brushed his cheek against hers. "I'll keep you safe, Meadow. It won't get you."

She closed her eyes and tried to control the ball of pain that wanted to escape her throat as a sob. She failed. Here she had thought there was only a thin veil of foil between her and the fire. But it wasn't so. Dylan stood between her and the flames. He protected her with his body and his promise and she loved him for it.

D1136672

FIREWOLF

BY
JENNA KERNAN

First Published in Great Britain 2017
By Mills & Boon, an imprint of HarperCollins*Publishers*
1 London Bridge Street, London, SE1 9GF

© 2017 Jeannette H. Monaco

ISBN: 978-0-263-92884-6

46-0517

Our policy is to use papers that are natural, renewable and recyclable products and made from wood grown in sustainable forests. The logging and manufacturing processes conform to the legal environmental regulations of the country of origin.

Printed and bound in Spain
by CPI, Barcelona

Jenna Kernan has penned over two dozen novels and has received two RITA® Award nominations. Jenna is every bit as adventurous as her heroines. Her hobbies include recreational gold prospecting, scuba diving and gem hunting. Jenna grew up in the Catskills and currently lives in the Hudson Valley of New York State with her husband. Follow Jenna on Twitter, @jennakernan, on Facebook or at www.jennakernan.com.

This book is dedicated to hotshots with special consideration to the Granite Mountain Hotshots and their families.

Chapter One

Dylan Tehauno would not have stopped for the woman if she had not been standing in the road. Her convertible was parked beside her, a black Audi of all things, impractical as her attire. It was impossible that she did not hear him crunching over the gravel road. Yet she continued to stare in the opposite direction, presenting him with a very tempting view of her backside and long bare legs.

Killer curves, he thought, as dangerous as the switchbacks between him and his destination on the mountain's ridgeline. Her pale skin had tanned to the color of wild honey. The Anglo woman wore no hat, and only a fool went out without one in the Arizona sun at midday in July. He let his gaze caress her curves again as she sidestepped and he glimpsed what he had not seen beyond that round rump. She was bent over a small tripod that had spindly black spider legs. Each leg was braced with a sandbag. On the pinnacle sat one of those little fist-sized mobile video cameras.

Her convertible blocked the right lane and her camera sat on the left. There was just no way around her as the graded gravel road dropped off on each side to thick scrub brush and piñon pine. It was a long way from his reservation in Turquoise Canyon to Flagstaff, not in miles, but in everything else that mattered. There were some pines down here, piñon mostly, not the tall, majestic ponderosas.

Up in the mountains they had water and an occasional cool breeze, even in July. The McDowell Mountains could not compare to the White Mountains in Dylan's estimation. The air was so scalding here he felt as if he were fighting a wildfire. He rolled to a stop. The dust that had trailed him now swirled and settled on the shiny hood of his truck.

He rolled down the window of his white F-150 pickup and leaned out.

"Good morning," he called.

But instead of moving aside, she turned toward him and pressed both fists to her hips. The woman's clothing was tight, hugging her torso like a second skin. Was that a tennis outfit? She looked as if she had just spilled out of some exclusive country club. The woman wore her hair swept back, a clip holding the soft waves from her face so they tumbled to her shoulders. It was blue, a bright cobalt hue. Mostly, but there were other hues mixed in including deep purple, violet and turquoise.

It seemed the only protection she did use from the sun was the wide sunglasses that flashed gold at the edges. These she slipped halfway down her narrow nose as she regarded him at last with eyes the color of warm chocolate. She had lips tinted hot pink and her acrylic nails glowed a neon green that was usually reserved for construction attire. A sculpted brow arched in disapproval. Was there anything about her that was not artificial?

Dylan resisted the urge to glance at her breasts again.

"Mind moving your vehicle?" Dylan added a generous smile after his request. It was his experience that Anglo women were either wary of or curious about Apache men. This woman looked neither wary nor curious. She looked pissed.

Had her car broken down?

"You ruined my shot," she said, motioning at her tiny camera.

She was shooting in the direction he traveled, toward his destination, the house that broke the ridgeline and thus had caused so much controversy. Dylan had an appointment up there that could not be missed, one that marked a change in direction.

"The dust!" she said, and dropped a cloth over her camera.

"I'm sorry, ma'am." Dylan's years in the Marines had taught him many things, including how to address an angry Anglo woman. "But I have to get by. I have a meeting."

"I can't have you in the shot."

Was she refusing to move? Now Dylan's eyes narrowed.

"Are you unable to move that vehicle?" he asked.

"Unwilling."

She raised her pointed chin and Dylan felt an unwelcome tingle of desire. Oh, no. Heck, no—and no way, too. This woman was high maintenance and from a world he did not even recognize.

"You'll have to wait." Her mouth quirked as if she knew she was messing with him and was enjoying herself.

"But I have an appointment," he repeated.

"I don't give a fig."

"You can't just block a public road."

"Well, I guess I just did."

Dylan suppressed the urge to ram her Audi off into the rough. That's what his friend Ray Strong would do. Ray spent a lot of time cleaning up after his impulsiveness. Right now Dylan thought it might be worth it. He pictured the car sliding over the embankment and resisted the urge to smile.

"Do you know who I am?" she asked.

He lowered his chin and bit down to keep himself from telling her exactly what she was. Instead, he shook his head.

"I'm Meadow."

She gave only her first name, as if that was all that mattered. Not her family name or her tribe or clan. Just Meadow.

He shrugged one shoulder.

"Meadow Wrangler?"

He shook his head indicating his inability to place the name.

Her pretty little mouth dropped open.

"You don't know me?"

"Should I?" he asked.

"Only if you can read."

Charming, he thought.

In a minute he was getting out of his truck and she wouldn't like what happened next. He could move her and her camera without harming a blue hair on her obnoxious little head. Dylan gripped the door handle.

"My father is Theron Wrangler."

Dylan's hand fell from the handle and his eyes rounded. She folded her arms. "Ah. You've heard of him."

He sure had, but likely not for the reason she thought. Theron Wrangler was the name that Amber Kitcheyan had overheard the day before the Lilac Copper Mine massacre. It was the name of the man that FBI field agent Luke Forrest believed was a member of the eco-extremist group known as BEAR, Bringing Earth Apocalyptic Restoration. But what was Theron Wrangler's profession?

"I'm not surprised. He won an Oscar at twenty-five. I'm working for him now. Documentary film on the impact of urban sprawl and on the construction of private residences that are environmental and aesthetic monstrosities." She motioned her head toward the mansion rising above the tree line on the ridge. "I've been here filming since construction. Timelapse. Sun up to sun down and today I finally have some clouds. Adds movement."

The wind was picking up, blowing grit and sand at them.

"I still need to get around you," said Dylan.

"And have your rooster tail in the shot? No way. Why are you going up there? I thought your people were protesting the building of that thing."

She was referring to the private residence of Gerald W. Rustkin, the man who had founded one of the social media sites that self-destructed all messages from either side of any conversation. The man who allowed others to hide had put himself in the center of controversy when he had donated generously to the city of Flagstaff and afterward quietly received his variances to break the ridgeline with his personal residence.

"My people?" asked Dylan.

"You're Native American, aren't you?"

"Yes, but we don't all think alike."

"But you're all environmentally conscious." she said, as if this was a given.

"That would be thinking alike."

"You don't want to prevent that thing from being built?" She pointed at the unfinished mansion sprawling over the top of the ridge like a serpent.

Dylan glanced at his watch. "I've got to go. You know you really should put on a hat."

She scoffed. "You think I'm worried about skin cancer? Nobody expects me to make thirty."

He wrinkled his brow. "Why not?" She looked healthy enough, but perhaps she was ill.

"Why?" She laughed. "You really don't know me?"

"Sorry."

"Don't be. It's refreshing. I'm the screwup. The family's black sheep. The party girl who forgot to wear her panties and broke the internet. I'm in the tabloids about every other week. Can't believe they didn't follow me out here. I thought you were one of them."

"I'm not."

"Yes, I can see that." She approached his truck. "Can't remember the last time I did this." She extended her hand. "I'm Meadow."

Dylan looked at her elegant hand. He considered rolling up his window because this woman represented all the trouble he tried to avoid.

Instead, he took her hand gently between his fingers and thumb and gave it a little shake. But something happened. His smile became brittle and the gentle up-and-down motion of their arms ceased as he stared into bewitching amber-brown eyes. After an awkward pause he found his voice.

"Nice to meet you, Meadow. I'm Dylan Tehauno."

Her voice now sounded breathy. "A pleasure."

Her eyes glittered with mischief. Now he needed to get by her for other reasons, because this was the sort of woman you put behind you as quickly as possible.

She slipped her hand free and pressed her palm flat over her stomach. Were her insides jumping, like his?

"What's your business, Dylan?"

"I'm a hotshot."

She shook her head. "What's that, like a jet pilot?"

"I fight wildfires. Forest fires. We fly all over the West—Idaho, Oregon, Colorado. Even east once to Tennessee. Man, is it green there."

"Really? So you jump out of airplanes with an ax. That kind of thing?"

"No, those are smoke jumpers. We walk in. Sometimes twenty miles from deployment. Then we get to work." In fact, he had most of his gear in the box fixed to the bed of his truck.

"That's crazy."

He thought standing in the sun with a GoPro was crazy, but he just smiled. "Gotta go."

"All right, Sir Dylan. You may pass. How long will you be up there?"

"Hour maybe."

"Time enough for me to get my shot then." She reversed course and moved her tripod behind her sports car.

Dylan rolled past. He couldn't stop from glancing at her in the rearview mirror. He kept looking back until she was out of sight. Soon he started the ascent to the house, winding through the thick pines and dry grasses.

His shaman and the leader of his medicine society, Kenshaw Little Falcon, had recommended Dylan for this job. This was his first commission in Flagstaff. He'd recently earned his credentials as a fire-safety inspector in Arizona. As a fire consultant, it was usually his role to give recommendations to protect the home from wildfire, identify places where wildfire might trap or kill people and provide fuel-reduction plans. Something as simple as trimming the branches of trees from the ground to at least ten feet or not placing mulch next to the house could be the difference between losing a home and saving it. But this consultation was different because so many did not want this house completed. Cheney Williams, the attorney who had filed the injunction, waited for him on the ridge. Dylan felt important because he knew that his report might prevent the multimillionaire Rustkin from securing insurance. At the very least it would buy time. That would be a feather in Dylan's cap. He lowered his arm out his window and patted the magnetic sign affixed to the door panel— Tehauno Consulting.

Dylan smiled and then glanced back to the road where he could no longer see Meadow Wrangler. He should be looking ahead. By the time he finished with the attorney, would Meadow be gone?

The flash of light was so bright that for an instant everything went white. Dylan hit the brakes. The boom arrived a moment later, shaking the truck and vibrating through his hands where they gripped the wheel. Artillery.

His brain snapped to Iraq. He had served two tours and he knew the sound of an explosion. He glanced up, looking for the jets that could make such an air strike and saw the debris fly across the ridgeline. A fireball erupted skyward and rained burning embers down from above. Rocks pelted the road before him.

Meadow.

Dylan made a fast three-point turn and was hurtling down the mountain as embers landed all about him, erupting into flames. It was July, over a hundred degrees today, and the ground was as dry and thirsty as it had been all year. Perfect conditions for a wildfire. But this was not one wildfire—it was hundreds. Burning debris landed and ignited as if fueled by a propellant. The flames traveled as fast as he did. Faster, because the wind raced down the mountain, pushing the growing wall of flames that licked at the trunks of the piñon pines. Once it hit the crowns of the trees it would take off. There was nothing to stop it. His only chance was to get ahead of it and stay there.

MEADOW GAPED AS the top of the ridge exploded like an erupting volcano. With her camera still running, she stood in the road, paralyzed by what she witnessed. The house that had broken the ridgeline collapsed, falling in fiery wreckage into the gap below. The steel skeleton vanished amid tails of smoke that flew into the sky like launching rockets.

Dylan.

He was up there. Her impulse was to flee, but the urge to reach him tugged against her survival instinct.

The rockets of fire flew over her head, and she turned to watch them land, each a meteor impacting the earth. The vibrations from the explosion reached her, tipping her camera and making her sidestep to keep from falling beside it. She lifted the running GoPro and held it, collapsing the tripod as she panned, capturing the flaming rock touching down and igniting infernos to her right and left, knowing the HDMI video interface and antenna in her car compressed the video data before sending it to the live feed.

The desert bloomed orange as it burned. She turned back to the ridge, seeing the smoke billowing up to the sun. Beneath the yellow smoke came a wall of fire and the cracking, popping sound of burning. A hot wind rushed at her, burning her skin. She felt as if she stood in an oven. She had to get out of here. Meadow turned in a circle and saw flames on all sides. The smoke was so thick she began to choke. Should she try to drive through the flames?

How had the falling rock and fire missed her? She stood in the road as she realized everyone had been right. She wasn't going to see thirty.

Chapter Two

Had she gotten out? Dylan wondered as he barely managed to navigate his truck along the thin ribbon of gravel to the bottom of the ridge and onto the straight stretch that led to Meadow.

He prayed that she had, but the fear in his heart and the flames already crowning in the pines warned him she was in danger. He listened to his instincts, slowed his speed, fighting against the urge to accelerate. Moving faster than he could see could cause him to crash the truck or to hit Meadow. He was close to her position now. He knew it. Where was she?

He saw her Audi parked exactly where it had been—only now the wall of fire to his left glimmered off the mirror surface of the black paint reflecting the approaching flames. Soon the paint would melt, along with every bit of plastic. The inferno was close to jumping the road. Dylan hit the brakes, sending gravel spraying from his rear tires.

"Meadow!" he shouted as he threw open the door. "Meadow!"

The blaze was loud now, sounding like a locomotive. His eyes burned as he swept the ground for any sight of her. Then he saw a flash of white. She was running. Strong legs pumping as she darted from behind her car and then in front of his truck. In one hand she held her camera by the folded, compressed tripod. She reached the passenger side, and his arms went around her instinctively as he pulled her into the truck and set them in motion again.

Not here, he thought. There was too much fuel. Too much energy for the flames to consume in the surrounding pines.

"There's no way out," she shouted.

He knew that. He knew they were trapped. It was not a question of if but when the fire would catch them.

Not here. Not yet.

He glanced behind them. The fire glowed red in the rearview. So close now. Ahead there was only smoke and the orange flames that raced along on either side of the road. Finally he saw it. The black earth he had been searching for. The fire had already burned the easy fuel there. He glanced back. How long did he have? A few minutes. He needed more earth, more black earth between him and what chased them. He needed a place to survive the burnover.

He went as far as he could, hoping, praying it was far enough. Knowing if he went any farther he would not have the moments he needed to prepare.

Dylan hit the brakes.

"What are you doing?" yelled Meadow. "Go! Go!"

He reached across the gap between them and dragged her out of the truck by her wrist. She didn't fight him, just locked her jaw and allowed him to pull her behind him. He grabbed his rake and thrust it at her. She clutched it in her free hand, the other still gripping her camera. Then he seized his pack and Pulaski ax from the utility storage box in his truck bed. No time to talk. No room for the bottles of water he always carried. He glanced about as he judged the wind and the flames, wishing the crowns of the trees had already burned. Then he rushed them off the embankment to the black earth. The road would help break the flames, but the truck… Were they far enough to be clear of the gas tanks? He tugged her along, running into the smoking black soil that crunched beneath his construction boots. Choosing his spot because he was out of time, he went to work with the ax breaking the soil, tearing away the burned vegetation by the roots, digging a trench. The ground was so hot. He'd never thought he'd have to deploy his fire shelter. After all the training films and practice and all the fires he had fought, Dylan really had believed that he could control the situation, stay ahead of the fire line and always have a viable escape plan. Yet, here he was.

"What are you doing?" she yelled.

The roar was louder and the hot wind rushed past them.

"Rake that away!" he yelled.

He broke more soil, digging deeper and glancing at the approaching wall of flame.

She pushed the tripod down the front of her shirt before using the fire rake to pull away the roots and brush he cleared with the ax.

"A grave?" she asked.

He paused to stare at her. She looked back with a calm that terrified him because he saw that she was ready to die.

"Fire shelter," he called.

Her brows lifted and he could not tell if she was relieved or disappointed.

No time now.

"That comes off." He tugged at her shirt.

"What?"

"Polyester. It melts." He dragged the shirt over her head. She dropped the rake. The camera tumbled free, and she stooped to her knees to snatch it up again and yelped at the contact of her bare knee with the smoking ground. He went for his pack, grabbing the flame-retardant shirt he wore to fight fires and tugged it on. It would be *his* back between the shelter and the flames.

"This, too?" She lifted the edge of the flimsy scrap of fabric that was her skirt.

He nodded and dropped the camel pack in the ditch, then took his gloves and radio, but nothing else. He'd never heard of two people deploying in a shelter that was designed for one.

He estimated the wind was reaching fifty miles an hour now. If he lost the shelter to the wind they were both dead. He dropped to his knees, already tugging the fire shelter from the nylon sheath.

"That looks like a Jiffy Pop bag," she said.

"Come!" he roared.

She dropped before him and he enveloped her, forcing her down to the earth and into the shallow ditch he had made. The roar grew louder, like a jet engine that went on and on.

He got the shelter over them and used the hand straps to tug the edges about them. His feet slid inside the elastic and he braced, holding himself up on his elbows.

"It's hot," she called, wriggling. "The ground—it's too hot. I'm burning."

"Stay still." It was hotter outside, he knew. Five hundred degrees and rising, he thought, his training providing him the information.

"This isn't going to stop it. It's thin as one of those emergency blankets."

Except this was two-ply. A silicon layer and the reflective outer foil.

"We'll cook alive!" she yelled.

It was possible. Not all deployed wildfire fighters survived. But mostly they died from the heated gases that scorched their lungs until they could not breathe.

"Stick your face in the dirt and take shallow breaths," he shouted in her ear to be heard above the roar. The explosion that shook them told him that his truck tires had blown. The gas tank would be next. Flying debris could rip the shelter. If that happened, they would die here.

The fire shield now seemed a living thing that he had to wrestle to hold down about them. The heat intensified until he felt as if the skin on his back burned. Every time the shelter touched him, it seared. He kept his elbows pinned and punched at the shelter, creating an air space. Each breath scalded his lungs. He took shallow sips of air and held them as long as possible, hoping the next breath would not be his last.

MEADOW FELT THE weight of him pressing down upon her. He was so big and the ground so hot. She couldn't breathe.

"We have to get out," she yelled, not knowing if he heard her. The air in her next breath was so hot she choked. He pushed her head down to the ground.

"Dig!" he ordered.

She held the neck of the tripod and used the collapsed legs to dig, making a hole, and then she released her GoPro to cup her hands over her face to inhale. How could he even breathe? The air above her head was even hotter. He needed to get his face down by hers.

She dug faster, using her hands now, her acrylic nails raking soft sand as she burrowed like a ground squirrel. "You, too!"

She gasped at the intake of hot air into her throat.

He wriggled forward, his cheek now beside hers, his nose and lips pressing into her cupped hands. She could feel his shallow breath. Their skin was hot and damp where their cheeks met.

From somewhere outside the balloon shelter came an explosion. She flinched.

Chapter Three

"Gas tank," he shouted, clarifying what had just blown up.

The roaring went on and the shield fluttered and bucked, reminding her of the slack sail on a sailboat.

Ready about, her father would call, and the boom would swing over her head. As the smallest and quickest, she was allowed to scramble up to the foredeck to tie off the lines and drop the buoy between the ship and the dock.

Something stung her chest. She clawed at her bra.

"Burning," she cried.

Dylan lifted, released the back fastening as she tugged it clear.

"Metal heats up," he shouted in her ear. "Buttons, rivets."

Underwire, she thought. The thing was so hot, like a brand against her flesh. She wondered if she had burned her skin. If she could just lift the edge of the cover and get some air. But he held it down with his forearms and legs. She reached for the shelter and he grabbed her wrist, forcing it to the hot, black earth.

"I need to breathe!" she shouted.

He said nothing. Just held her down along with the tinfoil roaster bag that was cooking them alive. It was an oven. Hotter than an oven. She pressed her face back in the dirt and tried to breathe through the fingers of her free hand. The rings were heating. She tugged at her captured hand. He resisted.

"My rings. Burning!"

He released her and she jerked off her silver, gold and platinum rings and pushed them away.

Beams of red light shone down in narrow shafts through the cover. She glanced up. There were holes in the shelter. She pointed and felt him nod.

"It will be all right," he said. "It will still work."

Had the roaring decreased? She wasn't sure.

"How you doing?" he asked.

She could hear him now. He wasn't shouting.

"I don't want to die," she whispered. The words came as a surprise to her. Yesterday there was nothing she'd wanted to do. Nowhere she'd wanted to go. And now she just wanted to see the sky again. Dive into cold water. Inhale the scent of peonies.

"We're both going to live." He brushed his cheek against hers. "I'll keep you safe, Meadow. It won't get you."

She closed her eyes and struggled to control the ball of pain that tried to escape her throat as a sob. She failed. Here she had thought there was only a thin veil of foil between her and the fire. But it wasn't so. Dylan stood between her and the flames. He protected her with his body and his promise, and she loved him for it.

"How long do we have to stay in here?"

He shifted, letting his hip slide to the ground, taking some of his weight from her. "A while. Have to be sure it's past us."

"How will you know?"

"The sound. The roar is fading. The heat and the color. It's orange now. See?"

She lifted her head to the pinholes and saw the light that had been pink and then red like the flashing light of a fire engine were now the orange of glowing coals. The sky shouldn't be that color. Never, ever. She let her head fall back to the breathing hole.

He stuck something against her face.

"Drink," he ordered.

It was a tube. She put it in her mouth and swallowed. Water—hot, stale and welcome. She drank until he took the hose from her. How much water had she lost in this tinfoil tent?

She marveled at him. In only minutes he had gathered from the truck exactly what they needed to survive.

"How do you know all this? How do you have one of these things?" *Hotshot*, she remembered. Walking twenty miles to deploy, he'd said. She needed to get one of these Jiffy Pop thingies. "You fight wildfires," she said, more to herself than to him.

"Yes."

"Dylan?"

"Hmm?"

She wished she could look at him, see his handsome face, those dark eyes and the clean line of his jaw, but he was so close that his nose was pressed to her ear and he lay half across her.

"Can you…talk to me? You know? Take my mind off…"

"What about?"

"Tell me about yourself."

"Well, I told you my name. I'm from the Turquoise Canyon Apache tribe. We are Tonto Apache. I live up there on the reservation between Antelope Lake and Darabee in the mountains."

His voice was like a song with a lyrical quality that calmed her. She felt the panic easing away as he continued.

"If I met you there I would say to you, 'Hello, I am Bear, born of Butterfly, and my father's name is Jonathan Tehauno. My mother's name is Dorothy Florez. They named me Dylan.' It's more important there to know your

parents and clans. Your name comes after all that or sometimes not at all. So when I say, 'Bear, born of Butterfly,'
you know my father's clan is Bear and my mother's clan
is Butterfly."

"I live in Phoenix. I am Wrangler, born of Theron and
Lupe. My mother's name was Cortez."

He chuckled and she felt herself smile.

"Tell me more." She felt herself relaxing, her weary
muscles twitching from the tension that now eased away
into the hot earth.

"I live in the community of Koun'nde in tribal housing. My friends make fun of me because my home has so
many books."

She chuckled because she had stopped reading the minute she realized no one could make her do anything.

"I own a truck, nearly, and have five horses in the community herd. Well, I did own a truck." He sighed and then
coughed. After a moment he kept talking, his breath cool
against her face. "I like to ride. I've won some endurance
races on horses and on foot. After high school, I joined the
US Marines. I was honorably discharged after two tours.
Decided not to reenlist. I missed home. It's cool up on the
mountain. Not like down here in Flagstaff or over in the
Sandbox. That's what we called Iraq."

His voice hummed in her ear, a deep, resonant song.
She closed her watering eyes.

"Let's see. I'm a member of a medicine society, the
Turquoise Guardians. We dance at festivals and perform
ceremonies. I sing in a drum circle."

She didn't know what any of that meant, but she wanted
him to keep talking.

"The people say I have a good voice."

Meadow agreed with that, though she had not heard
him sing. She wanted to ask him, but it was so hard for
her just to breathe, she didn't have the heart.

"I've been trying to get some of my friends to join me in August to go up to Rapid City for the Indian Relay Races. We'd need four good horses and a four-man team. One rider and each horse runs one mile with the same rider."

She tried to picture that, one man leaping from one horse to another.

"I keep telling Jack that he was born to be a catcher and Ray and Carter could hold the mounts. I'd like to ride, but if they're faster I'd let them go, instead. Only now Carter's in witness protection. So we need a fourth. I suggested Carter's brother Kurt. He's smaller but strong. Jack said he'd think about it. Jack Bear Den is a detective on our tribal police. His brother Carter and my friend Ray Strong are hotshots. Turquoise Canyon Hotshots. That's us. Kurt Bear Den is a paramedic with the air ambulance. I've been a hotshot since I came home but it's only six months, the fire season. So I need more work. I was supposed to meet Cheney Williams."

Her eyes popped open. "I know him."

"You do?"

"He works with my dad. He's a financial guy for the documentaries. Contracts, I think. Something. I'm not really sure. He's around a lot." Meadow felt a rumble in Dylan's chest, like a growl.

"I was told that he's an attorney in environmental law. Working to stop that house."

"You haven't met him?"

"No. My shaman recommended me."

She lifted her chin. It was easier to breathe. "Was he up there?"

The rough stubble on his chin brushed her temple. "Probably. He was meeting me there."

"Do you think he got out?"

Silence was her answer.

"Who would do this?"

His body tensed. "I'm planning to find that out."

"The whole ridge exploded. The rocks were flying everywhere. I can't believe they didn't hit me." She told him everything. About how she was filming and the red fireball and the house collapsing and the trees ablaze.

"You filmed the whole thing?"

"Yes."

"Why were you here today?"

"I've been here several times during the construction. My father sent me. He has a shooting schedule." She didn't say that her dad hadn't used any of the footage she'd shot. That she was beginning to think her assignment was a snipe hunt, designed to be rid of her, keep her busy and out of the clubs. That last headline had embarrassed them. Too much attention, her mother had said.

Too much was better than none at all, she thought, and she lowered her head.

"Your father sent you here. Today."

She didn't like the way he said that.

"Well, he couldn't have known this would happen."

His silence was her only answer. Meadow frowned. She didn't like that silence. There was something sinister and judgmental about it.

"My father is a saint. He's spent his whole life raising awareness of really important issues with his films."

Still no reply.

"What are you implying?" she asked.

"Heck of a coincidence."

"I could say the same for you."

"Yes. That occurred to me," he said.

The hairs on her neck lifted. She felt the need to fill the silence.

"Lucky you were here," she said.

"Yeah." There was a long pause. "Lucky."

"You saved my life."

"Not yet, I haven't." He moved again, trying his radio and getting nothing but static. He slipped the antenna out from under the fire shield and tried again. This time he got through to someone and she heard him give their position and ask for assistance. He also asked them to contact Detective Jack Bear Den on Turquoise Canyon Reservation.

He retracted the radio antenna inside the shield and she saw the black plastic tip had melted.

"I guess my car and Wi-Fi antenna is toast."

"You have internet out here?"

"I did. I was streaming my footage."

"You captured the explosion and streamed it…where?"

"My social media. Vine, Snapchat, Instagram. I also have YouTube, Facebook and Google+ and send footage to my remote server."

He went very still. "So anyone could see what you shot."

"Yes. That's the point."

"So you don't need to make it out of here alive for someone to see what you saw."

The hairs on her neck now began to tingle.

"What are you saying?"

"I think you and I were sent here to die."

Chapter Four

Dylan tried to put the pieces together. He didn't know if he was injured. During the worst of the burn-over he'd felt as if the skin on his back had burned. He knew from his training that it was not uncommon for a deployed hotshot to suffer burns. But the shelters worked. And theirs *had* worked. They were alive and the worst had passed. The worst of the firestorm. But now he wondered if by sending a distress call he had alerted whoever had sent them that they had survived. Radio channels were easy to monitor. If his hunch was right, they needed to get out of here before help arrived because the worst of the firestorm might still be out there.

The vehicles would be useless. He'd heard the tires blow and both gas tanks explode. His poor truck. He didn't even own it yet. Meadow would likely have a new Audi by morning.

If they lived that long.

Help was coming, but so too were the ones who had set that explosive. Dylan was sure.

"Tell me what's happening," she demanded.

Was she one of them? A WOLF or a BEAR? WOLF, Wilderness of Land Forever, was the less radicalized arm of the eco-extremists, who destroyed property but only if it did not jeopardize human life. BEAR made no such allowances. The FBI thought her father was a member of

BEAR, perhaps the head of the eco-extremist group. Jack had told him that. But they hadn't proved it—not yet.

Had she been sent here as a sacrificial lamb, to die for the cause as a martyr?

He remembered that look when she'd asked him if he was digging their grave. She'd been ready.

"Did you come here to die?"

"What?" she said. She made a scoffing sound and then gave a halfhearted laugh.

Dylan felt his upper arm tingle. Not because of the heat outside the shelter but because of the tattoo he had gotten after joining Tribal Thunder, the warrior sect of his medicine society. His shaman had suggested each new member have a spirit animal to help guide them. It was Ray Strong's idea to have them branded on their skin. Dylan's spirit animal was bobcat, and his tattoo was the track of the bobcat on a medicine shield, beneath which hung five eagle feathers. He loved having a cat as his guide but did not appreciate the reason. His shaman said Dylan was too overt and needed to be aware that not all things operated on the surface. Bobcat would help him see what was hidden and give him a quality he lacked—stealth.

Dylan had a reputation for being where he was supposed to be and doing what was expected, more than was expected. He wasn't reckless like Ray Strong or suspicious like Jack Bear Den or a natural leader like Jack's twin brother, Carter. He was predictable and he followed the rules. He was the conscience of the group. Was that so bad?

This woman beneath him was not what she seemed. A shadow figure. Appearing one thing while being another or existing on two planes at the same time. A woman with two faces. He felt it and Bobcat warned him to be cautious.

"Have you heard of an organization called WOLF, or one called BEAR?" he asked, and then kicked himself for

the overt question. But how would he know the answer if
he could not ask?

BEAR was much worse. Bringing Earth Apocalyptic
Restoration. That group was eco-terrorists. They'd or-
chestrated the mass shooting at the Lilac Copper Mine
to cover the long-term theft of mining supplies and then
paid a member of his tribe to kill the gunman of the mass
murder, breaking the link between the gunman and those
who sent him.

"WOLF? Yes. They burned that Jeep outfit in Sedona.
Right? Some kind of activist opposed to overdevelopment
of the land. Can hardly blame them. Damn red Hummers
rolling all over the fragile ecosystem." Her mouth dropped
open. She must have inhaled some of the sand on her face
because she coughed and spit. Then she turned, trying
to glance back at him. They were so close he could feel
every muscle in her back tense. So close he could press
his lips to her temple.

"You think they did this?" she asked.

He did not reply, but he could almost hear her mind
working.

"But the fire. They must have known that would cause a
fire. And they don't destroy the land. They protect it. And
the explosion. That was like something from a movie."

"Or a mine," Dylan said.

"Lilac."

There had been no mention of the loss of mining supplies from the Lilac mine in the media. Yet she had made
the connection with the speed of a lightning strike. Mines
had explosives, blasting cord and everything you needed
to do exactly what they had just both witnessed.

He swallowed as he accepted the confirmation. Why
did he think she could not be one of them? Because she
was pretty or pampered or seemingly suffering from a
terminal case of affluenza? Bobcat would see through all

that. Bobcat would proceed slowly without moving a single blade of grass.

Her father, Theron Wrangler, was the one person the FBI had successfully linked to BEAR because Amber Kitcheyan, an employee at Lilac and the only survivor, had heard that name spoken the day before the shooting. Dylan's friend Carter Bear Den had rescued her and the FBI now had both of them in protective custody.

This woman was Theron's daughter and she'd captured the explosion on film, then streamed it live. He thought of the suicide bombers in the Middle East. Had she planted those explosives?

"We have to get out of here," Dylan said.

"I'm all for that."

He glanced up at the holes in his fire shelter—the required equipment he had purchased a year ago and never expected to need. His crew was too careful, too experienced and too smart to be trapped by the living, breathing monster of a wildfire.

He dragged the camel pack from beneath his knees and drank, then offered Meadow a drink. Some deployed men suffered from dehydration, and, unable to leave the shelter as their bodies had lost too much vital fluids, they died. He was lucky to have had the seconds he needed to grab the water pouch.

Dylan thought about his truck and the sturdy utility box made of a polymer and likely now a melted lump of plastic. All his equipment and the water—gone.

He resisted the urge to lift the shelter as he estimated the temperature inside had reached over two hundred degrees and was now falling. Every rock and stone beneath them radiated heat like the bricks in a pizza oven.

"Couldn't it have been a gas explosion?" she asked.

"No gas lines."

"Welding tanks, for construction?"

"Maybe." Let her think that. He'd seen gas tanks explode on training videos. They were impressive but could not melt steel and bring down a 4500-square-foot home.

Dylan debated what to do. If he stayed, it gave whoever picked up his radio transmission time to get to them.

What would his friend Ray Strong do? Ray was the crazy one, or he had been until he met Morgan Hooke and became responsible for a woman and her child. Ray had changed. Perhaps his spirit animal, eagle, had really helped him see clearly and act, not on impulse, but with clarity and purpose.

Jack Bear Den would tell Dylan to be careful. To act on the assumption that the worst was coming and to be ready.

Jack's twin, Carter Bear Den, would tell Dylan to be ready to fight what came. Carter's tattoo was a bear track. Bears were strong. Carter had needed that strength to leave his tribe and go with the woman he loved. What would Carter do? He'd been their captain for the Turquoise Canyon Hotshots, a job Dylan assumed when Carter left them in February. They would be deploying without him today. He was sure. Who would be leading them now?

Dylan had joined the Turquoise Canyon Hotshots after his discharge. He had four full seasons fighting wildfire and two months and three fires as captain. But none like this. Back then fighting wildfire had been exciting. He had felt immortal. But his tours of duty in Iraq had shown him that none of them were and, lately, he had felt the weight of being the leader of his team. His decisions meant the life or death of members of his crew and he found himself questioning his ability to lead.

He held the shelter, feeling the time race by with the wind. If he was right and they stayed here too long, someone would come to finish what the fire had started. If they left too early, the heat would burn their lungs, saving the team from BEAR the trouble of killing them.

"HOW MUCH LONGER?" asked Meadow.

The sand and grit stuck to her damp skin. She'd never been so thirsty and she was beginning to feel dizzy.

"A few minutes more." He glanced at her. "Why don't you tell me about yourself? Pass the time." And get to know the enemy beside him. Bobcat would be pleased.

"Well, okay. I'm Meadow. My mom's nickname for me is Dodo, if that's any hint. You know, like the bird? I'm the last of six children. The oops baby. My next oldest sister, Katrina, is seven years my senior. My oldest brother, Phillip, is the CEO of PAN. My three sisters, Connie, short for Consuelo, Rosalie, Katrina, and my other brother, Miguel, are all professionals with promising careers." She had started to use air quotes but then dropped her hands back to the hot earth and the tripod.

Being so much younger sometimes made her feel like she was an only child with six parents.

"I'm closest to Katrina. She looked out for me when she could, or she used to before…you know, when I was a kid."

And when Meadow was home, which wasn't often.

"Your name isn't Spanish," said Dylan.

"What? No, it isn't."

"The others are, and your mother, Lupe."

She'd never really thought of that before.

"Anyway. Phillip is a CEO. Miguel is a doctor. So is Connie, Consuelo. Rosalie is an attorney and Kat has a business degree from Berkeley, undergrad and a law degree from…" She tapped her chin. "I forget where… Anyway, just passed the bar. They all went to private school here. Me, too, for a while. I got kicked out. I also got kicked out of schools in Westchester, Greenwich, Boston and Vermont."

"That's a lot of schools."

"What can I say? I'm good at what I do."

"So you cause trouble. Make a big fuss so everyone notices you."

"That's it." Only they didn't. Not often.

But getting sent home was the one sure way to get her father's attention.

"Oh, and colleges, too. I went to NYU for film. My dad made a contribution because my grades, well… I tried to be a chip off the old block. But my brothers have that gig all tied up. So I went to Berkeley for economics and then UCLA for marine biology."

"How'd you do?"

"I got mostly A's on the tests I took. Problem was I didn't take enough of them. I had trouble getting to class."

"Failed out?"

"Every time."

"But all A's. You're smart."

"If I was smart, would I be lying under an Apache hot-shot in the middle of a wildfire?"

"Good point."

"Maybe I'll go back to school. They have some in Hawaii. I could learn to surf."

"How old are you?"

"Twenty-six, but I'll be twenty-seven next month. Just in time to join the 27 Club."

"What's that?"

She turned to stare at him in disbelief. "You got to get off your mountain. Get your brain out of the smoke."

"Maybe. So…the 27 Club?"

"It's all the musicians who died at twenty-seven. Morrison, Hendrix, Joplin, Cobain, Winehouse. Only they were famous for creating something and I'm only famous for being the screw-up daughter of a rich man. Creating scandals. I haven't done anything else."

"Not too late," he said.

"Yeah. I'd like to see twenty-eight, even thirty."

He tugged her closer to him, adjusting his body to hold the shelter.

"Can I help hold it down?" she asked, and then realized this was the very first time she'd offered to do anything. She'd drunk his water, complained about the lifesaving shelter and whined about how hard it was to breathe. She sagged. Maybe he should have rolled her out from under the shelter like a log. She knew she would have been tempted if their situation had been reversed.

"You'd need gloves. The edges get hot."

Yet the thing had been flapping against him for what seemed like hours. He'd never uttered a word of complaint.

"How old are you?" she asked.

"Twenty-eight."

He seemed older, acted older, she realized.

"I'm going to lift the shield," he said. "Hold your breath."

Meadow drew as deep a breath as she could in the scalding hot air as Dylan lifted the edge of the shelter.

Chapter Five

A blast of hot winds rushed in below the fire shelter. The burning air made Meadow's eyes tear.

"Everything is black," she said, releasing her breath and then gasping at the heat of the air now rushing into her lungs. She hurried to be rid of it. The next breath seemed just as hot.

"Good. Did you see any fire?"

"No." She pressed her hands over her stinging eyes and rubbed. "Hot."

"Don't rub them. Just keep your eyes closed."

After a few minutes he asked her to hold the edge of the shelter. She tried but the metal was too hot. He piled some sand on the inner edge and she was able to press down the lip with her palm.

He used his free hand to retrieve his radio. She gaped at the melted top to the antenna. What did her car look like? It was miles to anything. A new fear tripped her heart rate. They couldn't walk out. It was too far.

"Help is coming. Right?" she asked.

"Someone will be here as soon as it's safe." He lifted the edge again. The air was hot, but not as hot. "Stay here."

"What! No!"

"Meadow, I'm wearing boots, a fire-resistant shirt, cotton jeans. You're naked."

That was true.

"Stay here until I tell you."

She nodded. "Be careful."

He slid off one glove. "Put that on. Use it to hold the shelter down. Use your feet to hold the bottom edge."

With that, he lifted the right side and rolled away. The edge flapped as she tried and failed to catch it. She felt as if her skin blistered. From outside the shelter the edge dropped and she was able to get her gloved hand down on the perimeter.

"Feet!" he yelled.

She spread her legs until her sandaled feet were in place. Meadow tried and failed to ignore the pain of her burning toes.

"Stay there," he called from outside the shield.

She heard the crunch of his feet on the scorched earth. Meadow's legs and arms began to tremble from the effort of keeping the shelter steady against the constant wind. How had he held the shield down all that time? It seemed impossible. Again she realized that Dylan Tehauno had saved her life. She knew he had come back just for her, and, because of that act, everything in her life that was good was a gift from him.

Meadow's eyes burned and she was surprised she had enough water left in her body to cry. But the tears came, sliding over the bridge of her nose and dropping into the dry sand. Even the tears were thanks to Dylan. The sobs came next. Meadow was so grateful and so undeserving.

How did a person like her repay a man like him? Money? Sex? A new truck? He said he was looking for a job. She could help him with that. Her father employed lots of people. Her brother Phillip, too. If she asked, her dad would give Dylan a job. Especially when he found out what he had done. She needed to call her father. But her phone was in her car. Or it had been.

The crunch of his boots signaled his return.

"Meadow. I'm taking off the shield."

The foil wrapper lifted away and the hot air rushed past her. She pressed her hands over her mouth to cool the next breath as she rolled to her side looking up at him.

He stood shirtless, his skin smudged with ash and glistening with sweat. Dylan dropped his shirt over her naked body.

"Put that on."

She drew to her knees, tugging the garment over her shoulders and holding it closed before her. The sand stuck to her skin and poured under her sandals. He offered his hand and, looking around, she rose beside him. The fire now raced far back along the road she had traveled, a line of orange glowing beneath the billowing gray smoke.

They were surrounded by a forest of tree trunks charred black and smoking. How many animals had died in that fire? She shivered at the thought. How many houses in the valley below them were now at risk? She'd driven through a new development that butted against the national forest. She remembered her father complaining about the expensive homes positioned with views of the sunset over the ridge. He'd called them hypocrites because they had objected to the mansion that broke the ridgeline for obstructing *their* views.

They were likely evacuating now.

Meadow glanced at the trench he had made. There lay the only patch of earth devoid of flammable vegetation. The only place the earth was not black. Her pink lace bra lay in the sand and a diamond on one of her rings twinkled. Then she spotted her GoPro. She stooped to recover it and paused. The camera was intact, but the tripod had not been wholly under the shelter and it had melted to a lump of black plastic. She stared at the evidence of how much hotter it had been outside the shelter than inside. Dylan crouched beside her and offered a wet bandanna, and she washed her face, horrified at the black soot that came away on the red cotton. He rinsed the cloth and used it to wipe off her throat. The simple act of kindness undid her.

She turned to him and fell into his arms, sobbing. He stroked her tangled hair. He whispered to her in a language she could not understand as she clung to him and wept. His hand stroked her back, rubbing up and down over the shirt he had given her. Everything she had and everything she was she owed to him. She lifted her chin to look up at him.

Why hadn't she seen the kindness in his dark eyes or the strength reflected in his blade of a nose and the strong line of his jaw rough with dark stubble and sand? All she'd seen was a nuisance ruining her shot. His black brows lifted and the corner of his mouth twitched upward. That mouth was so tempting and she was so lost.

Meadow threaded one hand in his thick, short hair and tugged, angling her chin, and rose onto her toes, pressing her mouth to his.

DYLAN STARTLED AT the unexpected contact and the unprecedented wave of desire that swept over him. Reflexively, his arms contracted, drawing her tight to his chest. Only after the contact of her bare skin to his did he remember she had not yet buttoned his shirt and he had removed his T-shirt to check his back for burns. Her bare breasts molded to the hard planes of his chest, setting off a firestorm inside his body. Her tongue flicked out and he opened his mouth, allowing her to deepen the kiss that soon consumed them both. When her fingers scored his bare back, Dylan's need overwhelmed him, but the fluttering in his belly and the stirring below that did not quite overtake the whisper of danger.

Bobcat growled a warning.

The overt. Her seeming desire.

The hidden. Her real purpose. Was this a distraction to

give her people time to reach them? A way to make him forget his unease and take what she offered?

She had told him she was a party girl. Now he saw her provocative nature. Sex to this woman meant no more than choosing what dessert to eat. Dylan pushed her away, not because of the danger or the hidden agenda but because he did not wish to be the flavor of the month. For him, the intimacy shared by man and woman was sacred.

"We need to go," he said.

She looked up at him with wide eyes, and a enticing pink mouth opened just enough to tempt him to kiss her again. But he wouldn't, precisely because he did want to so much. She seemed bewildered. Oh, this one was good. Very, very good. If he did not know better, he would believe the innocence and astonishment he saw in her face.

"Come on. Now."

He drew her away from him and then let her go. He allowed himself one long look at the swath of bare skin revealed between the edges of his shirt. His gaze stopped on the scrap of pink lace that covered her seemingly hairless sex. Then he met her gaze and saw the power in her eyes. She was used to men looking at her like this, completely comfortable now, as if she had regained her footing and stood on familiar ground. She stared at him with a kind of triumph melded with seduction.

He pointed at his shirt. "Button that."

Meadow gave a mock salute that revealed the bottom curve of a bare breast. Dylan met her gaze.

"Why did you do that?" he asked, brushing the sand from his chest and tugging on his T-shirt.

"I just wanted to thank you."

He shoved his bandanna in the back pocket of his jeans. "You don't thank a man by having sex with him, Meadow."

"Sometimes I do."

"I'm not like you, then. I'm not casual about such things."

"A real Boy Scout," she said, pink lips curling.

"You should have more pride and respect for yourself."

He saw his condemnation strike her. Her bottom lip quivered. Was this an act or real emotion? He rubbed his right shoulder, wishing Bobcat could tell him because his instinct was to take her in his arms again. Ridiculous. She was a wealthy, spoiled, lost woman-child and he was not interested.

Dylan dug in the sand, recovering her rings. "How many did you have?"

"Four." She accepted the offering in cupped palms and slipped the trinkets onto her long fingers.

Meadow looked from her hand to the ground.

"Is that your ax?" She pointed at the metal head that was all that remained of the Pulaski ax after the wood had burned away.

He lifted the ax head and then dropped it back to the sand.

"Fought a lot of fires with that. Like losing an old friend."

Meadow glanced to the road to the two burned hulls that had been his truck and her car. They were scorched gray and looked old, ancient, as if abandoned years and years ago.

She gasped, pressing one hand to her mouth as she pointed with the other.

"My car!"

"Totaled. But I suspect you have it fully insured."

She took a step closer. "The glass melted. The seats. Upholstery. Everything." Meadow gaped at him. "All the paint just… It looks like… Why is it on its side?"

"Gas tank must have been full."

"I topped it up on Canyon Road before coming out here." She lifted her digital recorder. All the acrylic nails had popped off her fingers in the heat, leaving small, ragged, natural nails glowing pink on her blackened, dirty

fingers. She fiddled with the buttons and the screen illuminated. "It still works!"

She beamed at him.

"We have to go," he said.

"But you called for help. They might be here soon."

If they could get through the fire wall and if the ones
who came were here to help them, he would stay. But
there was too much risk. Rescue might be hours, even
days, away, and the ones who had started this fire might
reach them first.

"You can stay. I'm walking out." He turned and headed
in the direction of the ridgeline, some two miles away.

"What? Wait up." She trotted along with him over the
smoking ground. "Wow. It's really hot. I can feel it right
through the soles of my sandals."

He stopped and debated. If he was wrong and she was
not involved, they might kill her. If he was right and he
brought her along, then she could report back to them everything he said and did.

"What?" she asked, those bright golden-brown eyes
seeming as honest as a child's.

"I think you should stay. Wait for your father. If I see
anyone, I'll send them to you."

She twisted a diamond ring from her finger and held it
out to him. "Take me with you."

He looked at the tiny circle of silver. "I don't wear silver."

"It's platinum."

"It's a bribe." She was used to buying what she wanted.
He could see that. Buying her way out of what she could
and letting Daddy clean up the rest. Had Daddy gotten
tired of wiping up after her?

"Why not wait here?" she asked.

Tell her the truth, a partial truth or a lie? He looked
down at her and lifted a hand to brush the soot from her

cheek. The touch of her skin made his insides twitch as the longing rose again.

"Because I think the men who did this are close, and I think they want you or me dead."

Chapter Six

Meadow gaped, uncharacteristically finding herself rendered speechless. She had been around long enough to spot paranoia when she saw it. The guy said he'd been in Iraq. Maybe he had a screw or two loose.

Play along, she decided.

"What men? And why would they want us dead?"

"I don't know the answers to those questions. I do know that you and I being here exactly when that explosion went off is something more than coincidence."

"How could you possibly know that?"

Her savior did not answer. Instead, he gave her a long, uneasy look and turned away.

"Keep the shirt," he said. Then he lifted his camel pack and shrugged it onto his wide shoulders and started walking. With him went all the water they had.

"Hey, wait." She trotted to catch him, wishing her sandals were less cute and more practical. Wearing a wedge that showed her slim calves to best advantage seemed unnecessary when her legs were streaked with soot and covered with grit and sand. She caught him and grabbed at his arm, her hand covered with the long sleeve of his shirt. "Do you know how crazy you sound?"

He kept walking toward the road and the twisted remains of a bit of the blackened skeletal metal infrastructure that survived the blast. She let her gaze travel over the place where the eighteen-million-dollar home had been. She had not seen the explosion. The flash had been so bright and the earth had been shaking. He was right. It had been an explosion. What had caused the blast?

He was a firefighter, and even he had admitted that a gas tank could be the cause. But, as she looked at the ridge-line that she had been filming on and off for months, she realized the size of the demolition. It could not have been caused by a small propane tank or reserve tank for gas. She knew it in her heart.

Which meant someone had gone up there with explosives and set charges and pushed some kind of detonator and let the fires and rock spray down on the pine trees in the driest, hottest month of the year.

"Who would do this?"

He looked back. "You believe me now?"

She nodded. "It's just too big. I need to look at the footage. Maybe I can see something."

"I'd imagine the FBI will want to see that footage, as well."

"It's up on my feed. Anyone could have seen it live. But the entire thing, it's only recorded on this." She lifted the camera. "And on my server."

"Can't the social media sites recall it?"

"I don't know."

He started walking again.

She spotted a phone sticking out of his back pocket and jogged to come even with him again.

"You have a phone," she said, pointing at his pocket.

"No service," he said without slowing.

"You think you'll have service up there?" She pointed to the ridge.

"Maybe. I know Rustkin's got a well. Only water within ten miles. The fire started there and moved with the wind. Top of the ridge and the far side will be untouched."

She looked at the climb ahead of them. Meadow already felt dizzy, and the prospect of the hike made her stomach twist. Maybe she should wait for help. A glance back showed the billowing smoke off to the east. How long until anyone could drive out here. The road they were on dead-ended at the mansion that had once occupied the ridge. Emergency and Fire would concentrate on the threatened town of Pine View and the larger community of Valley View, which lay between the fire and Flagstaff. But her father. He'd come for her. He knew where she was.

When she glanced back to Dylan, it was to find him another two hundred feet along the road. The man was quick as a jackrabbit.

She stretched her legs and walked. By the time she drew even with him, her mouth felt like cotton.

"I need some water."

"No."

Now that was a word she didn't hear very often.

"Are you crazy? I'm thirsty."

"We don't have much left. We need to make it up there first. Then, if I find the well, you can have a drink."

She stomped her foot, raising dust and his brow.

He was walking again. Meadow closed her dry mouth and lifted her stubborn chin. If he could make it up that mountain, then so could she.

SHE WAS TOUGHER than she looked, Dylan gave her that. The hike had to be four miles uphill, and she made it in those wedge sandals without another word of complaint or request for anything. In fact, it appeared that she would not even have taken the time of day from him if he had offered to give it to her.

Perhaps her strength was born of orneriness, but he still gave her credit for making the trek unassisted. He would have bet good money that she was going to start bawling like a branded calf or just stop so he'd have to bring water back to her.

Dylan glanced at the landscape surrounding them. He'd seen such a view before. Too often. The ground was scorched black and stank of charred wood. The fuel here had all been expended, the fire so hot that it had taken the crowns of every tree. The forest was gone, leaving denuded smoking trunks. The pristine view of the mountains, purchased at great expense, had now become bleak and ruined and would remain so for years to come.

Dylan lifted his phone and found a signal. He called Jack first, before his family and before his friend Ray, who was still a newlywed. He'd attended the ceremony in May. He knew now what no one but Ray and Morgan had known then. His new wife was already carrying his child. Seeing Ray happy for once, and settled with a wife and child, had been the deciding factor for Dylan. He wanted that. A wife. Children. And a job that didn't smell of charred trees and animals.

Jack picked up on the first ring. "Dylan!"

Dylan could tell from the echo on the connection that Jack was in his truck.

"Yes!"

"Where are you?"

Dylan gave him their position.

"Sit tight. I'm on my way."

It was over a 120 miles from Turquoise Canyon to Flagstaff and most of it on winding mountain roads.

Dylan told him he had a companion and relayed the name. Silence was his answer. Finally Jack spoke.

"Not good."

"Did you contact Kenshaw?" asked Dylan, inquiring about their shaman and the leader of Tribal Thunder, the warrior sect of Dylan's medicine society.

Jack said he had and that Kenshaw had been unable

to reach Cheney Williams. "Kenshaw said he was there, right at the epicenter."

"What is the news saying?" asked Dylan.

"Forest fire. Evacuations. No mention of the explosion yet."

Dylan told him about the live streaming.

"I should be able to get that feed," said Jack. "Have to submit a request. If it captured a major crime, they'll release it."

Dylan scanned the smoking landscape. He'd call it major.

"Cheney Williams's death qualifies," said Jack. "Was the home owner up there?"

"I don't think so. Cheney said it would just be the two of us and a caretaker."

"I'll look into that. You have the caretaker's name?"

"No. Sorry. Maybe you ought to call Luke Forrest." Forrest was the field agent in charge when they took Jack's twin brother, Carter, into federal protection. Forrest was also Black Mountain Apache.

"Maybe. Hey, they've already called in our hotshots. Ray's heading up the guys in your absence. I guess you won't be crew captain on this one."

The Turquoise Canyon Hotshots were going on assignment without him. That was what he had wanted, wasn't it? The reason he'd gone back for training as a fire-safety inspector. So why did his gut ache?

"Yeah."

"I can't get to you until the fire is off the road. You got water?"

"Soon."

"All right, Brother Bobcat. Hold on. I've got another call. It's Forrest."

Dylan heard a double beep indicating he was on hold. He disconnected and continued along. They needed water.

"So, Cheney was here?" asked Meadow. It was the first she'd spoken to him in over an hour.

"Yeah. I'm sorry. He's gone." Now Dylan was wondering if Williams was a victim or some sort of suicide bomber. Kenshaw had recommended Dylan for this job, but now Dylan wondered exactly how his shaman knew this attorney who had lived down here in the valley? And why hadn't Cheney sent one of his staff to meet Dylan up here on the ridge? If he worked with Meadow's father, he must have people to do such things.

"Why did he call you brother bobcat?" she asked.

"You could hear that?"

She nodded.

"Bobcat is my spirit animal." He pushed up the sleeve of his T-shirt, showing her the tattoo. "This is his track."

She stroked a finger over the muscle of his arm and purred, her hand lingering. Dylan's muscles twitched as he grappled with the tension now overtaking him.

He stepped back, breaking the connection between them.

She distracted him. Made it hard for him to think. Now the questions swarmed him again. Buzzing around his head like gnats when he reached the crest of the ridge. Nothing of the building had survived. The explosion had ripped away the rock beneath the building. The infinity edge pool that had floated above the valley on steel legs, the house, garage and guest suite—all gone.

Dylan checked his phone for calls and found the battery dangerously low. "I'm almost out of juice."

"Switch it off and then check it periodically."

"Will do."

Dylan made another call to his parents' home and reached his grandfather, Frank. He told him quickly what had happened, and that he was safe and Jack Bear Den was coming to get him. He remembered to tell the old man that he loved him before he disconnected. Frank Florez was the only father Dylan had ever known.

When he finished, he turned off his phone.

"That was sweet. Your father?" she asked.

"Yes, but officially he's my grandfather. My mother's father."

"What clan?" she asked.

"Butterfly."

"Same as your mother, of course."

Dylan could see how Meadow had gotten all A's in school. She was quick.

"Can I call my family?" she asked.

That was a bad idea. Her dad would find out she had survived eventually from his radio communication. But he didn't want her father knowing exactly where to find them.

"Not yet."

She lifted a brow but said nothing, keeping her thoughts to herself as they continued up the hill.

He moved farther up and over the ridge. He had left the road to climb past the wreckage and so had not seen beyond the epicenter of the blaze to the pristine pavers of the curving drive that led to the untouched gate and gatehouse beyond the flashpoint of the fire. His mouth quirked in a smile.

Meadow arrived beside him a moment later. Her face was dangerously red. He gave her the mouthpiece to the camel pack and she took a long drink. Then he led them to the gatehouse. The only standing structure had survived the blast by being well down the private road and back from the ridge. The fire had spared the gatehouse only because prevailing winds had carried the blaze in the opposite direction, westward from the epicenter of the blast.

The Rustkin gatehouse was larger than his home on the rez. Dylan knocked on the front door but received no answer.

"You said on the phone the guy would be here," said Meadow.

"That's what Cheney told me." Dylan tried again, knocking louder. Then they gave up and circled the home. He broke a window in the garage and crawled inside, then disconnected the opener and hauled up the door himself. Meadow stepped inside.

"Phew," she said. "Cool in here." She glanced around. "No cars."

Dylan hoped the caretaker was far away because the road that circled down the unscathed side of the mountain met the burning side at the break in the ridgeline. If the caretaker had evacuated, he would not get far.

She cupped her hands to her mouth and shouted a hello. There was no reply. She turned to Dylan. "Well, we have lights and AC."

"Generator out back. Saw it on the way in."

"Let's take a look around," she said.

She was a bold one, he'd give her that—perhaps a little too daring. Dylan didn't just charge forward. He was more of a planner.

"Maybe you should wait here."

"Hell with that."

Meadow pivoted and led the way down the hall and past the office facing the drive, through the small living space and into the kitchen in the back.

There she stuck her entire head under the sink faucet and soaked her hair making the blue and purple turn a darker shade. Then she drank until he thought her stomach might rupture.

When she drew back, she whipped her head up so that the ends sent a spray of water to the ceiling.

"How do you feel?" he asked.

"Alive, thanks to you. But I'm dizzy…and what a headache."

"Heat exhaustion." Or heat stroke, he thought.

"Never had it this bad." She stepped aside and Dylan drank. Then he soaked his head, letting the lukewarm water wash away the sweat and sand from his short hair. The water was heaven.

"I'm going to find a bathroom. I need a shower."

"I'll check the generator."

She cast him a glance over one shoulder and shrugged. "Suit yourself."

Had she been inviting him along? That idea should have sent him in the opposite direction because he did not want to listen to the water running while he imagined Meadow washing her tempting body clean. Instead, he watched her walk away.

She strode down the hall that presumably led to the bedroom and bath. On the way she dropped the shirt he had lent her, giving him an unforgettable view of her back broken only by the lace bra. He'd kept her from being burned. Every inch of her was perfect, if dirty. Her tan covered her skin all the way to her bottom, which seemed very white by comparison above the scrap of pink lace. She cast a final glance over her shoulder and gave him a wink.

"You're up next." She reached behind her back and unfastened the bra as she turned, heedless of the glimpse she gave him of her body in profile. She was smaller up top than he had imagined, small and round and perfect. Thanks to him.

Dylan found the generator ran on propane and had switched on automatically when the power quit. How long it would last was just a guess, but he thought this would be the place to bed down tonight. Still, he would be careful about what electricity they used. He did a perimeter check familiarizing himself with his surroundings, then returned to the house and checked the rooms. The kitchen had a small table and chairs, and both the living room and the single bedroom were furnished. Someone had been living here, judging from the books, laptop and half-full coffeepot. The mail on the counter was addressed to David Kaneda. Dylan used his camera to snap a shot and sent it to Jack Bear Den with the message that they had reached the caretaker's house, which was empty. Jack's replay was the letter K.

Okay.

He busied himself filling his camel pack and then checking the landline, which was dead. The security system was not yet functioning, though the metal gate across the drive was locked. Unfortunately, the wall was not finished and a temporary road had been graded beyond the gate for construction vehicles to complete one of the most expensive homes in Arizona—and the only one that broke the ridge. Was that why they had blown it up?

They'd achieved a two-for-one, endangering the affluent community in the valley, as well.

He searched the cupboards and refrigerator. The refrigerator had bottled water, some of those sixty-four-ounce soda-fountain drinks and leftovers from lunches, some fruit, two half sandwiches—one meatball and one roast beef that smelled edible. On the counter he found chips.

Dylan arranged some of the food on the kitchen table and listened but did not hear the water running.

"You done?" he called.

"I didn't start yet."

"Why?"

"No soap."

Meadow called from the shower. "Is there soap out there?"

He searched and came up with a bottle of liquid hand soap and was halfway down the hall when he paused as all kinds of erotic images flooded him.

Dylan debated his options. Sex meant nothing to her.

He patted his front pocket where his wallet held two condoms. He had principles, but he was still a man.

"Dylan?"

"I found some."

He stepped into the steaming air of the bathroom. The glass door gave him a pretty fair image of what she looked like naked and wet. He growled and lifted the soap over the top of the glass barrier.

"There are no towels," she said, accepting the soap and then tipping her head back to let the spray of water cascade over her crown.

"They're in the linen closet in the hall."

She rolled back the shower door. He didn't look away.

"So, do we have a bed?" she asked. She was so casual about her body and sexuality. *Do we have a bed?*

"There's only one."

"That'll do."

Now his skin was prickling and his body responding to the possibilities she raised.

"Is that all you ever have on your mind?" he asked.

She faced him, pressing herself against the glass, giving him a view he would never forget. "Only since I met you."

He didn't believe it, but he found himself growing hard.

"Why don't you step in? I'll wash you off."

"Meadow, I don't even know you."

"You will if you get in here."

Dylan untied his boots and stripped out of his clothing. He retrieved his wallet and one condom. Then he ignored his conscience, slid back the door and stepped into the shower with Meadow.

Chapter Seven

"Man," she said, her smile widening. "You are fine to look at."

"You sure about this?" His body pulsed with need.

"Totally."

He'd never slept with someone who said *totally*. It wasn't right. Dylan dropped the condom onto the tiled shelf and closed the shower door.

"I thought I had burned my back in the shelter." He presented it to her. "But I don't feel any burns."

Her hands caressed his shoulders as the water pulsed on his skin.

"Perfect," she said. She soaped him and lathered his skin from his neck to the back of his legs while his body built to a thrumming need to touch her.

Meadow's hand slipped down his arm pausing at the tattoo.

"I like this. It's well done. That's a medicine shield. Right? And eagle feathers?"

He nodded, watching her as she traced the design.

She slipped around in front of him and repeated her ministration on his chest.

"I've wanted to touch you since I saw you with that ax. Then you were on top of me and I could barely breathe."

"I'm sorry about that."

"Don't be."

"It's a one-person shelter. We might be the first to ever share one."

Her hands stilled on his chest.

"Dylan, I know you said you don't…you know. But I really like you."

"That why you wouldn't speak to me?"

"That was childish. I was so hot and thirsty." She lifted up on her toes and kissed his cheek. He tilted his head and kissed her back, their mouths melting and tongues dancing.

What was he doing? She was trouble. This was Theron Wrangler's youngest daughter. Chances were good that she was involved in this. Maybe he could find out.

It was an excuse to have her—and a thin one at that—but he took it. He broke the kiss and turned her so that her perfect white bottom molded to his hips. His erection slid between her legs and she pushed back.

"What is it you want, Meadow?"

"Isn't that obvious?"

He cupped her breasts, toying with her nipples, pinching until her head fell back against his chest and she cried out in excitement. Then he stroked her stomach, thighs, the inside of her thighs. She opened her legs and he flicked a thumb over the tiny bud of pleasure. Meadow rubbed back against him, making it hard to concentrate.

"Why were you here, Meadow?" he whispered. "Why today?"

"Bad timing," she answered.

"Whose idea was it, this filming of the construction?"

She gasped and braced her hands on the tile, giving him more pressure as she pushed back, her slippery thighs caressing his erection. He closed his eyes and tilted his head back.

"Who?" he repeated.

"My father. He said I'd be doing him a favor."

"What favor?"

"A fast-motion montage of the home breaking the ridge, spoiling the natural beauty of the mountains."

And a fast-motion view of it tumbling down again.

"He sent you today?"

She nodded, her vocalizations now tiny cries.

And Kenshaw had sent him today.

"No more talk," she said, and rubbed against him. His fingers glided over slick flesh and she trembled.

Meadow's cries grew louder and her body jerked as her pleasure took her. Dylan held her as she turned into his arms, pressing her cheek to his chest. She fit just perfectly against him, and for a moment he wished she was someone else, someone he could keep.

"You're good," she whispered.

She reached between them, grasping him with experienced hands. Dylan knew he should step away. He tried, but it only gave her better leverage. Her clever fingers and water all worked against his best intentions. She stroked and his body hummed with the building need.

"We'll save the condom for later," she said. "How's that?"

She glided against him, trapping his erection between her soft stomach and her hands. His head fell back and he knew he was lost.

He didn't last long and had to brace his arms against the glass and tile to keep his knees from giving way. The truth was that he'd felt something with Meadow that was unfamiliar…longing. He admitted to himself that he wanted her. Wanted all of her. Wanted to stretch her out on that bed and slowly explore every inch. He wanted to take her to see the sunset over Turquoise Lake and to see the spot where he dug out the best turquoise from the vein deep in the heart of his reservation and the vein of the sacred blue stone that threaded through the canyon along the river.

But he admitted what this was for her—just a quick,

meaningless encounter or, worse, a thank-you. Her hands fell away and the emptiness yawned inside him.

She smiled up at him. "You always talk so much?"

He shook his head. "Not usually."

"You're no expert interrogator, that's for sure. You should sneak up on things. Not just jump right at it." She lifted the bottle of hand soap. "Want me to wash your hair?" she asked.

Dylan sighed. He'd been too overt again. "No. Meadow. I'll do it. What you said before, was that all true?"

"I have no reason to lie, though I'm super good at it. Ask me something personal?"

"Have you done this before?"

Her eyes went wide. "Never. You're my first."

A shot of regret pierced him. She'd led him to believe she was experienced.

"I'm sorry. We shouldn't have…"

"Oh, relax. I was lying. I'd better get out." She handed over the soap.

"You're very casual about sex," he said.

She pressed a hand to her hip. "That wasn't sex, Dylan. That was a hand job. If we have sex, you'll see the difference."

He made a strangled sound that was his best attempt at a laugh.

She let her hand slide back to her side. "I'm starving. Find anything to eat?"

"In the kitchen."

She strode naked and dripping out the door. *Brazen*, his mother would say. Uninhibited, he thought. Did it bother him that she was experienced?

Double standard if it did, he thought. But he found himself unsettled by the encounter. It wasn't until the suds were streaming over his face and chest that he realized why. It wasn't that she had had other men—it was that he didn't want her to have any more. Except him.

"That's crazy," he said, and rinsed. "You have as much chance of keeping her as catching wildfire."

He shut off the water, using his hands like the blade of a squeegee to shuck off the excess water. He shook his head, sending droplets flying. He was only damp when he stepped onto the tile floor and reached for his jeans. The smell of smoke hit him instantly, but there was no help for it.

Meadow returned with a towel cinched about her hips. She extended a second one to him.

When he reached the hall, it was to find Mcadow standing half-naked in the corridor beside the open accordion doors. Inside the closet sat a stacked laundry and shelving with clean linens and bath towels. She tossed her bra and panties into the washer leaving herself naked.

He lifted the shirt so it draped on his index finger.

"Looking for this?" he asked.

"It stinks. Throw it in here." She stepped aside.

"Do you do everything naked?" he asked.

"Only the important things." She shot him a blazing smile full of perfectly straightened white teeth. She collected the rest of his clothing and tossed them into the washer.

"My dad could send a helicopter for us. Want me to call him?" she asked.

Dylan hadn't thought of that. Her family would be worried sick.

His gut told him no, but how could he deny her?

"Too dangerous," he lied. In fact, it would be safe to approach by helicopter from the east, skirting the plume of smoke. Dylan looked away.

She returned to washing his shirt.

"To land here or to trust my dad?"

He didn't answer.

She added the soap and started the machine.

"My father did not send me up here to get caught in that wildfire. So you are going to need another theory."

He said nothing.

"We were closest to the explosion. You filmed it and I was up there, or nearly." He would have been if she had not delayed him. Had she done that on purpose, knowing what would come?

He rubbed his neck and tried to decide what to believe.

"The police will want to speak to us," he said, and waited for her reaction.

She closed the washer door. "Fine. I've got nothing to hide."

Truth or lie? he wondered.

His friend Jack had suspicions that Kenshaw was using Tribal Thunder for his own purposes. He told Dylan he believed Kenshaw had sent Carter down there to rescue his niece because he had foreknowledge of the Lilac shooting. Then their shaman had arranged for Ray to protect Morgan before the FBI even knew that BEAR was targeting her for fear Morgan knew who had hired her dad. Dylan had been there with Morgan and Ray when two masked members of BEAR had shown up and told Morgan that they had determined she knew nothing. Now here he was with Meadow the day the ridge house exploded.

"I don't mind police. But the tabloids. Oh, man. Get ready, because you are about to get famous."

He didn't like the sound of that. He was not shy but would describe himself as a private person.

"My savior." She started the machine. "Don't worry. I won't tell them about our communal shower if you don't. Or that we slept together."

"We haven't..."

She smiled. "Day's not over yet."

He'd never met a woman so blasé about filling her sexual needs. Did she want him or would anyone do?

She glanced out the window. "Let that run while we get something to eat." She headed down the hall, releasing her towel and fixing it again under her armpits.

He stepped into the bedroom and retrieved his phone. He flicked it on and called Jack.

"You okay?" asked Jack.

"So far."

"Where are you?"

Dylan told him.

"Good spot. Listen. I spoke with Forrest. That video feed has gone viral. Ms. Wrangler caught the exact moment the hillside blew. Plus, because of your radio distress call, they know you both survived. Local law enforcement is calling the fire suspicious."

"That was quick. They haven't investigated."

"Dylan, the news is reporting that sources say you are wanted in connection. Both of you. So you're a suspect. One news program is speculating that you are one of those guys who starts a fire and then puts it out."

"Hero complex," said Dylan. He sure had the right background for that.

"Luke says it stinks. He wants you out of there before the locals take you."

"How do we do that?"

"That's the problem. All access is blocked by the fire. He's trying to get a helicopter. Agent Forrest told me he's got his doubts that if you are arrested, that you two will make it to a station. He's afraid the plan was to pin the whole thing on you two all along."

"Whose plan?" he asked.

"Forrest thinks it's BEAR because they have the explosives."

"If they match," said Dylan.

"Takes time to determine that. Time we don't have."

"Could it be her father?"

"Forrest mentioned that. He's the logical suspect. Already linked to the Lilac mine shooting. You think Meadow is involved?"

"I'm not sure. My impression is that her being here is her father's doing. She thinks she's working on a documentary film about the house that broke the ridgeline."

"What do you think?"

"I think her dad sent her here to die. Make her a martyr for BEAR's causes."

"You don't have to convince me or Forrest. You have to convince the police if they get to you first."

"They won't. What about Kurt and the air ambulance?" asked Dylan. Jack's little brother was a paramedic out of Darabee.

"They're evacuating the firefighters on the line. Heat illness. It was a hundred and three out there. You got water?"

"Yes. How's the fire?"

"Twenty percent contained." Jack gave him the details. "No one is getting in to you. Road is closed. Your crew is out there."

Without him. That was the first time he hadn't been with them. Twelve men working the line.

"Is Ray there?"

"Yes, he's the one who told me you should stay put."

That gave Dylan some ease, but the guilt was still there. The silence stretched. Dylan pressed a hand to his forehead.

"Listen. You can't be there, so forget it."

Jack was right.

"Did you find a phone charger?"

"Not yet."

"Okay. Concentrate on what you can do."

"What's that?"

"Don't get caught. Tomorrow, maybe you can try to jump the fire line and rejoin your crew."

"What about Meadow?"

"You need to get as far away from that one as possible."

Chapter Eight

Jack thought Meadow was involved. Even if she wasn't, Dylan's friend believed that her father was responsible for the fire. He said his instinct told him that the blast was caused by explosives stolen from the Lilac Copper Mine.

Meadow didn't seem like an eco-extremist to Dylan but, really, they were strangers. His mind replayed their encounter in the shower and he groaned. He switched the phone off to preserve the battery that was now in the red. If he could find a charger he'd be all set.

He searched the bedroom and came up empty. He found Meadow in the kitchen and searched again for a charger but with no luck.

"I found a pantry." She showed him the locked door she had shimmied open.

Dylan was going to tell her that was stealing, but emergencies required allowances. The food was cans and boxes, but the pork and beans and peas tasted better than anything in his memory. He tried to tell himself it was his hunger, but he knew it was Meadow. Truth be told, he enjoyed her company. She told him about being sent off to boarding school at ten. Even though she kept the stories limited to the predicaments she had found herself in and even though he laughed, because she was such an expert at telling a story, he kept wondering why she had been sent away.

Finally the meal was done, and still they sat across from

each other, wrapped in clean towels and sharing stories. He told her about Iraq and how he'd lost one of his best friends to insurgents. How his friend had been tortured and finally killed. It was a story he didn't share. He also told her about his dad, who had left his family when Dylan was seven. Dylan had not been the oldest but he had taken charge. His brother Danny had taken off at seventeen for the rodeo circuit. He told her how his younger brother, Donny, now danced professionally at powwows for prize money. "Even danced in DC at the American Indian museum they got there," he added.

"They both left you holding the bag."

"I was in the service for four years. But, yeah, when I got home, Donny left, too. He comes home from time to time. Mom and Gramps make his regalia. Sometimes he brings money." Most times Donny needed it, Dylan thought.

"That's why you were so good. Your mom needed you," she said. Then she sniffed. "Mine never did."

"Did your brothers and sisters all go to boarding school, too?"

Her smile dropped. He had a moment to see behind the fun-loving facade to the pain she hid beneath.

"Only me."

"Because you were so much younger?" Perhaps they just had not wanted to deal with a teen when all her siblings were grown.

"My mother's idea. She said I lacked discipline. The girls' version of military school."

"Had you been in trouble?"

She glanced away. "Not yet. That came after they sent me off. Back then I was Daddy's little girl. My mom said I was too needy and, well, nothing I did really pleased her."

How terrible, he thought.

"So why did you get into so much trouble at school?"

She looked at him as if he were dim. Then she forced a smile. "Just growing up, you know, testing the limits."

Then it struck him and he understood. "When you tested the limits, they sent you home."

She met his gaze and he knew he was right.

"For a while," she said.

"You ever get in trouble at home?"

She shook her head. "Am I that easy to read?"

"No, but it's funny. I've always been a source of pride for my family—but not because I always wanted to do what was right. I'm not a Boy Scout, despite what you think. I just never wanted to see the disappointment on my mother's face. Maybe that doesn't make me brave. There were times I wanted to do what I liked, take what I wanted."

She gave him a look charged with desire, and he felt his longing build.

"Take what exactly?" she whispered.

His breathing quickened, but he did not say that what he wanted right now was her.

"You can take me, Dylan. No one needs to know that the Eagle Scout stumbled. I'll never tell."

He believed her and he stood to go to her. He knelt beside her and stroked the petal-soft skin of her cheek all the way down her throat to the top of her chest, feeling the swell of her breast above the rolled top of the bath towel.

"I wish I could," he said.

She pressed her forehead to his and closed her eyes. "You can."

He drew back. "I don't just want sex, Meadow. I want a woman who will stand by me. One who understands me and who loves me. You and I, we'll be going in different directions soon."

She took his hand and laced her fingers to his. "I could stick around."

Now he smiled at the ridiculousness of that image. "You

gonna move onto the rez? Raise cattle? Maybe you could work in the cultural center or up at the ruins touring visitors. No, you aren't sticking around, Meadow. You aren't the type. You know it and I know it."

"No one ever asked me to stick around." Something in her tone made it seem to Dylan as if she really wanted him to ask. But he couldn't. He barely knew her and it wouldn't work. They were too different.

"You need to get back to your world," he said, and stood.

She lifted her chin and smiled. The mask returned to its place. The fun-loving party girl was back.

"Whatever you say. So who gets the bed?"

MEN DID NOT turn her down, Meadow thought. That made Dylan a challenge. She hated being rejected. But, if she were honest with herself, and she very rarely was, this man was different. He had a purpose and a depth of character that she admired. She even admired that he wouldn't sleep with her.

Refreshing. But his reticence had backfired and now she wanted more than sex. He intrigued her. With Dylan she glimpsed a different way, and somehow she wanted to earn his respect. Trouble was, she had no idea how to begin. He didn't respect her and why would he?

Meadow checked the washer and loaded the clean, wet clothing into the dryer. When she returned to the kitchen, she found that Dylan had cleared her place and was washing dishes. She found a towel and dried. The dryer buzzer sounded and she traded her towel for her under things and Dylan's clean fire-resistant shirt, while Dylan drew on his jeans and shrugged into his T-shirt. In the caretaker's closet he found her a pair of gym shorts, but she rejected them. His shirt was covering enough, and if she couldn't get close to him, she could be close to his things. She lifted the collar to her nose and inhaled the smell of soap, but not the man whom the garment belonged.

"It's clean," he said.

"Too bad," she replied.

He cast her that look, the one that mingled caution with intrigue.

They sat for a time in the kitchen and he shared with her tales of firefighting and soldiering and what it was like to be a boy who rode his horse to school.

When she suppressed a yawn, he called a halt and took her off to bed.

"You're sleeping here, too," she insisted.

"That's a bad idea."

"It's the only bed," she said. "And if you're such a paragon of virtue, you should be able to ignore little old me for a few hours."

"I have a feeling no one ignores you, Meadow." He gave her a smile.

"My mother does." She had meant it to be a flippant remark, but the truth of her words stuck in her throat and her next breath was a strangled thing.

His smile drooped and he stroked her cheek. Mothers were supposed to love their children unconditionally, weren't they?

The tears came next and Dylan gathered her up, tucking her head under his chin.

"She avoids me unless I'm in trouble."

"So, you're in trouble a lot."

"Yup. Then my dad swoops in and fixes things and I get to see him and everything is good, you know, although he's disappointed. Then my mom gets a hold of me." Meadow shook her head. "It's like she can't wait to see me leave. I've tried everything. She just hates me."

He stroked her back. "I'm sure that's not so. Maybe she is just worried about you."

"And disappointed. But when I do well, she's just as dissatisfied. Worse, actually."

"How do you mean?"

"I got all good grades at my first prep school, hoping I could come home if I did well. She said that my dad was a generous donor, so the teachers wouldn't dare fail me. Dylan, I earned those grades, but she just…" Meadow inhaled and then blew away the breath. "Once my dad had me working as an assistant on his documentary on the reintroduction of wolves in Wyoming. He said my filming was really good and so he was taking me on location with him. She threw a fit about how he handed me everything and I needed to make my own way. So he didn't take me."

"You need to do what is right for yourself, Meadow. Not for your mother or your father."

"Really? You don't know my family. My oldest sister, Connie, is an aid worker in Uganda. You know my oldest brother, Phillip, is CEO of PAN, Protecting All Nature. Next brother, Miguel, he's a pediatrician with Doctors Without Borders. My sister Rosalie oversees PAN's projects, all of them, including reintroducing wolves into their natural habitat. My other sister, Katrina, does pro bono work for convicts and helps with marketing campaigns for my father's documentaries. We've got a CEO, two doctors, two attorneys and then there is me."

"You could be any of those things."

"It won't make any difference. If you're right, they sent me out here like Gretel to get lost in the forest and be eaten by the witch."

That he could not deny, because he believed it.

He continued to rub her back. "On Turquoise Canyon we have strong traditions and a rich heritage. We also have poverty, substance abuse and one of the shortest life expectancies in the nation. Forty-eight. That's the average

for a man who stays there. It's why my brothers left and
why I left."

"You don't have sisters?"

"I do. Two of them. Both older. Rita and Gianna married young. They have kids. They never left the rez. But
I joined the Marines. I learned things, saw things, and I
am a different man than the one I might have been—but
I am still Apache. So I returned to my people and joined
a medicine society. I swore to protect my tribe and keep
my body strong."

"Eagle Scout."

"Bobcat, remember?"

She smiled and pressed her face against the warmth
of his muscular chest. If only she could just stay here in
his arms.

"You make your parents proud."

He didn't answer.

"Dylan?"

"My mom is proud. Dad took off when I was a kid, right
after Donny was born. You want to make your dad proud
while I want to be nothing like mine. I want to be there for
my children and teach them what it is to walk in beauty."

"Walk in beauty?"

"It is a way to live that is in balance with the natural
world."

"My father would approve of that."

The conversation lulled, but still she felt at ease. It didn't
seem necessary to fill the silences.

"Do you think you could just hold me awhile tonight?"

His silence stretched, and she felt needy and weak.

"Sure. Yes, I can do that."

Likely he could. She couldn't think of a single man
she had ever known who would have said yes to that and
then not used it as a way to get into her panties. But Dylan
meant he could do it and he would. She didn't know if

that should make her happy or bereft. A little of both, she supposed.

"Thank you."

He tucked her in and lay on top of the coverlet, one big strong arm wrapped around her shoulders. She laid a hand on his ribbed stomach and felt his muscles twitch through the thin cotton. Meadow smiled and released a sigh. The skin of his bare arms turned to gooseflesh. The temptation to stroke him was strong but she resisted. Gradually he relaxed and she did, as well. When was the last time she had lain beside a man like this?

Never. A first, and that was rare enough. And to her surprise she discovered that she had missed a kind of intimacy that went beyond sex. She was at ease with Dylan. She trusted him enough to let him see what others did not—her pain.

His breathing softened. His mouth gaped and she smiled. The night could not be long enough for her. She did not dream, but woke as the bright morning sunlight stole across her face.

Why hadn't they thought to close the blinds?

Sometime during the night she had rolled to her side and Dylan had rolled with her. He now spooned against her. Her bottom was pressed against his groin and, although she could tell from his breathing that he still slept, she could feel a spectacular erection. He had one arm around her and across her chest so that his hand held her shoulder as if he was a lifeguard preparing to tow her to safety. She smiled and stretched, rubbing her bottom against him.

His breathing stopped and his body tensed.

"Good morning," she said, looking back at him.

He released her and rolled to his back. She rolled with him, draping a hand over his chest. He blew away a breath.

"Sorry," he said.

"Mornings. It happens. Right?"

"Yeah." He pinched his eyes closed and pressed his forearm over his eyes. "You are such a temptation, Meadow."

She wanted to be. But she also felt anxious because she did not just want to sleep with him. She wanted…more.

Oh, boy. She was in trouble again.

Chapter Nine

Dylan needed a moment to compose himself. It had been a long time since he had lain beside a woman all night and never when he had not slept with her. His gaze fell on Meadow as the dawn crept over the sky, painting her skin pink and lavender. She was nothing like any of the others.

His three serious relationships had all ended badly when each woman expressed her wish for marriage, forcing Dylan to face the hard fact that he was not in love with any of them. Margarete had said he was afraid of commitment because his father had left them. But the commitment-phobic didn't sign enlistment papers, did they? Maybe it wasn't the same thing. He had decided long ago that if female company came at the cost of a marriage, he would not settle until he fell in love. He wanted kids but not badly enough to pick just anyone. So far, he had not been lucky enough to find a woman with whom he could imagine wishing to spend his life.

He had watched Meadow in the rising light as she slept and wondered at the strange feelings of intimacy. Before she had fallen into sleep had been the most difficult, his intentions to comfort battling with his need to possess. He blamed it on the fire. Ever since he had taken her into his shelter, he'd felt an overwhelming need to protect her.

Meadow slipped to the edge of the bed they had shared, just like newlyweds. Well, he admitted, nothing like newlyweds. If that had been their wedding night, he most certainly would not have stopped at a few kisses. Still, having her cuddle up to him in the night had broken loose something inside him and now he wanted…what? A date? Too late for that. A relationship? He imagined how his brothers in Tribal Thunder would laugh at that. He knew of no couple who were such a mismatch, unless it was Anglo Cassidy Walker Cosen and her husband, Clyne. She had married one of the tribal councilmen on Black Mountain, much to the consternation of many in his tribe. If he had done it…

But this woman was a little crazy and he liked that. Was surprised he liked it.

Meadow murmured, and when her eyelids fluttered open, their gazes locked.

"You all right?" she asked, and rolled toward him, placing a hand at his opposite hip. "You haven't changed your mind?"

He tried to keep his attention on her pretty, sleepy face, but his gaze dipped to slide down her body. Meadow had kicked off most of the covers during the night, revealing smooth, tight skin interrupted only by her pink bra and panties.

"About?"

"You know." She ran a finger down the center of his chest and paused where the sheets covered his pulsing erection.

He swallowed, trying to think with the rational part of his brain and not the animal part that roared to take what she offered.

"Meadow, you don't think this can go anywhere, right?" Had he sounded hopeful? *Please, no.*

"I think it can go any number of interesting places."

"What I mean is—do you want me just for this?" He motioned at the evidence of his preparedness.

Her gaze trailed down him, and he swore he could feel her attention like a caress.

"I don't know why you'd want anything else. No one else does. At first, men want sex or an introduction to my parents. Some latch on to me in hopes I might actually come into serious money someday. Those are the worst."

"I don't want those things."

She sighed. "Pity. Especially about the sex. I'd know how to handle you then." She allowed her hand to trail up his thigh, letting him know exactly what she intended to handle.

"I want to protect you, Meadow. That means keeping you from starting something that isn't going to work out."

Her hand splayed on his thigh. "It might."

He met her gaze and saw, reflected in her warm eyes, the need for a connection that matched his own. He sat up.

"No one will let us be," he said, still trying to be the voice of reason. "My mom, my friends, my tribe."

"My parents, friends and family would be shocked. But I'm not sure they'd be disappointed."

"But shocked," he echoed.

"That I finally picked a man of character. Sure would."

He switched to the language of his birth as he stroked her cheek. "I wish it could be you."

"What does that mean?"

"We don't have time."

The disappointment made him ache.

"Oh, right." She reached to the end table and handed him his phone. "You better check in. See if we can get through."

He booted up the phone, which now showed a red bar over his voice message page. The battery was nearly empty. Jack had left him a message. Ray Strong, too. Both were unread, but he never left his phone on the voice mail page.

She slipped to the edge of the bed and headed toward

the bathroom. He wondered if Meadow had used his phone. He'd never set the password protection. She'd had an opportunity to use his phone when he'd been in the shower. He glanced from the phone to the hallway where she had disappeared.

Again he wondered if he was sleeping with the enemy.

He checked the recent calls but found nothing. She could have deleted it. Then he checked his two messages. He listened to Ray's first and discovered where the fire was contained and where his crew was working. Jack's message was next and he listened as she reappeared and sat on his side at the foot of the bed.

"The road is opening at eight a.m. State police said they'll let the home owners through at around ten. Anyone could be heading at you. Pick up, Dylan. Listen. If you are at the gatehouse, you need to get out of there."

Dylan glanced at the phone's screen and saw it was only a few minutes after eight. He was up and dressed in moments. Unfortunately, Meadow still wore only her underwear.

He explained that someone was coming.

"That's good. Isn't it?"

"Not necessarily. We should be out of here before they arrive, just in case."

"In case of what?"

He explained it to her as Meadow slipped into her sandals.

"Find some clothing. Look in his dresser," he said motioning to the chest of drawers presumably belonging to the gatekeeper.

"They can't think we started this. It's ridiculous."

Dylan's people had been on the receiving end of many injustices. Unlike Meadow, he did not expect to get fair treatment.

"We have to go," said Dylan.

"I'm not going back out there."

"Wait here, then," he said.

"Maybe I think I will." That stubborn chin lifted again.

Dylan glanced out the window that showed the road that wound up to the gatehouse. That was when he spotted a rooster tail of dust. They were already here.

"It's a bad idea."

She followed the direction of his gaze.

"Cavalry has arrived?"

Looked more like trouble to Dylan. All his internal alarms were sounding.

He lifted his brows. "You realize the cavalry used to shoot my people on sight, don't you?"

"If you're planning on hiding, you better scoot before they get here," she said.

He grabbed her wrist. "Come with me."

She shook him off and he let her go. She thumbed toward the kitchen window. "Listen. I appreciate everything you did for me, but I am not going out there again unless there is air-conditioning." She lifted to her toes to peer out the window as Dylan ducked out of sight. "There, at the gate. Oh, a Hummer!"

It was, indeed. Not the commercial kind sold to posers in the cities but a Humvee that had armor plating. He had been in one when Hatch Yeager had been killed that night when they'd been ordered to secure the road. This vehicle was close to a mobile tank that could move across the desert or through the woods as long as there was a gap big enough in the trees. It also did not show any signs of having traveled through the fire.

There was only one road leading to this home to Pine View and between here and there the fire still raged. The road to from Valley View, through Pine Valley and then began hitched back and forth up the ridge, until the incline became too steep. The road then threaded between the ridges to continue up the gentler slope behind the mountain. This made practical sense and afforded an impressive view of the controversial home on approach. If the Humvee had driven over the valley road and through the wildfire, there would have been evidence, ash covering the surface, possibly pink fire retardant around the wheel wells or charring of the exterior paint. But there was none of that.

Dylan made the next logical conclusion. They had been inside the perimeter of fire. In other words, they had traveled down behind the ridge but never crossed into the valley of devastation beyond. So whoever was in that vehicle, they had been here since before the fire.

"Meadow. Listen, we have to go now. Those aren't friends."

"Dylan, I'm not going out there to scramble over those rocks again. My feet are blistered. Forget it."

The construction route remained open, leaving the security gate blocking an unfinished road. Even if theh perimeter was operational, that Humvee would blast right through it.

Meadow stepped past him. Dylan waited by the side door, slipping out as the Humvee roared through the missing section of wall and onto the flat, paved road beyond. It stopped in front of the main entrance as he crept around the back of the gatehouse, so he was there when the driver in combat boots stepped down from the vehicle. Dylan's eyes narrowed, knowing at a glance that this was not the home owner. The driver was dressed in desert camouflage, but the familiar name patch, black-and-white US flag and service insignia were missing. In other words, there was nothing to identify him. His designer mirror Oakleys were not regulation. His red hair was short but not buzzed, and his build was athletic. His stride contained a swagger of a young man.

His copilot emerged from the opposite side, similarly dressed with no soot or ash on his clothing. He was in his middle years, already well into the third quadrant of the medicine wheel. His hair was buzzed perhaps to hide the hairline that had receded back to his bald spot. He slipped on a cap with a brim that shaded his pale eyes. This one had the look of ex-military, right down to his crisp walk.

"Let's get this over with," said the passenger, who seemed to be the man in charge.

Dylan locked his jaw. *Get what over with?* He called on Bobcat to help him see what they intended and to be patient as he waited for his chance.

"I'm shooting him if he makes a move," said the young one.

"We don't even know if he's here."

"Survived the fire, though," said Red.

His commander searched the ground and quickly found the tracks that marked Dylan and Meadow's arrival.

"They said he's an ex-marine," said the young one, drawing his personal weapon and looking about as if Dylan would spring at him from behind the ornamental boulders that lined the drive.

There was no such thing as an ex-marine. Or that's what his sergeant had told him. Once a marine, always a marine. *Semper fi.*

"Put that away," ordered the one in command. "As far as anyone knows, they didn't leave the shelter. No radio contact from him since the distress call at twelve-hundred hours yesterday."

Dylan darted from the house to the grill of the Hummer, reaching the driver's side as the older man knocked on the gatehouse door like a service call instead of what Dylan judged him to be—a killer on a cleanup mission.

He heard them speaking as they approached the gatehouse. Dylan slipped the passenger door open and searched the interior, coming up with the keys that dangled from the ignition.

What was he doing? Jack had told him to hide. He could be over the ridge and down in those rocks by now. Instead, he was searching the rear seat and retrieving the shotgun he spotted there. Why hadn't he forced Meadow to come with him?

Meadow opened the door. She had found some clothing, beige jeans rolled at the ankle and an over-size T-shirt both of which only made her look smaller and more vulnerable.

"Well, here are my guardian angels. Did my father send you?"

"Yes, Ms. Wrangler. If you'll come with us."

He couldn't see her but he heard her sandals crunch on the gravel on the other side of the vehicle.

"Where is Mr. Tehauno?"

"Oh, he's down below looking for his friend, William Cheney. I told him he was gone."

Dylan tried to figure how her father's people knew that he and Meadow were together. He'd made one transmission. All other communication had gone only to Jack Bear Den, whom he trusted with his life. That meant someone had monitored the shortwave communication and sent these men.

Dylan checked the shotgun and found two rounds. He flipped the lever to single shot.

"We have orders to collect him, as well," said the second man.

Yeah. That is not happening, Dylan thought.

The sun was behind them now, making its ascent on one of the longest days of the year. Sweat beaded on Dylan's skin as he waited in the blistering hot morning sun. He bet it would be over a hundred today, too. The question was whether either he or Meadow would live to see it.

Dylan reached the back bumper of the Humvee and

glanced in the rear window, spotting an empty back compartment.

"Well, I'd like to get out of here, so you'll have to come back for him."

"Have a look inside," said the commander.

"He's not there, I said."

"After that, check the perimeter." He glanced at his smartphone. "He's close."

The driver pushed past Meadow, who managed to look indignant rather than frightened. She had to know that she'd made the wrong call remaining behind, but she held on to her persona as the powerful daughter of a powerful man.

The redhead disappeared into the gatehouse and returned a few moments later. "Not there."

"There's no cover but the rocks. Check the hill on the west." Then he turned to Meadow. "Right this way, Ms. Wrangler."

But, instead of going meekly along, Meadow screamed a warning.

"Dylan! Run!"

Her abductor dropped all pretext and slapped her across the face. Meadow staggered but remained standing. A few minutes later Dylan heard the crunch of boots on gravel as the second man returned.

"I didn't see him."

The one holding Meadow cursed.

"Get in the car," he said, presumably to Meadow.

"I'm not going anywhere with you. And when my father finds out that you struck me, you'll be sitting in a jail cell, mister." There was a scuffle and then Meadow's voice again. "Hey! Let go of me."

They were heading his way. Dylan raised the shotgun and took one breath in preparation. Then he stood, revealing his position.

The young driver did not look up as he muscled Meadow along and, behind her, the veteran soldier held a Taser pointed at Meadow's back. He spotted Dylan, his step slowing as they made eye contact.

"Don't!" said Dylan, but it was too late.

The older man pressed the trigger at the same moment his gaze flicked to Dylan. Meadow jerked and twitched, falling to her knees and then out of Dylan's line of sight.

Red, the young one, reached for his sidearm, still locked in the holster by a black nylon strap.

Dylan swung the shotgun at him, aiming at his face.

"It's the last thing you'll do," he said.

Red lifted his hands. Dylan swung the weapon to the real threat, who continued to press the Taser trigger. Dylan's heart hammered as he realized he was trying to kill Meadow by giving her enough juice to stop her heart.

"Drop it!" he commanded, and raised the stock of his rifle to his cheek, aiming for center mass.

The older one dropped the Taser.

Meadow went still. Was she even breathing?

Chapter Ten

Dylan held his aim on the one in charge as he spoke to the younger man.

"Put her in the Humvee," said Dylan.

Dylan had an adequate view of the ginger-headed man from his periphery. The man glanced at his supervisor, who gave a slight inclination of his head. Meadow was lifted, slack and limp, into the rear seat of the Humvee.

"Now step away," said Dylan.

If he had any doubt about Meadow's innocence in this, this attack had banished it. She was a victim here. At worst, she was a pawn.

"You going to kill us, son?" asked the older one. "No, I don't think so. You're the golden boy. Clean service record. Always making the right moves, even on the basketball court. Always following orders." He took a step closer. "Thing is, in all that time in the service, you never did have to shoot anyone. Look them in the eye and take their life. Because that would be wrong. And you don't do wrong."

"Stop," Dylan ordered.

"You aren't a killer. Give me the gun, son." He extended his hand and Dylan knew the man had badly underestimated him. Just because he *had* not did not mean he *would* not. He would—to protect Meadow, he knew he would do anything.

"I promised to protect her."

"She's not worth your time, son. Black eye to the whole family. Never held a job and she's got more men than a stray dog got fleas. You'd be the flavor of the month. And that's just not you."

Another step and his target would be close enough to take the shotgun barrel. Dylan knew a shot at this range would take his life and he knew the scatter pattern of shot from the years shooting on the rez. So, when he pulled the trigger, he aimed low and wide. The outside edge of the shot scatter struck his opponent in the leg and he went down howling like a wolf.

Dylan ordered the other man to lie face down beside his commander. Then he checked Meadow and found a pulse. He couldn't control the need to see her safe anymore than he could leave her here to die.

Flavor of the month? Maybe, but at least he'd be walking out of here.

The younger one was crying. Dylan took his pistol, phone and sunglasses.

"Pass code," said Dylan.

The crying man gave it to him. Dylan used the phone to call Jack but got flipped over to voice mail. That meant Jack was out of range. Dylan held the phone out, wondering how long the recording lasted.

"Your name," said Dylan.

"Vic Heil."

"Why are you two here?"

"Retrieve Meadow Wrangler."

"Who are you working for?"

"Wrangler. That's all I know. I swear."

The injured man howled and cursed at Vic. The only intelligible words were "Shut up."

"Did you two set the blast that started the fire?"

No answer.

Dylan pressed the pistol to Heil's temple.

"Did you?"

"Yes!"

"Why?"

"I don't know. Take out the snitch. That's what the captain said."

"What snitch?"

"Shut up," shrieked his commander. Dylan stepped on his bleeding thigh, and the man howled again.

"Williams," said Heil. "He's a snitch. Blabbing to someone. That's all I know. I swear."

"Blabbing to whom?"

"Don't know, I said."

"You don't know or they don't know?"

"I don't know."

Dylan removed the barrel from the man's head.

"Shut up!" yelled the captain, clutching his leg and rolling side to side on his back.

"Come on, man," said Heil to Dylan. "He's bleeding all over the place."

"Why do you want the girl?" asked Dylan.

"Just find her, is all."

Dylan lifted the phone and checked. The call had disconnected. He found the microphone app and pressed Record.

"What's the captain's name?"

"Rubins."

"First name?"

"Don't know."

Captain Rubins rolled from side to side as his leg oozed blood from the many punctures.

"Say it again," Dylan ordered. He held out the phone.

Vic started talking, telling what he knew, which wasn't much with the captain yelling at him that they'd just signed their own death warrants. Vic did admit to setting the fire and told him where they'd set the charges. He said he didn't know who they worked for and Dylan believed him. When he ordered him up, Vic pissed himself, but Dylan still sent him walking down the ridge. Dylan knew that Vic expected the second shotgun blast to hit him in the back. Dylan just wanted him far enough away to give him time to get Meadow out of here.

He turned to Rubins.

"You want to fill in the blanks?"

"Yeah," he said through gritted teeth, "you're a dead man. They won't stop."

"Why does her father want her dead?" asked Dylan.

The man's smile was a snarl. "Run, Bobcat. The BEARs are coming."

They knew he was called Bobcat. What else did they know?

Dylan took the man's phone and the pistol strapped to his bleeding thigh.

"I'll send help," he said as he climbed into the Humvee.

Rubins snarled. "You'll need it more than me."

Dylan commandeered their vehicle.

He needed to find the Turquoise Canyon Hotshots. Jack had given him their position, but he had doubts he could reach them on the main road. The Hummer gave him some leeway on the route. If there was any area of back burn, he might get Meadow through. But where to then? He didn't know. He only knew that they couldn't stay here.

They wound down the road that led toward the line of smoke billowing skyward. How many acres had already burned?

Halfway around they saw Heil still walking in wet pants. He watched them drive past and then reversed course. Dylan used the Humvee's satellite link to call 911 and report the injured man. He said the man had been injured by the discharge of a shotgun and gave the location. He had a feeling that Rubins was too stubborn to die. If

Heil slowed the bleeding and the shot pellets had missed the femoral artery, Rubins would likely survive.

Dylan pulled to a stop to check Meadow. Other than the two marks on her back from the Taser, she seemed fine. Her heartbeat was normal and so was her breathing. He used some of the water in the Humvee to wet her face. Her eyes fluttered open and she groaned.

"What happened?"

He told her.

She rubbed her jaw. "Feels like someone punched me." Her hand moved to her head. "Worst hangover ever."

"Drink some water." He offered the bottle to her and she drank.

"They Tasered me?" she asked.

"In the back."

She rubbed her forehead. "I should have listened to you. I'm sorry, Dylan."

"They hit you when you tried to warn me."

She glanced away.

"That was dangerous," he said.

"Yeah, well, reckless is what I'm good at. Remember?"

"That wasn't reckless. It was selfless."

Her artifice dropped with her smile and she gave him a serious look. "I didn't want anything to happen to you."

Now he was the one who had lost his mask. He didn't know what to say. He had never expected this woman—this woman he thought to be a spoiled little rich girl—to show such courage. Just like everyone else, he'd under-estimated her.

"How'd you get us away?"

He gave her the short version.

"What were they going to do with me?"

"Nothing good. Those guys set the fire."

She groaned. "Help me to the front seat."

He lifted her easily, then settled her into the passenger seat and buckled her in.

"How do you know they set it?"

Dylan wondered if he should tell her about the recording he had gotten. After a mental debate, he revealed he had Heil's confession.

"It implicates my father," she said.

He nodded.

She glanced away. "I can't believe this. I thought…I believed he loved me."

"Maybe he loves the cause more."

She said nothing to that.

Dylan called home and got his grandpa again after seven rings. His grandpa wasn't fast. But he was a wonderful fisherman and had also turned his turquoise claim over to Dylan. His older sisters Rita and Gianna didn't want it, but did want occasional nodules of the bright blue stone.

"Where are we going?" asked Meadow.

He told her his plan to find a break in the fire line, one as close to his home team of hotshots as possible.

She glanced ahead. "The fire line again?"

"We have to get through it. The crews will be on site. They'll have a break somewhere." He hoped.

There was only one road, so he followed it as far as he could. She turned to look at the place where the hull of her car sat. The ground was scorched now, black and stinking of smoke. He drove toward the fire, hoping he would get a signal but knowing the smoke would interfere with reception.

Dylan got them as far as the ridge of smoke, looking for a break or a crew at work. The last thing he wanted was to get himself into another spot where they would be trapped. He couldn't tell if the smoke was worse or if it was only because the winds had shifted. It grew so thick he needed the headlights to keep going. Meadow pointed to the sky.

"Look!"

He glanced up at the helicopter flying with the red collapsible bucket beneath. A moment later it released the load and red fire suppressant spilled from the sky. The compound was sticky and slimy, but it worked. He headed for the spot the chopper had dropped the payload. A few minutes later he saw the place where the ground was coated with the viscous red fluid. Then he saw the men behind it making a line.

The phone Dylan had taken from Rubins rang and he lifted it, not recognizing the number. He picked up.

"Yeah," he said.

"You got them?"

"Yeah."

"Where the hell are you?"

"Heading for the fire line."

"Fire line? You're supposed to call for a chopper."

"Send it."

"Who the hell is this?" There was cursing. Then the line went dead.

"Well, that didn't work."

"You don't speak like them."

"I was trying."

"Your speech pattern is more lilting, like a song."

Dylan didn't know if he liked that.

"Can we get through the fire line?" she asked.

"Jack says so. He also says the main road is open, but it will be covered with highway patrol. We don't want that."

"Won't they help us?"

He came from a place where the police were not often helpful. He supposed her parents had told her to look for a policeman if she were in trouble.

"You and I are wanted for starting this fire," he reminded her.

"But we didn't do it."

He thought that was irrelevant.

"We just have to explain."

"Meadow, a man was killed up here. Your father sent killers to finish you. He won't help you and, without your father's money, you will be represented by an attorney appointed by the court. You could be in jail a very long time while they investigate the case—that is, if someone doesn't get to you while you are locked up. Do you have anything to prove your innocence?"

"You can't prove you didn't do something."

"Exactly."

"I was with you."

"You were in position to film the explosion. You had an opportunity to set the charges. I did, too. Plus, if those men are to be believed, your father not only set you up to die in this fire, he sent men to be certain you didn't reappear with a different story. He might try again."

"I could go to my sisters or brothers."

He didn't know them and so didn't trust them.

"If you like."

"They might be with him." She sank into her seat. "I have no one. That's what you're saying."

"You have me."

"All right, Bobcat. What do we do?"

"Find out who set the fire. Clear our names. Bring the guilty to justice."

"And how do we do all that?"

"Working on it."

Chapter Eleven

"I've never seen anything like it," Meadow said as she glanced out the window.

Dylan had. Many times in many states, he realized as he left the main road to weave through the charred remains of standing trees. The odor of smoke seeped in through the vents.

"Hard to believe now, but the vegetation will come back."

"Ruined the view from the valley. I suppose that was the point."

That seemed very likely. Dylan followed the helicopters, judging where they had been and choosing his route from that. When they reached the area that had received a coating of the red fire retardant slurry, the first crew he met was out of Flagstaff. They directed him to the Apache crew, but that turned out to be the Navajo boys out of Fort Defiance. They knew where the Turquoise Canyon crew was working and Dylan found them, making a line with their axes, their motions smooth and efficient. He paused a moment to see how well they were managing without their former crew chief.

Ray Strong left the line to speak to him. His face was streaked with sweat and soot, making his teeth appear especially bright. Even without trying, there was a kind of perpetual devilment in his twinkling eyes and mischievous smile. Ray had been in and out of trouble most of his life, owing to a reckless nature coupled with a stubborn streak. But he was one man Dylan knew he could rely on. In his current situation, he needed a friend who didn't care very much for rules or laws.

Dylan left the vehicle to greet his friend, with Meadow close behind him.

Ray hugged him, and Dylan accepted a thump on the back.

"We've been looking for you all night," said Ray. "News reported you both dead. I see Jack was right, again. Man, you gave me a scare." Ray broke away and gave Meadow a long look. Dylan tried to tamp down his possessiveness as Ray moved closer, and failed. He objected to the way Ray smiled at her and gripped her hand during the introduction. He held on a little too long, in Dylan's opinion.

"How's Morgan?" asked Dylan.

Ray was now a married man with an instant family, since Morgan had a daughter from a previous relationship.

Ray seemed to be holding back a laugh as he regarded Dylan. "Just fine. Worried about you, too. Let's get you two back to base. It's not too far."

Ray rode with them. The base was just a grouping of tents, a temporary shower area and a food drop. Ray left them to return to the line, as Dylan and Meadow shared a ready-made meal. They were still eating when Ray re-appeared.

"Highway boys are here. They're looking for you two. They already have your Humvee."

Dylan was on his feet looking for an escape route. He needed a vehicle.

"Your truck here?"

Ray shook his head. "Came in by bus."

They were trapped.

"Hide in plain sight," said Ray, holding up two fire helmets.

Dylan wrapped Meadow's blue hair in a bandana then adjusted a helmet to fit her head. In short order, Dylan was dressed in familiar attire, borrowed from Ray, and Ray had a quick version of all that had happened since Dylan and Meadow had been forced into the fire shelter. Well, not everything. He'd left out what had happened in the shower and what had been happening to him since. If they survived this, he'd like to take her out.

The voice of reason scoffed. Where? Where in the wild world would an Apache hotshot take a celebrity heiress? The impossibility of a relationship weighed on him as much as the fear of pursuit.

"We need to get you into protection. Like Carter. Until then, you two hide on the line."

Meadow slipped into a pair of battered boots that Ray offered. She could keep them on if she laced them tight.

"Jack said Forrest is here somewhere. The feds are out here looking for you, too. We need to be sure that Jack finds you first."

"Our crew chief is right up here," said one of his men, a little too loudly as he came up the hill in their direction. "Captain?" he hollered. "There are two detectives from the Highway Patrol wanting to see you."

Ray waved Dylan and Meadow away and they retreated in the opposite direction.

"Mr. Strong, we need the location of the two fugitives that arrived in a Hummer."

Dylan heard Ray speaking to one officer.

"Where's the other one?" he whispered to Meadow.

"What?"

"Ray's man said there were two. Where's the other one?"

The male voice came from behind him. "Right here."

Dylan had a weapon. Two, actually, but he would not draw on a law enforcement officer. He raised his hands. Meadow did the same.

"Facedown on the ground. Both of you."

Dylan stretched out. Meadow hesitated.

"Meadow, do as he says," said Dylan.

The officer took out his Taser and Meadow dropped down beside Dylan. In a moment they had their hands zip-tied behind their back, they were frisked, read their rights and were then hustled into the back of an Arizona Highway Patrol vehicle.

He saw Ray make an attempt to get to them. They were both members of Tribal Thunder, and he knew Ray would do whatever it took to get him out.

Ray called out to Dylan in Tonto Apache.

"I will call help. Do not worry, Brother Bobcat."

Dylan replied in Tonto, "Hurry, my brother. Her father wants her dead."

The last he saw of Ray was his worried face as he drew out his radio. Then they were gone, driving past the staging area and away from the fire.

"Where are we going?" asked Dylan.

"Flagstaff."

"I want a lawyer," said Meadow. Then she turned to him and said, "Don't you say a thing to any of them until I get you an attorney."

She still didn't understand. All her money and power and influence flowed from her parents and that tap had been shut off. Meadow now had only her reputation and her fame. It wouldn't be enough.

They were met en route by the Flagstaff police and escorted to the station. Once there, they were greeted by news crews with cameras and microphones pointed at them like artillery.

For the first time in his life, Dylan found himself on the

wrong end of the law. He had always done what was expected, what was right and legal. He'd helped Ray Strong out of more situations and scrapes than he could count, but Dylan had never been the one facing a prison cell.

They were separated for processing. Dylan's one call at six that evening was to his grandfather, who said he would send help. Dylan asked him to get to their shaman, Kenshaw Little Falcon. He then spent much of the next day refusing to answer questions. The police did furnish him with some information. The vehicle they had taken was found to have carried explosives. Some of the blasting cord was still in the back. They told him that they believed he was one of the eco-extremists involved with the theft down at the Lilac Copper Mine. They were testing the explosives and expected a match. He did not confirm or deny his ownership of the Humvee, but it didn't matter, because the registration bore his name. Clearly, he and Meadow had more than just terrible timing. They were the fall guys for this and were supposed to die like good little patsies. He expected someone would be sent to get to them. That was what had been done to the Lilac mine shooter. The hit had been made as the mass gunman was transported to the police station in Darabee. Sanchez had been assassinated by one of Dylan's own people, and whatever Sanchez had known died with him.

The police needed the guilty and BEAR needed a scapegoat. Dylan thought they had found two. And the fact that he had been driving the vehicle and that Meadow's brother headed PAN, the organization known in the Southwest for Protecting All Nature, and that her father was an environmental documentary filmmaker did not help her cause. She came across as some Patty Hearst–like character. The rich-girl-turned-terrorist. Oh, boy, would that sell papers.

Dylan wondered how long they would keep at this. It

seemed like hours since he'd arrived, but in the window-less interrogation room it was difficult to tell.

The interrogating officer started asking him the same questions again from the beginning. Dylan exhaled his frustration and kept his mouth firmly shut.

The impact from something heavy shook the building. The detectives stood and looked at the door.

"What was that?" asked the younger detective.

"See what's up," said the one with the sprinkling of gray in his short stubble of hair.

"Felt like a bomb." The man already had the door open when they heard the sound of automatic weapon fire. The older man shot out the door and then turned back to the junior man and aimed a finger at Dylan.

"Watch him!" Then he vanished from sight.

The younger detective watched him go and so did not see Dylan rise from his seat and charge him. The impact of that attack brought them both out into the hallway, where Dylan landed on top of him. He stood preparing to stomp the guy if he needed to, but the officer had the wind knocked out of him, giving Dylan the moment he needed to retrieve the man's wallet and the handcuff key. That was where his friend Jack Bear Den kept his key. Dylan also took the guy's car keys. If the fob was right, the guy drove a Dodge. Dylan had one wrist out of the cuffs when the detective reached for his gun. Dylan hit him in the jaw and then dragged him back into the interrogation room. Then Bobcat went hunting for Meadow.

Where was she? He didn't know what was happening, but he knew who they were after—him and Meadow, the loose ends that could ruin their plans.

The police returned fire now. Automatic weapon blasts mingled with the discharge of shotguns. Dylan checked one room after another. He found her in an interrogation room with a wide-eyed female officer. Dylan ordered her back and she went for her weapon. Meadow was up and diving for the female officer, causing her to fall to the ground and her pistol to skitter across the floor.

Dylan dragged Meadow off and hustled her out. Her hands were cuffed, but he didn't stop to address her captured wrists.

"What's happening?" she asked.

"Don't know." He turned away from the gunfire and made it to the end of the hall that led to an emergency exit and then stairs. The Flagstaff joint police and sheriff building had only two floors. They were halfway down the flight when they heard the door above them open. Dylan glanced up as they made the turn around the landing and saw Vic Heil, one of the two men who had crashed the gatehouse.

"They're here," Vic yelled over his shoulder.

Then Vic aimed the automatic weapon at them. Dylan pushed Meadow to the wall as the blast of gunfire hit the concrete stairs above their heads.

"Who is it?" she asked.

"Guy from the gatehouse. Run, Meadow."

They burst out the side door, triggering another alarm. Dylan blinked at the bright sunlight and the blast of hot air.

Meadow stumbled, her hands still cuffed behind her back. Dylan kept a hand on her elbow to assist her balance as they darted into the parking lot. Meadow was quick and they made it out the door to the rear parking area. They darted between the closest cars and kept low as Dylan retrieved the fob and pressed the door release. They heard a beep and headed for the sound as the back door of the building banged open. Their pursuer had reached the parking lot.

Chapter Twelve

Dylan did not hit the lock release again for fear of alerting the gunman of their destination. Instead, he searched for Dodge vehicles. His second try found a car that was unlocked. He got Meadow into the passenger seat and then ducked around to the driver's side, praying that this was the detective's vehicle and not just an unlocked car.

The key turned and the motor engaged. His relief was short-lived as he saw the gunman's head turn in their direction. An instant later, the gunman was running. Dylan saw him clearly now, the younger man from the gatehouse— Vic Heil. Behind him came a second man that Dylan did not know.

Dylan threw the muscle car into Reverse and flew backward in the Dodge Challenger. Thank goodness the detective liked fast cars. This one was a V-8.

Dylan burned rubber and fishtailed on his exit from the lot. Meadow looked back, yelped and ducked low as bullets peppered the trunk.

Vic had missed the tires, Dylan realized as he made the main road and screeched out into traffic amid the sound of horn blasts. They barreled away from the station. Dylan didn't know where he was headed yet. He just wanted to put distance between him and the men who hunted them.

"Hit men," said Meadow. "Honest-to-God hit men."

She let her head sink back to the seat and turned to look at him. "You saved my life again."

"You're welcome," he said, and cast her a grin. He drove them out of the city before stopping to release the second side of his cuffs and set Meadow free.

"Where should we go?"

"Two choices. Your family or mine," he said.

"My family has financial resources."

"They also might have sent those men to kill us."

"I've always wanted to see those reservoirs in the mountains," she said. "And the ridge of turquoise you spoke about."

With the destination decided, Dylan set them in motion. Twilight found them driving south. It was well past dark when they reached Indian land. Dylan thought it was the first time he had taken an easy breath in two days.

Dylan drove straight down I-17, the fastest way home from Flagstaff. He stopped to make a phone call at a truck stop east of Phoenix and reached Jack. His friend met them at the boundary of their land. He flashed his lights and escorted them toward tribal headquarters. Their tribe was small—only a little over 900 members living on the rez—so the tribal seat included a small police station in a wing of the building, but it was enough for the nine officers on the payroll.

Dylan needed a shower, a hot meal and a warm bed. The thought of bed made his gaze slide to Meadow.

"How are you holding up?" he asked.

"Exhausted. Do you think he'll interrogate us again?"

"He'll have questions, but I'll handle them."

She levered her palm under her chin as if she needed to brace herself to keep her head up. Her yawn triggered one of his own.

He pulled into tribal headquarters behind Jack. His

friend Detective Jack Bear Den stepped from his vehicle. Meadow's gasp at the sight of him was audible.

"He's…he's…" She was pointing now, leaning forward.

"I know. He's big."

"Big? That's a giant. He's Apache?"

"There's some debate about that," he muttered.

She turned to him, her voice conspiratorial. "Really?"

Dylan must be more exhausted than he realized, revealing Jack's business.

"He has brothers, but he doesn't really resemble them."

She nodded, those pretty brown eyes wide. "Gotcha."

Jack was at her door now, drawing it open.

"Miss Wrangler?"

She nodded.

"Welcome to Turquoise Canyon. I'm tribal police detective Jack Bear Den. I'm sorry to hear of your troubles."

He extended a hand. Dylan could not explain why it pleased him that she looked to him before accepting. He nodded and she took Jack's hand, her small one all but disappearing into his.

"Thank you," Meadow said.

Dylan got out of the car to join them as they made their way into the station.

"I ordered some food," said Jack. "Should be waiting."

Dylan wanted a shower, but he thanked his friend. Jack was a fellow member of Tribal Thunder and a warrior by nature. It was because of Jack that his brother Carter had survived the insurgent attack that had killed their translator and their friend Hatch Yeager. Carter had rescued their sergeant, and Jack had passed the wounded man to Dylan, then grabbed a hold of Carter to keep him from charging into the enemy forces that had already overtaken Hatch's position. It was exactly the kind of cool thinking under pressure that made Dylan so relieved to have reached the tribe and Jack's protection.

Jack escorted Meadow into the station and then introduced her to his police chief, Wallace Tinnin. Once in the staff room, Dylan was greeted by three members of the tribal council. As was custom, they spoke of generalities until their guest was fed. Only after their meal did they speak of what had happened, and they chose to speak in Tonto Apache.

The short version was that they believed Dylan was innocent of all charges and were prepared to protect him from any and all Anglos. Meadow was a different story, however. They looked at her with suspicion and feared that this outsider would bring trouble. It was only through Dylan's refusal to desert her that she was permitted to stay.

Dylan made the decision to take her to his home. Jack arranged police protection for them. Dylan knew resources were tight and appreciated Tinnin approving the decision.

His home was in a remote area, past the tribal community of Koun'nde. Access was via a single road. One way in. One way out. Jack escorted him home and Dylan was relieved to see his place was empty. He'd been half-afraid that his mother, sisters and grandfather might be there to greet him. He loved his family, but his energy was waning. He needed rest.

Jack went in first while Dylan and Meadow waited outside.

"He's like a pit bull," said Meadow.

"Just bull. No pit."

"He's in your warrior society?" she asked.

Dylan nodded and stretched his tight muscles.

"What's his spirit animal? Wait, let me guess. Buffalo."

Dylan shook his head, his smile turning sad. He rubbed the back of his neck.

"Bear?" she guessed.

"No. Our shaman, Kenshaw Little Falcon, did not

choose an animal for Jack. Jack was given the medicine wheel."

Her brow wrinkled. "That's what?"

"It looks like a compass, divided into the four directions. But the symbol is more inclusive, with many meanings."

"Why did he choose that?"

"I do not know. I only know what Jack told us, that Kenshaw said it would help him find which direction to go."

Dylan was about to tell her that there was one more difference between Jack and the three other newest members of Tribal Thunder. Jack's tattoo was not on his right arm, but emblazoned on his back, between his shoulder blades. But somehow that seemed even more private than the mystery of his birth, so he remained silent.

Jack's return ended Dylan's internal quandary.

"All clear," said Jack. "See you in the morning. Kenshaw wants to speak to you tomorrow."

Dylan stiffened. He had never had any trouble with their shaman until February, when Jack had mentioned his suspicions that Kenshaw was an active member of WOLF.

WOLF, which stood for Wilderness of Life Forever, was the less extreme of the two groups. Their aim was the same as BEAR, but they made all efforts to preserve human life while BEAR made efforts to destroy as many lives as possible in their efforts to protect and preserve nature.

If their shaman was an eco-extremist, seeing him might put Meadow in danger.

Dylan switched to Apache. "Do you still suspect he is a member of WOLF?"

"No. I no longer suspect. I know he is."

Dylan lifted a brow.

"I will not put her in danger."

Now Jack lifted a brow, and Dylan found it hard to hold his gaze.

"Really? Do you know what you are doing?"

"I used to think so."

"You saved her, so she is your responsibility. But be careful. Even I have heard of this one." He inclined his head toward Meadow, who seemed to know she was the subject of conversation as she looked from one to the other.

"I am always careful," said Dylan.

Jack smiled. Did he think he was speaking to Ray? One or the other of them was always reminding Ray to be careful. To follow the rules. To do as he was told. No one had ever felt the need to issue such advice to Dylan. Suddenly he understood the sour look he always gleaned when he gave his unsolicited advice to Ray. He glared at Jack and switched to English.

"We will see you in the morning."

"I'll call first." He let that one sink in and then tipped his cowboy hat to Meadow. "Sleep well, Ms. Wrangler."

They watched him walk away.

"He doesn't like me," said Meadow.

Dylan didn't deny it. But what mattered was that Dylan liked her. She wasn't what she believed herself to be. He recalled her tackling the female officer in Flagstaff and running through the parking lot. Meadow was a warrior and a survivor, just like Dylan. But there were so many differences between them. Too many, he reminded himself. Still, reason didn't stop him from admiring her, and, if he was honest, he'd admit his feelings did not end with a growing respect. He was beginning to like her. And for the first time since he had met her, they were safe and alone together.

Chapter Thirteen

Meadow explored his living room, feeling his gaze follow her as she moved through Dylan's space. The furniture was sparse, nearly Spartan with the exception of a long, sagging couch and an upholstered chair and ottoman. The back of the sofa was draped with a woolen blanket in a bold geometric pattern that reminded her of a Navajo rug. Behind the chair sat a floor lamp angled to pour light on the occupant. On the ottoman were three stacks of books and on the floor, in the place where an end table might be, sat another pile of books reaching up to the level of the armrest. She saw mysteries, thrillers, books about American history and a travel guide on fishing in Alaska. Dylan had more books on his ottoman than she'd read in the past six years. She hadn't read anything much since her schooling ended and she no longer had to state the theme of the fish in *The Old Man and the Sea* or describe the meaning of irony using Lord Byron's *Don Juan*. She looked to the place where a television would be and found only a speaker system that attached to an MP3 player and a charging station for digital devices.

"You don't watch TV?" she asked.

"On my tablet, sometimes. I like college hoops."

"News?"

"Online mostly. Can I get you a drink?"

"Wine would be wonderful. Red, if you have it."

He glanced away. "I don't. Never drank alcohol."

She did not succeed in stifling a gasp. "Never?"

Now she wondered if he had a problem, but he'd said he never drank, not that he didn't drink or didn't drink anymore. She had given up hard liquor while in detox, after a late-night swim lead to an indecency charge. She now only drank wine and held herself to a two-glass limit.

"Because you're Native American?"

He smiled. "Because alcohol is bad for you and makes you do things you later regret."

"That's true."

"No one in my family drinks."

"Is everyone in your family Apache?"

"Yes, all."

"And you only date other Apache?"

"That's a small gene pool. I don't limit myself or discriminate by race. Though my mom would prefer..." He glanced away and made a face.

He didn't have to finish. His mother wanted a nice Native American girl. She certainly didn't want a spoiled white girl with Smurf-blue hair whose main talent seemed to be generating income for the tabloids.

"Maybe I can meet her sometime." She felt singularly inadequate. Generally, she only felt this way when with her siblings. Her wealth often put men off balance, but lately her lifestyle had attracted men who liked money and especially liked spending hers.

"Oh, I'm sure you will. The minute she finds out I'm home, she'll be at the door."

Meadow looked at the door in question and swallowed hard. She glanced down at her clothing and grimaced. She thought she could still smell the odor of smoke clinging to her.

"I can't meet her like this," she said.

Dylan smiled. "I think you are safe for the night."

She didn't want to be safe. And she wanted more than a night. More than a few days, a lost weekend. Oh, she was in so much trouble. He was a warrior, a hotshot, a man of character with morals strongly rooted in his community. She was a punch line.

"So, tomorrow we speak to your shaman?"

"That's right."

"Is there any protocol or anything?"

"It's not like meeting the Queen of England. You don't have to curtsy. He's a regular guy, mostly."

"So women can speak to him?"

He smiled. "Again, not Hassidic. Not Amish. Apache."

She flushed. "I don't know anything about shamans."

"They learn by apprenticeship. It's a calling, like priests, but they are not celibate. They preside over ceremonies like the Sunrise Ceremony, which is a woman's coming of age. He advises, prays, heals, and is a spiritual leader. He preserves our language and culture by teaching the youth."

Somehow she could see Dylan doing all those things.

"Are you considering it?"

He inhaled. "How did you know that?"

"Just the way you looked when you spoke of their responsibilities."

"I've considered it. I'm a little old to begin."

"Have you spoken to your shaman?"

"Yes, and he's agreed to accept me as an apprentice."

"But you can still marry?" As soon as she said it, she recognized her mistake. Was it the haste of her words or the worry in her eyes that told him her thoughts? She didn't know, but she saw the confusion break into speculation as he considered why she asked this question.

When she realized she was wringing her hands, she

dropped them to her sides. Now she felt small and inadequate again.

"What?" she asked.

"You're a puzzle," he said. "You could have any man. I'm struggling to understand your interest in me. Is it just physical?"

Something told her to withdraw, protect her ego. If she said yes, he might sleep with her, but he might also tell her that he was not that kind of guy. But to admit that she wanted more than to share his bed was to show a kind of need and vulnerability that frightened her nearly as much as the fire shelter. She looked at him.

He waited, his dark eyes cautious. Was that the glimmer of hope?

She bit her bottom lip and then jumped in headfirst, like always.

"It's not just physical. I'm attracted to you, physically, of course. Powerfully, and since I first saw you."

"You were rude when you first saw me."

"I was showing off. Trying to get your attention."

"You succeeded."

"I acted like an ass."

"But back to your attraction," he said, stepping closer.

"I've never met anyone like you," she said.

"Apache?"

"Yes, but no. You're protective, perceptive, sensitive."

"Sensitive? I'll deny that if you tell anyone."

"You shouldn't. It's rare."

He took her hand and led her down the hall. "Let's finish the tour."

"Kitchen is through there."

She had a glimpse of a dark room with empty counters.

"I have two bedrooms and one bath. The tribe provides housing through HUD. We own the land and property on the land communally. Unlike most tribes, we do not have a shortage of housing and so a single man like me can live in a single home."

"That's good."

"We have a surplus because of a falling birthrate and because unemployment has caused many of our young men to leave us to find work elsewhere."

"Like Alaska?"

His eyebrows lifted again and then he glanced back to the living room. "You got that from the book on salmon fishing?"

"And knowing that there are jobs there."

"There are. But I would not like to leave the tribe for so long. I see what happens. Men leave. They find work or a woman and…" He shrugged. "Men go to the woman's family. It's tradition here and common out there, too."

Like his brothers. They had both left and never come back.

"You speak as if it's another country. We live in the same state."

"But a different world. I don't know if I could blend my life with an Anglo."

She let her hand slip away.

"But maybe the right woman could change that," he said.

The hope bubbled in her chest like a tiny gem. The oyster making a pearl of possibilities inside her hard shell. Was she the right woman?

Her skin was tingling and she felt the flush of excitement.

"You are a fascinating woman. Brazen. Independent and very brave."

"I never was brave."

"Maybe you never had anything worth fighting for before."

There was truth in that.

He motioned to a door. "Guest room."

She glanced in and saw a full-size bed made up with military precision with a striped red, black and turquoise wool blanket and white sheets. There was a desk with a computer.

"Office?"

"Something like it. My room is across the hall. Bathroom is between the two. We each have a door lock. You can use it if you don't want company."

His smile faded as his joke turned into possibilities. Was he also remembering the shower they had shared? Did he regret setting her aside? She took a step toward him, vowing that if she ever got him naked again, she wasn't going to let him go.

"Need anything else?" he asked, and then pressed his lips together as he realized what he had offered.

"Yes," she said, and looped her arms around his neck. The kiss she gave him was full of sensual need and promise. He responded instantly, gathering her tight in his arms so she could feel every muscular curve and contour and hard ridge.

She hummed with satisfaction as he deepened the kiss, bending her over his arm. Her fingers raked his back, calling on his spirit animal to take his mate. The sound he made was a growl, deep, low and dangerous. Oh, she wanted to unleash that danger. Meadow raked her fingers downward.

He gasped and then pushed her back. She felt the past repeating and wondered if she'd ever recover from the humiliation of throwing herself at him twice.

But this time he didn't reject her. The heat in his gaze made her stomach tremble.

"Are you sure, Meadow?" he asked.

She shivered with desire fused with anticipation. In answer she used one index finger to graze down him midline, stopping at his waistband, where she hooked that finger inside the fabric of his trousers and tugged.

"Very," she said, just before his mouth claimed hers again.

She savored the sweet velvet glide of his tongue on hers. Dylan's hand angled up under the shirt and unfastened the oversize jeans she wore. She broke the kiss to kick out of her borrowed boots and stepped clear of the men's pants, returning to him and their kiss.

The pads of his fingers grazed over her thigh, making her stomach tremble. She wanted him to touch her there at the epicenter of the pulsing need he stirred.

Meadow rubbed against the hard muscle of his thigh and was rewarded when he splayed his fingers over her bottom and lifted her until their hips met. She wrapped her legs about him, locking her ankles behind his back as he turned them toward the bed.

He was whispering to her in his language, his breath stirring the hairs on her neck. The anticipation beat inside her like a living thing, the need pulsing with her blood.

"Hurry," she said.

"No. This is not going to be fast. When you look back on your life, Meadow, I want you to remember me."

Was he already planning their separation? Perhaps he was just wise enough to see the number of obstacles between them. A realist, when she had always been a dreamer.

And her dreams were full of Dylan, now and forever. Oh, she would remember him. How could she ever forget?

She only hoped that she would look back and remember this as the beginning and not the end.

What would convince him to stay, to give them a chance? Certainly nothing in the bed that even now rushed up to greet her. She needed to touch more than his body.

But his body was what she needed right now—the warmth and comfort and protection. He'd never denied her those things, and she knew that he would deny her nothing tonight.

Chapter Fourteen

Dylan explored Meadow's body with both hands. She wanted him, and tonight it did not matter that there was no future in it. His time in the service had taught him the tenuousness of life. Since his return, he'd forgotten this lesson. But the wildfire had made him remember that life was sweet and short and never to be taken for granted.

They were safe and she was in his arms. What more could he wish for? A future with her. Well, yes, but he'd whisper that only to himself, the irrational desire that told him this woman was placed on this earth only to walk at his side.

He longed to give her so much more than his protection. He wanted to give her his heart. And that would be foolish, indeed. She'd made it clear she was not the sort of woman to be trusted with something as fragile as a man's love. She was giving him this night and he would take what he could, knowing that his family would not approve of her or of his actions. Knowing that his medicine society would be shocked to see the golden boy make such an obvious mistake.

He let the pads of his fingers graze over the soft, yielding flesh, stroking down her midline, pausing at her navel and feeling her stomach muscles ripple under his touch. He followed with his lips, tasting the sweetness of her skin, savoring the velvet of the tiny hairs.

She sighed and arched to meet him, her hands clenching in his hair. Here was a woman who knew what she wanted and was prepared to take what she liked. The knowledge that she was experienced aroused him further as she planted her feet on the coverlet and let her knees splay. The earthy scent came to him as he tasted her. He moved his fingers and tongue, all to increase her pleasure, savoring the sounds of her growing need.

She spoke to him in a tone husky with passion, encouraging him, saying things he wished were true, calling him her sweetheart, her darling, and when she found her release it was his name she called. He let her rest awhile, using the firm muscle of her thigh as a pillow, drawing what he could not say with his fingertip on her opposite thigh and stomach. Gradually her breathing slowed and then she made a humming sound.

"Come back up here," she said, and he did, gliding along her slick flesh, letting his hips press her down to his bed. He had never brought a woman here, to his home, his refuge, his sanctuary. But it seemed right with Meadow and that troubled him. Getting her here would be easier than convincing her to stay. He almost laughed at the image of her, the party girl, tabloid princess and goat of all goats, living here on the reservation. Riding with him along the river on horseback. Coming to dance when he beat the drum at gatherings.

He could not see any of it.

"That's a serious face," she said.

"Yes, loving a woman is serious business." He had not meant to say it that way. Would she think he meant the act of making love to her? He hoped so. She held her quizzical look for a moment and smiled.

"Why don't you kiss me again?" She lifted her hips and his erection slid along her cleft. The sensation made him suck in a breath.

He kissed her, angling his mouth to show her exactly what he intended to do, his tongue stroking hers in long thrusts. She broke away, whispering against his temple.

"I can't wait. I want to feel you inside me. Dylan, please tell me you've got protection."

He shifted to open the drawer in the bedside table and offered her a foiled condom. She showed strong white teeth as she tore into the packaging, then pushed at his shoulder to encourage him to roll away.

If she wanted to do it, he was willing. Her clever hands stroked down his shaft and before he could make his next move she had straddled him, risen to her knees and then slid down over him. He grasped her hips, setting a pace that was slow and deep. She didn't fight him but whimpered as her fingers curled to rake his chest. The sensations overwhelmed him. He struggled not to finish what they started. But he waited for two reasons. He wanted to watch her ride him, see her body sink down over him with a force that made her lovely full breasts bounce. He didn't know if it was her self-assurance or his passion for this woman that made him so hot, and he didn't care. She was moving faster now, her head thrown back as she took and gave. They seemed to lock in place and then she rose up on her knees again, nearly losing him.

The secret, internal rippling started an instant before she cried out. They rode the wave of ecstasy home together, and then she fell forward to sprawl across his chest, her blue hair rippling down his torso like a wave. He closed his eyes at last, held her there, limp and sated, knowing that he wanted her again, still, forever.

He understood the difference between want and need. His desire for Meadow was too strong to be forgotten or cast aside. That meant that he would need to fight to keep her. Fight her family, his family, his friends and clan and—very possibly—Meadow.

Dylan had never loved a woman before, but he recognized the truth. She had captured him as she had likely done to others before him. He knew he could only keep her if she wanted to be kept.

There was as much chance of stopping a wildfire single-handedly as capturing a woman with a heart as wild as this one's.

MEADOW WOKE WITH a start, not knowing where she was. There, in the dark with her heart hammering, she felt the arms of a man and the familiar scent that reminded her of the one good thing to come out of all this chaos—Dylan.

He drew her in, cradling her against his chest and pressing his lips to her forehead.

"Safe now," he whispered.

She released a breath and felt her racing heart slowing to a strong, steady beat.

"I have you." And here he switched to the language she could not understand.

"What does that mean?"

"Hmm?"

"The words you were saying."

His voice was gravel and slow as if struggling against the grip of a deep sleep.

"Endearments. Like *sweetheart* or *darling*. Literally means…my…heartbeat." His breathing puffed out in a way that told her she had lost him to sleep. But still he held her close, his thumb stroking her shoulder.

His heartbeat? She smiled. What a lovely thing to say.

DYLAN WAS NOT done with her. He knew that her father was not the wealthy philanthropist he pretended to be. Or, if he was this, that was not all he was. That alone was enough to divide them. But there was so much more. He felt the passage of time, the seconds and minutes adding to the moment they would part. If holding her in his arms was enough to keep her here, he would never let go. But soon, very soon, the day would come and the forces of division would appear with the sun.

He closed his eyes, promising himself he would rest only a few moments and knowing from the weariness of his body that he lied. He told himself that she needed some rest before he showed her how much she now meant to him, acted out the devotion and adoration he could not speak aloud.

Once more, he thought, and then once more after that. It would have to be enough. In the end, it was not the sun but those few hours of necessary sleep that stole away his chance to love her again.

Dylan woke to the pounding on his front door.

The gray glow of morning provided enough light for Dylan to recognize Jack Bear Den's white SUV. The words *Tribal Police* were printed across the rear door and back panel in blue lettering, and on the front door was the great seal of the Turquoise Canyon tribe. Detective Bear Den stood on his front step, blocking Dylan's view of the rest of the drive, his arm lifted to beat on the door again.

He flipped open the lock and let in the friend he'd had since grade school. He scrutinized Jack's expression, trying to anticipate the reason for his visit, and thought that the massive man's face seemed thinner, and there were dark smudges under his eyes. Why hadn't he noticed that yesterday? Dylan looked more closely. Was it a trick of the light or the loss of his twin brother that had caused the change in his appearance?

Jack issued a greeting in Tonto Apache.

Dylan returned the greeting. Then he rubbed the palms of his hands into his tired eyes and peered at Jack, studying his posture and expression for clues. He did not like what he saw. Something was wrong.

His thought was that something had happened to Carter, who was now in witness protection, but then he had another thought. It shot through him like an electric current, startling him to alertness. Ray Strong was on the line fighting that fire, the crew chief in his place.

"Ray?"

"No," said Jack, understanding the question, but whether from the panic that must have shown on his face or the tone of his voice, Dylan did not know. "He's fine. Fire is still raging, though. They are hoping the rains will kill it."

"That could be weeks," said Dylan, sick at the possibility that the fire started by a group that purported to protect the environment would burn thousands of acres.

Dylan turned to the next possible reason for his early visit.

"Carter?"

Jack's mouth turned down. "No word."

"Will you come in? I'll make coffee." Dylan hoped he would go away so he could return to his bed and the woman waiting in it.

"I'm sorry, I can't. I need you to come with me."

Dylan's heart cried out as his body braced for some new threat.

"What time is it?"

"Five thirty. Morning paper just arrived. Kenshaw called me. He needs you and the Anglo."

"Her name is Meadow."

"Yes, I know." Jack lifted a folded newspaper and let it drop open so Dylan could read the two-inch-high headline:

Heiress Meadow Wrangler Missing
Casualty or Cause of Fire?

Dylan snatched the paper. The article reported that Meadow had been filming for one of her father's projects when she was caught in the wildfire. Her car had been recovered but no remains. Dylan scanned the article further, seeing that a search was hampered by the active wildfire and road closures. Her father had posted a reward for information.

"They don't know she was in custody?"

"Apparently not," said Jack.

"Twenty-five thousand dollars?" asked Dylan.

"Yup."

"He's after her," said Dylan. "Who saw us come in?"

"Enough people to cause me concern. She can't stay here."

Dylan gripped the door to help him regain control, because his instinct was to fight Jack or anyone else who tried to take Meadow from him.

"Where is Kenshaw?" asked Dylan. Now he needed Tribal Thunder to agree to protect Meadow, an outsider, from her father. That meant convincing their shaman not to let her off the reservation.

"I'll take you to him," said Jack. "He said to hurry. He doesn't have much time."

"He doesn't?" What did that even mean? "Jack, you need to fill me in."

"Can't. Not my place. Get what you need. Pack for traveling."

"What kind of traveling?"

"Unknown. But travel light."

Dylan had the unpleasant task of shaking Meadow out of bed. He paused in the door to his bedroom to try to memorize what she looked like sprawled on his mattress, the covers tangled in her tanned legs and her cobalt-colored hair cascading over his white linen pillowcase. She had one hand raised with curled fingers pressed to her forehead and her mouth was parted as she breathed with slow, even breaths. Her cheeks glowed pink in the rising light and he wondered if that was from the scratch of the stubble on his chin and cheeks. He wanted nothing more than to crawl into bed beside her and love her again.

Instead, he touched her bare shoulder. Her eyes opened and she turned an unfocused gaze on him, casting a sleepy smile.

"Good morning," she said, and then stretched. She sat up and the coverlet dropped away.

His body reacted to the sight of her, naked to the waist. He sucked in a breath as the fire raced through him.

"Come back to bed," she whispered, looping a finger in his boxers and tugging.

He resisted and she frowned.

"Jack's here."

Her finger slipped away and her brow knit. "Here? Why?"

"My shaman has asked to see us right away."

"What's happening?"

Dylan didn't know what was happening or why his shaman needed to see them both right now. He didn't know if he could convince the others of Tribal Thunder to protect Meadow. All he did know was that *he* would protect her. Because over the miles and the minutes, Meadow had risen from responsibility to necessity and Dylan could no longer imagine letting her go.

Chapter Fifteen

Jack Bear Den drove them from Koun'nde. The sun broke over the ridge of pine as they passed the upper ruins. His friend Jack was not good at small talk and Meadow was too worried to be polite so Jack switched to Tonto Apache and spoke to Dylan.

"Is she all right?" asked Jack.

"Afraid of what will happen next. She's been through a lot."

"You both have."

"You really don't know what Kenshaw wants?" asked Dylan.

"I know he sounded out of breath and asked me to meet him in an unusual place. I sent my men first to be sure it was safe for you and the woman."

"Meadow," said Dylan.

She looked at him from the backseat and he smiled, reading concern clearly across her pretty face.

"Yes. Her father is searching for her. You can't keep her a secret for long."

That was true. Most secrets were hard to keep. Jack had secrets, ones he wanted revealed.

"Ray won't be there. Carter, either."

"No. Just you, me and my brother Kurt."

"Have you heard anything from Carter?"

Jack shook his head. "Field Agent Forrest says he's well and they are awaiting the trial to testify."

"Then what?"

"He isn't sure. BEAR is still a credible threat. Carter's wife is the only one who can link Wrangler to the Lilac mine." Jack glanced in the rearview at the woman whose father was the most likely head of BEAR. That made her a threat, too.

"She's not involved."

Jack turned to Dylan. "Oh, no. That's not true. She may be just a pawn or something more. But she is definitely implicated, because someone wanted her killed." They slipped into silence as they reached the Hakathi River and turned toward Piñon Forks.

Jack broke the oppressive stillness first. "I got back the test results on the sibling DNA."

Dylan glanced from the road to Jack. Ray had told him that Carter had complied with Jack's request to take the test. Jack had a theory to explain the fact that he did not resemble his brothers. He thought he had a different father. The simplest way to prove this was to take a sibling DNA test. As Dylan understood it, that was only a swab of the cheek. It would show if you and your sibling shared two parents or only one.

"What did it say?"

"I don't know. I haven't opened it. I carry it around in my wallet. Every day I hold it in my hands and then I put it back."

"But I thought you needed to know."

"I do. But maybe I need not to know more."

Dylan shook his head, not understanding.

"As long as that envelope stays closed, I can pretend…"

As long as the envelope remained closed, then Jack was still Bear Den, still Roadrunner born of Snake, still Tonto Apache. Yes, Dylan understood.

"No hurry, Jack."

Jack met his gaze and smiled.

"I'm with you no matter what you decide." He switched to English. "Hey, have you considered my idea to bring a relay team up to the Brule Sioux Rez? With you as catcher and me as rider, I think we can win." The Indian Relay Races were gaining popularity and he did not want the Sioux to have all the glory.

"The other two?" asked Jack.

"Ray has agreed. I wanted Carter, but if he will not be back by September, maybe Kurt or Tommy," Dylan said, referring to Jack's younger brothers.

"What about Danny?" asked Jack.

"I'll ask Danny. But he won't come home from the rodeo circuit."

"Maybe meet us there?"

"I can ask if you ask Tommy."

"Deal. You really think we can win?"

"Of course."

Jack was smiling again. But he lost his good humor as they pulled into a cutoff leading to a portion of the reservation off-limits to outsiders. This road led to the Turquoise River, one of the few rivers in Arizona that ran year-round, though not as it used to before the series of dams were added in the forties. They were met by a roadblock made of two orange traffic cones and a branch. One of his fellow officers left his unit to greet them.

"They're waiting," said Officer Wetselline. "Chief Tinnin, too."

Jack cursed. If he had hoped to keep something from his boss, Wallace Tinnin, he had failed. None of his force of nine officers moved without him knowing.

Wetselline removed the branch and they rolled past.

Dylan did not know what to expect, but he had packed

light, as Jack had requested. He splayed his hand over his duffel and glanced back at Meadow.

"Almost there."

She gave a quick little nod, her brow knitting.

"It will be all right," he said.

Her reply was a wide-eyed expression and clenching jaw that silently relayed she believed it would be anything but.

He turned to Jack. "If we need to make a run for it, will you help us?"

Jack lifted a thick brow. "You'd run, for her?"

Dylan nodded and Jack's expression turned blacker still. "Yes."

"Mexico?"

"I don't know. I haven't thought it through. Will you?"

Jack nodded. "Hope it doesn't come to that. But yes, I got your back. Always."

They drew up to the lodge and pavilion utilized by the tribe for celebrations and ceremonies. Beyond, a string of cabins sat along the river. Past that, in the trees, was the sweat lodge used by their medicine society, the Turquoise Guardians, and the smaller, elite warrior sect of Tribal Thunder.

Dylan thought he could benefit from a good sweat to remove the poisons of the fire from his body with the ritual cleansing of the sacred sage and cedar smoke. But there was no time. There, in the road beside the pavilion, stood his shaman, the chief of tribal police, Wallace Tinnin, and, beside them, an outsider, FBI field agent Luke Forrest of the Black Mountain Apache Tribe.

"What's he doing here?" asked Dylan.

"Don't know," said Jack. "Nothing good."

"He can't arrest us here. Not on our land."

Jack nodded the truth of that. "But he can arrest her," he said, his chin indicating the passenger in the backseat.

"Jack, you can't let that happen."

His friend lowered his chin, but whether in reply or in preparation for a fight, Dylan did not know. Dylan was always the peacemaker in the group. He'd pulled Ray Strong's fanny from the fire more times than he could count and Jack's, too, on occasion. Now he was the one who was preparing to do something stupid, and he pitied anyone who got between him and Meadow.

"Let's see how this plays out," said Jack, and exited the vehicle.

Dylan glanced to Meadow. "I don't know if you should stay here or…"

Meadow shook her head. "I'm staying with you for as long as I can."

Dylan helped her out and brought her into the gathering of serious men, all Apache and all dour as mourners at a funeral. He made introductions.

"Meadow Wrangler, this is my shaman, Kenshaw Little Falcon."

His shaman did not offer his hand. That was an Anglo custom and Kenshaw did not believe in such greetings. He said an open hand was not assurance that a man did not have a weapon. Kenshaw was the only one in the bunch without a blazer or sport coat and looked the least official. His white cotton shirt covered him from the sun, and the turquoise beads he always wore fell in heavy cords about his neck. He looked the elder he was fast becoming because of his sour expression and the threads of white hairs that mingled with the black in two straight braids adorned with nothing more than hair ties. Jeans and boots completed his outfit.

"I know your father," said Kenshaw to Meadow. "He is a powerful speaker."

Meadow held her smile as she met Wallace Tinnin, who did shake her extended hand and lifted his drooping features for a moment into a kindly smile before his face fell back to the perpetual look of a man on the hunt. He and Luke Forrest both wore their hair very short and dressed like the Anglos Kenshaw said they were becoming.

Forrest was Dylan's last introduction. The man was lean and compact with a power that came from his bearing as much as his body. Dylan had to resist dragging Meadow behind him when Luke took her hand in a brief greeting. Suddenly Dylan found himself facing off against religious, local and federal authorities all at once. It was a scenario he could not have imagined even three days ago. But so much had changed, and all since he'd met this woman.

"Shall we go into the lodge?" asked Tinnin.

Dylan glanced to Jack, who nodded and then led the way. Inside, they gathered in the office conference area that provided them a wide circular table inlaid with turquoise and set to reveal a spectacular view of the river and the high ridge of gray stone that rose on the opposite bank.

The men waited for Meadow to sit. Dylan flanked one side and Jack took the other. On the opposite side of the table sat Tinnin and Forrest. Little Falcon chose a place between the two parties.

"Why is the FBI here on our land?" asked Dylan.

Kenshaw gave a weary sigh. "Bobcat should be more observant and more patient."

Dylan cautioned himself to patience and stealth. Now more than ever he needed to see what was hidden.

"I am here with my informant," said Forrest.

Dylan looked at Meadow, who met his gaze and then cast him an expression of incredulity peppered with annoyance. Dylan looked from one man to the next. Tinnin could not be an informant, could he? He did not look to Jack, because Jack had no one on whom to inform. In fact, the only one who had access to that kind of information was Little Falcon. But he was their shaman, a religious man who sought to preserve their culture and heritage.

Dylan met Kenshaw's gaze and saw the man's mouth twitch. "Very good, Bobcat."

"You're working with the feds?" Dylan did not manage to keep the distain from his voice.

Once he had thought to join the agency. What had prevented him was the sure knowledge that he would run into conflicts with his people and the mission of the FBI. He wanted to serve his country but balked at being an agent and so had turned down the recruitment that had come after leaving the service and again after Carter Bear Den entered witness protection.

"I have a confession to make to you, Dylan," said Kenshaw. "I did not send you to Cheney Williams for a fire-safety survey for that building site."

Dylan absorbed this blow to his ego and then fielded the curious expression from Jack. Dylan had not told his friend of his intensions to leave the hotshots as crew chief and work in the private sector.

"I was going to tell you," he said to Jack. "I passed the test. I'm accredited now. Ray knows. I just never found the right time."

"Okay. Later," said Jack, and turned to Kenshaw. "So why *did* you send him?"

"Cheney and I were old friends and activists. We worked on the water rights together in the eighties. He and I both joined PAN together."

PAN, Protect All Nature, the environmental group headed by Meadow's oldest brother, a seemingly innocent organization working to preserve wild places. And Cheney Williams had died on that ridge in the explosion that had started the fire that still raged. He had been Kenshaw's friend and he'd worked with Meadow's father on legal matters related to documentary financing and on filing the preliminary injunctions to prevent the building that broke the ridgeline. What else had he been involved in with her dad—the mass shooting in Lilac? Hiring the assassin to kill that shooter?

Cheney was dead. Had Wrangler killed him?

Bobcat waited.

"He and I both joined WOLF in the nineties. I'm still a member." Kenshaw glanced to Forrest who held his expression impassive as he studied Meadow.

"You blew up that dealership in Sedona?" asked Jack.

"Yes." Nothing in Kenshaw's expression or posture held any hint of remorse. But a man had died in that fire. "WOLF targets attacks on groups that encroach on nature."

"Like the first home to break the ridgeline," said Dylan. "Cheney died up there. Was that an accident?"

"I don't think so," said Kenshaw. "I think someone knew he was informing. He was my contact in BEAR. They don't know he was speaking to me."

"How do you know that?" asked Tinnin.

Forrest took that one. "Because he's still alive."

Dylan wondered if he really knew anything about the man who led their warrior sect. Then a more disturbing notion rose to the surface. If Kenshaw worked with WOLF and he controlled Tribal Thunder, then they might have unknowingly done WOLF's bidding.

"I never mixed the two, son." Kenshaw sighed again. "We have to work on that poker face."

Forrest picked up the telling. "Kenshaw has been helping us since Carter Bear Den and Amber Kitcheyan became witnesses."

"Amber Bear Den," corrected Jack. His brother had married Amber, with Kenshaw and Jack as his witnesses, to keep from being separated from Amber when she entered witness protection.

"Yes, right," said Luke. "Kenshaw had foreknowledge of some attack in Lilac." The copper mine was where Ovidio Sanchez had gunned down seven people and then hunted down and shot Amber's boss, narrowly missing Amber.

"But I didn't know what was happening. Only when, so I sent Carter to get my niece."

"Your niece?" asked Luke.

Dylan realized that Field Agent Forrest did not know the family connection between the woman Carter rescued and married and their shaman.

"Amber Kitcheyan Bear Den is the child of my sister, Natalie," said Kenshaw.

Forrest absorbed this. "You should have called the FBI."

"And say what—a friend told me there's going to be trouble in Lilac?"

"Anonymous tip line," said Forrest.

"Ha," said Kenshaw. "Anonymous. That's funny."

Dylan wondered if Kenshaw was working with the FBI only to prevent himself from going to prison. Tinnin and the tribal council could protect him to some extent. They decided which cases to turn over for federal prosecution. Had they turned over Kenshaw?

Police Chief Tinnin brought them back on track. "You were saying?"

"I recommended the man who killed the Lilac Copper Mine mass gunman."

"Morgan Hooke's father," said Dylan. Morgan was the woman Kenshaw had sent Ray Strong to protect. He had done too good a job. Morgan was alive and they were married.

"WOLF had wanted a man with no family, or someone who was terminally ill."

That was the case with Morgan's dad, Dylan knew. He'd had only months to live when he had turned assassin for hire. But his plan to provide for his daughter and granddaughter had backfired and nearly gotten them both killed. Ray had prevented that.

"And that was the last one you set up without us knowing about it," said Forrest.

Dylan thought that sounded more like a warning.

Kenshaw nodded. "Back to Cheney. He was trying to stop that construction with legal action. He needed the fire report to file with the court. I set up the meet so he could get his report and I could get the information he had on BEAR's next target. Cheney said they were planning something big for the explosives they stole from the Lilac mine."

"The house wasn't the target?" asked Meadow.

"My superiors think that the explosion was a warning to others not to break the ridgeline," said Forrest. "And a way to dispose of Cheney."

"What do you think?" asked Meadow.

"It was a test."

A test for what? wondered Dylan. His heart thudded at the possibilities. They had to find out, had to stop BEAR.

Forrest raked his fingers through his thick hair, leaving track marks. "Now we've lost our contact with BEAR. We're blind. We need someone else on the inside."

"Do you know any other members of BEAR?" asked Tinnin.

Kenshaw nodded and looked to Forrest.

"Just one—we suspect he's their leader," said Forrest.

"Who?" asked Jack.

"Meadow's father, Theron Wrangler."

Chapter Sixteen

"No," said Meadow, the outrage shuttering through her voice. "My father would never have set that fire. He's an environmentalist."

"A radical one," said Forrest. "We believe that this explosion was only a test. Cheney had information on the real target. He was supposed to deliver it to Dylan."

Dylan scowled. "It would have been nice if someone had told me that."

"He's fought to protect wild places all his life," she said as the outrage turned to dread. What if they were right?

"Cheney told me that Theron headed BEAR. Theron took over after Walter Fields went to federal prison for manslaughter."

"What did you get him on?" asked Jack.

"Carelessness. He ran down the owner of a fur farm and claimed it was an accident. Jury thought otherwise. Guy had two young kids."

Meadow knew that man. She used to call him Uncle Walt. Now her sense of dread turned to fear. This couldn't be. She would not believe her father could do something like this.

"Why would he endanger his daughter?" said Dylan.

"She broadcast some spectacular footage. It's all over the internet. You've gone viral, Miss Wrangler, and we would very much like to examine that footage more closely. Did anything survive the fire?"

She nodded. "My GoPro."

"Where is it?" asked Forrest.

"I hid it in the gatehouse when those men arrived."

"Where exactly?" asked Forrest.

Meadow described tucking the recorder in between the sheets in the back of the gatehouse's hallway linen closet. Forrest jotted some notes.

"But why her?" asked Dylan. "He could have sent anyone. Why his own daughter?"

"We have a theory," said Forrest.

They waited. Meadow was afraid to breathe.

"Make her a martyr for the cause. The builder had two acetylene tanks on site. The newspapers are theorizing that they blew. The lawsuits are already flying. The builder is facing reckless-endangerment charges. The state sent a fire-and-explosion investigator." He snapped his fingers, thinking. "Albert Waltz. He's on site with our men. We don't believe the tanks were the cause," said Forrest. "They only contributed."

"Do you know what the investigator thinks?" said Dylan.

"He thinks you did it," said Tinnin.

"Why?"

"Means," said Tinnin. "You know how to weld. Learned in the Marines, and you picked up a few jobs here, too. Motive. You're Apache and everyone knows we are opposed to assaults on the environment."

"That's weak," said Jack.

Tinnin went on as if his detective had not spoken. "Opportunity. You were there when it blew and yet somehow miraculously survived."

"It wasn't a miracle. I deployed a fire shelter."

"Which you happened to have along," said Forrest.

"I always do."

"Most folks don't carry them," countered Forrest.

"Most folks aren't hotshots."

"All right," said Tinnin. "Point being, that explosives guy, Waltz, is going to arrest you the minute you leave the reservation."

Meadow's anxiety switched from her father to Dylan.

"He didn't do it."

The chief of tribal police gave her an indulgent smile. "That likely won't matter. Waltz has a warrant and has applied to the tribal council for Dylan's release to his custody, which they won't accommodate. Makes him a prisoner here, though."

"Only way around that is to clear his name," said Jack.

And that meant getting Waltz a new suspect—her father, she realized.

"My video!"

"It shows me heading to the site," said Dylan.

"And coming back. You didn't have time," she said.

"Could have done it earlier," said Jack.

"We need to see that footage," said Forrest. "Excuse me." He stepped away to make a call.

"His partner is at the epicenter," said Tinnin. "With that inspector, Waltz."

Forrest returned to the table and spoke to Meadow. "Can you tell me what you shot?"

She gave him a summary. She'd filmed the ridge before construction and then the house in various stages of development.

"Oh, there's other footage on there, too. Unrelated. I'm working on two projects."

Forrest quirked a brow. "What's the other?"

"A documentary—in its early stages—on the effect of damming the Hakathi River. They modified it to prevent floods and generate hydroelectric power. But they changed it irrevocably."

"What did you film?" asked Jack.

"The power company gave us permission to film the exteriors of all four dams and I got some interior shots at the Skeleton Cliff and Alchesay Canyon Dams. Those guys up there were really friendly. Even took me in a crane basket for some of my footage."

Jack straightened and Forrest met his gaze. They both looked to Kenshaw.

"Maybe," he said.

They didn't like that information. Meadow waited for someone to speak. Instead, their shaman motioned for her to continue. So she described the footage she had taken.

"The inside of the powerhouse isn't very cinematographic, just cooling turbines and sluice gates to control water flow and a lot of compressed air in big tanks. That's on there, too. Just in between the ridge footage."

"You stream any of that?" asked Forrest.

"No. It's for research on the next project. Nice guys up there, the engineers."

Dylan said something to Detective Bear Den in Tonto Apache and the detective shook his head and replied, looking to Forrest. The next thing Dylan said was a question. She could tell that much.

"Skeleton Cliff is right above our reservation," Dylan said in English. "It will be at capacity after the summer rains."

He'd gone pale. Meadow recalled the ridge explosion and suddenly felt sick. If the dams were the real target, the target Cheney would have revealed to the shaman through Dylan, then his tribe, his people, his home—everything and everyone in his entire world would be washed away if Skeleton Dam failed.

"What do you mean?" asked Meadow.

Dylan shook his head as if words just failed him.

"My father didn't blow up that house. Neither did Dylan," said Meadow to the FBI agent.

"Well, if you really believe that, then you'll want to clear your father," said Forrest. "You'll want to help us out with the investigation."

Meadow hesitated. Her actions could incriminate her father. What would she do if it became a choice between her father and the man who had saved her life? Meadow prayed she would never have to make that choice.

"I won't do anything to incriminate my father."

"We just want the truth, Meadow. We all want the truth."

"What is it you want her to do, exactly?" asked Dylan.

Forrest switched his attention to Dylan. "We want her to go home."

"That's it?" said Meadow. Some of the tension eased from between her shoulders.

"And wear a wire."

Her muscles tensed again. A wire? Like those things she saw on TV. She'd then be some kind of family narc. How had her life become a crime drama? Forrest's phone chirped and he glanced down at the screen.

"We have your camera," he said to Meadow. "Thank you for providing us the location. We'll make a copy of the footage for you and get the hardware back to you soon."

Meadow snorted as if she doubted that and stuck to the topic of the wire.

"You want me to be an informant against my father."

"We want you to prove us wrong."

She wasn't falling for that bait.

"What if I don't?"

"Nothing. You can go home, alone, without FBI protection to your loving family."

Meadow glanced to Dylan.

"Oh, he stays here. He leaves, he loses tribal protection. Remember?" said Forrest.

Dylan placed his arm across the table, a visible barrier between Meadow and Forrest, just to let Forrest know he wouldn't let her go without a fight.

"She stays here," said Dylan.

"No. Whether or not she cooperates, I'm placing her into custody. Whether that becomes public knowledge is also up to Miss Wrangler. Of course, I could arrange for Waltz to back off for a while."

Meadow understood the threat. If she cooperated and wore a wire like a good girl, she'd get Dylan and the FBI's protection. Refuse, and she'd be left alone and everyone would know she'd been detained by the FBI—everyone, including her father. Meadow rubbed her hand over her mouth as she considered her options.

"Don't, Meadow," said Dylan. "It's too dangerous."

But it was also a chance to clear Dylan's name and, if she was right, her father's, as well.

"Under the condition that you get Dylan cleared of charges before we leave the reservation."

"I can't clear him. I can only buy him time."

"But you know he didn't do it."

Forrest leaned in. "You don't get it, do you, Meadow? I don't care who did it. I want to know who has the rest of those explosives and where they plan to strike next. Someone out there has dump trucks full of explosives and a moral obligation to send the entire Southwest back into the Stone Age. That's not happening. Not on my watch. So you can help me or you can watch it happen."

"Okay," she said. "I'll do it."

DYLAN DID NOT like the plan, but he waited as Meadow was outfitted with a wire, and then he stood placidly as Forrest applied one to him, as well.

When she returned, she was given a burner phone to call her father. Dylan listened on headphones with the rest of them. He picked up on the first ring, his greeting taciturn.

"Yeah?"

"Daddy?"

Everything in his voice changed. "Princess. Is it you? I knew it. Oh, baby, are you all right? Where are you?"

If he was acting, it was darn convincing. Dylan read only relief and joy in Theron Wrangler's voice.

"I'm okay. I'm sorry if I worried you. I only just got the phone replaced."

"They found your car. But not you... Sweetheart, what happened?"

She relayed the lie as it had been set up.

"I got out before the fire. Some guy picked me up and we just made it out."

"Thank God. Thank God." He was mumbling to himself now. "I knew...I just knew it." There was a choking sound.

"Daddy?" Meadow's eyes rounded as she listened to her father weep. She held Dylan's gaze and he saw her eyes fill with tears. "Daddy? I'm sorry. I should have called right away."

"I'm so glad you're safe."

Dylan thought again that this did not sound like a man willing to martyr his daughter for the cause. But if he was not the one, then who?

"You need to come home," he said. "Tell me where you are."

"I'm in Darabee."

"Darabee? In the mountains?"

"Yes. The guy that got me out, he lives up here. I lost my phone and my wallet and everything but the camera. Did you see the footage, Dad?"

"The hell with the footage. I'm sending Jessie to pick you up. They have a small airport. Can you get there?"

"Yes. Daddy, can I bring him?"

"Who?"

"The man who saved my life."

"Heck, yes. I want to meet that young man."

She lowered her voice. "Daddy, he's Apache, from the Turquoise Canyon tribe."

Dylan's eyes narrowed at the long pause.

"Apache? That's a heck of a thing. What's his name?"

His tone had changed now, seemingly casual but with a hard undercurrent that Jack and Luke also caught because their eyes flashed to him and then each other.

"Dylan Tehauno. He's wonderful."

"Sure he is. He's a hero. Saved my baby girl. Tell him there's a reward in it for him."

"He doesn't want money, Daddy." Her face wrinkled in disapproval and she shot Dylan an apologetic look.

"Well, what does he want?"

"Nothing."

"Hmm." Dad had been around long enough to know that everyone wanted something, and if it wasn't money it was something worse. "A job?"

"No. Daddy, we're dating."

Another long pause. "I don't think so."

"What?" Her expression read absolute disbelief.

"You're not dating a boy from the rez."

"He's a man."

"Without a job, likely, who latched on to the best thing that ever came his way."

"I'd better go," she said.

"I'm sending Jessie."

"Don't bother. I'll find my own way home."

Forrest was waving at her as Meadow went off script.

Silence stretched as Meadow affected a look of petulance Dylan had never seen. The grit and intelligence of this woman dissolved as she reverted into a child on the verge of a tantrum.

"All right," said Wrangler.

Meadow's mouth curled in a smile. The victor, Dylan realized.

Wrangler continued, conceding. "He can come. But do not introduce him to your mother as your newest flame. She won't have it. You know that."

"She doesn't have to date him."

"You need her approval."

"Only if I want a wedding with five hundred people."

"Wedding! Princess, we need to talk."

Dylan's eyes widened at this turn and his gaze flashed to Jack, who was now scowling. Dylan shook his head, wondering what game Meadow was playing.

"Isn't that what we're doing?" asked Meadow.

"Have you met his family?"

"Some," she lied.

"Did you meet a man named Little Falcon up there?"

"No. Just his mother. She's lovely. Very gracious and welcoming. She didn't seem to mind that I was a white girl."

"Of course she didn't. I'm sending Jessie. Get to the airport."

"With Dylan."

"Great." His voice belied his words.

"Love you, Daddy."

"Oh, Princess, I am so damn glad you are alive."

"See you soon." She disconnected.

Forrest slumped in his chair. Jack shook his head in disbelief, and Dylan wondered if he was as easily manipulated as her father.

"What?" she said.

"You're used to getting your way," said Dylan.

"With Daddy, yes. But Mom is tougher." Meadow

tucked away her new smartphone in the pink sparkle case. "She's very hard to please."

Was that why she'd given up trying, playing the family screwup, instead. Any attention was better than no attention after all.

"I'm sorry," said Dylan.

"About what?"

"Your mom."

"Yeah, well, you'll be sorrier after you meet her. She's going to eat you for lunch and send me to a nunnery."

"She doesn't like Apache Indians."

"She likes professional men with their own money. You got any money, Dylan?"

"I got this?" he said, lifting the choker of silver and turquoise beads that ringed his neck. "And a claim from my grandfather to get more of the same."

She hugged him tight. "This will be hard. I don't usually bring a man home unless I want to get a rise out of her."

"She'll think I'm there to upset her, then."

"Probably."

"I can play that part. Might enjoy it."

"You won't," she whispered.

Dylan lowered his chin and she lifted up to kiss him. Suddenly the danger they faced slipped away in a haze of desire.

Forrest cleared his throat. Dylan broke away and cast him an impatient look.

"We have to get you two over to the airport."

"I'll drive them," said Jack.

"We've got a team in Phoenix. They are in position to surveil and assist, if necessary. Just use the code word and we'll pick you up."

Destiny, he recalled. That sent the FBI into attack mode. He hoped he wouldn't need it. But if they were right, he and Meadow were flying into a lion's den.

Chapter Seventeen

Meadow pressed her hand over the wire that had been affixed between her breasts with paper tape. The helicopter blades made any conversation impossible, and anything she said into the headset was also heard by Jessie. She felt as if she had dropped down the rabbit hole. Everything seemed familiar but changed when, in truth, only she had changed.

The suspicion tainted everything. As the runners touched down she spotted her father's Mercedes sedan, big and white and pretentious. He had a Jeep and a Range Rover and also the Ferrari. The Mercedes was the vehicle her mother used for impressing potential donors to PAN and meetings with film producers. She swallowed her dread at the possibility that her mother was waiting behind those tinted windows.

The blades slowed and Dylan touched her wrist and shook his head, glancing at her chest. She dropped her hand. The involuntary action, touching the wire, could get them both killed—if the FBI was right about her father.

Were they?

The FBI said her father was the head of BEAR. Could he head an organization so violent and that had such a bleak outlook on the human condition that they called for a do-over? One that did not include people. They did not just incidentally kill people while protecting the natural world. According to Forrest, they encouraged it.

And the FBI really believed that her father had sent her up there, to the mountains outside Flagstaff, to die.

Her father stepped from his vehicle, his salt-and-pepper hair blowing in the artificial wind of the slowing chopper blades. His hair had once been the same soft brown color as hers. Her brothers and sisters had inherited the thick black hair of their mother, and her deep brown eyes. Her mother didn't like Meadow's hair, calling it mousy brown. It was one of the reason she'd died it ocean blue. Not surprisingly, her mother had not liked that any better.

Their eyes met and he smiled, flashing white teeth that now looked dangerous in their brightness. He extended his arms in welcome and she forced down her apprehension. This was her dad, the one who always indulged and pampered her to the point that her brothers' and sisters' jealousy hardened into disdain and disapproval. Only Katrina managed to look past her favored status and keep their relationship alive.

When would she grow up? When would she do something with her life?

Her brother Miguel's lecture ran in a loop in her mind. Well, she had grown up, suddenly and all at once, in that fire shelter when the man beside her had used his body to protect hers. She had come to appreciate her life and found her purpose. She wanted to know the truth, and she was willing to do whatever was necessary to discover who had sent her to die.

She was here to prove her father guilty or innocent, and she really, truly, did not know which he was. Her heart prayed for innocence as her mind spouted facts. He had asked her to film that day. He had sent her up there. Him.

Jessie stepped out first. She waited for him to open her door and then climbed down, keeping low.

"Princess Meadow!" called her father, and met her halfway. He enfolded her in his arms, squeezing so tight she could not breathe. Did he feel the transmitter taped to her torso? "I'm so happy to have you home."

He kissed her forehead and she pulled away. Dylan was out of the chopper.

She slipped naturally under her father's arm and motioned to Dylan. His transmitter was inside his truck's key fob, which had been clipped to the loop of his jeans.

"Daddy, this is my hero, Dylan Tehauno of the Bear Clan."

The minute she said "bear" her heart skipped. Her father's arm tightened and then he stepped away to shake Dylan's hand.

"Bear, huh?" he asked.

"Bear born of Butterfly. My tribe is Turquoise Canyon."

"Beautiful country, except for the river. They've ruined that, the salmon runs, the migrations."

"Yes, sir."

"Well, I want to thank you for getting my girl out of the fire. I'm in your debt, Mr. Tehauno."

"My pleasure."

Her father's smile hardened. Their hands remained clasped a beat too long as the men sized up each other. Her father's smile reemerged as he dropped his hand and returned to her side.

"Well, we need to get you home, Princess." He gave her a squeeze. "Can we drop you somewhere, Mr. Tehauno?"

Dylan's gaze flicked to her.

"That's not funny, Daddy."

Her father's smile held, but his eyes stayed pinned on Dylan. He didn't like her new beau and it wasn't really a joke. He looked like he would love to drop him somewhere. That was certain.

"In we go." He motioned to his limo and the man in uniform who held open the back door.

"Where's Mom?" asked Meadow, feeling both relieved and disappointed her mother had not come to greet her.

"She's working, Princess. But we'll see her tonight. Big welcome-home dinner just for you. Your brothers and sisters will be there, and some of your friends."

Dylan wondered if that might be worse than confronting the man. As it turned out, he would have been happier battling a wildfire on the line with Ray. At least then he would have had a clear escape route.

Dylan remained silent as Wrangler and Meadow conversed about the revised version of events since she had left to film.

"What about the camera?" asked her father.

Meadow looked away to lie. "Gone."

"Well, no matter. Great footage. Best you ever shot."

And it had nearly killed her. Dylan felt sick as he saw Meadow beam with pride. They used the highway to circle the outskirts of Phoenix and then headed up into the gated luxury communities that lay south of the city in the pine forest and mountain meadows. The Wranglers' home sat on a golf course, which Dylan found ironic. The log-and-stone exterior included a huge portico, where they were greeted by staff. Dylan trailed behind Wrangler, who looped his arm in Meadow's as they strolled through a home larger than his tribe's headquarters. The interior was rich with polished wood, flagstone and wrought iron. Sculptural glass pieces filled niches above the fireplace, and he spotted a beautiful Navajo rug draped over a leather couch that looked as if no one ever sat on it.

In the back of the house, between the golf course and the huge outdoor seating area was a lap pool. It was there he met her mother, who had been "working" on her tan.

Lupe Wrangler floated on a pink raft in the shallow

end in a two-piece neon-orange suit that showed a full figure. Her raven hair was pulled into a ponytail that fell over the visor shading her eyes and onto the headrest of the float. Mrs. Wrangler did not bother to leave the pool as they appeared but paddled to the stairs, where she stood in knee-deep water to meet Meadow with a perfunctory kiss, accompanied by a cutting comment that she still smelled of wood smoke. Likely, Dylan thought, from the fire in the tribe's meeting house. She did not bother to greet Dylan but lowered her glasses down her nose to stare.

"So this is the latest. Interesting choice." The glasses slid back into place. The woman exited the pool and dragged on a sheer cover-up that did little to hide the neon-orange bikini beneath. Her dark skin came either from her lineage or a dedication to tanning. With her black hair and deep brown eyes, she did not look like the mother of the fair-skinned Meadow. Suspicions rose immediately in Dylan's mind.

Meadow resembled her father, Dylan realized, and perhaps someone else?

"Your father insisted on a party," said Lupe Wrangler. "I told him that the less attention we draw, the better. But you know your father."

Dylan watched as Meadow's smile became brittle and her eyes glassy. Lupe sank into her lounge chair with her drink. She did not offer her daughter or her guest a drink or ask them to join her. It made him think of the adage his grandmother often repeated: *Assume that your guests are tired and hungry and act accordingly.*

"You'll want to clean up and dress before dinner," said Lupe, lifting a magazine.

Meadow remained where she was. Her mother glanced at her and a raven brow lifted above the tops of her sunglasses.

"Well?"

"This man saved my life, Mother. He's not an interesting choice. He's a hero."

Her mother frowned. "Don't be dramatic, dear. Your father told me all about it. All he did was stop to pick you up. Anyone would have done the same."

Not here, Dylan thought. She'd have driven right by Meadow. Maybe over her. Was she intentionally trying to be cruel?

Lupe flipped the pages of her magazine, dismissing her daughter and ending the conversation.

Meadow's face reddened but she said nothing, just turned and retreated into the house.

Her father waited there, arms folded as he watched the exchange.

"She was worried about you," he said.

"Yes. I can see that. Did she miss a manicure waiting for news?"

Her father's smile seemed sad to Dylan. Lupe Wrangler was beautiful and cold as an ice sculpture.

Theron walked them through the foyer, the polished wood tile echoing with their steps.

"Guests are arriving at eight. That will give you some time to rest. Have a swim."

Dylan thought of swimming in front of the ice queen and found the prospect left him cold.

"If you need anything, Mr. Tehauno, please just ask—something more appropriate for dinner, perhaps?"

Dylan gave a half smile. "I'll be wearing this." He plucked at his cotton shirt, causing the heavy multistrand necklace of turquoise mingled with silver beads to thump against his chest.

"Of course."

Meadow took him upstairs, and they spent the afternoon resting in her suite of rooms. The sitting room and bedroom looked like a magazine spread but nothing like a home. Meadow selected a silver dress from her cavernous closet and tossed it on the bed. Then she slipped out of the shirt he had given her and into the metallic sheath, transforming before his eyes from the woman he had come to know to the party girl she had claimed to be. The low-cut cocktail dress accentuated her slim figure and revealed her long legs. He wondered if the dress was selected specifically to irritate her mother. She applied a generous coating of makeup, a red lipstick and silver earrings that brushed her shoulders. She waited until eight thirty to leave her bedroom suite. One of the waitstaff stood holding a necktie and blazer out for Dylan. He accepted the jacket and refused the tie. Together he and Meadow descended the grand staircase with her arm in the crook of his elbow. Meeting the guests, Dylan felt as out of place as a fish in the Mojave Desert.

Her friends were all Anglo, well-educated and oh-so-careful to appear socially conscious and forward thinking as they surreptitiously checked their text messages every few minutes. Her brother Phillip was short and fat and old enough to be Meadow's father. Dylan found him to be a blowhard and his handshake seemed to be compensating for something. He let Dylan know how important he was by spouting statistics like a whale spouts water as he yakked about their operating budget, his staff and the very necessary efforts and successes PAN had managed as cocktails were served and appetizers offered by the waitstaff.

He was seated for dinner between Katrina and Rosalie, Meadow's attorney sisters, who interrogated him like a witness to a crime, and so far across the enormous table that he could not touch or speak to Meadow. Dessert was served in another room entirely but at least he could leave the witness chair and return to Meadow. As the evening dragged along, her friends grew louder and her mother more catty. Lupe Wrangler cornered him in the dining room after dinner.

"You won't have her for long. No one does."

"Thanks for the warning."

"You must think you died and went to heaven." She swept her hand about in the air, indicating the opulence all about them.

"Should I?"

"Of course. I've visited some of Arizona's reservations. Garbage everywhere, filthy little hovels of houses. The government should be ashamed."

"Should they?"

"I think so. I don't know why you don't rise up against them."

"We tried that in the 1870s. Didn't work out."

Her lips curled in a mirthless smile.

"Well, you're more interesting than her usual fare, I'll give you that. My girls tell me you fight wildfires."

The gathered intelligence had already been received, he thought.

"Yes. I'm with the Turquoise Canyon Hotshots."

"Do you ever think that fire is nature's way of cleaning the palate?"

"I've heard that argument. But nature doesn't start most of the fires I fight. Men do."

Her smile never faltered as she inclined her head as if giving him a point. Catlike eyes regarded him then swept away.

"It's mine, you know?" she said, surveying her home over the rim of her glass. "My husband is a self-made man, but he was wise enough to marry money. *My* money."

"Good to know." Dylan glanced around for rescue.

"Dirty money mostly," said Lupe. "Great-Granddad had oil-drilling companies in Mexico before they nationalized. My grandfather built offshore drilling platforms for the Mexican government. One of them had a blowout and the oil ignited. Massive spill in 1979." She paused and lifted her brows expectantly.

He shook his head.

"Too young to recall it, then. Wish I was, but time marches on." She stroked her hand under her jaw as if judging the texture of her skin. "I don't do anything much except invest in my husband's films and follow the golden rule, Don't Touch the Principal."

Dylan thought he understood why Lupe might marry a man with an environmental agenda. She had a family legacy that would give anyone pause. He looked about for Meadow, but she was nowhere in sight.

"Do you know Kenshaw Little Falcon?"

"Yes." He tried not to tense.

"He did some good work stopping the land swaps. We couldn't have prevented that Canadian mining company from coming in here if not for the efforts of the Turquoise Canyon and Black Mountain tribes. I hear he's negotiating the water rights up there in Turquoise Canyon."

"He's very active in a number of worthy causes."

"He came down here to protest that house breaking the ridgeline. Did you know that?"

"I did not."

"What do you think about the encroachment of housing into wild places?"

Meadow rescued him. Her mother's expression went sour the instant she spotted her youngest.

"Here she comes. The prodigal child returns." She slipped an arm around Meadow and gave her shoulder a little pat. Then she leaned in and whispered, "What are you wearing?"

Meadow ignored her. "I'm going to steal Dylan. I want him to meet my friend Veronica."

Her mother waved her away.

"Sorry about that," said Meadow. She steered them up the stairs to the balcony over the portico. The breeze was absent and the night so much hotter than up in his mountains. They looked out at the city of Phoenix twinkling in the distance.

"Do you want me to meet your friend?"

"Not really. But you will. My friends are all curious about you."

They had only a few minutes of peace before Rosalie and Katrina found them and the interrogation resumed. If he did not know, he would not have guessed these two were Meadow's sisters because she was taller, lighter in skin tone and a completely different body type. Where Meadow's frame was model thin, her sisters had full figures and wore clothing that hugged those curves and revealed enough cleavage to make a man lose his concentration. They were short, and even the high-heeled sandals did not bring them eye level with their youngest sister.

He tried to ask Rosalie about the projects she oversaw at PAN and to discover what kind of fund-raising Katrina organized for her parent's upcoming release, but they carefully steered all conversation to his rescue of Meadow and his work with the hotshots. They barely acknowledged their little sister. When they finally glided away on four-inch heels he felt as if he'd just survived running the rapids on the Snake River.

He blew out a breath.

"That goes double for me," she said. "Want something to drink?"

"Water with lemon." He didn't drink and, though tempting, he wasn't starting now when he was in a nest of vipers.

Meadow flagged a waiter, who returned a few moments later with two drinks on a silver tray. Meadow lifted the wine, swirling the burgundy liquid before taking a long swallow. He took a large gulp from his drink and found it tasted of chemicals. He grimaced and set the tumbler aside. Meadow had already finished her drink and signaled for another.

"Bad idea," he said.

"Two-glass limit. Also, my mother hates it when I drink."

They had a few minutes alone as Meadow nursed her second glass of wine. Then she made her excuses to her mother and kissed her father, then led him to the room he would use while under her parents' roof. It was too far from Meadow, so he followed her back to her room.

"My head aches," she said, her words slurred.

He'd been battling an upset stomach since just after dinner.

"Did you have anything else to drink?" he asked.

"Two glasses. That's it." She blinked slowly and her lids remained half-closed.

His stomach pains escalated. Dylan spoke so that FBI field agents Forrest and Cosen could hear.

"I think we've been drugged. Meadow is blacking out. I've got stomach pains. Destiny. Destiny," he said, repeating the code for help.

"What?" she said, her eyes widening.

Dylan wasn't taking chances. He lifted the phone on her desk and got no dial tone.

"Cell phone?" he said, wanting to call Jack.

She motioned at her satiny silver cocktail dress. "Don't have it."

He lifted her by the shoulders and took her to her bathroom. There he told her to make herself vomit. He did the same. But it was too late for Meadow. She was already dropping into a drug-induced slumber. He lifted her, determined to take her out of this house. He got his arms under her legs and lifted, but she was so heavy. Instead of bringing her up into his arms, he fell to his knees on the bathroom floor.

"Forrest," he said. "Help."

Had the agents heard them?

The door to her room banged open. Dylan managed to get one knee under him. His vision was bad and the two men seemed a blur of motion, coming at him too fast for him to react.

"This one's still conscious," said the one in blue.

"Knock him out, then check him for a wire."

Dylan roared and lunged. He caught the one in blue around the waist and drove him through the doorway and knocking him to his back. The jolt of their landing made his head pound, but he lifted a fist to finish the job. Something heavy hit him in the back of the head so hard he saw stars. The wide wood-floor planking rushed up to greet him. He tried to rise and someone hit him again.

Chapter Eighteen

Meadow woke to the smell of smoke and a stomach that heaved with every jolt. She'd had her fair share of hangovers—okay, more than her fair share. And she'd woken up in some unexpected places. But she didn't do that anymore.

Why not?

Then she remembered. Dylan Tehauno. Since she had met him she had lost much of her inclination toward reckless self-destruction.

The car hit another jolt and she groaned.

"Sleeping Beauty is waking up."

She knew that voice.

"Won't matter. We're here."

The car pulled to a stop, bumping along on uneven ground.

Meadow could not get her eyes to stay open. It took all her effort just to lift her lids a slit as the door beside her head swung out. She was hauled from the vehicle by her wrists. Her legs banged into the wheel well and then onto the ground. Next, her heels dug twin trenches in the sand. She managed a sound that was more mew than cry.

"Jeez, I can barely see through the smoke," said the first man.

Who was that?

She was dropped unceremoniously on the ground. Her cheek hit hard and the sharp sting of pain helped rouse her.

She opened her eyes and saw yellow grass and two legs clad in gray trousers. Either the light was bad or it was her vision. Was it still evening or early morning?

"Come on. Let's get him and then get them both into the house."

Him? Were they talking about Dylan?

"What'd you give the guy at the roadblock?"

The other man snorted. "Money. They evacuated this neighborhood yesterday. Wrangler says it's a goner. Smoke should kill them even before the fire gets here. Either way, we'll be on our way back to Phoenix."

She did cry out this time.

"You hear that, Princess? Should have died up here the first time. You recognize it? The ridge fire outside Flagstaff? Welcome back."

She tried and failed to roll to her back. What had they given her? It was like she was paralyzed, unable to get her body to listen to the commands of her mind.

They walked past her and then returned, dragging Dylan. They dropped him on his back beside her. His head lolled and she saw the drying blood that had run across his forehead and into his eyes. He didn't move, and for a moment she thought they had killed him. But then she saw it—the blood leaking from a wound on the back of his head. Dead men didn't bleed, did they?

Really, she didn't know.

"Dylan," she cried, her words only a whisper.

He remained completely still. Tears leaked from her eyes. This was her fault. She'd wanted to prove her father's innocence, and Dylan wouldn't have let her go alone. She didn't care if she had to join the 27 Club if only she could save Dylan. He was so much better than her in every way imaginable. And she loved him.

The tears now choked her as she admitted the truth. She loved him and it was going to get him killed.

Beyond her tiny view of the world, she heard the sound of a motor and the clang of metal. The men returned.

"Is he alive?" she asked.

"Not for long," said her captor, and then she knew him. It was Joe Rhodes, one of the soundmen on her father's documentary projects.

"Joe. Don't do this."

"I'd say sorry, but I'm not. You cannot believe what I'm getting for this." He scooped her up and then carried her from her resting place, past the truck and up a driveway made of paver stone. She controlled her head, but the rest of her body did not seem attached. Her legs swung and her arms dangled. She couldn't really feel them. When Joe passed the driveway and carried her around toward the back of the large ornate Spanish-style home, the smoke came directly at them, a hot rush of air, like the kind from a blast furnace used to fuse glass. The skin on her face tingled.

"Why?" she asked Joe.

"Wrangler's orders. I guess someone is tired of cleaning up after your messes. I would have put you over my knee about twenty years ago. Someone should have. But they never cared enough about you to do that. Did they, Princess?"

Joe shifted her over his shoulder to maneuver through a wrought-iron gate and then draped her across a lounge chair with what should have been a fine view of the ridgeline. Instead, it gave her a horrific picture of the approaching line of orange flames that would soon overtake this home.

Joe left her. She screamed at him to come back and choked on the acrid smoke. Seconds ticked by as she tried to get just her little finger to move. The gate creaked open and then banged shut. The next time she heard the gate, Joe and the second man had returned carrying Dylan between them. She now recognized the second guy, as well. Mark Perkinson, her sister Rosalie's legal assistant. He leaned down and stroked her cheek.

"Just drop him here," said Joe, releasing Dylan's knees. Mark grunted and then lowered Dylan to the flagstone patio. Mark approached and stood over her, hands on hips.

"Not too good for me now, are you?"

She vaguely recalled turning him down at a holiday party some years ago.

"Mark. You have to help us."

Mark turned to Joe. "She's talking. I thought she'd be out the whole time."

"So hit her on the head," said Joe.

"She's not a catfish," said Mark.

"But she's going to fry like one," said Joe, and snorted at his joke. Then he turned toward the gate. "Come on. We don't want to get trapped up here, too."

"Should we put the camera near them so it looks like they were filming the fire?" asked Mark.

"Just set it up." Joe's coughing was worse. "Then turn it on."

"Why on? It's just going to burn up."

"I don't know. Wrangler wants it on."

There it was again. Wrangler. She squeezed her eyes shut against the stinging smoke as her heart split in two. Her father had done this to her. He was exactly what the FBI had told her, a madman, an extremist bent on returning the earth to pristine glory before humans interfered.

She did not know what her death would achieve. Perhaps she would be a martyr for his cause.

Then she had a thought. The wire. The FBI. They'd be listening. They'd know where to find them.

But then why hadn't they come already?

She looked down at her dress and found the back zipper open so the low neckline gaped. The skin between the pink cups of her bra was bare. The wire was gone.

"She's moving," said Perkinson.

The wire...was gone. They were on their own and no one knew where to find them.

"Won't matter. Come on." Joe disappeared and she heard the gate creak. Mark spared her a backward glance.

"Sorry," he muttered, and followed Joe.

Meadow rolled her head back to the approaching wall of flames, the pungent stench of charring wood now hauntingly familiar. Death was coming for her and she was filled with regrets, so many they ate away at her like termites in rotting wood. Even as the smoke stung her eyes, she came to a certain clarity that Dylan was the one good thing in her life. He had treated her with the respect and tenderness that was absent in her family. Why did her father want her dead?

They had always been so close. He had never denied her anything and that had been a constant source of contention between her parents. Her mother could not and would not approve of her lifestyle or her accomplishments, few as they were.

Up on the ridge, the dry piñon trees had no chance against the fire that consumed them, crackling through their branches and turning the crowns into torches. Behind the flames lay a hillside of blackened earth.

Why weren't their firefighters here trying to save this neighborhood? She tried to think. Sometimes the fire teams deemed an area unsalvageable and offered it as sacrifice to the gods of fire. That would please her parents because she knew how her mother and father felt about the overdevelopment in this canyon. Though they didn't object to their own older gated community and the golf course that sucked up precious water.

Meadow reached out and clasped Dylan's limp hand and

squeezed. He did not move. She looked at her hand clutching his and realized she had moved her hand.

What would Dylan do?

She didn't know, but she was sure that he would not be mourning a misspent youth. He'd be fighting for their lives. And that was exactly what she intended to do.

Chapter Nineteen

Someone was calling his name from a long way off. Dylan roused to the feeling that his head had been cracked open like a goose egg. He squeezed his eyes shut, smelling smoke and blood. He lifted a hand to wipe away the sticky fluid pooling in his eye sockets and then moved his fingers beneath his nose to smell the drying blood. His fingers then raked through his hair to the gash that sat on a lump at the back of his skull.

"Don't touch it. It's still bleeding."

He blinked open his eyes to see Meadow kneeling beside him, her features tight with worry as her amber eyes met his.

Dylan registered the unmistakable smell of a wildfire and looked about.

"Where are we?"

"Back at the ridge fire. Two of my father's men dropped us here."

"Why?"

"I think they'd like us to die."

Dylan swung his legs off the padded lounge chair and onto the flagstone. Meadow still wore the pretty satin cocktail dress she'd had on last night and he was still in his clothing, necklace plus the borrowed blazer. His shirt had been opened and the wire that had been affixed to his chest had been removed.

"Someone hit me from behind. Twice." He grappled with the pain and dizziness that came with each tiny movement.

"I was drugged. I couldn't even move until a few minutes ago. It was like some nerve toxin."

Dylan looked at the line of fire rushing down the hillside in their direction. They had to get out of here.

"Have you tried the phones inside?" he asked.

She shook her head. Dylan opened the locked glass sliders by using the base of the wrought-iron side table as a battering ram. The force needed to shatter the glass made his eyes water as the pain flipped the contents of his stomach. His coordination was dismal as he staggered inside the ornate dining room using the upholstered chair backs for support. In the kitchen, Meadow found a phone on the wide expanse of black honed granite. She lifted the handset and pressed the call button. She gripped the counter with her opposite hand and swayed as if she stood on a ship's deck in rough seas. What had they given her?

"No service," she said, her words slower than usual. She squeezed her eyes shut and gave her head a shake.

He reached her and drew her close.

"We have to go," he said. Maybe the residents had left a car in the garage. He wouldn't have. If he'd had two cars and this house, he would have loaded up everything he could carry and left when the evacuation was called. Still, they stumbled to the garage and found the three bays empty except for a golf cart.

She looked at him and he made a face.

"Terrible escape vehicle," he said, glancing at the open sides.

"It's that or the bikes," she said, motioning to the expensive mountain bikes neatly stored on hooks beside the ski equipment and golf clubs. "And my balance is off."

He took her arm and guided her to the cart, where they

found the ignition key missing. A search of the tiny glove box, cup holders and beneath the seats yielded nothing.

"I'll bet it's on his key chain."

"Hot-wire," he said.

Dylan watched with growing appreciation as Meadow located the two wires running from the battery behind the seat and yanked. Once free it was an easy matter to touch the exposed ends together. The engine turned over.

"You ever drive one?" asked Meadow.

He shook his head and she climbed into the driver's seat.

"Where'd you learn that trick?" he asked.

"It's why I got thrown out of the Canton-Wesley Academy. Stole the dean's cart and drove it into the outdoor pool on a dare."

Dylan returned to the entrance to the garage and hit the button to open the automatic door. Outside the lifting door was a white Range Rover, and beside the vehicle stood Meadow's father, holding a pistol.

"Get in," he ordered.

"Daddy?" Meadow slid from the seat of the cart and stood on unsteady legs.

Dylan dragged a golf club from the closest bag, a wood, with a nice solid-looking head.

"What are you doing here?" she asked.

"No time. Let's go." Theron Wrangler looked behind him, down the road as if expecting company. He was sweating and pale, and he held his left hand across his middle as if he had suffered some injury.

This made no sense. He'd brought them here and now he wanted to move them. Dylan tried to puzzle out a reason and a possibility flickered in his mind. He slipped the club behind his back as Wrangler turned his pistol in Dylan's direction.

"You, too. Come on." He stepped back, giving them room to exit. "Who else is here?"

Meadow shook her head. "Your men already left."

"My men?"

"Joe Rhodes and Mark Perkinson. They said you paid them to leave us here. Why, Daddy?"

"No time now."

If Dylan didn't know better, he would think he was looking at a man who was truly frightened.

Dylan wondered at the choice of words, which made it seem as if Theron's life was also at risk, though he was the one pointing the gun.

The blast of a car horn was unmistakable. Through the smoke that swirled about the house, Dylan saw the white Mercedes sedan draw into the driveway, boxing in Wrangler's Range Rover. The rear door swung open and Dylan saw Lupe Wrangler, dressed in charcoal-gray slacks and a tailored orange blouse, lean from the compartment and motion wildly to her daughter, shouting to be heard above the approaching maelstrom.

"Niña, hurry."

Her father swung the pistol to aim at his wife. She lifted her hand as her eyes widened. A moment later her face went scarlet with rage.

"Don't go, Meadow. She's the one who drugged you," said her father.

Meadow looked from one parent to the next as confusion knit her brow.

What had Carter told Dylan, the name that his new wife had overheard…? *Wrangler.* Not Theron Wrangler. Just Wrangler. Could it have been Lupe Wrangler all along?

Meadow took a step toward her mother. Dylan grabbed her arm. She stared up at him. He shook his head.

"I think your father is telling the truth."

"What?" she asked.

Because poison was a woman's weapon, he thought. And because he'd never seen a mother so hostile toward a child, and because Meadow did not resemble her siblings, who all favored their mother. And because Lupe had the money and the legacy of environmental ruin. The pieces of the puzzle snapped into place. Daddy's little girl and the reason Meadow could never please her mother.

"Come on Meadow," called Lupe. "Right now. He won't shoot you."

Theron kept the gun aimed at his wife.

Meadow inched closer to Dylan, the only one she seemed to trust at the moment.

"Mama, did you drug me?" she asked.

"Don't call me that. Not ever again."

Meadow recoiled as if shot. Dylan wrapped an arm about her as she leaned heavily against him.

"Your father brought you home after his little chippie died. Said he'd be a good boy and help the cause if I just took you in as my own. Ha. Easier said than done."

"You're not my mother."

"Ding-ding." Lupe's voice chimed like the bells on a carnival midway.

Why hadn't Katrina ever told her? She must have known. They all must have known.

"You hate me," said Meadow.

Lupe rolled her eyes in disgust. "Drama. Always drama." Lupe said something into the vehicle's open door. Theron headed for cover, making it behind the stucco wall inside the garage as two men holding pistols left the sedan in unison. They stood flanking the sedan, using the doors for cover. Dylan dragged Meadow behind the golf cart.

Lupe's orders were clear. "Kill her and the Indian. Get my husband. Don't kill him."

Meadow gasped. "It's her. She did all this."

From his position, Dylan could see Theron waiting beside the open bay door.

"She's the head of BEAR," said Dylan.

Wrangler cast him a glance, his jaw set tight as he nodded. He was caught between his daughter and his wife.

"She took the explosives?"

Theron kept his focus on the approaching gunmen but answered. "Yes."

"Why?"

"She wants to restore the river."

"Which river?"

"Shut up, Theron," said Lupe.

"Your river," said Theron.

"Ruined with their hydroelectric plants and man-made reservoirs," said Lupe. "Dammed and filled with speedboats on lakes that never should have existed in the first place. It's a crime against the earth. Man doesn't own that river."

Lupe stepped into the garage and faced her husband.

"Give me the gun, Theron."

He didn't. Instead, he moved to open ground, standing between his daughter and his wife.

"You can't shoot them," said Theron. "The coroner will see the bullet hole."

"Not if you're burned badly enough."

"They'll see it, Lupe. Even your connections won't stop them from an autopsy."

She gave a half shrug. "They've served me well thus far."

Lupe was used to playing God, thought Dylan.

"If you don't put down that gun, I'll leave you here with them," she said.

Theron now faced the two armed men both with weapons aimed at him.

Without warning, he shot one of the two men in the

chest. The wounded man fell as the second man fired. Theron spun.

"Don't shoot him," yelled Lupe.

Theron fell to one knee, the gun now trapped between his open hand and the garage floor.

"Get his gun, Joe," ordered Lupe.

Dylan waited until the remaining gunman stooped in front of Theron to retrieve the pistol. Then Dylan stood and threw his club. It flew end over end and hit the second gunman. Joe managed to get an arm up to shield himself from the worst of it. Dylan rushed him, lifting a putter from the bag as he charged forward. He'd practiced with a war club for many years, and he'd learned hand-to-hand combat in the US Marines. And he knew that he had a chance to break the shooter's arm before he redirected his aim from the floor. It all depended on how fast his opponent could move and how well he could aim.

Dylan swung the club with all his might.

Chapter Twenty

The blow connected with the raised arm at the same instant Dylan saw the flash from the barrel. There was a burning pain at his neck. The shooter's arm went slack as both bones in his forearm bent as if on an invisible hinge. The gun clattered to the floor and Lupe scrambled to retrieve it as Dylan's forward momentum took him into his opponent. Dylan straddled his attacker and Joe screamed in agony as he attempted to splint the broken bones by cradling his injured arm.

Dylan spun in an effort to recover the pistol, but Meadow already held the weapon.

"Theron!" shouted Lupe.

Lupe fell to her knees beside her husband as Meadow's father sprawled to the cement floor clutching his side.

"You idiot!" Lupe wailed. "Stay with me."

Lupe fell across her husband's chest as blood welled bright red from a wound on the left side of Theron's abdomen.

She lifted her bloodshot eyes to Meadow. "You killed him. With worry and now with this. I should have drowned you in the bathtub when you were a baby." She looked back to her husband whose breathing was coming in short pants. Clearly he was not dead. "But I didn't want to hurt him. He's my only weakness. My compass." She glared back at the child of her husband's infidelity. "And you stole him. Part of him was always yours. I hate you for that."

The hot wind now howled past the building. Dylan knew the sound, like a locomotive. The fire had reached them.

"Meadow, we have to go," he called.

Meadow dropped to her knees opposite her mother. Dylan could see her father's chest heaving in a labored, an unnatural rise and fall as his color went from pink to a ghostly gray. Dylan had seen that before, after an IED had taken out the Humvee in front of his, killing all the passengers. Her father was dying.

Dylan left his combatant writhing on the floor and went to Meadow, who had forgotten the gun in her hand, which now rested on her father's still chest.

"Daddy!" she shrieked.

Lupe reached for the gun that lay in her husband's cupped hand. Dylan kicked it clear. The weapon skittered across the floor and under the cart beside them.

Dylan took the pistol from Meadow's hand and lifted her to her feet. He kept the weapon raised and on Lupe as he checked for a pulse at Theron's throat and found none.

"He's gone, Meadow." He shouted to be heard above the shrieking wind.

She screamed and tried to drop back to her knees beside her father, but he pulled her away. Lupe's black eyes remained fixed on his.

"Come with us if you want to live," he said.

Lupe shook her head and draped herself over her husband.

"Mama. Come," cried Meadow.

Lupe closed her eyes against the sight of the child she had tolerated and raised on a diet of bile and neglect. Dylan pulled her to the Mercedes. The flames now rose up behind the house, taking the trees below the roofline and sending black smoke swirling into the sky.

Dylan pushed Meadow into the passenger seat. As he reached the driver's side, he saw the one Lupe had called Joe carrying the struggling Lupe over his shoulder. His other arm hung limp at his side.

He jumped over his fallen comrade as he ran toward Theron's white SUV.

Dylan reached the road as Joe got Lupe into her husband's abandoned Range Rover. He did not know if they had a weapon but preferred not having them behind him, so he reversed the sedan far back on the road as the Range Rover roared backward out of the drive.

"They left him," she cried, looking back at the open garage and the black smoke that made it impossible to see the two fallen men within.

Dylan jerked the shift into gear and hit the gas.

"He's gone, Meadow. I'm sorry."

She covered her hands and wept while Dylan faced the problem before him. The inferno was racing up the hillside and the only escape through the fire.

The houses on the winding road below their original position were already engulfed in flames, the telephone poles burning as flames spiraled upward to the sky. The trunks of the trees burned orange, sending plumes of fire into a scarlet sky.

"Put on your belt, Meadow," he said.

Ash and burning embers now rained down upon the hood of the sedan, reflecting orange and red as they skittered from the metallic surface to fall to the road.

"I can't see through the smoke," she said, clicking her belt across her middle.

Dylan knew the roads to this development because he had driven through them on the way to his appointment with Cheney. That clear day, under bright blue skies, he had seen the houses tucked into the rolling pine-covered hillside. All roads led down to the main highway. And that was why, at every intersection, he headed down. He didn't know how far up they had been transported or where the fire had jumped the road. But he did know that the highway was below them and that it was the only way out.

Meadow coughed and pointed away from the thick smoke blocking his view.

"That way," she said, choosing the clear road that led away from the fire.

"I spoke to Ray last night before the party. He said they were letting Pine View Springs go."

"But all these homes."

Built in a tinderbox of dry forest that had not had a fire in decades. The ground cover alone had enough fuel to take the development. Add the piñon pines and it was impossible. The very thing that drew them to this place, the green trees and mountain views, was what made the landscape so deadly. And her mother had tossed the match that started it all.

"Have to get to the highway," he said.

He wondered if her mother's driver had headed into the fire or away?

The visibility dropped to zero as he steered to where the road should be. The smoke lifted in time for him to see the fire at the shoulder sending yellow flames slithering across the asphalt like some living creature. He accelerated across the stream of fire, praying it did not ignite their gas tank and that the thick black smoke beyond came from a fire beside and not on the highway.

The smoke was so thick it no longer looked like day but some eerie combination of twilight and hell. He flicked off the lights because the beams were reflecting back against the gray smoke. They shot through the fire wall and into a blazing inferno to their right. A car sat before them fully engulfed in flames. Dylan veered around.

The blaze beside them was not orange. This was white

with pink flames bursting skyward. He had seen this and it was very bad.

"My God," said Meadow.

This was the burn-over. The fire sweeping from one side of the road to the other, flying on the winds of its own making. Fire and burning debris whisked from one side to the other. Dylan wondered if his decision to make for the highway had been a mistake. It seemed already too late.

He glanced to Meadow and felt a strangled hope mixed with bitter regret. He could see a life with her if they could escape the flames but he could also see their chances of escape burning to ash.

"I'm sorry," he said.

She lowered her chin as the significance of his words reached her. She did not look frightened or torn with sorrow. She looked pissed.

"Don't you give up on us. We are getting out of this."

Dylan nodded and pushed the sedan to greater speeds. He couldn't see the road at times, but he could see the blackened earth on either side of them.

"It's been past here," she called, her voice elated. "The fire."

Meadow was a fast learner. She understood what that meant.

Nothing left to burn. Not the shells of two-by-fours that had once been luxury housing or the smoldering trunks of denuded trees that had once been green with pine needles or the blackened smoldering frames of automobiles stripped of rubber and glass by the raging wildfire.

They had reached a burn-over.

"Keep going. The highway can't be far."

She was right. The smoke now hung above them like the anvil head of a huge electrical storm. But the road before them was clear. Dylan allowed himself to exhale.

"Do you think they got through?" Meadow asked.

Her mother. The woman who had drugged her and dropped her in the path of a wildfire—twice.

"Meadow," he said.

"I know." She cradled her head in her hands. "She hated me. Now I understand why."

Dylan exhaled slowly, trying to unravel the tangle of emotions that came with family. Her mother despised her. But Meadow couldn't do the same. No matter how awful, that was her mother—or the only mother she had ever known. Perhaps with her father's death, she might never find the name of her real one.

"I'm sorry, Meadow. And, yes, they might have gotten through." If they had come down the hillside, he thought.

Ahead, Dylan spotted flashing blue lights and slowed as the emergency vehicles came into view. The roadblock was staffed by a female officer, who wore a yellow vest over her uniform and waved a flashlight to help him see her. Dylan slowed and rolled down his window.

"You both all right?" she asked, bending to speak to Dylan. "Mister, you're bleeding."

Dylan touched the wound at his neck, feeling the clotting blood in the gash carved through skin and muscle by the bullet.

"I'm all right. Anyone else come this way recently?"

She shook her head, still staring at his neck.

"That looks bad."

"I'm on my way to medical now. Can you radio the FBI?"

"FBI? Why?"

"There are two people still up there. One is wanted. The other shot me."

"You two better pull over."

Dylan did and answered her questions while accepting some gauze from her medical kit. She let him use her mobile and he got through to Forrest, flipping the call to speaker and then explaining their situation.

"She's up there?" asked Forrest.

"I think so. Only one way out and we're at it."

"So she still might get out?"

"Possibly."

"Tell the officer not to stop them but to notify me if that Range Rover passes her position. I've got people en route. You two head for Flagstaff and our offices there."

Meadow shook her head and spoke up. "Hospital. He's been shot in the neck and there's a gash on the back of his head."

"You better drive, Meadow," said Forrest. "I'm sending help. They'll meet you."

Dylan returned the phone to the officer who did not detain them.

They switched seats. Meadow drove them toward help and they were intercepted twenty miles outside of the city by an ambulance. Dylan's headache had only gotten worse and the smoke and the blood loss made him woozy and sick to his stomach. He needed help to stand and to get onto the gurney. Meadow abandoned the sedan to ride with him to the hospital. He didn't remember much of it, just the IV going in.

Meadow sat beside him, her face smudged with ash and soot. But they had made it out. Dylan closed his eyes and let himself drift. But drifting was dangerous. You never knew which way the current would take you.

He heard Meadow calling him back, but he just couldn't summon the strength.

AT THE FLAGSTAFF HOSPITAL, they took Dylan through a double door and into Emergency, where she could not follow. She called Jack and told him what had happened. He said they would send his family and tribal leadership.

She was treated and released to the custody of the FBI. Neither Field Agent Forrest nor Field Agent Cassidy Cosen arrived to interview her. Instead she was grilled by Special Agent Virginia Bicher. It became apparent quickly that she did not believe one word Meadow said.

"I want a lawyer," she said.

"You're not under arrest, Miss Wrangler. We're just investigating a crime you allege was committed."

"Did you find my mother?"

"Let me ask the questions, please."

After that Meadow closed her mouth. Following another barrage of questions she would not answer, she stood up to leave.

"We're not finished yet," said Agent Bicher.

"I'm finished." Meadow walked out, expecting to be arrested or detained. But they let her go. She still wore her silver satin dress, now torn, soot covered and smelling of smoke. She had no shoes and her stockings had run at both knees. It was this picture that was captured by the news media waiting outside FBI headquarters. Meadow was forced to return to the lobby. Then she faced a dilemma. She had no money. No credit cards. She called her sister Katrina for help.

Katrina came in a limo ninety minutes later, having driven up from Phoenix with a driver and a bodyguard, who plowed a path through the reporters and herded Meadow into the backseat where her sister was waiting.

"What did you do now?" Katrina said by way of a greeting. "Mom is furious. She could barely speak to me."

"Mom's alive?"

"What?"

"You talked to Mom?" Meadow felt she had dropped down the rabbit hole again. "When?"

"She said you called Dad out of bed last night and you two took off to film the fire." Katrina waved a hand before her face. "God, you reek."

The bodyguard climbed into the passenger seat and glanced back at Katrina. She nodded.

"Go," she said, and then touched the button to lift the privacy shield between them and the men seated in front of them.

The limo pulled away from the throng of photographers still snapping photos.

"Why did you go back up there?" asked Katrina.

Meadow shook her head in denial. "I didn't. I was drugged."

"You mean you drank too much."

"I had two glasses of wine."

"More like six. I was there, remember."

Meadow's skin began to crawl. "Take me to the hospital."

"More reporters there. Mom said to bring you home. She actually said to leave you, but I talked her out of that. You can thank me later."

"Katrina, Mom had me kidnapped and she tried to have me killed."

Katrina gave Meadow a long, steady stare. With that frown, her older sister looked exactly like their mom. Meadow corrected herself. Lupe Wrangler was not her mother and that explained so very much, because no matter how good or bad she was, Meadow had never managed to earn more than Lupe Wrangler's disdain.

Her sister lifted one of Meadow's eyelids. "Are you high?"

Meadow pulled away. "No." She captured her sister's hand. "You have to take me to your apartment. I can't see Mom."

"You have to face her sometime."

"But you spoke to her. Really?"

"You are acting so odd."

"What time is it?" asked Meadow, glancing at the dashboard clock.

"Three. Why?"

"Saturday?"

"Yes, of course."

Katrina's phone jangled a tune and she glanced down.

"It's Phillip." She lay an elegant, manicured finger over the screen and then lifted the smartphone. "Hi, Phil. What's up?" Katrina listened. "Yes. I have her. Reporters everywhere." A pause. "I didn't know about the press until I got there." Another pause as her eyebrows lifted. "I'm putting you on speaker. You can ask her." Katrina switched the call to speaker. "Go ahead."

Phillip's voice emerged. "Meadow? Dad's missing. Mom said he left with you in the Range Rover last night. Do you know where he is?"

Meadow blurted out her story, choking on tears.

"Wait. Wait," Phillip said. "Start from the beginning. You left with Dad late last night, and you two drove into the neighborhood that had been evacuated. Then what happened?"

"That's *not* what happened. I was kidnapped from my room."

"I saw you leave with him, Meadow."

"I was taken by Joe Rhodes and Mark Perkinson."

"Who?"

"Joe. Dad's sound guy."

"I don't know him, Meadow. What was the other name?"

"Mark Perkinson. He's Rosalie's legal assistant."

"Her legal assistant is Jessica Navade. I know because I approve all hires. I'll check with HR, but I don't know anyone named Perkinson."

"That's impossible. I've met them. You've met them."

"Katrina? Take me off speaker."

Her sister instantly complied.

"Yes. Mmm-hmm. I agree. Okay. Will do."

Meadow's mind spun as she tried to make sense of what was happening.

"Where was Mom last night?" asked Meadow.

"At your party."

"Today, I mean."

"Rosalie said they had breakfast and then Mom left to see Phillip about the gala."

"Phillip said she was with him?"

There was no disguising the impatience as Katrina hissed out a yes. "Why?"

"Someone is lying. She wasn't there."

Katrina sat back in her seat and gave Meadow a look of displeasure.

"So Phillip's lying and Rosalie is lying? Everyone. Right?"

Meadow stared at her sister. Either Katrina really didn't know what was happening or she was a part of this. Suddenly Meadow felt as if she was back in that fire shelter struggling to breathe. What was happening?

Chapter Twenty-One

Meadow inched closer to the door as her older sister huffed out a breath. Katrina sank back in the plush leather seat and folded her arms as she tapped out her impatience with her index finger on her sleeve. She stared at the ceiling as she spoke, her voice laden with reproach.

"Of all the attention-getting stunts you have pulled, this takes the cake." She rolled her head on the headrest to stare at Meadow. "What's wrong with you?"

"Me? Katrina, have you seen Dad? He's gone."

"What did you do to him?"

Meadow faced the obvious truth. Either her mother had played Phillip and Katrina, or they were fully informed and this was some kind of mass cover-up. Well, they couldn't hide two bodies or her father's absence. But they could pin both on her. She sucked in a breath as she realized they might also pin the murders on Dylan.

"I have to make a phone call," said Meadow, reaching for Katrina's phone.

Her sister held it back. "Not yet." Katrina lowered the privacy shield between the front and rear seating area and passed her phone to the bodyguard. Then she spoke to her driver.

"Change of plans, Ralph. Could you take us to this address?"

The driver glanced down and his eyebrows lifted.

"Yes ma'am."

"Where? Where are you taking me?" said Meadow, her voice taking on a hysterical edge.

"Take it easy, Meadow."

"I want out of this car. Right now!"

Katrina rolled her eyes. "So dramatic." Then she spoke to Ralph. "Hurry, would you?"

"Yes, ma'am."

The car sped on and Katrina lifted the privacy shield. "You're embarrassing me."

Meadow tried to explain again, from the beginning. Katrina rolled her eyes up and away and folded her arms.

"Where are we going?"

"To a hospital."

Meadow sat back as dread slithered in her belly, cold and slippery as an eel. "What kind of hospital?"

"FMHH."

She gasped. She'd spent time at Flagstaff Mental Health Hospital before, when she was just seventeen. Her mother had taken her for a drug test that had come back positive for opiates and she'd been admitted. She'd learned that going in was a lot easier than getting out, especially for a teen. She'd spent three months there.

"You need my permission."

Katrina shrugged. "Phillip says you need help. I agree. We think you're drinking again."

"I'm not!"

"You had wine last night."

"So did you," said Meadow.

"I'm not an alcoholic."

"This is Mother's idea, isn't it?"

Katrina didn't deny it. "She's worried about you. And Dad's missing. Now you're making up stories and people. You never made up people before."

"I'm not making this up. Katrina, you have to believe me."

Her sister just shook her head. "You'll be all over the newspapers again. A media frenzy. Congratulations. You'll be in the tabloids all week. Front page. Just look at yourself." She swept a hand toward Meadow. "Who goes to a forest fire in a satin cocktail dress? Oh, my baby sister, that's who."

They left the highway and Meadow considered her options. They couldn't admit her if she refused treatment. She was an adult, after all. She didn't think diving out of a moving car would improve her chances of looking sane. She would need to convince the doctors to contact the FBI and tribal police.

"But what if Mother had gotten to them, too?" she muttered.

"Gotten to whom? A hospital? Meadow, you sound crazy. You know that, right?"

At the hospital admissions, she was muscled into an exam room by two goons. Once in an exam room, it was explained to her that they did not need her permission for an evaluation because three of her family members had requested one.

She was told that she was being admitted because her family believed her likely to suffer mental or physical harm due to impaired judgment and that she had displayed symptoms of substance abuse.

Meadow refused evaluation and was told that her inability to appreciate the need for such services only strengthened the argument for involuntary placement. Her best option was to cooperate.

Then the intake physician showed her a petition for involuntary emergency admission signed by her mother, Phillip and Katrina. It was in that moment, as she held the page between her two trembling hands, that Meadow recognized that even if she explained the truth she would sound paranoid and, well, crazy.

Once admitted—she had no doubt that the evaluation would recommend admission—she would be either locked away here or killed in some accidental fashion. A suicide, perhaps. Her family had done an excellent job in discrediting her. What police detective, FBI agent or jury would believe a woman twice institutionalized?

It was in that moment of betrayal by her family that her mind turned from convincing others of her sanity to plans of escape.

THE SUNLIGHT FROM the window hurt Dylan's eyes even through his closed lids. Gradually he realized the sounds around him were unfamiliar and there was something wrong with his neck. The dull ache at his elbow caused him to bend the joint, sending off an alarm beeping beside him.

"You awake?"

Someone straightened his arm and the beeping stopped. He knew the voice. That was Jack Bear Den.

Dylan cracked open an eye and stared. He tried to speak and the movement caused his neck to throb.

"What?" asked Jack. "Don't talk yet. Just listen."

Jack sat in the chair beside his bed. Two more people sat behind him on a bench beneath the window. The railing between him and Jack confirmed his suspicion. He was lying in a hospital bed.

"You were shot in the throat. Lost a lot of blood from that neck wound. The bullet grazed muscle mostly but nicked the artery. You're lucky, Brother Bobcat. Very lucky."

Dylan tapped his wrist and then raised the wrist to his ear.

"Time? It's still Sunday. Seven p.m. You came in by ambulance yesterday morning and went right in to surgery.

After that they kept you in the ICU overnight because of your blood pressure."

"What was wrong with my blood pressure?" he whispered.

"You didn't have one."

Dylan lifted a hand to touch the bandage at his neck. His voice had sounded strange. The pain told him that something was wrong with his throat.

THE TWO PEOPLE at the window rose and approached him. As soon as they moved past the flood of late-afternoon sunlight through the open blinds, he recognized his mother, Dotty, and his maternal grandfather, Frank Florez.

His mother took his hand and began to cry. His grandfather rested a gnarled hand on Dylan's thigh and forced a smile.

"Welcome back, grandson," he said in Tonto Apache.

"Where's…?" His voice rasped like sandpaper across stone.

"They stitched up your neck. A gash. The rest is bumps and bruises."

Dylan pressed a hand to his throat, feeling the thick bandage, and then moved his fingers to rub over his Adam's apple and winced.

"They had to open your airway in the ER to get more oxygen into your blood. They stuck a tube down your throat. Oh, and you had some transfusions."

"Meadow?" he whispered.

Jack bowed his head. "Can't find her."

"What?" He tried to get up, and both his friend and grandfather pushed him back down. The fact that he was so easily subdued scared him almost as much as learning that Meadow was missing.

"I've got Forrest looking. She was with you here. The ER nurse I spoke to said she tried to get to you. But she wasn't family so…she was treated for minor injuries and released. The FBI questioned her. Dylan, where's Theron Wrangler?"

"Shot," he said.

Jack winced. "That's what Forrest said, and that Meadow told one of their investigators, Field Agent Bicher, the same. They've been out searching for evidence to confirm her story, but the fire has made it impossible to reach some places. Meadow didn't know where exactly you two were. Do you know?"

"Pine View somewhere." He winced at the pain words caused him but it didn't stop him. "Her mother?"

"Here. Here all the time, according to her statement. She's got witnesses."

"No," he whispered. "Lying. Her man. Shot me."

"Could Theron Wrangler have been the one who shot you?"

"What? No." Dylan held a hand to his throbbing neck and clamped the other around Jack's wrist. "Find her."

"Working on it. Family asked for privacy."

"They have her? They'll kill her," rasped Dylan. "Call Forrest."

"I did. He's investigating Meadow's story. So far he hasn't found a shred of evidence that any of this happened. He has no bodies and no crime scene."

Dylan pointed to the bullet wound. "He has this."

"I'll call him again. Already left four messages."

Dylan threw back the white sheet and thin cotton blanket.

"What are you doing?" asked Jack.

"I'm going to find Meadow."

"No, you're not."

Dylan was going. Jack wasn't stopping him. Dylan did not wait for the discharge papers, but he was delayed while his mother went to buy him some jeans and a shirt because they'd cut off his clothing in the ER. Luckily, his boots and turquoise necklace had both survived. Once she returned, he dressed and slipped the multistrand of turquoise over his head before he tugging on his boots.

"Your neck is bleeding," said Jack, raising a finger to point at the bandage.

Dylan flashed an impatient glance from Jack to his mother, who stood at the foot of his bed with a newspaper clutched to her chest. Dylan paused. Her mother never bought the newspaper, preferring to get her news from Native Peoples Television and NPR. This particular one had the distinctive shape of the tabloid news.

"Mom?" Dylan rasped.

"She's in the paper." Dotty slowly lowered the paper so that he could see the headline and photo beneath— Meadow Burnin' Down the Houz!

Beneath was Meadow still in her tattered soot-smeared party dress, lifting a hand to shield her face from the flashes of the paparazzi's camera.

Dylan scanned the article. Meadow had been photographed leaving the FBI office in Flagstaff yesterday afternoon with two "handlers," who looked like gorillas in suits.

He read aloud. "No comment from family." He lifted his head. "She's disappeared. The reporters were waiting at her parents' home. She never showed." He flipped the page, read the continuing article. Then his hands dropped and the paper crumpled in his lap.

"What?"

"Unidentified source claims she checked into rehab."

Jack snatched the paper. "Where?"

Dylan shook his head. "We have to get her."

"Hold on. Let me get my hat," said Jack.

Jack's phone rang and he drew it from his front pocket. "It's Forrest."

Jack answered the phone and kept his eyes on Dylan.

"Yeah."

Dylan could hear Luke speaking, but the words were unclear.

"Okay." Jack disconnected. "We gotta get out of here. Now."

Dylan had been ready to leave, but now he hesitated. "Why?"

"Forrest is on his way. They found two bodies up in Pine View. He has orders to bring you in for questioning."

Chapter Twenty-Two

"Why did Forrest call us first?" asked Dylan as they reached the parking lot and Jack's tribal police unit, a large white SUV with blue lettering on the sides.

"I'd say to give us a head start," said Jack, opening the passenger door.

Dylan was about to object to being driven around, but it hurt to talk, and even climbing up into the seat made him sweat.

"He told me that agents interviewed Lupe Wrangler. She was seen retiring last night a little after eleven and her staff confirmed she ate breakfast at six at her home. She provided access to her cook and housekeeper and driver. All corroborated her version of events."

"Lying," said Dylan, and he winced.

"Well, then so is her family. She met with one of her daughters in the morning and the caterers for a gala that PAN is having in the fall. She's got a solid alibi."

Dylan shook his head. It didn't happen that way. He had seen her. But when? Early Saturday morning in the hours before she had breakfast? He didn't know what time he'd woken on that patio beside Meadow. The smoke had been so thick it might have been morning or night.

"How'd she get from the fire to Flagstaff?" asked Jack. "She never passed the roadblock."

"Helicopter? Meadow's father picked us up outside the

rez in one." Dylan had to hold his throat against the pain and felt the blood soaking through the bandages.

"Maybe. I'll ask Forrest to do some checking. She can't cover flight records."

"Want to bet?" asked Dylan. He climbed into the passenger side and buckled up, waiting with impatience for Jack to get them moving. Then he realized he didn't know where to start.

"Any ideas?" asked Jack.

Dylan bowed his head to think. Who would know something and be willing to tell them?

"She told me Katrina looked out for her when they were kids."

"Where does she live?"

"I don't know."

Jack started typing on his computer. In a few minutes the database search provided Katrina's vehicle registration, violations, and property.

"Katrina likes to drive too fast," said Jack.

Dylan leaned in and found her residential address. "Let's go."

The drive to Phoenix seemed endless. Finally they pulled up before the complex. Katrina's posh apartment was located on the top floor. Jack's badge got them access, but Katrina knew they were coming.

She met them at her door and escorted them to her living room, glancing several times over her shoulder toward the kitchen.

"Who else is here?" asked Jack.

"My housekeeper," said Katrina. "My mother picked her."

The implication was clear. Katrina was worried her mother would find out she was speaking to the enemy.

She swept them past her housekeeper and told the young woman that she was not to be disturbed. Once inside, she

shut the door and pressed her back against it as if to bar
the castle gates.

Dylan glanced about the room, seeing a white leather
couch edged in chrome opposite a glass coffee table from
two matching chairs. The banks of windows provided impressive views and were anchored with a long, curving
cabinets in ivory, which hugged the bend in the exterior
wall. Her glass-and-chrome fireplace dominated the room.
The only color was a cheerful bouquet that sat on the coffee table beside her television remotes.

"What are you two doing here?" She spoke in a whisper that held a definite edge.

"Where is she?" asked Dylan.

She lifted a finger. "You're bleeding." She stared at his
neck and spoke as if to herself. "I should call security."

"She said you looked out for her," Dylan said.

Katrina sucked in a breath and her chin trembled.

Dylan bowed his head and spoke in a calm, gentle voice.
"She needs you now more than ever."

Katrina folded her arms around herself and began to
rock, thumping back against the closed door. Finally she
shook her head. "You should go."

He wasn't going. Not until he knew where to find her.
"Katrina, they're going to kill her."

"You're as crazy as she is."

"If you're right, it won't matter. But what if I'm right?"

Katrina stopped rocking and glared. He waited, knowing that the one to speak first in this standoff would lose.

"She's at Flagstaff Mental Health Hospital," said Katrina, her voice low and conspiratorial. "They're holding
her for observation and I never told you. Now get out."

"A psychiatric hospital?" asked Jack.

"She asked me to bring her."

"Your mother?" asked Jack.

Katrina nodded.

"Because Meadow trusted you," said Dylan.

Katrina flinched, then lifted her chin in an attitude of defiance. "They found barbiturates in her blood."

Dylan paused. "Want to know who put them there?"

Katrina turned her worried eyes away. "You should go."

Dylan was already heading for the door and Katrina swept out of the way. "You won't get her out. It's very secure."

Dylan didn't know how he'd get to her, but he knew one thing for sure—he would get to Meadow.

Jack followed him out. Once back in the tribal police unit, Jack hit the lights and then the highway, driving at high speeds and using the siren to move distracted drivers out of their way.

Dylan turned to his friend.

"We need to break her out."

"You have a plan?" Jack asked. "Because I have zero jurisdiction and no friends down here. I might as well pull up on a Segway dressed as a mall cop."

"Steal someone's ID card?"

"Illegal."

Dylan swore. "Every plan I come up with will be illegal." He wondered what they were doing to her right now. "They could stage a suicide attempt."

"Not if she's under observation. She'd be under added supervision and it will be harder for anyone to hurt her."

Dylan hoped Jack was right.

Dylan felt his stomach drop. "Drive faster," he said.

Jack pressed the accelerator slowing only when they reached their exit. He took them to the facility, which had a high metal gate and security booth at the entrance.

"That's bad," said Jack.

"Obviously." Dylan scratched his head and found the smooth surface of the staples they had used to close up his scalp. "What about a laundry service or food service truck?"

"Still check ID and we wouldn't have access past the delivery area. What you need is someone who can go anywhere, even to the lock-in floors."

"Impersonate a doctor?"

Jack gave a halfhearted shrug.

Dylan's throat hurt. His head hurt. But, most of all, his heart hurt. Meadow was in there alone, and he had to get to her before her mother finished what she had started.

Someone who could go anywhere, he thought, and then the idea came to him, all at once and completely formed.

"That might work," Dylan muttered.

"What?" asked Jack.

"Fire inspector," said Dylan.

"I don't follow," said Jack Bear Den, still staring at the front gate to the mental-health facility.

"I'm a certified fire inspector."

"On Turquoise Canyon," said Jack.

"No. Statewide. I can inspect any public facility, including group homes, residential-care facilities and medical facilities."

"But not at night," said Jack.

"Oh, yeah. Especially at night. If they do business in the evening, like a bar, or 24/7, like a hospital, I can inspect them anytime, any day."

Jack sat back and smiled. "Ain't that a kick?"

"They're inspected quarterly and they are not supposed to know ahead of time."

"What if they just got inspected yesterday?" Jack asked.

"Doesn't matter. I tell them that there has been a complaint of a code violation."

"You have a badge or something?" asked Jack.

"I do, but not with me. But I have an ID card in my wallet. Two, actually—state and international."

"My vehicle says Tribal Police," said Jack.

"Yeah, we need to lose this. Where's Ray?"

"He's back on the line, fighting the fire. They're making progress now. He says it's seventy percent contained. We could rent a vehicle."

"A red or white SUV."

"City vehicle would be better," said Jack. He threw the SUV into Reverse. "Shouldn't be very hard to find one to borrow at this time of night."

"Sounds like a plan."

"Once we find her, how do we get her out?" asked Jack.

"I might need your help on that one."

Dylan used Jack's phone to find city hall. Round the back on West Aspen Avenue was a really nice parking lot with a variety of white vehicles all with the city's colorful insignia on the door panel. They had vans and mid-size cars, SUVs and several pickups. Dylan walked along with Jack as he selected a pickup that was shielded from the street by three other cars.

"They'll have cameras on this lot," said Jack.

Which was why they had left the tribal police car down the street and walked here with Jack's bag of tools. His friend routinely broke into cars for various reasons.

Dylan glanced about as Jack used the slim jim to pop the door open. He wedged his big shoulders between the seat and wheel well and had the truck started soon after. Dylan drove the truck, pausing only to drop Jack at his vehicle before retracing his course back to the facility holding Meadow.

He felt the pressure of time pushing down on him. Was her mother's plan merely to discredit Meadow or did she mean to kill her?

Jack flashed his lights and then passed him as he turned into the residential neighborhood close to the hospital. He parked on the street and then joined Dylan.

"Okay, let's go."

At the gate they found a sleepy attendant who snapped into action as Dylan identified himself and presented his ID.

"Usually we know ahead," said the pink-faced attendant as he studied the red-and-white identification card.

"You're not supposed to have advance warning. Who's been doing the inspections?"

That got the young man twitching. He closed his mouth and scribbled down Dylan's name and ID number. Then he lifted the phone in the booth.

Jack leaned across the seat and yelled, "Gate!"

A moment later the lever arm lifted and they drove on.

He did and they rolled up to the facility. They had not even disconnected the starter wires when a woman came rushing out to meet them.

Chapter Twenty-Three

Meadow woke with the taste of copper in her mouth. Her head pounded and her vision rippled like moonlight reflecting on deep water. The cotton dressing gown stuck to her wet skin and sweat puddled beneath her flushed body. The movement of her eyes caused sharp pains at her temples. She hadn't felt like this since she'd stopped drinking Jack.

This was a hospital. She knew the look of the sterile walls and room layout. Meadow tried to lift her hand to scratch her nose and found her wrist secured to the bed rail with a clear plastic tie. Above the fastening was a white hospital bracelet.

The panic bubbled up inside her as the intake process rose in her mind like a backed-up toilet. She'd been stripped. She'd been searched. They'd taken her clothing, earrings, underwear, blood and, finally, her dignity. When she'd refused their tests they'd injected her with something.

Where was Dylan? Did he know what had happened to her? What if they had hurt him? The last she'd seen him was in the emergency room, where he was being treated for a bullet wound. Shot by her mother's crony.

Oh, the blood. So much blood.

Meadow squeezed her eyes shut. This was all her fault. She'd dragged him into this nightmare and he'd stayed and it had nearly gotten him killed.

She prayed he was alive and safe. But in the meantime she needed to get out of here.

"Hey," she yelled. "Hey! I need to use the toilet."

Someone stepped into her room. She knew him. Meadow gasped as the face of Joe Rhodes came into focus. He was dressed like a male nurse or orderly in green scrubs and white tennis shoes. His left arm was casted and now rested in a black sling. If Meadow found any solace, it was in knowing that Dylan had broken Joe's arm in the fight at the ridge fire.

"Good evening, Princess."

"Joe, whatever my mother is paying you, I'll double it."

He smiled. "She said you'd try to bribe me, so she cut off your funds. They're her funds. You don't have anything without her." He stepped nearer. "Oh, your blood work came back." He ticked the items off on the fingers of his injured arm. "Oxy. Barbiturates. Pot, of course. And heroin. Looks like you've moved up from binge drinking."

"You know she put all that in my drink."

"No, actually, I did. I had a tranquilizer in there, too, but it didn't come up on the test. Must have worked it out of your system."

He stepped nearer.

"I'll scream."

He grimaced. "Oh, please. Someone is screaming in here about every three minutes."

"Stay back." She used her legs to push as far away from him as her bonds allowed. Panic zinged through her like speed and her heart crashed into her ribs. She was going to die here in this stupid bed with the sheets tangled about her legs and everyone in the world would believe she was just another train wreck.

"You're on suicide watch," Joe said, now at her bedside. "I wrapped the IV tube around your neck, but someone came in before I finished. Got you restrained, though."

"How are you going to explain my killing myself while restrained?"

"Bit your tongue." He reached for her, grabbing her head and sealing her nose shut.

She struggled and finally had to open her mouth. He pushed a wedge of plastic between her jaws. Meadow was not ready to die. She rolled her knees to her chest and then exploded outward like a diver before entering the water. Only, instead of extending toward a perfect entry, she kicked Joe's casted arm with all her might.

Joe screamed and fell back, landing hard on the floor. Meadow spit out the wedge and shimmied down in her bed, gnawing at the restraint on her right wrist. Joe was on his feet and cradling his arm as she pulled one wrist free.

There was murder in his eyes as he approached her bed for the second time.

DYLAN ADDRESSED HIS attention to Louisa Crane, the night manager on call, who had drawn the short straw for taking the inspectors throughout the facility. She was dressed in a black skirt and maroon blouse, and her black hair was drawn back in a neat ponytail. She was young with anxious eyes.

"Let's start with the sprinkler systems," said Dylan to Louisa. He knew that the sprinklers were on every floor and every room. It was a way to get to Meadow quickly. But, when and if he found her, how would he get her out?

"Oh, all right," said Louisa.

"And the fire exits. You can't have equipment blocking stairways."

"Oh, we never do," said Crane, but she was sweating now, her dark blouse showing even darker stains down the center of her back.

She swiped her employee card in a slot to summon

the elevator and again inside to access the top floor, level three.

"This is a lock-in ward with some of the residents who wander. It can be noisy."

"When was your last fire drill?" asked Dylan.

Crane wiped her upper lip. "I'd have to check the records. I'm only here at night."

"You have to run drills day and night. Practice is important," said Jack, sounding as if he knew what he was talking about.

Crane's hand went to the junction of her neck and shoulder where she rubbed. Dylan smiled. Apparently Jack and he were becoming a pain in her neck.

"I need to check the dates on the extinguishers and see the sprinkler heads in every room," said Dylan.

"Every room?" Crane did not keep the exasperation from her voice. "That will disturb the patients."

"I need to see eighteen inches of clearance under each sprinkler head."

He began his inspection in the room to his left and continued to the next and the next.

The crash brought them all around. A male voice roared and a woman shouted for help. Dylan glanced at Jack and nodded. He knew that voice. It was Meadow.

Dylan turned in the direction of the commotion and charged down the hall.

"Hey!" called Crane.

The sound of something striking metal reached him as he barreled into the room.

Jack followed Dylan and the two men skidded to a stop in front of the hospital bed and the two struggling combatants.

A man in a sling choked Meadow as she thrashed, her heel striking the bed rail and making it ring as she clawed at the hand clamped to her throat.

Crane arrived and gasped. "What is going on here?"

Her attacker released Meadow, but she continued to swing, her arms and legs flaying as she fought for her life. His brave warrior would not go down without a fight.

"Meadow," Dylan called.

At the sound of his voice, her eyes popped open and her body stilled.

Crane gaped. "You know her? What is this?"

The man now faced them. Dylan braced as he recognized Joe Rhodes.

Crane drew out her phone and started pressing buttons.

Dylan inched along the opposite side of the bed from Rhodes as Jack stepped past the foot of the bed to block Rhodes's exit.

Tears rolled down Meadow's face as she looked at Dylan.

"You…you came," said Meadow,

Had she doubted that he would?

Dylan reached for the small knife clipped to his belt and flipped open one of the blades.

"Weapons are not allowed in here," said Crane.

Dylan ignored her as he sliced the bond holding her left wrist to the bed rail.

"You can't do that," said Crane.

Meadow threw herself into Dylan's arms. He gathered her up and held her, whispering in her ear.

"I got you."

"I need your ID badge. Now," said Crane to Rhodes.

Rhodes spoke to no one in particular. "We've got company."

"He just called for backup," Jack said.

Rhodes reached into the sling. He drew a pistol at the same time Jack drew his sidearm from his shoulder holster. Rhodes pointed his weapon at Meadow, now on the opposite side of the bed, as Jack leveled his service pistol at Rhodes.

Crane closed her mouth and inched back toward the door.

Jack did not move. Dylan knew Jack was an excellent shot, but he was not fast enough to stop Joe from firing at Meadow.

Stalemate.

"I'll step aside and you can go," said Jack, who did not move aside but kept his weapon raised and ready.

"Lower your weapon," said Rhodes.

Jack didn't move. Dylan eased Meadow to the floor and then stepped in front of her.

Rhodes shifted his attention to Dylan. "Bullet will go right through you and then hit her. It won't even slow down."

Jack spoke again. "You should go."

Rhodes did not take his eyes off his targets. "Put the gun on the floor, Bear Den."

Dylan knew that Jack would not do so. If he did, there was nothing to keep Rhodes from shooting all of them.

Dylan spoke in Apache. "Shoot him."

Jack said nothing, just kept his weapon poised and ready. Rhodes was sweating now, the beads rolling down his face and into his eyes. He shrugged his shoulder, but with the cast he could not wipe his face.

Crane continued her backward tread until she inched from Dylan's view behind the wall and the corridor that led past the bathroom and into the main hallway. A moment later, Dylan heard a shot coming from the hallway. Rhodes's gaze shifted away from Meadow and toward the door.

Jack fired.

Chapter Twenty-Four

Rhodes crashed to the floor on the opposite side of the bed.

"Check him," said Jack as he moved toward the door. "Crane is down."

Dylan rounded the bed toward the motionless Rhodes, catching a glimpse of the woman's body sprawled in the hall outside Meadow's room and of Jack pressed to the wall beside the door, weapon raised.

Meadow followed Dylan as far as the foot of the bed.

"Get down," said Dylan, and Meadow crouched.

Dylan checked Rhodes and found no pulse. Jack had hit him in the breastbone. Dylan retrieved the man's pistol from the floor.

"Two heading this way," said Jack from the door. "Armed with rifles."

Dylan went to the window and glanced out at the night. Meadow's room sat directly over the entrance, three floors down, but there was a flat portico one story beneath them.

Dylan used the chair to smash the window and lowered Meadow over the window casements.

"Get ready," he said. She nodded, and he dropped her. She landed on her feet and then fell to her side. He turned to Jack. "You're next."

"What have we got?" said Jack, retreating backward toward Dylan's position.

"Portico on two, about ten feet down."

"Together, then," he said.

They went out the window, using the casements to dangle to full length before dropping beside Meadow.

Gunfire sounded above them.

"They're in the room," said Jack, raising his weapon and aiming at the windows above them.

Dylan helped Meadow to her feet. She was unsteady and pale as moonlight. What had they given her in there?

He helped her to the edge of the portico. Jack was already on the ground beside the entrance with his service pistol raised. He fired three shots as Dylan lifted Meadow and sent her over the edge once more.

The instant she landed, he dropped beside her, and all three made it under cover as the two gunman above returned fire.

"They'll be down as fast as they can take those stairs," said Jack.

"Let's go."

Dylan never let go of Meadow's hand as they raced along the sidewalk, close to the building and then out to the lot. Alarm bells sounded behind them. Their pursuers had reached ground level.

Jack opened the door to the city vehicle and Dylan lifted Meadow inside before scrambling up beside her. When Jack reached the driver's seat, he touched the exposed wires together and the truck engine turned over. They pulled away and out of the gate, making the turn as the lights of the police units swarmed past them.

"Your neck is bleeding again," said Jack.

"We need to lose this car," said Dylan.

Meadow clung to Dylan, burying her face against the muscles of his chest. He rubbed her shoulder and held her tight.

"I've got you, Meadow. And I'm not letting go."

They switched vehicles at Jack's police unit near the

Flagstaff lot and headed east toward their reservation, taking the winding route past the series of reservoirs until they reached Turquoise Canyon land. Meadow slept on his shoulder much of the way. Dylan kept one arm around her and the opposite hand pressed to his neck wound, which had come alive with a throbbing ache now that the adrenaline had ebbed away to nothing.

Jack called ahead and a welcoming committee waited at the tribe's health clinic. The group included Jack's brother Kurt, the paramedic, Kenshaw Little Falcon and Jack's boss, the chief of tribal police, Wallace Tinnin.

"You about to get fired?" asked Dylan, eyeing the sour expression on Tinnin's face.

"Or promoted. Hard to tell."

"Is that Forrest?" said Dylan, looking at the man standing beside tribal police chief Wallace Tinnin.

Jack sighed. "Yup, and he's got jurisdiction to investigate federal crimes on the rez."

"With permission," said Dylan.

"Technically. Get ready to be arrested."

Jack parked the SUV and Meadow roused, her words slurred. "We here?"

"Yes, darling," said Dylan.

Jack gave him an odd look and Dylan lifted his chin. Jack's brow quirked in silent question and Dylan nodded.

Yes, this was his woman.

"Okay then," said Jack. "Glad I didn't risk my butt for just anyone."

"I don't expect she'll stay," said Dylan.

Jack looked at Meadow, who rubbed her eyes with both hands. Her wrists were red and raw from the restraints. Her hair stuck up on top like a breaking blue wave and she was still wearing the hospital gown.

"She might surprise you."

Chief Tinnin reached Jack's door. "We have medical. Anyone need a stretcher or wheelchair?"

Jack gave Tinnin a rundown of their injuries as Dylan helped Meadow to a wheelchair. Inside, Dylan refused to leave her as they checked her over and drew blood to determine what they'd given her at the mental-health facility.

Dylan needed his neck wound sutured as he'd torn out several of the staples. Kurt took care of that as Dylan sat at Meadow's side. Late that night, Meadow was moved to a room and Dylan took the bed beside hers. He had planned to keep watch but dozed and woke to someone calling his name. He blinked his eyes open, trying to shake off the grogginess of slumber. Jack stood at the foot of his bed looking worn-out. A glance at the windows showed that morning had come—Monday morning, he realized.

"What time is it?" asked Dylan.

"Nearly nine. I let you sleep as long as I could."

Meadow did not rouse, but her breathing was steady and slow.

Dylan's neck twinged when he sat up, but his throat no longer hurt as much as the soft tissue at his neck. He swung his legs over the side of the narrow hospital bed.

Jack gave him the short version of events.

"We are wanted for the shooting at the facility in Flagstaff. Rhodes's body was not found on the scene. But Crane's was. She's dead."

Dylan knew that meant there was no one to corroborate their version of events.

"Video surveillance?"

"Surprisingly, they have cameras on every corridor. Forrest has a team there."

"They'll see the gunman," said Dylan.

"Maybe."

"You know her mother sent those men. She planned for Meadow to die in there."

"Hard to prove," said Jack. "Her mother is contending that she was worried about Meadow. Her actions come off as those of a concerned parent dealing with a drug-addicted child."

"Meadow doesn't do drugs," said Dylan.

"She's been in detox once after a public indecency charge. She was swimming naked in a fountain at a private country club. According to Forrest her family pulled strings and she got community service."

Dylan realized that no one would believe a thing Meadow said. Not a judge. Not a jury.

"What do we do?"

"You're a war hero. Highly decorated. I'd say your word is good. But Forrest said that the press is spinning you as a PTSD vet with a gun. Morning papers are out. Her mom is good."

"So she's cleared of her husband's murder and she's clear of any charges of wrongdoing regarding Meadow?"

"She will be. I'm certain."

"And we are both wanted?"

Jack nodded. "That's right."

"What does Lupe say about the explosives?"

"She denies any knowledge of her husband's radical involvement."

Dylan swore.

"Oh, and she is suing the papers for mentioning that PAN might be a feeder organization for recruitment to WOLF and BEAR. Forrest says she'll win."

"So she gets away with it all?" asked Dylan.

"The FBI has found nothing to implicate Lupe. But they don't have the explosives, either. Forrest is trying to convince his superiors that the ridge fire was a test and that the real target is one or more of the reservoirs."

"How's that going?" asked Dylan.

Jack shook his head. "Not good."

"If they take out either of the dams above us, it will flood our land."

"Wipe out Piñon Forks completely. Might go as high as Koun'nde."

The two men stared at each other. They both knew they could not let that happen. It was their duty to their people to stop BEAR from destroying their home.

"Skeleton Cliff Dam isn't on our land," said Jack.

"But we have to protect it."

"And Alchesay Canyon," added Jack, naming the dam above Skeleton Cliff and holding back the enormous Goodwin Lake. Below that dam lay Two Mountain Lake, Skeleton Cliff Dam and then their rez, bordering Turquoise Lake. And just beyond their western border was Red Rock Dam, Antelope Lake and, finally, the Mesa Salado Dam. The entire system provided drinking water for both Phoenix and Tucson and supplied the electricity for much of the state. If that was the target, it was a good one. Taking out the dams would send them all back to the 1800s. No air-conditioning, no clean water, no refrigeration. Southwestern Arizona would go from a thriving web of cities to the largest refugee camp in the nation.

Dylan swallowed back the dread at the possibilities. Then he drew a deep breath. The targets were spread over forty of the roughest, most inhospitable miles of territory in the state.

"We need more men," said Dylan.

"Kenshaw is recruiting now. I called my brother Tommy to come home. Kurt is already a full member of Tribal Thunder. Wallace Tinnin wants to move from the Turquoise Guardians to Tribal Thunder, as well. Kenshaw thinks it's a good idea."

The chief of tribal police had always been a leader of the medicine society, but now he wished to join it to the warrior sect.

"He knows it will be bad," said Dylan.

"We'll need him."

Dylan nodded.

Jack motioned toward Meadow. "She can't go home."

Dylan looked at Meadow's sleeping face and felt a squeezing pressure behind his breastbone.

"I know that. I wanted her to stay because she wanted to, not because she had no other choice."

"You love her?" asked Jack.

Dylan nodded, not taking his eyes off her.

"Always pictured you with an Apache girl."

Dylan looked at Jack.

"Well, sometimes things don't turn out like you plan."

"That's true enough," said Jack.

"You ever going to open that DNA sibling test?" asked Dylan.

"Sometime. Soon maybe."

Dylan knew he'd been carrying the results around with him for weeks.

"Carter would want you to have your answers," said Dylan, certain his twin would not have provided the sample if he objected to Jack discovering the truth.

"What are you going to do?" asked Jack.

"Stay here. Protect the tribe. Protect Meadow. Ask a certain heiress to marry me."

Jack didn't look surprised, rather like he expected Dylan to say something like this.

"Forrest and Cosen won't arrest us on federal land, but they can't keep state officials from trying."

"We have to stay on Indian land."

"For a while."

"Suits me." He wondered how Meadow would do without her parties and clubs and private limo.

"You marry her and she's protected, too," said Jack. "Otherwise, the sheriff can execute a warrant here."

"I don't want her to marry me because she has to."

Jack shrugged. "She doesn't seem the sort not to do what she pleases."

"How will I know?"

"What?"

"If she is marrying me for me or because I can protect her?"

Jack scratched the back of his head. "Don't know."

Dylan moved to stand over Meadow. He stroked her tangled hair from her face.

"I love her, Jack. And I want her to love me back."

Chapter Twenty-Five

Meadow opened her eyes to find herself lying in a twin bed beneath a familiar red, black and turquoise blanket. She fingered the wool and sank down against clean sheets that smelled of bleach and soap. This was Dylan's guest room and library. He had brought her here after the fire.

"You awake now?" The woman's voice was melodious, almost a song.

Meadow opened her eyes to see an unfamiliar Apache woman sitting beside her. The woman lowered the sewing she had on her lap and met Meadow's gaze with directness. There was something very familiar about her.

"My son asked me to watch over you. He is meeting with the FBI and tribal leadership. I'm Dotty Tehauno, Dylan's mom."

Meadow pushed herself up to her elbows and blinked at the woman. The resemblance between mother and son was remarkable, especially around the eyes and mouth, but in Dotty the generous mouth seemed more welcoming and her eyes were more speculative.

"You've been asleep all day. It's Tuesday afternoon now."

Meadow vaguely recalled being lifted from a vehicle and carried through the bright afternoon sunlight. Was that yesterday?

Jack had woken her at the medical clinic and the doctor had checked her over before releasing her. They had wanted her out of there before the sheriff came looking for her and Dylan had driven her here.

The woman offered her a drink and Meadow swallowed one mouthful after another. Apple juice, she realized, sweet and wonderful. The woman helped her set the glass on the side table.

"He's never asked me to watch over a woman before. He said you're important. So what I want to know is if you are important to this investigation or important to my son."

Both, she hoped. "Dylan saved my life."

"More than once, if I can believe Ray Strong, and usually I don't. He just got back from that ridge fire. It's out but burned fifteen thousand acres. Be some mudslides with the rain, I'll bet. Dylan should have been there, too. Fighting that fire. Now he won't get paid." Her expression showed reproach. Both women knew why Dylan was not on the line with his crew.

"I have money," said Meadow.

"No, you don't. You used to have money. Now you've got a crazy mother who wants you dead, a brother who is planning to blow up the parts of the state that they didn't burn down and a father who died trying to save you. I'm sorry to hear about your father. But what you don't have is money. Not anymore. So that might make you think that you need to find someone who can protect you, because you don't have money to do that anymore. So I wanted to tell you this. My son is not your protector. My son deserves a woman who loves him and who can defend herself."

Meadow felt herself being judged and found lacking. But why not? What had she done with her life but screw up? She tried to think of one redeeming act she had accomplished with her advantages and could not come up with a single thing.

Her head bowed. "I think you're right."

She was met with silence. Meadow looked up to find Dotty regarding her with cautious eyes.

"Your son is a wonderful man. He's smart and brave and selfless. He deserves someone like that."

"But you're not smart?"

"I'm smart. But I didn't do well in school. Schools," she corrected.

"I heard you went to the FBI and told them about your mother."

That made her look like a traitor, Meadow knew, turning in her own mother.

Meadow nodded.

"I think that is brave."

Meadow narrowed her eyes at Dotty. Was she playing some game with her?

Dotty lifted the fabric on her lap and placed another row of careful stitches.

"That leaves selfless." She flicked her gaze from the scam to Meadow. "What are you prepared to sacrifice?"

"I'd give my life for Dylan."

"Very dramatic. Sticking around would be harder. His father left us when he was young. My son has always felt that loss. He needs someone who will stay. If you can't do that, you'd better go sooner rather than later."

"I don't even know if he wants me to stay."

Dotty lifted the stitching. "He asked me to watch over you."

Meadow puzzled over this cryptic reply.

"I need to go find him,"

"No. You need to eat and to bathe." Dotty stood and set her work on the chair. "I'll fix you some lunch. Shower is that way." She pointed toward the door.

"Thank you, Mrs. Tehauno, for your kindness."

Dotty harrumphed and then disappeared down the hall,

muttering that she hoped her son had some food in the house.

Meadow showered, working out the kinks and examining the bruises she'd gotten during their escape from the mental hospital.

The water poured down on Meadow's body as she added shampoo to her hair.

Two more people dead and her mother was responsible for it all. No, not her mother. Her father's wife. That meant the siblings who had always looked just a little different than she did shared a father.

So who was her mother? Meadow rinsed the shampoo away. She didn't know who her mother was or what had happened to her, but she intended to find out.

Dylan had told Meadow about his friend Jack. He had suspected most of his life that his father was not the same as his brothers. Why hadn't Meadow ever suspected? Why had she spent most of her life trying to get the only woman she ever knew as her mother to notice her?

To love her.

Meadow let the water wash away her tears along with the soap. Lupe hated her because she was the visible reminder of her husband's love for another woman. An infidelity. A betrayal.

Meadow turned off the taps and reached for a towel. She borrowed Dylan's deodorant and brush, then used the toothbrush he had given her during the first time she'd been here. When she returned to Dylan's spare room it was to find her bed made and a clean set of clothing placed on the blanket.

The jeans were big on her, but the sports bra and underwear fit perfectly. She had fastened the pearl snaps of the green-checked Western-style cotton shirt when she smelled the mouthwatering aroma of fresh-brewed coffee, eggs and sausage. She followed her nose to the kitchen and discovered that Dotty had added fried potatoes to the offering.

"This smells wonderful."

"Everything does when you are hungry." Dotty handed her a plate and motioned to the frying pans. "I made this because it is quick. You eat meat, don't you?"

"Yes, I do," said Meadow as she helped herself to some of everything.

"Fine. You must be starving."

"I'm going to burn that hospital gown," said Meadow.

"I already threw it in the trash," said Dotty.

They shared a smile.

"Thank you for the clothing."

"Those belonged to my youngest daughter, Rita, when she was a teenager. She wore it for barrel racing. I never throw anything out."

"Well, lucky for me," said Meadow, and she settled in at the table before her full plate.

"Eat," said Dotty, and Meadow dug in.

Meadow was on her second helping when Dylan arrived and joined her. Dotty said her goodbyes and left them alone.

Suddenly Meadow felt afraid. She wasn't brave or smart or selfless. She was a trainwreck about to blow the one chance she had with a man whom she loved with every ounce of her being.

The men in her past had been interested in her for the obvious reasons. Sex, of course, but also her money and all that came with it. Dylan wasn't like them. But who was she now that she was not the youngest daughter of Theron and Lupe Wrangler?

"How you feeling?" asked Dylan.

"Clearheaded for a change." *And terrified*, she thought. "Thank you for getting me out of there.

"Why'd you come back for me?" she asked, and then

she stilled at the intent look he cast her. She couldn't seem to draw a full breath under the incredulous stare.

"You needed help."

She bowed her head. "Oh, yeah. I really did. You must get tired of pulling my fanny from the fire."

He said nothing.

Meadow glanced up. "I heard Ray Strong is home."

"Safe and sound. He wants to see you, but I held him off."

His friend wanted to check on her. That was good, wasn't it?

"That'd be great."

Dylan grabbed a plate and filled it with eggs and potatoes, then joined her. He polished off the food in short order. When he had finished his meal, he retrieved his coffee mug, cupping it between both his strong hands as he settled across from her once more.

Her belly twitched at the urge she suppressed to stroke those long elegant fingers.

"You spoke with the FBI?" asked Meadow.

"Yes. Forrest and Cosen will want to talk with you again. They have some options for you."

She swallowed and placed a hand over her quaking stomach as she met his gaze across the table. This was bad.

"Options?"

"Yeah. Like you could be relocated as a protected witness."

Meadow felt her heart clench. His friend Carter and his wife, Amber, had entered that program. They had been gone for months and had still not testified in the federal case against the surviving gunman. The thought of being separated from Dylan for such an extended period made her entire body ache. What would she do if he sent her away?

But why would he want her to remain? She'd been trouble for him since the moment they met. That's what she was everywhere she went. Her one true gift was her ability to make a mess.

"I'd rather not," she said.

He exhaled and his hold on the coffee mug tightened. Had he hoped to have someone take her off his hands?

"I can't go home."

"No, you sure can't. Trouble is that Forrest's superiors are not convinced of your mother's involvement. She is contending that she was unaware of her husband's illegal activities."

"What about last night? Rhodes was there to kill me, and my father could not have sent him or the other gunmen."

"She denies any knowledge of why he might have attacked you or of the two men who killed Louisa Crane at the medical health facility. If she's as good as Forrest suspects, there will be nothing to connect any of this to her. She's used your dad as a shield between her and the operation for years. As far as the FBI can determine, Rhodes worked for your father."

"What about the other two?"

"Gone."

"What about the explosives?"

"All I know is what Cosen told me. The traces from the ridge-fire explosion match the type taken from the Lilac mine."

"Did you tell them that the reservoir system is the target?"

"They know. Our word against your mother's, and there is zero evidence she was up there with us that day."

"But the FBI will protect the reservoirs. Right?"

Dylan pressed his lips together. "I hope so. Forrest is worried the bureau might not find the intel credible."

"That's a fancy way to say that they think we made it all up."

He nodded.

"Sure," she said. "Why wouldn't they? I'm crazy. Right? Just broke out of a psych ward. All hopped up on who knows what." Meadow found herself pacing across the kitchen floor.

Dylan stood and captured her in his arms and drew her back so that his mouth was beside her cheek.

"*I* believe you."

She turned toward him, lifting her arms to loop around his neck. How she wanted him. Deep down and with every part of her.

"Our tribal leadership has met with our medicine society. Tribal Thunder will protect the reservoirs."

"All of them?"

Dylan nodded. "Yes, all. Because if any of the dams above our reservation fail, they will take out the next and the next."

How many of his people might die in such a flood?

"Dylan, I don't want to be relocated."

His expression gave away nothing as he continued to stare.

"I want to stay here and guard the reservoirs…with you."

"It's dangerous."

"I know."

"And boring. Guard duty isn't like, well, the life you are used to living."

"I know that, too."

"And it's not your land."

"My mother and father did this. I have a responsibility to set this right."

"Is that why you want to stay? Out of duty?" He leaned forward, as if her answer was important to him.

"Partly."

"What's the other part, Meadow?"

She looked away and realized she was not as brave as Dotty gave her credit for. Not brave enough to say that she loved Dylan, because to say that aloud was to risk her heart. And that was something far more fragile than a life.

"Forrest said that as long as you stay on federal land he can keep the sheriff and highway patrol from getting to you. You won't be arrested or detained. But you are wanted for questioning in the death of your father."

She felt her skin prickle. "They think I killed him?"

"Forrest says they think that Mark Perkinson shot him and that your father shot Perkinson. You and I are witnesses."

"I see."

"Both Forrest and Cosen think your mother might try again. That's why they are recommending witness protection."

"I see." She drew back. His hands brushed her hips as he released her. "I suppose she canceled my credit cards."

"I would. Your father left no will. His estate will go to probate, but…"

"She gets it all."

He nodded.

"It was all hers to begin with." She raked her fingers through her drying hair. "I want to find out about my real mother."

"We can try. There have to be records."

"I need to know who I really am."

Dylan nodded. "Everyone does. But you are who you make yourself. We choose who we will become."

She nodded. There was truth in that. Who did she want to become? Her gaze met his.

"You could stay here with us."

"Your tribe, you mean?"

"With me."

He looked frightened for the first time since she had met him. His fingers drummed on his thighs like a piano player practicing scales, and his entire body looked as tense as one big muscle spasm.

"Dylan, do you want me to stay here with you?" She bit her lower lip as she waited for his reply.

She watched his Adam's apple bob.

"I want you to stay with me, and not because you have to or because you'll be arrested if you leave. I want to know that you..." He pressed his hand to his forehead as if taking his own temperature. Then he blew out a breath.

Hope swelled in that place behind her breastbone, right beside her heart. Dylan wanted her to love him and to stay because there was no other choice but to be where he was—always.

She stepped forward, filled with a hope that he wanted her as much as she wanted him. Meadow took both her hands in his and squeezed.

"Dylan, if I stay it will not be because of the danger of leaving, or because the FBI recommends it, or because you are willing to protect me. It will be because you love me, too."

"Too?" he asked.

She nodded.

He sucked in a breath of surprise and then wrapped her up in his arms so tight she could barely breathe. Then he gripped her shoulders and pushed her back so he could look at her upturned face.

"You love me?" he asked.

"I do. So much that the thought of leaving you hurts. I need to be with you and I'll help you fight them."

"I was afraid you'd have no choice. Marrying me would give you the protection of a full member of the tribe."

"And you thought I'd do that to save my own skin."

He lowered his head until his forehead pressed to hers. "I just wanted you to have a choice."

"I do have a choice."

"And you'll marry me?" he asked.

She stepped back. "No."

His smile fell away.

"No?" he asked.

"No. I won't. I'll stay here and fight with you. I'll love you until you have no doubt, and when we have stopped them and I'm free, then I'll marry you."

"We don't have to wait."

"Yes, we do. Not just for you, Dylan. For me, too. I want everyone to know why I choose you. I won't have your tribe thinking you married me from pity or that I had to be your bride. I won't marry you—because I love you too much."

Dylan smiled and then he nodded. "Once they know you, they'll know why you stay."

She was giving him what he needed. Dylan would keep his dignity and she would find pride in doing something of use.

"This will be a new experience for me," she said. "I'm more the immediate-gratification kind of gal."

"Patience comes with its own reward." There was a certain twinkle in his eyes that made her blood rush.

"Oh, yeah?"

He looped an arm around her shoulder and leaned in, taking the lobe of her ear into his mouth. Tiny ripples of pleasure cascaded along every nerve, and she trembled with anticipation.

Dylan drew back and looked down at her, his smile wicked.

"Withholding personal gratification makes the pleasure more satisfying," he said.

"I'm looking forward to trying that sometime," she said as she steered him down the hall toward his bedroom. "But not today."

She thought about the first time she'd laid eyes on him, when she'd blocked his way up that ridge, delaying him just enough that he had survived the blast, and then he'd rescued her.

It was important that he know her heart, and it would take time to show him—and his people—that this outsider had changed her ways and was here for the duration.

They were a team and they were in love. She didn't need a wedding band as evidence of his devotion. His mouth and his hands and his heart were proof enough.

She knew the July monsoons were coming. Knew, too, that the reservoirs would be full to bursting after the storms. This would be the time to strike, when the damage would be most great.

Meadow knew all that, and she knew that they must stop her mother and the extremists of BEAR because Meadow and the brave warriors of Tribal Thunder would protect what they loved.

Meadow's heart beat with hope and excitement. She was no longer lost or alone because she had found her place and her purpose. Dylan had given her so much more than his love. He had given her respect, a mission larger than herself and a chance to make a difference in the world. She felt ready for what would come; ready to join Dylan in this fight and ready to become the woman worthy of his love.

Bobcat had found a mate.

"You are my heartbeat," she said and kissed him long and slow.

* * * * *

Prepare as tribal police detective Jack Bear Den goes undercover with FBI field agent Sophia Fowler in the final showdown between the eco-extremists of BEAR and the warriors of Tribal Thunder in book 4,
TURQUOISE WARRIORS,
coming June 2017.

"You think I need backup?"

"Everybody needs someone watching their back. Especially stubborn redheads who keep poking at mysteries no one wants to talk about." Duff circled the table. "You've officially got me."

Melanie palmed the center of his chest and kept him at arm's length. "I suppose you expect me to have your back now, too?"

"I expect you to keep being my friend." He leaned into her hand, dropping his voice to a drowsy timbre. "But make no mistake, Melanie Fiske—I will be kissing you again."

Anticipation skittered through her veins. "Friends don't kiss each other like that."

"You don't want me to kiss you again?"

Her blush betrayed her. "You know I can't hide that I like you. Maybe becauses you're not one of them. Or maybe because you say what you think." She snatched away the fingers that were still clinging to the firm muscles of his chest and turned a pleading gaze up to him. "Just don't lie to me, okay? I want to be able to trust you."

NECESSARY ACTION

BY
JULIE MILLER

First Published in Great Britain 2017
By Mills & Boon, an imprint of HarperCollins*Publishers*
1 London Bridge Street, London, SE1 9GF

© 2017 Julie Miller

ISBN: 978-0-263-92884-6

46-0517

Our policy is to use papers that are natural, renewable and recyclable products and made from wood grown in sustainable forests. The logging and manufacturing processes conform to the legal environmental regulations of the country of origin.

Printed and bound in Spain
by CPI, Barcelona

Julie Miller is an award-winning *USA TODAY* bestselling author of breathtaking romantic suspense—with a National Readers' Choice Award and a Daphne du Maurier Award, among other prizes. She has also earned an *RT Book Reviews* Career Achievement Award. For a complete list of her books, monthly newsletter and more, go to www.juliemiller.org.

For Tracey Marie Oberhauser.
Because you make my son happy.

Prologue

"This is some kind of Valentine's Day curse." Duff Watson stuck his finger inside the starched white collar of his shirt and tugged, certain the tux the rental shop had given him for today was a size too small.

He wondered what his family would think if he tossed the red bow tie and unbuttoned the collar of this stupid monkey suit. His sister, the bride, would be ticked, and his father would be embarrassed, Grandpa Seamus would laugh, and he'd never hear the end of it from his brothers. So he endured.

Duff—no one had called him by his given name, Tom, for years—was all for celebrating his sister's happiness. He'd even agreed to stand up as best man for her fiancé. But the only things that felt normal about Liv's wedding day were the gun holstered at the small of his back and the KCPD detective's badge stashed in his pocket. And, oh yeah, watching his two younger brothers, Niall and Keir, tagging along behind him as they escorted the bridesmaids down the aisle to join him at the altar.

The three Watson brothers, all third-generation cops following proudly in their father's and retired grandfather's footsteps, couldn't be more different if they tried.

Niall was the brain, a medical examiner with the crime lab. He seemed clueless about all the pomp and circumstance surrounding the wedding. He looked as though he was doing some sort of mental calculation about the distance to the altar or how many guests were seated in each pew. Keir was the social one, and he was eating this stuff up. He flirted with his escort and blew a kiss to the older woman in the second pew, Millie Leighter, the family cook and housekeeper who'd helped raise the four of them after their mother's senseless murder.

Duff was the self-avowed tough guy. He didn't have the multiple college degrees Niall did, and he'd never win a sweet-talking contest against Keir. But neither could match him for sheer, stubborn cussedness. Duff was the survivor. He'd been old enough when Mary Watson had died that he could see his father's anger and grief, and had stepped up to help take care of his younger siblings, even after their father had hired Millie, and Grandpa Seamus had moved in to do whatever was necessary to hold the fractured family together. Hell, even now that they were all grown-up, he was still doing whatever was necessary to protect his family—listening to his baby sister when her devil scum of a former partner had seduced and then cheated on her, making sure the man she was marrying today was worthy of her. He'd written a personal recommendation for Keir to one of his academy buddies when the ambitious youngest brother had been up for a promotion to the major crime unit. And there was no end to the coaching Niall required as the shy brainiac negotiated the intricacies of interpersonal relationships.

Duff had the street smarts, the gut instincts that helped him get through numerous undercover assignments for the department. He read people the way Niall read books. Only once had he misjudged someone he'd tried to help, and he'd paid for that mistake with his heart and a beat down that had put him in the hospital for nearly three weeks.

But facing a drug dealer's wrath hadn't killed him. Being betrayed by Shayla to her brother had only made Duff stronger and a hell of a lot smarter about falling in love. He'd been played for a fool, and he owned the repercussions of his mistake. Maybe his colossal screwup—when it came to love on this day that was all about love—was the reason he couldn't get his tuxedo to fit right.

"Natalie is married to Liv's partner, you know." Niall, an inch taller than Duff, adjusted his dark glasses and whispered the chiding remark about flirting with the bridesmaid to Keir, who stood a couple of inches shorter.

"Relax, charm-school dropout." Keir clapped Niall on the shoulder, grinning as he stepped up beside him. "Young or old, married or not—it never hurts to be friendly."

"Seriously?" Niall turned that same whispered reprimand on Duff, eyeing the middle of his back. "Are you packing today?"

He'd tucked his ankle piece into the back of his itchy wool slacks. At least he wasn't wearing his shoulder holster and Glock. "Hey. You wear your glasses every day, Poindexter. I wear my gun."

"I wasn't aware that you knew what the term 'Poindexter' meant."

"I'm smarter than I look."

Keir had the gall to laugh. "He'd have to be."

Duff shifted his stance, peering around Niall. "So help me, baby brother, if you give me any grief today, I will lay you out flat."

"Zip it. Both of you." Leave it to Niall to be the cool, calm and collected one. Liv had probably put him in charge of corralling her two rowdier brothers today. The smart guy scowled at Keir. "You, mind your manners." When Duff went after the collar hugging his neck again, Niall leaned in. "And you, stop fidgeting like a little kid."

A sharp look from the minister waiting behind them quieted all three brothers for the moment. With everything ready for their sister's walk down the aisle, the processional music started. Duff scanned the crowd as they rose to their feet. Millie dabbed at her eyes with a lace hanky, making no effort to hide her tears. He knew a hug could make those tears go away, and he would gladly go comfort her, but he was stuck up here at the altar.

Grandpa Seamus was sneaking a handkerchief out of his pocket. The old man was crying, too.

And then Olivia and their father, Thomas Watson Sr., appeared in the archway at the end of the aisle. A few strands of gray in his dark hair, and the limp from the blown-out knee that had ended his frontline duty with the department far too soon, couldn't detract from the pride in Thomas's posture as he walked his daughter down the aisle. Duff's sinuses burned. *Be a man. Do not let your emotions get the better of you. Do not cry.*

But Olivia Mary Watson was a stunner in her long beaded gown and their mother's veil of Irish lace. Who knew that shrimp of a tomboy would grow up into such a fine, strong woman? He took after their father with his green eyes and big, stocky build. But Liv was the spitting image of the mother he remembered—dark hair, blue eyes. Walking beside Thomas Sr., he thought of the wedding picture that still sat on his father's dresser.

He blinked and had to say something quick to cover up the threat of tears. "Dude," Duff muttered. He nudged the groom beside him. "Gabe, you are one lucky son of a—"

"Duff." Niall's sharp tone reminded him that swearing in church probably wasn't a good idea.

Gabe sounded a little overcome with emotion, too. "I know."

"You'd better treat her right."

Yep. Liv must have put Niall in charge of keeping him in line today. "We've already had this conversation, Duff. I'm convinced he loves her."

Gabe never took his eyes off Olivia as he inclined his head to whisper, "He does."

Keir, of course, wasn't about to be left out of the hushed conversation. "Anyway, Liv's made her choice. You think any one of us could change her mind? I'd be scared to try."

The minister hushed the lot of them as father and bride approached.

"Ah, hell," Duff muttered, looking up at the ceiling. So much for guarding his emotions and watching his mouth. He blinked rapidly, pinching his nose. "This is not happening to me."

"She looks the way I remember Mom," Keir said in a curiously soft voice.

Duff felt a tap on his elbow. "Do you have a handkerchief?" Niall asked.

So he'd seen the tears running down Duff's cheeks. "The rings are tied up in it."

"Here." Niall slipped his own white handkerchief to Duff, who quickly dabbed at his face. He nodded his thanks before stuffing the cotton square into his pocket and steeling his jaw against the embarrassing flare of sentiment.

When Olivia arrived at the altar, she kissed their father, catching him in a tight hug before smiling at all three brothers. Duff sniffed again, mouthing the word *beautiful* when their eyes met. Keir gave her a thumbs-up. Niall nodded approvingly. Olivia handed her bouquet off to her matron of honor and took Gabe's hand to face the minister.

The rest of the ceremony continued until the minister pronounced them husband and wife and announced, "You may now kiss the bride."

"Love you," Olivia whispered.

Gabe kissed her again. "Love you more."

"I now present Mr. and Mrs. Gabriel Knight."

Duff extended his arm to the matron of honor and followed Liv and Gabe down the aisle. He traded a wink with Grandpa Seamus, silently sharing his commiseration over the public display of emotion. He nodded to his dad and exchanged a smile with Millie before unbuttoning his jacket. The tie was going next.

He was halfway to the foyer and the freedom to unhook the strangling collar when he spied a blur of movement in the balcony at the back of the church. A figure in black emerged from the shadows beside a carved limestone buttress framing a row of organ pipes. The man opened his long duster coat, revealing the rifle and handgun he'd hidden underneath.

Duff was already pushing the matron of honor between the pews and pulling his weapon when Niall shouted, "Gun!"

The organ music stopped on a discordant note and the organist scrambled toward the opposite balcony door. The man's face was a black mask, his motives unknown. But when the stranger raised his rifle to his shoulder and took aim at the sanctuary below, his intent was crystal clear.

"Everybody down!" Duff ordered, kneeling beside the pew and raising his Beretta between his hands. "Drop it!" But the bullets rained down and he jerked back to safety.

"I'm calling SWAT," Keir shouted. Duff glanced back to see him throw an arm around Millie and pull the older woman down behind the cover of a church pew with him. Gabe Knight slammed his arms around Liv and pulled her to the marble floor beneath his body. Niall was reaching for their father and grandfather.

He heard panicked footsteps, frightened shouts and terse commands as bullets chipped away marble and splintered wood. Flower petals and eruptions of dust floated in the air. Half the guests at the wedding were cops, active duty or retired, and every man and woman was taking cover, protecting loved ones, ensuring everyone was safe from the rapid barrage of gunfire.

Duff waited for a few beats of silence before swinging out into the aisle again and crouching at the end of the pew. The gunman was on the move. So was he.

"I've got no shot," Duff yelled, pushing to his feet as the shooter dropped his spent rifle and pulled his pistol. He pointed the other officers on the guest list who happened to be armed to each exit and zigzagged down the aisle as the next hail of bullets began. "Get down and stay put!" he ordered to everyone else, and ran out the back of the sanctuary.

"Niall!" Duff heard his father shout to his brother as Duff charged up the main stairs to the second floor. By damn, if that whack job had hurt his brother, he was going down.

Signaling to another officer to cover the opposite entrance, Duff pushed open the balcony door. But he knew as soon as they entered that the balcony was clear. The chaos down below echoed through the rafters, but Duff tuned it out to focus on the staccato of running footsteps. The shooter was gone. He'd taken his weapons with him and fled through the massive church.

Duff returned to the darkened utility hallway, where a wave of cold air blew across his cheek. Outside air. Close by. The clang of metal against metal gave him direction. The perp had gone up to the roof.

His instinct was to turn to his radio and call in his location and ask for backup. But he was wearing a black tuxedo, not his uniform. He'd have to handle this himself. Leaving the other officer to see to the frightened organist, he sprinted down the hallway and climbed a narrow set of access stairs to the roof. If the perp thought he was getting out this way, he'd corner the chump before he reached one of the fire escapes.

Duff paused with his shoulder against the door leading onto the roof, reminding himself he'd be blind to the perp's position for a few seconds. Nobody shot up his sister's wedding, put his family in danger, threatened his friends. No matter what screw was loose in that shooter's head, Duff intended to stop him. Heaving a deep breath, he shoved the door open.

Squinting against the wintry blast of February air, he dove behind the nearest shelter and pressed his back against the cold metal until he could get his bearings. The glimpse of gravel and tar paper through the kicked-up piles of snow were indicators that he wasn't the first person to come out this way. The AC unit wasn't running, so he should be able to hear the shooter's footsteps. Only he didn't. He heard the biting wind whipping past, the crunch of snow beneath tires as cars sped through the parking lot and the muted shouts of his fellow officers, circling around the outside of the church three stories below. The only labored breathing he could hear was his own, coming out in white, cloudy puffs, giving away his position like a rookie in training.

He was going to have to do this by sight. Clamping his mouth shut, he gripped his gun between his chilling hands and darted from one cover to the next. Instead of footprints, there was a wide trail of cleared snow, as if the man had been dragging his long coat behind him. But the trail was clear, and Duff followed it to the short side wall of the roof. He peered over the edge, expecting to find a fire escape. Instead, he found a ladder anchored to the bricks that descended to the roof of the second floor below him. But he spotted the same odd path transforming into a clear set of boot prints, leading across the roof to the wall that dropped down to the parking lot.

"Got you now." Duff tucked his gun into his pocket and slid down the ladder.

He rearmed himself as he raced across the roof. He could make out sirens in the distance, speeding closer. Backup from Kansas City's finest. Ambulances, too. That meant somebody was hurt. That meant a lot of somebodies in that sanctuary could be hurt. This guy was going to pay.

Duff swung his gun over the edge of the roof and froze. "Where the hell...?"

The only thing below him was a pile of snow littered with green needles at the base of a pine tree, and another officer looking up at him, shrugging his shoulders and shaking his head.

The perp had vanished. Poof. Disappeared. Houdini must have shimmied down that evergreen tree and had a driver waiting. Either that or he was a winged monkey. How could he have gotten away?

"Son of a..." Duff rubbed his finger around the trigger guard of his Beretta before stashing it back in its holster. He was retracing his steps up the ladder, fuming under his breath, when his phone vibrated in his pocket. He pulled out his cell, saw Keir's name and answered. "He got away. The guy's a freakin' magician."

"Grandpa's been shot."

"What?" The winter chill seeped through every pore of his skin and he broke into a run. Seamus Watson, eighty-year-old patriarch, retired cop who walked with a cane, followed Chiefs football and teared up at family weddings the same way Duff did was a casualty of this mess? No. Not allowed. "How bad?"

"Bad. Niall's trying to stop the bleeding. Get down here. Now."

Duff had no one left to chase. The shooter's trail had gone as cold as the snowflakes clinging to the black wool of his tuxedo.

"On my way."

Chapter One

"Who cleans up a scuttled boat?"

Frowning at the smell of bleach filling her nose, Melanie Fiske waded barefoot into the ankle-deep water that filled the wreck of her late father's fishing boat each time it rained and opened the second aft live well, or rear storage compartment where fish and bait had once been stored. She expected to find water, rust, algae or even some sort of wildlife that had taken up residence over the past fourteen years, like the nest of slithering black water moccasins she'd found hidden inside three years ago.

Poisonous snakes had been reason enough to stop her weekly sojourn to the last place her father had been alive. But too many things had happened over the past few months in this idyllic acreage where she'd grown up—the rolling Ozark hills southeast of Kansas City— for her not to explore every available opportunity to find out what had happened to her father that night he'd allegedly drowned in the depths of Lake Hanover and was never seen again.

Now she was back, risking snakes, sunburn and the

wrath of the uncle who'd raised her, to investigate the wreck, tipped over on the shoreline of Lake Hanover next to the old boat ramp that hadn't been used since the boat had been towed ashore to rot.

All these years, she'd accepted the story of a tragic accident. She'd been so young then, motherless since birth, and then fatherless, as well, that she'd never thought to question the account of that late-night fishing expedition. After an explosion in the engine, he'd fallen overboard, and the eddies near the dammed-up Wheat River power plant had dragged him down to the bottom. It had been a horrible, unfathomable tragedy.

But she'd caught her aunt and uncle in too many lies lately. She'd seen things she couldn't explain—arguments that hushed when she entered a room, trucks that arrived in the middle of the night to take handcrafts or baked goods to Kansas City, fishing excursions where no one caught a thing from the well-stocked lake. And maybe most importantly, her uncle's control was tightening like a noose around her life. There were rules for living on the farm now that hadn't been there when she'd been a teenager, and consequences for breaking them that bordered on abuse.

Yes, there were bound to be flaring tempers as they transitioned from a simple working farm to a stopping place for tourists from the city seeking outdoor fun at the lake's recreational area or a simple taste of country life without driving farther south to Branson and Table Rock Lake. There were reasons to celebrate, too. The farm had grown from a few family members running a mom-and-pop business to a small community with enough people living on the 500-acre property to be listed as an unincorporated township. But Uncle Henry still ran it as though they were all part of the same family. Their homes and small businesses were grouped like a suburban neighborhood nestled among the trees and hills. Instead of any warm, fuzzy sense of security, though, Melanie felt trapped. There were secrets lurking behind the hardworking facades of the family and friends who lived on the Fiske Family Farm.

Secrets could hurt her. Secrets could be dangerous.

When she'd hiked out to the cove to look for fourteen-year-old bloodstains or evidence of a heroic struggle to stay afloat after the engine had blown a softball-sized hole in the hull of the boat, Melanie hadn't expected to find new waterproof seals beneath the tattered seat cushions that closed off the storage wells. The first fiberglass live well she'd checked had been wiped clean. Blessedly free of snakes, this second storage compartment also smelled like bleach.

Only this one wasn't completely empty.

Curiosity had always been a trait of hers. Her father had encouraged her to read and explore and ask questions. But her uncle didn't seem to share the same reverence for learning. The last time she'd been caught poking around for answers up in her uncle's attic, she'd been accused of stirring up painful memories of a lost brother, and not being grateful for the sacrifices her aunt Abby and uncle Henry had made, taking in an eleven-year-old orphan and raising her alongside their own daughter. Melanie had moved out of the main house that very night and things had been strained between them ever since. And though she wasn't sure how much was her imagination and how much was real, Melanie got the sense that she had more eyes on her now than any bookish, plain-Jane country girl like her ever had.

Squinting into the thick forest of pines and pin oaks and out to the glare of the waves that glistened like sequins on the surface of the wind-tossed lake, Melanie ensured she was alone before she twisted her long auburn hair into a tail and stuffed it inside the back of her shirt. Then she knelt beside the opening and stuck her arm inside the tilted boat's storage well. The water soaking into the knees of her blue jeans was warm as she stretched to retrieve the round metal object. Her fingers touched cold steel and she slipped one tip inside the ring to hook it onto her finger and pull it out.

But seeing the black ring out in the sunlight didn't solve the mystery for her. Melanie closed the live well and sat on the broken-down cushion to study the object on her index finger. About the circumference of a quarter and shaped like a thick washer with a tiny protrusion off one edge, the round piece of steel had some surprising weight to it. Unravaged by nature and the passage of time, the ring couldn't be part of the original shipwreck. But what was it and how had it gotten there?

With a frustrated sigh, she shoved the black steel ring into her jeans. Her fingers brushed against a softer piece of metal inside her pocket and she smiled. Melanie jumped down onto the hard-packed ground that had once been a sandy beach and tugged the second object from her pocket as she retrieved her boots and socks.

It was her father's gold pocket watch. She traced her finger around the cursive *E* and *L* that had been engraved into the casing. A gift from her mother, Edwina, to her father, Leroy Fiske had never been without it. From the time she was a toddler, Melanie could remember seeing the shiny gold chain hooked to a belt loop on his jeans, and the prized watch he'd take out in the evenings to share with his daughter.

But the happy memory quickly clouded with suspicion. The workings of the watch had rusted with time, and the small photograph of her mother inside had been reduced to a smudge of ink. Melanie closed the watch inside her fist and fumed. If her father's body had never been found, and he always had the watch with him, then how had it shown up, hidden away in a box of Christmas ornaments in her uncle's attic?

Had this watch been recovered from the boat that fateful night? Why wouldn't Leroy Fiske have been wearing it? Had it gone into the lake with him? Who would save the watch, but not the man?

The whine of several small engines dragged Melanie from her thoughts.

Company. She dropped down behind the boat to hide. Someone had borrowed two or three of the farm's all-terrain vehicles and was winding along the main gravel road through the trees around the lake. Maybe it was one of the resident fishing guides, leading a group of tourists to the big aluminum fishing dock past the next bend of the lake, about a mile from her location. It could be her cousin Deanna, taking advantage of her position as the resident princess by stealing away from her job at the farm's bakery and going out joyriding with one of the young farmhands working on the property this summer.

"Mel?" A man's voice boomed over the roar of the engines. "You out here? Mel Fiske, you hear me?"

"Great," she muttered. It was option C. The riders were out looking for her. As the farm's resident EMT-paramedic, she knew there could be a legitimate medical reason for the men to be searching for her. Minor accidents were fairly common with farm work. And some folks neglected their water intake and tried to do too much, easily overheating in Missouri's summer heat. But she really didn't want to be discovered. Not here at her father's boat. Not when her aunt had asked her to leave the past alone, since stirring up memories of Henry's brother's drowning upset her uncle when he needed to be focusing on important business matters. Finding her here would certainly upset someone.

Like a swarm of bees buzzing toward a fragrant bed of flowers, the ATVs were making their way down through the trees, coming closer. Melanie glanced up at the crystal blue sky and realized the sun had shifted to the west. She'd been gone for more than two hours. No wonder Henry had sent his number-one guard dog to search for her.

It wasn't as if she could outrun a motorized four-wheeler. She glanced around at the dirt and rocks leading down to the shoulder-high reeds and grasses growing along the shoreline. She couldn't outswim the men searching for her, either. Her gaze landed on the sun-bleached wood dock jutting into the water several feet beyond the reeds. Or could she?

Melanie unzipped her jeans and crawled out of them. After tucking the watch safely inside the pocket with the mysterious steel ring, she stripped down to her white cotton panties and support bra and sprang to her feet. With a little bit of acting and a whole lot of bravado, she raced onto the listing dock and dove into the lake.

The surface water was warm with the summer's blistering heat, but she purposely swam down to the murky haze of deeper water to cool her skin and soak her hair so that it would seem she'd been out in the water for some time, oblivious to ATVs, shouting voices and family who wanted her to account for all her time.

She didn't have to outswim anybody. She just had to make up a good cover story to explain why she'd gone for a dip in her underwear instead of her sensible one-piece suit. Melanie was several yards out by the time she kicked to the surface.

As she'd suspected, she saw two men idling their ATVs on the shore near the footing of the dock. The bigger man, the farm's foreman and security chief, who thought shaving his head hid his receding hairline, glared at her with dark eyes. He waved aside the other man, telling him to move on. "Radio in that she's okay. Then get on over to the fishing dock to make sure it's ready for that group from Chicago tomorrow."

The other man nodded. He pulled the walkie-talkie from his belt and called into the main house to report, "We found her, boss," before revving the engine and riding away. Meanwhile, Melanie pushed her heavy wet hair off her face and began a leisurely breast stroke to the end of the dock.

Silas Danvers watched her approach. "What are you doing out here?"

It wasn't a friendly question. As usual, Silas was on edge about something or someone. But, then, when wasn't the short-tempered brute ticked off about something?

Melanie opted for a bimbo-esque response he seemed to find so attractive in her cousin. She treaded water at the edge of the dock, even though she could probably stretch up on her tiptoes and stand with her head above the water. "It's a hundred degrees out here. What do you think I'm doing?"

She was getting good at lying. Maybe it was a family trait she'd inherited from her uncle.

"Why can't you just take a bath like a normal woman? Get your ass out of the water," he ordered. "You're out of cell range here."

Melanie stopped moving and curled her toes into the mud beneath her, feeling a twinge of guilt. "Is there an emergency?"

"No, but Daryl's been trying to get a hold of you. He's got a question about those medical supplies you asked him to pick up in town. No sense him making two trips just because you decided to go skinny-dipping."

Melanie nodded and paddled to the tarnished copper ladder at the edge of the dock. "Okay. I'll get out as soon as you leave."

"You got nothin' I ain't seen before." Well, he hadn't seen hers, and she wasn't about to show him. Still, she had a feeling that Silas's reluctance to turn the ATV around and ride away had less to do with her being nearly naked and more to do with his egoistic need to make sure his orders were followed. "Don't keep Daryl waiting."

Melanie held on to the ladder until he had gunned the engine and disappeared through the line of trees at the top of the hill. *Victory.* Albeit a small one. Once his shiny bald head had vanished over the rise, Melanie wasted no time climbing out of the water and hurrying back to her pile of clothes and newly acquired treasure. She was dressed from T-shirt to toes and wringing out her hair in a matter of minutes. Despite the humidity, the air was hot enough that her clothes would dry off soon enough, although her hair would kink up into the kind of snarling mess that only Raggedy Ann fans could appreciate. Funny how she'd grown up without being noticed—she'd always been a little too plump, a little too freckled, a little too into her books to turn heads. Now she was counting on that same anonymity to allow her to return to the farm without drawing any more attention to herself.

Pulling her phone from her lace-up work boot, she verified that she was, indeed, far enough out in the hills, away from the cell tower on the farm, that she had no service. So Silas hadn't lied about his reason for tracking her down. She'd give Daryl a call as soon as she was in range, and then, even though an internet connection was spottier than cell reception in this part of the state, she'd try to get online and research some images to see if she could identify the object she'd found inside her father's boat.

Putting off her amateur sleuthing for the time being, Melanie cut across to one of the many paths she and her father had explored when he'd been alive. She followed a dry creek bed around the base of the next hill and climbed toward the county road that bordered the north edge of the property.

As she'd hoped, she was able to get cell reception there, and she contacted her friend Daryl to go over the list of items she needed to restock her medical supplies. But it was taking so long to connect to the internet that she reached the main homestead and had to slip her phone into her hip pocket so that no one would see her trying to contact the outside world.

As the trees gave way to land cleared for farming, buildings, gravel roads and a parking lot, Melanie headed to the two-bedroom cottage she called home.

But, instead of finding everyone going about their work for the day, she saw that a crowd had gathered near the front porch of her uncle's two-story white house. She could hear the tones of an argument, although she couldn't make out the words. Suddenly the crowd oohed and gasped as if cheering a hit in a softball game, and Melanie stopped. "What the heck?"

She changed course and headed to the main house, looking for a gap where she could get a clear view of whatever they were watching.

She spotted Silas near the bottom of the porch steps, slowly circling to his left, eyeing his unlucky target. What a surprise, discovering him in the vicinity of angry words. It was a fight, another stupid fight because somebody had ticked off Silas. More than likely, her cousin had turned him down for another date, and his opponent was merely the outlet for his wrath. Typically, her uncle didn't allow the tourists visiting the bakery and craft shop to see any kind of dissension in the ranks of the people who lived and worked on the farm. But the hot day made it easy for tempers to rile, so maybe Henry was letting one of the hands or Silas himself blow off a little steam.

Shaking her head at the testosterone simmering in the air, Melanie turned to leave behind what was sure to be a short brawl. If it even came to fists. The men around here were smart enough to end any argument with Silas with words and walk away before it escalated into something they'd regret. If these folks had gathered for some kind of boxing match, they were going to be disappointed.

Melanie halted in her tracks when Silas's opponent shifted into view.

He was new.

Her stomach tied itself into a knot of apprehension as she took in the unfortunate soul who'd been foolish enough to stand up to the farm foreman. Only it was pretty hard to think of the narrow-eyed stranger mirroring Silas's movements step for step as any kind of *unfortunate*.

The stranger was almost as tall as Silas. The faded army logo T-shirt he wore fit like a second skin over shoulders and biceps that were well muscled and broadly built. With military-short hair and beard stubble the color of tree bark shading his square jaw, he certainly looked tough enough to take on the resident bully, and she felt herself wanting to cheer for him. She caught a glimpse of a navy blue bandanna in his back jeans pocket, and her gaze lingered there long enough to realize she was gawking like a hungry woman eyeing a new batch of cupcakes in the bakery window.

Feeling suddenly warmer than the summer weather could account for, she forced herself to move away from the circle. She didn't want to watch a fight and she didn't want to be interested in any man who'd shown up here, especially since her goal was to find out about her father and then get away from this pastoral prison.

"This is how you welcome somebody to your place, Fiske?"

Melanie stopped at the stranger's deep, growly voice. *Welcome?* The apprehension left her stomach and siphoned into her veins. But she wasn't feeling pity over a pending beat down—this trepidation was all about her. If Henry had hired this guy to work on the farm, then he'd be one more Silas-sized obstacle she'd have to outmaneuver in order to keep digging for answers about her father.

Chapter Two

Duff spit the blood from his mouth where the bruiser with the shaved head had punched him in the jaw, scraping the inside of his cheek across his teeth. He eyed the older man who'd invited him here for this so-called interview standing up on the porch watching the scuffle in the grass with a look of indifference. "Forget it. I don't need a job that badly."

He wanted to get hired on at the Fiske Family Farm. If this undercover op was going to be a success, he *needed* to get hired here. But he couldn't seem too eager, too willing to kowtow to the owner's authority or to the bruiser with the iron fist's intimidation tactics. Otherwise, nobody here in the crowd of farmhands, shopkeepers and tourists—along with a man in a khaki uniform shirt sipping coffee and noshing on a Danish—would buy his big-badass-mercenary-for-hire persona. He'd spent the past few weeks cultivating his world-weary Duff Maynard identity in the nearby town of Falls City. Portraying a messed-up former soldier looking for a job off the grid, he'd even slept several nights in his truck, solidifying his lone-drifter status so that he could infiltrate the suspected illegal arms business being run behind the bucolic tranquility of this tree-lined farming and tourist commune. Playing his part convincingly was vital to any undercover op.

So he scooped up the army-issue duffel bag that had been taken from him and strode over to the porch, where Baldy had retreated to stand in front of his boss, Henry Fiske. Duff nodded toward the keys, wallet, gun and sheathed hunting knife lying on the gray planks, where the man with the shaved head sat in front of the railing, panting through his smug grin. Removing the weapons from his bag and identification from his pockets when the big man had patted him down and gone through his things had given Duff reason to start the fight in the first place, solidifying his tough-guy character in front of a lot of witnesses. "I'll be taking those."

Baldy rose to his feet, looking ready, willing and eager to go another round with him. "I don't think so, Sergeant Loser," he taunted.

He heard a few worried whispers moving through the onlookers as he and Baldy faced off. But the man on the porch, Henry Fiske, raised his hand and quieted them. "Not to worry, folks. We're just gettin' acquainted. Had a bit of a misunderstanding that we'll work out." He gestured to the uniformed man standing near the end of the porch. "Besides, we've got Sheriff Cobb here. So nothing bad's gonna happen. Go back to your cars or get to shoppin'." He tipped his nose and sniffed the air. "I smell fresh baked goods y'all aren't going to want to miss."

With murmurs of approval and relief, most of the touristy types separated from the crowd and headed toward the shops on the property. But others—the men and women who lived and worked on the vast complex, perhaps—merely tightened their circle around Duff and the front of the house. Why weren't they dispersing as ordered? What did they know that Duff didn't?

"You've got everything under control, Henry?" the sheriff asked.

"I do."

"Then I'll be headin' back into town." He gently elbowed the sturdy, fiftysomething blonde woman beside him. "I just drove out to get some of Phyllis's tasty cooking. My wife doesn't fix anything like this for dessert."

The woman waved off the compliment and turned to follow the tourists. "Come on, Sterling. I'll pack a box of goodies to take with you."

That's why the Hanover County sheriff hadn't been included in the task force working this case. Either Sterling Cobb was being paid to overlook any transgressions here, or the portly man who'd refused to step in and break up a fight was afraid, incompetent or both.

"Ain't nobody here to back you up, Sergeant Loser," Baldy taunted as soon as the sheriff was out of earshot. "You still want to give me trouble?"

In real life, Duff had been an officer, not a noncom, and he bristled at the dig. But he was playing a part here on behalf of KCPD and the joint task force he was working for. His fake dossier said he'd enlisted out of high school and had seen heavy action in the Middle East, which had left him disillusioned, antisocial and a perfect fit for the homegrown mafia allegedly running arms into Kansas City.

Like the guns that had been used to shoot up his sister's wedding and put his grandfather in the hospital.

Duff had to play this just right. Because he was not leaving until he had not only the job, but the trust—or at least the respect—of the people here so that he could work his way into Fiske's inner circle. He'd need that freedom of movement around the place to gather the intel that could put Fiske and the operation he was running out of business.

Although his mission briefing for this joint task force undercover op between KCPD, the Missouri Bureau of Investigation and the ATF hadn't mentioned any welcome-to-the-family beat down, Duff had worked undercover enough that he knew how to think on his feet. He'd originally thought this assignment had more to do with his familiarity with the terrain of the Ozark Mountains, where he'd spent several summers camping, hunting and fishing. But he also knew how to handle himself in a fight. And if that's what the job called for, he'd milk his tough-guy act for all it was worth.

He stepped into Baldy's personal space and picked up the Glock 9mm in its shoulder holster, stuffing both it and the knife inside his duffel bag. He kept his gaze focused on Baldy's dark eyes as he retrieved the ring of keys and wallet with his false IDs and meager cash. Interesting. Baldy's jaw twitched as though he wanted to resume the fight, but the man standing above them on the porch seemed to have his enforcer on a short leash.

"In town you told me I had a job here at the farm if I wanted it." He shifted his stance as Baldy spit at that promise and pushed to his feet. There had to be somebody here he could make friends with to get the inside scoop. Clearly, it wasn't going to be Baldy. "Tell him to back off. You said you needed a man who knew something about security. I didn't realize you offered blood sport as one of your tourist attractions."

"I believe you were the one to throw the first punch, Mr. Maynard." Fiske gestured to the people waiting for the outcome of this confrontation. "We all saw it. Silas was defending himself."

Henry Fiske might have looked unremarkable in any other setting. He was somewhere in his fifties, with silvering sideburns growing down to his jaw and into his temples. He wore overalls and a wide-brimmed straw hat that marked him as a man who worked the land. The guy even had an indulgent smile for the platinum blonde leaning against the post beside him. The aging rodeo queen would be his wife, Abby. Despite Fiske's friendly drawl, Duff had seen the cold expectation that his authority would not be challenged in eyes like Fiske's before.

So, naturally, Duff challenged it. He swung his duffel bag onto his shoulder. "I'm out of here."

"Don't let the muck on my boots fool you, Mr. Maynard. I'm a businessman." Duff kept walking. "A lot of money and traffic pass through here in the summertime, making us a target for thieves and vandals. Hanover is a big county for the sheriff to patrol, and since we're a remote location, we're often forced to be self-sufficient. It's my responsibility to see the property and people here stay safe." A mother pulled a curious toddler out of the way and the crowd parted to let him pass toward the gravel parking lot in front of the metal buildings where he'd parked his truck. "I needed to see if your skills are as good as you claim. You don't exactly come with reputable references."

"The US Army isn't a good enough reference for you?" Duff halted and turned, reminding Fiske of the forged document that was part of the identification packet the task force had put together for him to establish his undercover identity—Sergeant Thomas "Duff" Maynard. His army service was real, but the medical discharge and resulting mental issues that made him a bad fit for "normal" society had been beefed up as part of his undercover profile.

"I trust what I see with my own eyes. Silas?" Henry Fiske called the big man back into action and gave a sharp nod in a different direction.

The crowd shifted again as a second man approached from the right. This twentysomething guy was as lanky as Silas was overbuilt. But the scar on his sunburned cheek indicated he knew his way around a brawl. So this was what the crowd had been waiting for—a two-on-one grudge match. This wasn't any different than a gang initiation in the city. If Fiske wanted Duff to prove he had hand-to-hand combat skills, then prove it he would.

Duff pulled the duffel bag from his shoulder and swung it hard as Skinny Guy charged him. The heavy bag caught the younger man square in the gut and doubled him over. He swung again, smashing the kid in the face before dropping the bag and bracing for Baldy's attack. The big man named Silas grabbed Duff from behind, pinning his arms to his sides. He hoped Baldy had a good grip on him because he used him as a backboard to brace himself and kick out when Skinny Guy rushed him a second time. His boot connected with the other man's chin and snapped his head back, knocking him on his butt. Utilizing his downward momentum, Duff planted his feet and twisted, throwing Baldy off his back.

But the big guy wasn't without skills. He hooked his boots around Duff's legs and rolled, pulling him off balance. The grass softened the jolt to Duff's body, but the position left him vulnerable to the kick to his flank that knocked him over.

Baldy was on him in a second and they rolled into the wood steps at the base of the porch, striking the same spot on his ribs. Duff grimaced at the pain radiating through his middle, giving his attacker the chance to pop him in the cheek and make his eyes water. Okay. Now he was mad. Time to get real.

He slammed his fist into Baldy's jaw and reversed their positions. Duff pinned his forearm against the big man's throat, cutting off his air supply until his struggles eased, and he slapped the bottom step as if the gesture was his version of saying *Uncle*.

Silas might be done with the fight, but by the time Duff had staggered to his feet, Skinny Guy had, too.

"Stay down!" Duff warned. But when he swung at him, anyway, Duff dropped his shoulder and rammed the other man's midsection, knocking the younger guy's breath from his lungs and laying him flat on the ground.

Duff was a little winded himself, and damn, he was going to be sore tomorrow. But as far as he could tell from the cheering hoots from a couple of teenage boys, he'd passed this part of the job interview with flying colors. He was brushing bits of grass and dirt from the thighs of his jeans and checking the dribble of blood at the corner of his mouth when the cheers abruptly stopped.

He heard a grunt of pure, mindless fury behind him and spun around. He saw the glint of silver in Baldy's hand a split second before a slash of pain burned through the meat of his shoulder. Duff dodged the backswing of the knife, and jumped back another step when the blade was shoved toward his belly.

He was poised to grab Baldy's wrist on the next jab when a blur of warm auburn hair and faded blue jeans darted into the space between them. "Stop! Silas, stop!"

Instinctively, Duff snaked his uninjured arm around the woman's waist and pulled her away from the thrusting knife. "Are you crazy?"

Baldy, too, seemed shocked by the interloper. He

grabbed the redhead by the wrist and jerked her from Duff's one-armed grasp before pushing her to the side. "Damn it, girl. You get out of my way."

She stumbled a few feet. But as soon as she found her footing, the redhead jumped right back into the fray. She shoved at Silas's chest and wedged herself between the two men. "I said to stop!"

Duff's arm went around her again, snugging her round bottom against his hip as he spun her away from the danger and pulled her to a safer distance. "Listen, sweetheart, I appreciate the effort, but you're going to get yourself killed. And I can't have that on my con—"

"Melanie!" Henry Fiske shouted from the porch, warning the woman to stand down instead of telling Baldy to lower the knife that was now pointed at both of them. "You forget yourself, girl. You get out of there now. This doesn't concern you."

Silas's dark gaze bored into hers and Duff retreated another step, dragging his foolhardy savior farther from that blood-tipped blade. Silas snapped his gaze up to Duff's, over the top of her head, before he flicked the knife down into the ground and walked over to the edge of the porch. Cursing Duff and the woman under his breath, Baldy dipped his hands into a bucket of water and splashed it over the top of his dirty, sweaty head.

A damp wisp of wavy auburn hair lifted in the hot summer breeze and stuck to the sweat on Duff's neck as his chest heaved against the exertion of the fight. The woman's breath was coming hard, too, but she kept her eyes fixed on Silas, making sure he wasn't going to try another sneak attack. She sagged against Duff's chest, and he realized the front of his khaki T-shirt was soaking up moisture from the long cords of hair caught between them. As quickly as he sensed the woman's relief, he realized he was still holding on to her with a death grip. He released her and she turned to inspect the torn, bloodied cotton of his sleeve. Well, hell. She might be a lot of tough talk, but she was gutting her way through this brave little rebellion against his violent welcome.

"I'm forgetting nothing, Uncle Henry. The new guy put Silas down fair and square. He proved what you wanted him to." Despite her succinct words, there was a soft drawl to her *ng*'s and vowel sounds, indicating her Ozark upbringing. "You put me in charge of the infirmary and I'm doing my job. I know you sent Daryl on a supply run, but until we restock, I don't have the supplies to treat more injuries like this."

She reminded him of a long-haired Irish setter after a bath, with the dripping ends of her long hair making dark spots on the front of her gray T-shirt. She was of average height and definitely on the full-figured side of things. Her face was nothing remarkable to look at. Ordinary brown eyes. Simple nose and apple-shaped cheeks dusted with freckles. Pale pink lips.

But her fingers worked with beautiful precision. She ripped the sleeve away and pulled the material down off the end of his arm before wadding it up and pressing it against the slice across the outside of his shoulder. She didn't even hesitate at his grunt of pain. The woman certainly knew how to make a field dressing. "As it is, I may not have enough sutures to seal this cut. And I'm completely out of antibiotics. We should take him to the hospital in Falls City."

"Is he dying?" Fiske asked.

The redhead's mouth squeezed into a frown. "No."

"Then you're not going anywhere. You're a resource-

ful girl. Figure it out." Fiske's tone made that sound
more like an annoyance than the compliment it should
have been. And there was nothing girlish about the
curves straining the damp T-shirt she wore. "Have you
been in the lake again, Mel?"

"I took a dip to cool off." That explained the wet hair.

"Melanie?" Fiske chided, apparently requiring a different sort of answer.

She dropped one hand from the makeshift dressing
over Duff's shoulder and lowered her head to a more
deferential posture. "I'll find a way to take care of him
without going to town."

Without the pressure of her grip, the cut throbbed
and blood trickled down his arm again. Thinking she'd
given up on defying her uncle to help him, Duff snagged
the wadded cotton from her grip and reached over to
cover the wound with his own hand. But she surprised
him by stretching around him and palming his backside. Her heavy breasts squished against his chest as
she patted one cheek and then the other. The grope was
unexpected but far more pleasurable than Silas's fist
had been. Duff turned to keep her eyes in sight, gauging her intent. "Not that I don't appreciate a good butt-
grab, sweetheart, but I don't even know your last name."

"It's Fiske...oh." Rosy dots appeared beneath her
freckles as her gaze darted up to his. Her fingers stroked
him as she curled them into her palm, and his buttock
muscle clenched at the unintended tickle. She pulled
back, dangling the blue bandanna she'd stolen from
his pocket. "Um..."

"You stopped that girl's mouth from runnin', Mr. Maynard." Fiske chuckled from the porch. "You're hired."

Chapter Three

"Mr. Maynard."

With his brain sidetracked by the blush creeping up Melanie's neck, Duff didn't immediately answer to the name on his fake driver's license. She not only hadn't been getting fresh with him, but she looked mortified for him to believe that she had been. Duff backed away a step, silently cursing how easily her bold touches had distracted him. And this feisty mouse wasn't even trying! *Reel it in, Watson.* She was being resourceful, just as her uncle had directed, not putting the moves on him.

He knew better than to let any woman get in his head and derail his focus on his assignment. He looked over the top of Melanie's wild red hair and nodded his thanks to her uncle. "I trust the open space and quiet time to think you promised me starts now?" He glanced around the circle of lingering onlookers and hardened his voice to a steely timbre. "Or does anybody else want to try to get their licks in?"

Fiske laughed as a few less-daring souls skittered away from the audience. "I promise we have a predictable routine and plenty of opportunities for you to make a living away from outside influences here." The laughter ended as Henry eyed the slender young woman who had hurried over to help Skinny Guy off the ground. No doubt suffering from battered pride in addition to his bloody nose, he seemed only too happy to drape his arm around the pretty brunette's shoulders and limp toward the side of the house. "Roy?" Skinny Guy turned. "You did well today. You didn't quit. I can't ask for anything more."

Roy nodded. "Yes, sir. Thank you, sir."

"But you aren't going anywhere alone with my daughter," he warned. "Silas, you take Deanna on into the house."

"Yes, sir." The big guy seemed eager to obey that order.

"Silas will do nothing of the kind." The blonde who'd been leaning against the post walked to the edge of the porch to rest her hand on her husband's arm. "Young people need a little time to themselves."

Henry patted his wife's hand before seeking out his daughter. "All right, then, tend to Roy. But, remember, dinner's at six, and I expect to see you there. We have company coming."

"Who? Silas?" the young brunette whined. "He's not company."

"You do as I say, young lady," Henry ordered.

"Daddy—"

"Deanna Christine…"

The young brunette looked from her mother to her father. "What if Roy and I have plans? I'm not a baby, anymore. I'm almost twenty-two. You can't tell me what to do."

"Six o'clock, young lady. Or you won't be seeing Roy at all."

Deanna pouted out her copper-tinted lips. "Yes, Daddy." She wound her arm around Roy's waist and leaned into him. "Come on. I'll make those boo-boos feel all better."

Abby squeezed her husband's arm before retreating to the corner of the porch to watch her daughter leave. "She'll be fine, dear. I promise."

Leaving his daughter's love life up to his wife's supervision, Henry repeated his order. "Give Mr. Maynard his bag and get cleaned up."

Silas waited for a moment, then pulled the knife that was stained with Duff's blood out of the ground. He held the blade down at his side as he picked up the duffel bag. Since Melanie was working on a field dressing for his cut again, Duff reached out to take the bag. "Thanks, Baldy."

The big man didn't immediately release the strap. His eyes sent the message that he was top dog at this place. "You may have the job, but you're still on probation, Maynard. And you'll be reporting to me."

Duff was a big man, too. And backing down wasn't part of the role he needed to play. He yanked the bag from Silas's grip. "Just don't expect me to salute you."

Silas's nostrils flared. He muttered something under his breath before wrapping his big bear paw around Melanie's elbow and pulling her away from her work. "You're going to that dance with me in a couple of weeks."

It wasn't a question. Despite Duff's vow to keep his hormones in check on this assignment, he dropped the bag to pry Silas's hand off the woman.

"Are you kidding?" But the curvy redhead didn't need his help. She smacked Silas's hand away and gestured toward the corner of the house where the young couple had turned out of sight. "Ask Deanna if she's who you want to be with. I'm not interested in being her substitute."

"Silas." The vein throbbing in the big man's forehead receded at Henry's summons. "Now's not the time to be thinking about who you're taking to the Hanover Lake festival. On second thought, you clean up later. We have work lined up that needs to be dealt with today. There's a truck coming in later tonight."

"Yes, sir."

"Wipe your feet," Abby reminded the two men as they entered the main house. "And take your hat off, Henry. Don't worry, dear. I'll keep an eye on Deanna."

The two men disappeared into a room on the left side of the hallway before the front door closed. Fiske's office? Definitely a place Duff wanted to get a firsthand look at. And he wanted eyes on that truck, to see whatever was being shipped in or out. But it was too soon to make a move without raising suspicions. Fiske and his lieutenant were probably discussing him and where they could put him to work. Hopefully, something on a night shift so that there'd be fewer people to see his comings and goings when he left the compound to meet with his task-force handler.

"Welcome to our farm, Mr. Maynard." Abby Fiske offered him a silky smile as she came down the stairs. She swung her long hair off her shoulders and glanced at the redhead. "You couldn't spare a minute to put on a little makeup, dear?" she chided before giving him a head-to-toe once-over that made him feel like some kind of prize bull that was up for sale. "My husband will send someone for you when he's ready. Now all of you—the show's over." She shooed the remaining onlookers back to their jobs before she, too, disappeared around the corner of the house.

Once Duff confirmed the key players and uncovered how the illegal operation worked, he'd be one step closer to finding the man who'd pulled the trigger that had left Seamus Watson with a traumatic brain injury and a long road to recovery. Grandpa Seamus had learned to walk again, and was regaining some use of his left hand. But retraining himself to speak and enduring months of painful physical therapy had left the once-vibrant octogenarian a white-haired shell of his former self.

No one else had been shot at Liv's wedding. Only Seamus. That afternoon in February had been all about creating terror, about destroying his family's happiness and leaving them in a state of guarded vigilance in the months that followed. Somebody had to pay for that. Although his brother Niall had saved their grandfather's life and uncovered the type of weapons used in the shooting, and Keir had gotten them a lead on the shooter himself, the KCPD detectives officially working the case hadn't gotten the shooter's name. All indications were that the shooter was a hired gun going by the code name *Gin Rickey* and that the weapons he'd used could be traced to this backwoods retreat—the Fiske Family Farm.

Maybe everyone here was part of the arms-smuggling ring, including the sheriff. Or maybe most of these people were innocent, unaware of the crimes being committed right under their noses. And maybe they knew, but were too cowed by Fiske and the tag team of Silas and Roy to do anything but look the other way. No matter what, Duff intended to get the evidence he needed to report back to his task-force contact the next time he—

"Ow." Duff's shoulder throbbed as Melanie Fiske pinched the bandanna around his deltoid. Right. There was one other player in the mix here—Fiske's niece, Melanie. Out of every person here—man or woman— she'd been the only one to stand up to Silas and her uncle. Maybe she was part of the smuggling ring, too, and had stepped in before they wound up with a dead body to dispose of. Or maybe she just had the brassy temperament to match her red hair. "Easy, sweetheart. I've only got two arms."

"How's your tetanus shot?" she asked, tying off the short ends into a square knot.

His red-haired rescuer picked up the heavy duffel bag before he could grab it and hefted it onto her shoulder. "Your bedside manner needs a little work. You sure you've got training for this?"

"I'm a registered EMT-paramedic. Uncle Henry's goal is to make the farm a completely self-sufficient community. I'm what passes for health care here." She crossed the yard, heading toward the row of cabins and bungalows on the other side of the gravel road that ran in front of the Fiskes' house. "Come with me. I need to stitch up your arm. You could use an ice pack on that cheekbone, too."

"Yes, ma'am."

She halted and spun around. "I don't appreciate being mocked. You can call me Mel or Melanie or Miss Fiske. Save the *ma'am* for my aunt Abby, and the *sweethearts* and jokes for one of the other girls if you want to impress somebody." With that bossy pronouncement, she turned and headed out again.

His gaze dropped shamelessly to the butt bobbing beneath his duffel bag as he fell into step behind her. She might dress and talk like a tomboy, but there was nothing but shapely woman filling out those jeans. Not that her curves made any difference to his assignment, but he wouldn't be much of a man if he couldn't appreciate the scenery around this place.

"Okay, Mel. I'm Tom. Tom Maynard." Using his real first name and an old family name was supposed to make this undercover profile easy to remember so he wouldn't slip and make a mistake that could give him away. But they still felt like foreign words on his tongue. That's why he liked to blend his fake persona with a little bit of reality—to make the role he had to play as real as possible. "My friends call me Duff."

"I'm not looking to make friends, Mr. Maynard." With a tone like that, she didn't have to worry. Surely, there'd be someone else at this place who'd be an easier mark for developing a relationship with to get the information he needed. He followed her to the cottage at the end of the crude neighborhood street and headed up the brick pathway bordered by colorful flowers. She pushed open the unlocked door and held it for Duff to enter before closing it behind him.

The blast of cool air that hit him after the heat and humidity outside raised goose bumps on his skin. For some reason he hadn't expected to find air-conditioning at this remote location. He sought out the source of the welcome chill in the steady hum of a window unit anchored over a small shelf crammed with books beside an empty brick fireplace. He used his survey to also identify a small dine-in kitchen area and a pair of open pinewood doors that led into a bedroom and a bathroom.

The flowered love seat and white eyelet curtains at the front window seemed to indicate Melanie lived alone.

She dropped his bag beside the love seat. "Welcome to the infirmary."

"Quaint little place you've got here. Does everybody get his own house?"

"Married couples and families get their own place. Henry will probably put you up in the bachelor quarters near the equipment shed for now. You'll be able to eat meals there, too. Phyllis Schultz, who runs our bakery, cooks a big dinner for anyone who doesn't have his own kitchen."

"How did you luck out?" He nodded toward her left hand. "You're not married."

"No. I'm not. I doubt I'll ever be."

Now that was an odd addendum to make. Melanie Fiske might not be a beauty like her cousin, but the woman had fire and plenty of curves that would tempt the right man. *Not me*, he reminded himself. But even in this backwoods Eden, a woman in her midtwenties surely didn't think of herself as an old maid.

"I give people nicknames," he explained, telling himself not to be curious about what her cryptic comment might mean. "Baldy. Old Man. I ought to call you Red."

"You can call me Melanie," she drawled, slipping into that invisible armor again. Amusing him with her sass more than she knew, she opened a glass-paned door that was also hung with eyelet curtains for privacy off the west side of the tiny living room. "In here." She gestured to an examination table that looked as though it had come out of some old country doctor's office. "This is why I get to have my own place. Since I have to be on call around the clock, it makes sense to live in the quarters where all the medical supplies and sickbeds are kept."

He took in the two beds that were little more than metal cots made up with crisp white sheets and blankets, and the metal cabinets that were marred with rust around the hinges and corners. She washed her hands at a tiny porcelain sink before opening a dorm-size refrigerator and pulling out a vial of medicine. Then she opened drawers and the cabinet, which were, as she'd claimed, sparsely stocked and pulled out sterile gloves, alcohol, gauze bandages and a syringe packet. Duff was all for playing his part as a grizzled vet looking for some peace and quiet away from the crowds and noise of the city, but did he really want to get medical treatment from a woman who wasn't even a registered nurse, much less a doctor?

She faced him again, frowning when she saw he was still standing. "You're not afraid of needles, are you?"

He wasn't. Duff leaned his hip back against the table and sat. "You're sure you know what you're doing?"

Her chin came up and she pointed to the framed document on the wall. "I may not have all the medical training I'd like, but I have enough to do this job. There's my certification from the Metropolitan Community College in Kansas City."

So she'd been to school in KC. Someone commuting back and forth to classes could certainly smuggle a trunkful of guns into the city. He'd have to check to see if her schedule coincided with any of the suspected weapons deliveries. "When were you in Kansas City?"

But she wasn't interested in getting friendly. "We're talking a shot of topical anesthesia, cleaning the wound and eight, ten stitches, tops. I don't have antibiotics on hand to administer right now, but if you show signs of infection, there's a doctor in Falls City who does."

There was also a medical team on call for the task force. Duff would ask for one of those doctors to check him out when he made his scheduled report to his handler later tonight. In the meantime, if he thought about how confident her hands had felt checking his wound outside, and not how iffy the modernity of this infirmary might be, he had a surprising degree of confidence in her ability to heal him.

"Do your worst, Doc. I can take it." He reached for the hem of his T-shirt and peeled it off over his head, gingerly maneuvering the soiled material over his injured shoulder. By the time he'd wadded up the bloodied shirt and tossed it into the trash can, he had two big brown eyes staring at the center of his chest.

Well, I'll be damned. Melanie Fiske wasn't all cold and prickly and disinterested in men, after all. Although he could guess that a woman with medical training had seen a half-naked man before, her eyes seemed more than professionally curious about the particular dimensions of his bare chest and torso. He *was* built like a tank. Maybe she'd just never seen this much exposed male skin in her infirmary before.

"You, um—" she swallowed, and he watched the ripple of movement down her throat as a telltale blush moved in the opposite direction "—never answered my question about a tetanus shot. Is yours up-to-date?"

Maybe he could play off the innocence peeking through her tough tomboy facade and make a friend here, after all. "I'm good. That's one thing the army does right."

She tended to him for several minutes in silence,

keeping her eyes carefully averted from bare-naked-chest land as she untied the bandanna and irrigated the wound. While she waited for the area where she'd given him the shot to grow numb, she shifted her attention to the tender swelling on his cheek and gently cleaned the scrape there. "How did it feel to punch Silas in the face?"

Interesting that that should be the first personal question she'd asked him. "Like it needed to be done."

"I can't tell you how often I wished I could…" Her fingers paused for a moment and he thought he glimpsed the dent of a dimple, indicating a brief smile before she went back to work. "I'm surprised he didn't pull the knife sooner. He hates to lose. Let me see your hands."

"They could use a little TLC. But I'll live."

After cleaning his hands and putting a bandage on one finger, she touched the boot-sized bruise on his flank. Duff sucked in a sharp breath as her fingers brushed across his skin. "Sorry." She'd thought she'd hurt him, but that eager response was all on him and the years he'd gone without a woman's tender touch. She prodded the skin all around the bruise, and Duff gritted his teeth at the exploration. "I'll get an ice pack. If it starts to swell, or you feel like you're struggling to breathe…"

She suddenly drew back her fingers. Had she maintained contact more than was medically necessary? Duff hadn't noticed. Or minded. Instead, he'd been thinking that the space between them smelled of the summer heat coming off her skin. And beneath the tinge of perspiration and antiseptic that lingered in the air, he detected a soft scent reminiscent of baby oil. That was her. The curvy tomboy with the plain features and wild auburn hair smelled like that. Sweet and down-to-earth, yet sexy—like she'd be soft to the touch if he reached out and brushed his fingertips across *her* skin. He hoped she wasn't one of the bad guys here. Because he was seriously tempted—

"I don't have an X-ray machine to check for internal injuries."

Now he was the one swallowing hard to regain his equilibrium. "I know what a cracked rib feels like. I'm breathing fine. This is just a bruise."

She pulled a tray of ice from the minifridge and wrapped the ice in a thin towel, placing it gently against his aching side. "You've been in a lot of fights?"

"A few."

"I'm sorry." She took his hand and placed it over the ice pack to hold it in place so that she could set up a tray with sutures. "That you've been hurt, I mean. I'm not sorry that somebody was able to put Silas in his place for once." She tilted her eyes up to his. "Does that make me a bad person? That I feel like I should thank you?"

Maybe the woman was more bluff than any real experience with men. Since she wasn't attached to anyone here, he could take advantage of her apparent interest in him. She seemed to be at odds with Henry Fiske, but she was part of his family. And, clearly, she had some kind of history with Danvers. She'd know everyone here and have access to most, if not all, of the facilities. And this conversation was giving him the feeling that he could get close to her, after all.

For a split second, Shayla Ortiz's face superimposed itself over Melanie's. He'd used her, too, to get close to her drug-dealing brother. And that had turned into the worst sort of disaster an undercover cop could face.

He'd lost his focus on the case when he'd fallen in love. Shayla had betrayed him and blown his cover to protect herself, and he hadn't seen it coming until it was too late.

But Duff was a decade older and wiser now. He didn't have to trust Melanie Fiske—he just had to make her think he did. He had to make her believe he cared about her. He didn't have the suave charm of his youngest brother to draw on, but how sophisticated could a woman who'd grown up in the boonies of Missouri be? She just needed somebody to be nicer to her than Danvers had been, and that wouldn't be much of a challenge. If he paid attention to a few details, he could figure out what was important to her and pretend those things were important to him, too.

Melanie tucked a damp tendril behind her ear and held it there as her freckled cheeks colored with a rosy blush. "I guess that makes me a hypocrite—trying to stop the violence, yet wishing I could have done it myself."

Duff realized he'd been staring long enough to make her uncomfortable—just the opposite of what he needed to be doing if he was going to woo her into becoming an ally. He ignored the stab of guilt that tried to warn him away from involving her in his investigation. "Has Danvers given you trouble before? Do you know how to fight?"

"So far I've relied on outwitting him. It isn't that hard."

Duff wanted to grin at her sarcasm, but the fact that the man who'd cut his arm open had threatened her, as well, didn't sit well with him. "I could give you a few pointers on defending yourself."

"You'd teach me to fight." Now that was a skepti-
cal look. "Like you were doing out there with Silas?"

Realistically, he doubted she could take Silas down
the same way he had. But there were ways. "You just
have to be smarter than your opponent, do the unexpected and be fierce about committing to the attack. I
could show you escape maneuvers—and you probably
already know some of the key targets if you want to
incapacitate a man."

Her gaze dropped down to the zipper of his jeans
and up to the column of his throat.

"I see you already know a couple of vulnerable
spots." He really should feel guilty about saying things
that triggered that graphic response on her skin. Instead,
he was wondering what else he could say or do to make
her skin color like that.

She quickly averted her face. "I'd appreciate that. If
you have the time."

Her hip brushed against his thigh as she inserted the
first stitch. Duff turned his nose to the crown of her
hair, inhaling the scents of baby shampoo and damp
summer heat. "I'll make the time for you."

"You don't even know your work schedule..." Before
she made the next stitch, she tipped her face to his. Her
breath caught with an audible startle at how close he
was to her, but Duff made no effort to retreat.

Her eyes weren't ordinary at all. Their cool brown
color, spiked with flecks of amber, reminded him of the
fine Irish whiskey he and his brothers liked to sip on
special occasions. With her sweet scent and eyes like
that, he wouldn't have to pretend that this woman had
some pretty about her, after all.

"When I say I'm going to do a thing, I do it."

He lowered his gaze to the quiver of her lips and felt a twist of hunger low in his belly. He could kiss her right now if he wanted to. Maybe the bold move would shock her into kissing him back. Or she might just slap his face for doing without asking.

"Don't make promises you can't keep." Her hands were suddenly very busy with the cut on his shoulder.

"I don't."

Yep. Busy, busy. She didn't know what to do about her interest in him. She didn't know how to hide it, either. As long as he didn't spook her, he could give her a few lessons about how to indulge that awareness she was feeling. And, damn it, he was going to take advantage of that attraction. Because the mission required it.

But that meant ignoring his conscience and his errant libido, and taking it slow so he wouldn't frighten her off before he had the chance to solidify a connection between them. So he dialed back his own curiosity about what her lips might taste like and thought about the vanishing man who'd shot his grandfather and the reason he was here in the first place. Duff set the ice pack on the bed beside him and captured a strand of Melanie's auburn hair, pulling it away from the damp spot on her left breast. The kinky tendril was thick and soft as he rubbed it between his thumb and fingers, stirring up the scents he'd noticed earlier. She must use baby products for all her personal toiletries. If he needed any further testament to her innocence...

Melanie pulled away at the same moment he forgot that touching her was supposed to be an act.

"Give me a sec." She exited the room for a minute or so, and came back in, sans the blush, tying a rubber band around the long braid that hung over her shoulder. Without another word, she pulled on a new pair of sterile gloves and prepped the needle for the next stitch. Her tough-chick armor was back in place.

But Duff wasn't about to surrender the opportunity to get closer to her. "That's a shame, winding up all that wild hair like that." He reached out and twisted the heavy braid between his fingers, using it to tug her into the vee of his legs. "I liked it better down."

Chapter Four

"You liked…?" Melanie caught her breath when the back of Tom Maynard's knuckles brushed across her breast as he played with the braid of her hair. The caress tingled over her skin, tightening the tip into a tender pearl. Was that an accident? Or had that touch been intentional? She cringed at the sound of denim rasping against denim. She was nestled between his thighs and she wasn't making any effort to move away from the warmth surrounding her.

"Are you hitting on me?" With an awkward push and a nearly stifling amount of embarrassed heat creeping up to her cheeks, she stepped around his knee. A half-sewn suture linking her hands to his shoulder kept her from bolting across the room. "You'll make me mess up this stitch."

She'd been stripped down to wet undies that were transparent to the skin an hour or so ago and hadn't felt as exposed as she did fully dressed with Tom Maynard. Of course, no one had touched her, accidentally or otherwise, when she'd been swimming in her skivvies. And this man seemed to keep finding reasons to touch her. Where was that sharp tongue she'd used to tell off Silas and her uncle? Was she really so starved for some tender attention from a man that she'd forget her vow to steer clear of any entanglements on the farm?

She stopped herself from reaching inside her pocket again to touch her father's watch. It was a superstitious habit, really, thinking that holding on to the busted watch could bring back either of her parents. The scratched-up piece of gold couldn't really channel her father's spirit and give her clarity and reassurance when she needed it. She had to be smart enough to remember all the life lessons her widowed father had taught her right up until the night he'd died.

Except that she'd been a girl of eleven when Leroy Fiske had drowned. And, somehow, the lessons she'd learned as a little girl never included how she was supposed to react to a man who stirred things inside her. Even when he didn't mean to. Or did he? She'd been secretly cheering for Tom Maynard when he'd stood up to Henry and Silas's authority. They'd had to gang up on Tom and pull a weapon to turn the tide of power back in their favor. For a few moments, she thought she'd found her hero—the perfect ally—a way out of the nightmare unfolding around her these past few months. No wonder she'd been so eager to defy her uncle's authority and step into the middle of a fight.

Then she realized he was going to be like the other men here—overlooking her uncle's lies and accepting his questionable dictates in exchange for a share of the farm's profits—or whatever a man like Tom needed.

But the promise of a hero must have lingered inside her because she'd been ogling Tom's imposing chest and the T-shaped dusting of brown hair that tapered into a line that disappeared beneath his belt buckle, imagining being held close to all that muscle and heat again.

Did her reaction to his touch mean she liked Tom? Had catching her admiring the muscular landscape sent her patient the message that she wanted to be touched? If so, how did she change that message? Because it really wasn't in her plans right now to...to what? Make a friend? Have an affair? Completely embarrass herself by revealing that she'd reached the age of twenty-five with more experience fishing than kissing?

"Hey, Doc, you okay?" His voice rumbled in a drowsy timbre. "You got quiet on me."

She hated how her skin telegraphed every emotion, putting her at a disadvantage when she couldn't read whatever Tom was thinking or feeling. "I did?" She cleared her throat to mask the embarrassingly breathless quality of her own voice. "I'm sorry. What were we talking about?"

"Why you tamed all that hair into a braid like this. You've sure got a lot of it." Was that supposed to be a compliment? Or a remark about how the Missouri humidity could wreak havoc on too much naturally curly hair? And, goodness, was he still twirling the tail end of her braid between his fingers?

She couldn't summon her father's spirit to guide her, but she could muster up a little common sense. Melanie pulled the braid from his fingers and swung it behind her back. "It's not practical to have it flying all over the place when I have to do work like this. I can't tell you how many times I've been tempted to cut it all off."

"Now *that* would be a shame. It's like earthy fire."

Melanie lowered her needle and tipped her gaze past the brown stubble dusting his jaw to meet his smiling green eyes. "Is that your best line? That *is* a line, isn't it?" She understood a brute like Silas pawing at her and barking orders more than she ever had men who pretended she was pretty or special so that they could get something from her. And this man with his neat military haircut and unshaven face, his mature body and boyish grin, his eagerness to fight *and* flirt, definitely wanted something. "You give people nicknames because refusing to use their real name is a way to put distance between you. I'm not a doctor, so stop calling me Doc. You told Henry that you wanted to get away from people, and yet you're trying to make friends with me. I need you to watch where you put your hands, and my hair is *earthy fire*? What does that even mean? If you want to say something, just say it. I don't understand why men can't be honest."

He put up his hands in surrender. "Whoa, sweetheart. I think I just got lumped in with some bad history. You don't even know me. Not all men are dishonest."

She wanted to believe that. But, after a few run-ins with her uncle and Silas, she doubted it. She got a sense that even this one who'd protected her from Silas's knife was lying about something.

"And I'll start keeping my hands to myself once you stop putting yours on me," he said.

"I'm treating your injury."

"That's not all you're doing, Doc."

Melanie groaned as he teased her with the nickname again.

"Sure, I'm trying to be friendly," he said. "We're going to be seeing each other almost every day, right? And giving you those self-defense lessons? Trust me, they'll go easier if you don't think of me as the enemy. You gotta give me a chance."

She knocked his left hand down and moved closer to sew another stitch. "No, I don't."

His arm flinched against his side and he swore. "Easy, Doc—er, Mel. Melanie. *Miss Fiske.*" That snippy tone of mockery she understood. "That one pinched."

She stopped before cutting the end of the suture, appalled that she'd let this man's teasing and touching, and her own distrustful thoughts, get in the way of her doing her job with the care and accuracy in which she prided herself. No matter what her issues were with her uncle, she had no right to take her frustration out on a patient. "I'm sorry." She quickly analyzed the neat row of stitches to make sure she hadn't aggravated his injury. "Did I hurt you?"

"I'll live. But I felt the tug." He dipped his square jaw to line up his gaze with hers. "Why are you so mad at me? I figured you'd be grateful."

"For what?"

"Danvers was more than happy to cut you, as well as me. I got you out of there."

"I thought I got *you* out of there."

"You do like to argue a point. How is that any different than me giving you a nickname? You're workin' awfully hard to keep your distance from me, too." He scrubbed his fingers over the top of his hair, leaving a trail of short spikes sticking up in a dozen different directions. "When I think you might actually like me."

"Whatever gave you that idea?"

He traced her collarbone around the neckline of her T-shirt. "That blush creepin' up your neck."

Melanie's hand flew to her throat as he pulled his finger away, grinning at her inability to hide the truth.

"I don't know you well enough to decide whether or not I like you."

He sat back on the table. "You're not even going to give me a chance to find out if we can get along?"

"I thought you told Henry that you were here for peace and quiet—that you wanted to be left alone."

Grim lines appeared beside his eyes as his teasing smile faded. "I get a little paranoid in a crowd—but I do pretty good one-on-one."

What kind of *good* was he talking about? A good friend? A good boyfriend? The wannabe nurse or doctor in her tempered her determination to resist him. This man was a veteran, after all. With the few hints he'd dropped already, he was probably suffering from some degree of post-traumatic stress. Maybe he was reaching out to her because he felt safe with her. Maybe he saw some kind of kinship with her already because she'd jumped in on his side of the fight when no one else had. It kind of made sense. He probably didn't see her as any threat. "That's all you want? A chance?"

"That's all a man ever wants." The angry lines softened. And though the teasing smile didn't reappear, he dropped his voice to a growly whisper that indicated some sort of intimacy. "Unless he's one of those jackasses who's lied to you."

Men didn't talk softly to her. And they certainly didn't share anything that resembled intimacy. The hard walls of defense she'd lived with every day since finding her father's watch crumbled just a little bit. Remembering the professional training she prided herself on, Mel placed the ice pack in Tom's hand and guided it up to the violet-red mark on his cheekbone. "All right, then. We can try to be friends. But maybe you shouldn't talk for a while. I'll finish faster if you let me concentrate on my work."

"In other words, zip it?"

He held her gaze until she nodded. Then he looked away, ostensibly taking in every corner of her mismatched but clean treatment room. A crooked smile softened the square line of his jaw, and she had to tamp down those little frissons of infatuation that tried to take hold of her again. She wouldn't say Tom Maynard was handsome, exactly. But he was overtly male in a way that woke up feminine impulses inside her that she'd ignored for a very long time.

But ignore them she would. She was agreeing to a trial friendship—nothing more. Making sure to gentle her touch, Melanie sewed in the last few stitches until the blood oozing from the wound had completely stopped. She inspected the neat line of the mended cut and cleaned the area again before opening the antibiotic ointment and prepping the gauze and adhesive tape to cover it.

"Out of all the men you've ever known, every last one of them has lied to you?"

Tom's deep voice startled her as much as the probing question. Melanie fumbled the roll of tape she'd been using and it rolled away underneath the sink. Glad she could move away from the distracting body heat that even the air-conditioning couldn't seem to diminish, she got down on her hands and knees to retrieve it. "In my experience, they say what they want you to hear. Or else they make stuff up because they think it's what *I* want to hear. Like saying I'm pretty when I know I'm not." She stood and returned the tape to its spot inside the barren storage cabinet. "Half the men around here think that sweet-talking me will get them closer to Henry. Or to my cousin, Deanna. Every single man here has his eye on her. And why not? She's gorgeous and outgoing, easy to like. She eats up the attention."

"Danvers was hitting on *you* when he mentioned that dance."

"He was asserting his authority and assuaging his pride. If he thought dating one of the dairy cows in the south pasture would secure his position with Henry, he'd do it."

Tom chuckled, and the warm laugh sounded genuine enough to make her want to smile in return. "You've got a pretty wicked sense of humor when you're not busy pushing people away." He drew a cross over his heart with his finger. "No lie."

Keeping her smile to herself at the childish gesture, Melanie carried the soiled supplies to the trash. She peeled off her gloves and tossed them, too, before facing her patient again. "My father was an honest man."

"Was?"

"He died when I was eleven."

"I'm sorry." The lines of sun and stress reappeared beside his eyes as he narrowed his gaze. "Your mom?"

"Why do you ask?"

"That's how you make friends. You ask questions and get to know a person. So does your mom live here?"

Melanie shook her head. "She died when I was born. There were complications. The midwife couldn't stop the bleeding, and Dad couldn't get her to the hospital in time. It's what motivated me to get emergency medical training. When something like that happens, it feels like we're a long way from civilization out here."

"That's rough."

She took the ice pack from him and emptied it before draping the towel over the edge of the sink. "It wasn't all bad. I have wonderful memories of Dad. He taught me about the trees and wildlife here, how to run a fishing boat. He told me all about my mother, read to me at night. He took me swimming, hiking, canoeing..."

And then she couldn't talk about it anymore. Not with the fear that something horrible had happened to her father, and she'd never suspected—never even thought to suspect—a crime, or at least a cover-up, until just a few months ago. With the grit of unwanted tears stinging her eyes, Melanie excused herself to retrieve Tom's bag from her living room. She lifted the sleeve of her T-shirt and dabbed it against her eyes until she'd replaced sorrow and guilt with the determination to do right by her father.

"So Henry and Abby raised you." She jumped as Tom palmed the small of her back and reached around her to pick up his bag before she could reach it. "Sorry. Gotta work on that hands-to-myself thing. So, no nicknames, no touching, and any time I have a conversation with you, I need to be brutally honest."

Melanie was still gaping with surprise. She hadn't even heard him follow her into the room. "I prefer that."

"All right, then. I'll tell you something real about me."

Manners aside, the man didn't have much to do with modesty, either. He unhooked his belt and slipped on the knife Silas had taken from him before digging inside the bag a second time to pull out a rolled-up black T-shirt. When he reached for the zipper of his jeans, she turned away to face the eyelet curtains at her front window.

"My mom was murdered when I was in high school,"

he said. "By a couple of druggies robbing a convenience store where she'd gone to pick up milk."

"Oh, my God." She turned right back. "That's awful. I'm so sorry." If he was trying to gain her sympathy or show they had something in common, he might be succeeding. She understood that lonesome ache, that empty space in her heart where unconditional love used to reside. Did he? Could he truly understand how torn she was inside—wanting to get away from this place that had caused her such pain, yet needing to stay and do whatever was necessary to uncover the truth? She waited for him to pull on the shirt so she could read the sincerity of his expression. But it was the same craggy face with the same unreadable green eyes that she'd seen earlier. "Is that true?"

He carefully adjusted his sleeve over the gauze bandage before tucking in the hem and fastening his jeans and belt. He pulled his gun from the bag and slipped it on over his shoulders, completing the look of a warrior before his gaze settled on hers. "I never lie about my mama."

There was a hard edge to his eyes and mouth and even in his posture that made her believe he was telling the truth. She tightened her grip around the end of her braid, fighting off the impulse to reach out and offer some sort of comfort. Right now, though, he didn't look like the sort of man who needed or wanted comfort. This was what a soldier who'd seen too much looked like. This was the man who wanted a job away from the bustle of too many people, too many buildings, too much noise. This glimpse of what she suspected the real Tom Maynard was like beneath the crude charm and nicknames was, frankly, a little scary. But she'd take this *brutal* honesty over sweet-talking lies any day. Maybe she could use an ally like that in her quest to find the truth. Not that she could ever fully trust him—not while he worked for Henry. "I'm sorry about your mother. Did the police find her killer?"

"Yes."

"You found closure after her death?"

"I guess." The steely set of his shoulders relaxed with a heavy exhalation, and he knelt to pick up the flannel shirt and balled-up socks that had fallen from his bag and stuffed them inside. "I'll always be pissed off at the lowlife who shot her, and I'll always miss her. But it happened a long time ago, and the shooter and his partner will be in prison for the rest of their lives, so, yeah, I guess that's closure." With a firm tug, he cinched the bag shut and pushed to his feet. "Why do you ask?"

She wanted the same kind of justice for her father—or proof beyond a reasonable doubt that Leroy's death *had* been an accident. Maybe her uncle had found the watch on the boat after it had been towed ashore, and he'd simply helped himself to the memento of his brother. But if there was a sentimental reason for keeping it, why stuff it in a forgotten box in the attic? Other relatives had swarmed in to take things that had belonged to her father—as a child, she'd been helpless to stop them. As a grown-up, she wondered if any of their motives had been sentimental—or if taking pretty much anything that wasn't nailed down had held a more sinister purpose. As much as she felt compassion for Tom's loss of a parent, she wasn't ready to share her suspicions with a stranger. It was dangerous to share them with anyone around here.

Instead, she countered with a question of her own. "Why did you tell me about your mother?"

"You asked for a truth. And that's one I'm willing to share." So there were other truths he didn't intend to tell her? "You want to know another one?" He pointed to her left ear. "You've got a kink of hair stickin' up like a horn on the side of your head." Her hand immediately flew there. She snagged the wayward strand and stuffed it into place behind her ear. A slow grin spread across his face, breaking the somber mood. "But I do love the color of it. I don't know if I've ever touched red hair before. And this is the real deal, isn't it?" He caught the braid she'd been fidgeting with a few moments earlier and held it up in his palm to study it. "Don't know why I thought it'd feel different from any other color. Is that honest enough for you?"

Melanie tugged the braid from his fingers and, this time, despite her best effort, she smiled back. "I don't know what to make of you, Tom. I can't tell if you're trying to shock me or seduce me."

He arched an eyebrow. "Is that second one an option?"

Melanie was silently cursing the embarrassing heat crawling up her neck when someone knocked on her front door.

"Mel? Are you in here?" The door swung open before Melanie could reach it. A wave of hot air rushed in, followed by very pregnant blonde woman.

"SueAnn?" She took one look at her friend's pale cheeks and grabbed hold of her arm. Melanie kicked the door shut and guided her into the living room, unsure if this was a friendly visit or a medical one. "Did you run over here? Are you all right? Is the baby okay?"

Rubbing her heavy belly, SueAnn Renick wheezed for breath and leaned against Mel. "Is he here? I heard you had a patient. Is it Richard?" Tom lifted his duffel bag out of her path and SueAnn tilted her head back to greet him. "You're the new guy?"

"Yes, ma'am. Duff Maynard."

Melanie urged her to sit. "I thought I told you to stay inside during the heat of the day. Catch your breath and I'll get you a glass of water."

But SueAnn rolled to her feet and tottered right after her. "I heard you were treating an injured man. Is Richard okay?"

"Richard isn't here." Melanie turned to see her panicked friend swaying on her feet and quickly linked her arm through hers to walk her toward the infirmary door. "I was taking care of Tom. You need to relax. I'll get you a cool compress."

"I know I'm really emotional with the baby. But I have a right to be, don't I?" SueAnn moved her hand from her belly up to her forehead to lift her sunny gold bangs off her face.

Melanie couldn't tell if that was perspiration or tears beading on her friend's cheeks. But she could tell the woman was overheated and dangerously close to hyperventilating. "Of course, you do. But Richard's a grown man who can take care of himself. You need to think of yourself and the baby right now."

"How can I? What if he's in trouble and needs me? It's been four months since he left. A man doesn't get a job just a few miles away and never return home. We've always been close. He'd call or send a letter if he could, wouldn't he?" SueAnn braced her hand against the doorjamb and stopped. She looked inside the empty infirmary, then back up to the armed man still standing in the middle of Melanie's living room. Her breath rushed out in a sharp gasp. "Oh. He's your patient. I guess I wasn't thinking straight."

"Sorry to disappoint you." Tom stepped forward and extended his hand. "Like I said, I'm Duff. Is everything all right, ma'am? Who's Richard?"

"My brother." She shook his hand. "I'm the one who should apologize. SueAnn Renick. Resident crazy lady."

Melanie tried to get her moving again. "Tom, you'd better go."

"I know something's wrong." She spun, grabbing on to Melanie's arm with a sweaty palm as the color drained from her face. "Something's happened to Richard. It's this horrible place. He saw his chance to leave and…" She rocked back against the wall. "I am feeling a little light-headed…" She cradled her belly and slid toward the floor.

Chapter Five

Melanie barely had time to cradle her friend's head and keep it from hitting the wall when a blur of black shirt and big shoulders nudged her aside.

"I've got her." Tom caught SueAnn in his arms and tipped the unconscious woman against his chest.

"Be careful of your stitches," Melanie warned.

Without so much as a grunt of discomfort, he pushed to his feet, lifting her pregnant friend. "What's wrong with her?"

"Put her in here and let me check." Pushing aside the fleeting thought that Tom Maynard seemed to have a knack for rescuing women, Melanie pointed to the nearest cot. SueAnn's blackout had been only temporary, but the woman was still woozy from the heat, exertion and fear that had brought her running in a few minutes earlier. Once Tom had laid her on the cool sheets, he backed up to let Melanie work. While she wrapped a blood-pressure cuff around SueAnn's arm, she nodded toward the sink. "Grab that wet towel and fold it up for me."

Thankfully, he was quick to obey the order. He handed her a neat compress that was still cool from the melted ice. "You really are the doctor around here."

"I wish." She sat on the edge of the cot and placed the compress on SueAnn's forehead. The frantic woman's blue eyes opened, then drifted shut again.

"Is she all right?"

Melanie plugged the stethoscope into her ears and listened to the rapid beat of SueAnn's pulse. Her blood pressure had spiked to 160/100. Not good. Melanie shook her head and pointed to the file cabinet across the room. "Look under *R* for Renick and pull SueAnn's file. I'll need a pen, too." As eager to help now as he'd been a recalcitrant patient himself, Tom brought her the requested items. She listened to the baby's heartbeat, as well as SueAnn's, before adding the vitals to the record she was keeping. She was seeing a pattern here that was as troubling as the idea of secrets surrounding her father's death.

She moved the compress to SueAnn's neck and wrists, trying to cool the pulse points. "She's worried about her brother. He's been missing for several weeks."

"Missing?" Tom's shadow towered beside her. "Did you report it to the sheriff?"

The disappearance of Richard Lloyd wasn't Melanie's main concern. "SueAnn, you need to see a real doctor. I can't control these blood-pressure spikes without medication. They're not safe for you or the baby."

SueAnn blinked her eyes open. "Our home is here. This is where I want to raise my baby."

"That doesn't mean you shouldn't go to a hospital to deliver him or her. A real doctor could tell you if it *is* a him or her. You need to go to Henry and ask him to let you and Daryl go to Falls City or, better yet, Kansas City."

"He'll never agree to that." She dropped her voice to

a nervous whisper and glanced up at Tom. "Besides, you know Daryl can't get a job that pays as well anywhere else. And if we leave, how will Richard find us when he comes home?" Melanie felt her friend's pulse beating faster beneath her fingertips. SueAnn swatted aside the compress and pushed herself up on her elbows. If it weren't for her awkward balance and Melanie blocking her way, she would have climbed right off the cot and probably fainted again. "You don't think Sheriff Cobb put him in jail for getting drunk again, do you? What could he have done to keep him imprisoned all these weeks?"

"We don't know that he's in jail. The sheriff would have said something. Richard would have been given a phone call."

"I just know something terrible has happened to him." SueAnn gulped in a sob of breath and fought against Melanie's helping hands.

"Ma'am? SueAnn?" A deep voice sounded beside Melanie as Tom knelt beside her. His big hands replaced Melanie's on the other woman's shoulders and lowered her to the bed. "You need to think of your baby. Take deep breaths." He inhaled and exhaled along with her. "That's it. Now why don't you tell me a little bit about this brother of yours."

Melanie stared at the jut of Tom's shoulder moving between her and her patient, eyeing the strip of white adhesive tape peeking out between his tanned skin and the snug fit of his sleeve. He was certainly a man of contrasts, able to handle the violence of a fight as easily as he comforted a hysterical woman. Melanie should suspect his motives for still being here when he could have left several minutes ago, but right now she was grateful for the soothing resonance of his voice and the calming effect it seemed to have on SueAnn.

Encouraging Tom to take her place on the edge of the cot, Melanie got up. "I'll get her something to drink."

She pulled out a fresh towel and ran it beneath the faucet while SueAnn rattled on. "His name's Richard. The night before he left he told me he was taking on an extra job in town. Henry had arranged it. Or maybe it was Silas. I can't seem to remember. A lot of the men pick up extra work when money's tight around here."

"Is money tight?" Tom was frowning when Melanie glanced back at him. "I thought this looked like a pretty prosperous place."

"Did you come from Falls City? Did you see a young man with blond hair?"

Tom shook his head. "I was just passin' through when I met Mr. Fiske and got word about a job doing nighttime security work here."

"Night security?" SueAnn collapsed against her pillow. "That used to be Richard's job. I wonder if he borrowed money from Henry. He had that new truck when he left. Maybe he thought he had to take the job in order to pay Henry back."

"Do you know what kind of job he had?" Tom asked. "Or what kind of truck he was driving? I could go back to Falls City and look for him."

"Enough. She needs rest." Melanie pressed the damp towel to SueAnn's lips. "Here. Suck some water out of it if you can."

Her front door swung open to the clump of footsteps and a deep, worried shout. "SueAnn!"

Daryl Renick dashed through the infirmary door before Melanie could meet him. He pushed a heavy box into her arms and moved right past her, eyeing Tom away from his wife and taking his place at the side of the bed. He tossed his shaggy brown hair out of his eyes and captured SueAnn's hand between his. "Honey, I heard you were in the clinic. Is everything okay? Did something happen with the baby?"

"It was just a silly mistake. I'll be fine."

Daryl smoothed SueAnn's bangs off her face and pressed a kiss to her forehead. He rested his palm on her distended belly before raising his dark eyes to Melanie's. "Silas didn't do something stupid to scare her, did he? I got those disposable phones he asked for."

Tom frowned. "Why would Silas want to scare your wife?"

Melanie jumped in when she saw Daryl's deer-in-the-headlight expression. She wouldn't put it past Silas to coerce someone into doing what he wanted, and, clearly, Daryl's trip into Falls City hadn't all been about fetching medical supplies. She set the box of supplies on the exam table before offering him a rueful smile. "SueAnn passed out in my living room." She nodded toward the muscular man lurking in the doorway. "Tom brought her in and helped me calm her down. But she needs to see a doctor."

"I know it." Daryl extended a hand to Tom and nodded to Melanie, including them both in his thanks. "Thank you. I'll talk to Henry again about visiting that specialist in Kansas City."

"I don't need Dr. Ayres." Despite her wan color, SueAnn was all smiles now as she reached out to Melanie. "You're all we need, Mel. You've taken care of me for eight months. You'll take good care of my baby, too. You delivered Alice's baby."

Melanie took her friend's hand. "One baby doesn't make me an expert. What if there are complications?"

SueAnn gave her hand a weak squeeze. "Then I know you will fight harder to save my baby—and me—than anyone else. I believe in you."

Maybe she shouldn't. Melanie gently squeezed back before releasing her hand. "You rest here for a while. Daryl, you stay with her. Make sure she drinks some more water."

"I will."

Melanie led Tom out of the infirmary and closed the door. But her frustration erupted in a noisy groan as she stormed across the room to pull out the obstetrics textbook she'd been poring over these past few weeks.

Tom planted himself in the middle of the room while she turned to the index and searched for the information she wanted to double-check. "If she needs to see a regular doctor, why doesn't she just go?"

"Things are complicated around here. Henry and Abby—they make deals. They do nice things for people. But they expect loyalty in return." She set the open book on top of the shelf and flipped through the pages. "They helped Daryl and SueAnn get a house. The yellow one at the end of the lane."

"I saw it. Looks like a new build. That's a pretty expensive bribe to ensure someone's loyalty."

"Daryl spent time in prison for stealing cars. He served his time and all—before he met SueAnn. She knows his background, and he's so good to her. But it's been hard for them to get credit anywhere because of his record."

"So your uncle bought him the house. And now Daryl owes him. They have to stay."

She paused in the middle of skimming the page and turned. Maybe it wasn't too late for Tom to do the smart thing and get out of here. "Henry worries that if people leave, they won't come back. Like SueAnn's brother. Richard left the farm four months ago, and we haven't seen him since. He's a screwup sometimes, probably drinks more than he should, but I can't believe he'd upset his sister like this."

"A man doesn't disappear for no reason." Tom splayed his hands at his waist, drawing her attention to the gun, the knife and the threat of danger that emanated from his very posture. "He either doesn't want to be found—or something's keeping him from contacting the people he cares about."

"You want to disappear."

"I've got a reason."

She supposed he did if he suffered from PTSD. But the Richard Lloyd she knew was a different sort of man. "Richard likes to have a good time and laugh and be with people. He and Daryl hunt and fish all the time. He's a relentless flirt, even though every girl around here knows not to take him seriously. I can't see him ever wanting to be alone like you do."

"You're that worried about SueAnn and her brother?"

Melanie turned back to her textbook to recheck the information she'd already memorized. But she wasn't a physician and she didn't have access to any of those medications. "I used to think this was an idyllic place. Life was simple, but productive. I was honoring my father's legacy by staying here and helping the farm become a success." She closed the heavy book, feeling helpless to fix anyone's problems. "Now things are so…"

"So what?" Before she realized he'd even crossed the room, Tom's fingers wrapped around her elbow. He turned her to face him, leaving Melanie no place to retreat. "Is there something going on here I need to know about before I join the team? What did Henry do to ensure your loyalty?"

Didn't the man have any notion of personal space? His shoulders blocked her view of the infirmary, and every breath she took was tinged with the scents of musky heat and antiseptic coming off his skin.

She tilted up her chin to meet the scrutiny in his moss-colored eyes. She probably shouldn't tell him how much she was questioning her loyalty to her uncle right now. "He paid for my schooling and the expenses of living in Kansas City for a year and a half. He put a roof over my head and raised me after Dad's death. I should be grateful."

"Should be?"

That was a stupid slip of the tongue. "I *am* grateful. The Ozarks are a beautiful place to grow up. And I always wanted to do something in the field of medicine. I owe that to him."

"But?"

Melanie flattened her hand in the middle of his chest and pushed him back a step so she could think and breathe properly. "Why can't you just accept the answers I give you? Why does every answer lead to another question?"

"Because I don't think you're telling me everything."

And she wasn't about to. No matter how tempting his strength and penchant for rescuing a damsel in distress might be, she didn't really know Tom—*my friends call me Duff*—Maynard. If she didn't trust the people she knew well around here, why should she trust an outsider?

But Tom had protected her from Silas's temper and helped SueAnn, and she had silently agreed to make the effort to be his friend, so she settled for sharing a different truth. Turning her back to him, she picked up the textbook and hugged it to her chest. "I wish I could get out of this place and go back to school again. I'm trained for basic medical procedures and illnesses— not a hypertensive pregnant woman who may need an emergency C-section. I'm reading everything I can to help SueAnn. But it's not the same as having the real experience and a sterile operating room."

The creak of leather in his belt or holster was the only sound to give him away as he moved in beside her. He ran his fingertip across the spines of the top row of books. "Have you read all these?"

"Why have books if you're not going to read them?"

He pulled out her tattered copy of *Jane Eyre*, checking the last page number and frowning before handing it over to her. "You liked going to school?"

"I take it you didn't?"

"I got through it well enough to play football and graduate. But the classwork wasn't really my thing."

She plucked the novel from his hand before sliding both books back into their places on the shelf. "I came home to work off the debt I owed my aunt and uncle since they paid for my classes. But I'd go back to school in a heartbeat if I could—back to KC to finish my nursing or even premed degree."

"I grew up in KC."

Melanie's pulse picked up at that casual pronouncement. "You know Kansas City?"

"Chiefs football. Jazz. Barbecue." He glanced around her humble home with its handwoven throw rugs and rustic decor. "I guess I figured you lived out here all your life. The city traffic didn't scare you? You weren't overwhelmed by all the crowds and noise?"

Melanie shook her head. The city had been an exciting place for her. She'd made friends, and had learned so much about so many things beyond her books and professors and practicums. This could be dangerous territory for her, finding one more thing she had in common with Tom. "What was your favorite part of KC?"

"I guess I never really thought about it before," he said.

"I loved exploring it," she gushed. "The Plaza lights on Thanksgiving night. Union Station and its science center. The museums. Maybe there's something in my genes. I've got an ancestor who was a wagon-train master on the Santa Fe Trail. I grew up learning all the waterways and trees and paths around these hills. The city just has different terrain—and a different sort of wildlife."

He arched an eyebrow at that comment, making her wonder if she sounded foolish to him. But she wasn't going to apologize for possessing a sense of adventure. She wasn't ashamed of hoping for something better than the life she had here. "I'm going back to Kansas City to finish my degree one day. When the time is right, nobody will be able to stop me."

"When the time is right?" Those sharp green eyes seemed to be reading more into this conversation than she wanted him to. "If you've got a dream that big, why don't you go for it? You can get a job, scholarships, loans if money's the issue."

"I have other reasons for staying here."

He nodded toward the infirmary door. "Like your friend?"

"Somebody has to take care of SueAnn."

"You put your dreams on hold for a friend?"

And a father.

He captured the tendril of hair that must have sprung free again and tucked the independent lock behind her ear. Why did this man keep finding reasons to touch her? And why wasn't she protesting his boldness?

"You are one surprise after another, Doc."

Melanie groaned at the teasing misnomer. "I told you I wasn't—"

Her front door swung open without so much as a knock and Silas Danvers strolled in. Although she was expected to keep her door unlocked during the day in case there was a medical emergency, she was thinking seriously about installing a dead bolt on her door. "Don't tell me you're hurt now, too."

The bruise swelling around his cheek and left eye said he was, but that wasn't why he was here. She interpreted Silas's clean shirt and too-busy-for-niceties glare as a no. "I heard Daryl was back. He didn't check in. Is he here?"

Tom beat her to the infirmary door, planting himself in Silas's path. "His wife wasn't feeling well. Give them a few minutes."

"Was I talking to you? I need to know if he got everything on the list I sent with him."

"What list is that?" When Tom rolled his shoulders as if he was willing to go another round with Silas, Melanie tapped his forearm and urged him to step aside.

With eight new stitches in his arm, he didn't need to

be going another round with anybody. She didn't want a fight in her home, and she certainly didn't want these two in a ruckus that would upset SueAnn further. "It's okay. He can go in."

Now why had she turned to Tom for help in averting an argument? Was she so certain Silas wouldn't listen to her that anyone else would make a better ally? Or was she really buying into Tom's efforts to become her friend? With a glance down to where her hand touched his skin, Tom nodded and stepped away.

Silas must have interpreted his response to her request as a sign of weakness. Smirking, he brushed past Tom and opened the door. "Meet me on the porch of the main house. I'll show you where you can bunk and park your rig." He eyed the leather straps of Tom's holster. "And find a less conspicuous way to wear that gun. You'll scare the tourists."

"You get a lot of visitors on the property after dark?" Tom's question was riddled with sarcasm. Silas closed the door with only a sneer for an answer. "I'm glad I punched him in the face, too. Guess that's my exit cue."

Melanie followed as he scooped up his duffel bag and swung it onto his uninjured shoulder. "Thanks for helping with SueAnn. And for sharing about your mother."

"Thanks for puttin' me back together, Doc." He put up a hand in apology at using the nickname. "I know. Can't seem to help myself. You can call me Duff if it'll make you feel better."

"We'll see." Melanie opened the door for him. "What does Duff mean, anyway?"

"Oh, now that I'm leaving, she's interested. Meet me again sometime, and I'll tell you." He stepped outside. "You know, maybe you've got it all backward with that nickname rule. I don't think it has anything to do with putting distance between us. It could mean I want to be a little closer."

"You want to be closer to Baldy?"

He laughed and Melanie felt a genuine smile forming on her lips.

"I like you, Melanie Fiske. You make me laugh. I haven't done enough of that lately. I'll see you around."

"You'll see me tomorrow when you stop by for me to check those stitches."

He touched his forehead in a salute. His gaze shot past her head and his grin faded as Silas opened the infirmary door behind her. There seemed to be a definite purpose when Tom reached out to catch the end of her braid and give it a little tug. "I'll stop by in the morning, Doc, and give you that first defense lesson."

"See you then." Melanie followed Tom out into the stifling heat, standing on the porch and watching him stride down the gravel road toward the parking lot. She squatted to pull the dead heads off her geraniums, hoping Silas would get the hint to leave.

He didn't.

Silas joined her on the porch before she'd pruned her way to the third plant. "You're getting mighty cozy with the new guy."

She shrugged off the accusation in his tone. "We were having a conversation."

He clamped his hand like a vise around her upper arm and pulled her to her feet, spilling the wilted flowers from her fingers. "Make sure that's all you have. If Roy gets Deanna knocked up before she gives my proposal the attention it deserves, I'm coming for you.

Your uncle promised I'd inherit. That means marrying one of you."

She jerked her arm from his grasp. "Plead your case with Deanna."

She knelt to pick up the mess of flowers on her front walk.

But Silas couldn't stand hearing sass from a woman. "You don't want to cross me, Mel. Henry said you needed to be getting married and making babies. I'm your best choice here."

There was a whole wide world out there, bigger than the virtual prison of these 500 acres. If this bully was the best she could do… If she had to lie with him and bear his child… Melanie pushed to her feet. "You don't love me. I don't even think you like me. How could you ever possibly be happy with me?"

"Because your last name is Fiske."

"That's insulting. I'm a person. I have feelings. If you stop to think, so do you."

He turned away to spit into the grass. "Deanna thinks I'm too old for her."

So the big brute was capable of an emotion beyond greed and anger. "If your sales pitch to her wasn't any better than the one you just gave me, it's no wonder she won't give you the time of day. Neither will I."

"It's not like men are knockin' down your door to get to you. Henry is going to make you marry someone to keep you here, and it might as well be me."

"Never. Going. To happen." She was on a roll today—pushing limits, asking questions, getting herself into trouble. Why not poke the bear one more time? She tipped her gaze to Silas's black eye. "Have you heard anything more about Richard? Any idea where he is? SueAnn doesn't need to be stressing about her brother's disappearance right now."

Silas might have a temper, but he was no fool. He wouldn't be riled into admitting anything. "I'm more interested in what you were doing out at your daddy's boat."

"I was swimming."

"You're lying."

But Melanie wouldn't be taunted into revealing anything, either. "Richard was sober when he left. He was cleaning up his act for SueAnn's sake. He wanted to be a good role model for his niece or nephew." She took a step toward Silas and dared him to tell her the truth. "Do you know where Henry sent him to work? Do you know if Sheriff Cobb arrested him? Was there an accident?"

"Why are you asking me?"

"You keep telling everyone you're in charge of things around here."

"I don't keep track of hard cases like Richard once they leave the farm."

She backed him right off the edge of her porch. "I think *you're* lying. I think you *do* know something."

He raised his hand and Melanie flinched. "You watch your tone with me, girl."

The door opened behind her and Daryl came out. Silas lowered his hand as her friend moved up beside her. "SueAnn's taking a nap. We can talk now."

Silas pointed a thick finger at her. "This conversation isn't over."

Which part? Refusing to tell her what he knew about Richard? Or *threatening* to marry her?

Feeling sick to her stomach from the stress of yet

another confrontation, Melanie watched the two men head toward the main house. She walked around the side of her cottage and tossed the dead flowers in the compost bin. She winced as she lowered the lid and pushed up her sleeve to see the clear imprint of Silas's hand on her arm.

She hadn't grown up in a world filled with threats like this. Or maybe she had, and she'd been too naive, too consumed with loneliness and unfulfilled wishes to notice it around her. But she was aware now. She was aware of the violence and secrets, the missing friends and the lies.

She was aware of being watched. Right now.

Inhaling the smell of the fetid compost as she steeled her resolve, Melanie turned to see Tom Maynard, standing at the open door of his black pickup, watching her. Even from this distance, she could read the grim look on his face.

The man who'd no doubt witnessed that entire interchange with Silas wasn't the distracting Tom with the crooked grin and familiar hands. He wasn't even the friendly Tom with ties to Kansas City. That was scarysoldier Tom. The man who wore a gun and a knife and made her think she'd finally met someone besides herself willing to stand up to Henry and Silas.

He scraped his palm over his spiky hair and gave her a curt nod before locking up his truck and strolling across the gravel road to meet up with Silas and Daryl.

Why was Tom so fascinated with her?

And why did it unsettle her so much that he was?

Chapter Six

"Thanks." Melanie took the icy glass of lemonade from Deanna and scooted over on the porch railing at Henry and Abby's house to make room for the younger woman while they enjoyed the view of the men loading a truck in the parking lot. Now that the fishing dock and shops were closed for the day, they could relax. "I can use a cold drink."

"Not a problem." Deanna swung one long leg over the railing and then the other. Melanie buried her smile behind a long swallow of the cooling liquid. Deanna was risking splinters in her backside wearing denim cutoffs that short. But the daring change of clothing paid off. Roy Cassmeyer tripped with the crate he was carrying and stumbled into the loading dock on the back of the truck because his eyes had been glued on Deanna's legs instead of his destination. "What is the temperature out here this evening? A hundred?"

"At least." Maybe a little hotter from Roy's point of view. Melanie had to take another drink of the tart liquid to hide her amusement.

Melanie appreciated the shade as much as the raised perspective on the Jackson Trucking semi parked in front of the bakery and craft shop. Phyllis Schultz was checking off a manifest on a clipboard while the pot-bellied driver chowed down on a slice of pie beside her. Phyllis and her friend Bernie Jackson, however, weren't the scenery Melanie was watching from her perch. Her eyes had latched on to the men moving furniture and boxes of trinkets made by the craftsmen on the farm from the shop into the back of the truck for distribution to outlets in Falls City, Warsaw and other small towns around the lakes. Truth be told, she was watching one man, in particular.

With a square of white gauze and tape sticking out like a tattoo against his tanned skin, Tom was easy to spot. With Silas off on an errand for her uncle, Tom was easily the biggest man here. Although she couldn't hear the words, she read the teasing remark he aimed at Roy's klutzy maneuver, and heard the resulting laughter among all the men.

Tom had a clever sense of humor that had tempted her to smile on more than one occasion. How unfair was it that someone so ruggedly built could also tell her an adorable story about being a toddler who'd stripped off all his clothes on an outing with his mother to go skinny-dipping in one of the fountains on the Plaza in Kansas City? Although it was impossible to ignore that body, which was fit enough to handle the farm's physical workload—and strong enough to make a believer out of her when he'd shown her how to break a man's nose or strangle him with his own shirt if she needed to defend herself—it was that sense of humor he shared in their morning meetings at the infirmary that spoke to something inside her. Tom seemed to have made more friends around the farm the past few days than she'd made in the past year. Strange for a man who preferred the solitude of the night shift.

After dinner, it had been all available hands on deck to help Bernie Jackson unload boxes of groceries and paper goods from the back of his truck and get them into Phyllis's walk-in pantry inside the bakery before any of the food supplies were tainted by the heat. Now speed had given way to muscle as the men loaded the craft pieces into the truck for transport.

"He's hot." Deanna must be equally mesmerized by the show of testosterone.

"I bet they all are."

Deanna peeked over the top of her sunglasses, rolling her eyes at the joke. Then she pushed the frames onto the bridge of her nose and turned her gaze back to the men. Most of them had taken off their shirts in deference to the heat. All of them were glistening with sweat. "I'm talking about the new guy."

Melanie was surprised at the resentment that soured the lemonade on her tongue. She looked forward to Tom visiting her cottage for a check of his injury, then sharing coffee and some conversation about KC. She'd even had a few naughty fantasies about turning the impersonal contact they shared when he gave her those self-defense lessons into something very personal.

But that didn't mean she had a monopoly on his company. She'd given him directions to a quiet spot at the lake, and he'd promised to help her and Daryl keep an eye on SueAnn. Those were the kinds of things friends did. The way he touched her hair or brushed against her just meant the man had no sense of boundaries—not that he was interested in her.

She had no claim on Tom, but if Deanna set her

sights on him, then Melanie would have no chance at all to lure him over to the dowdy-cousin side. Not that she really wanted to get attached to any man here. Her plans to learn all she could about her father's death and then leave depended on her ability to stay unattached. Still, she heard a jealous voice inside her, and pointed out, "I thought you were into Roy right now."

"He's got muscles that Roy doesn't. Plus, he's got that whole bad-boy vibe going for him."

"Silas has that same bad-boy vibe," Melanie said. "And he wants to be with you."

Deanna dismissed Silas's obsession with a toss of her dark hair. "Do you suppose Duff dances?"

"How would I know?" With a stab of something that felt like an impending sense of loss, Melanie's gaze zeroed in on Tom's broad back as he hefted one end of a dining room table onto the truck. He released the table and turned to her. Even at this distance she could see his gaze narrowing, as if he knew she'd been staring at him and was wondering why. Melanie swung her legs back over the railing to face the house instead of those curious green eyes. Even with the cold drink, she could feel her temperature rising. This conversation was getting under her skin a lot more than it should have. "You call him Duff?"

"All his friends do."

Was Deanna simply repeating the party line Tom made with every introduction? Or had her cousin already gotten extra friendly with him? After working here for a week, was Melanie the only person still calling him Tom?

"I wonder if he's going to the Lake Hanover dance. I think I'll ask him." Deanna looked over at her and laughed. "Relax, Mel. I'm not making plans to steal your man."

"He's not my man."

"I bet he could be if you tried. He's really into you for some reason. But you know, there's such a thing as playing *too* hard to get. If you need some makeup tips, or want to borrow some clothes or— Oh, wait. Nothing I have would fit you, would it?" Her frown transformed into an excited smile. "We could go shopping in Falls City. I wonder if Duff would prefer you in a dress or tight-fitting jeans."

"Stop trying to be helpful," Melanie muttered.

When the front door swung open, she nearly leaped to her feet at the chance to escape the unsettling conversation. "Aunt Abby."

"Girls?" Her aunt peeked out the screen door. With her hair drawn back into a ponytail, Abby was clearly in cleaning and planning mode. "If you've had enough of a break, I could use your help. I need to get the decorations for the dance down from the attic. Since we're hosting it this year, I want everything to look just right."

"I'll go." Melanie handed her lemonade glass off to her aunt and went inside. She'd have volunteered to scrub the toilets if it meant getting away from Deanna's *helpful* observations about Melanie's shortcomings when it came to getting a man to notice her. But her mood shifted from thoughts of escape to the opportunity to do more exploring to see if she could find anything else that had belonged to her father. "What am I looking for?"

"Three boxes marked Independence Day," Abby called after her as Melanie hurried up the stairs. "I know it's past the Fourth, but I thought the red, white and blue would make colorful decorations around the barn. The boxes should be on the metal shelves."

"I'll find them." Abby turned her attention to Deanna while Melanie went to the end of the hallway and tugged on the rope to lower the attic stairs.

The air on the house's third floor was heavy and warm. Melanie picked up one of the flashlights stored on a shelf beside the opening in the floor and switched it on. When her beam of light bounced off the window in the back wall, she briefly considered opening it to get some sort of breeze. But if she was up here long enough to need a breeze to cool off, someone would surely start to question her disappearance and come looking for her.

She'd have to settle for quick rather than thorough when it came to her search for clues. Melanie spotted the boxes as soon as she pulled the string to turn on the bare lightbulb overhead. She carried them to the top of the steps one by one, using each trip to study the shelves, furniture and hanging storage bags to see if she spotted anything that reminded her of her father.

The box where she'd found the watch seemed to have conveniently disappeared, but she read every label, hoping something would draw her attention. Halloween. Deanna—High School. Rodeo Pageants. Melanie lifted the lid on that box and found several mementos from her aunt's career as a beauty queen. Although her winning crown and hat were displayed in a hutch downstairs, this box contained framed certificates from county-fair contests, along with a couple of photograph albums and some of the decorative tack Abby had used when she'd competed.

Something about the carved grommets that had once decorated a show saddle, and the pockmarked chain of a bridle with the bit still attached, reminded Melanie of the ring of black steel she'd found out on her father's boat. She tucked the flashlight beneath her chin and dug into her jeans to pull out the ring, holding both it and the chain up to the light. Not that the ring matched in terms of age or style, but the shape was similar. With the oblong protrusion on one side of the ring, and a tiny hole like the eye of a needle in the middle of that protrusion, it could be a link in some other type of chain.

If so, how did that help her? What would a chain be doing on her father's boat? The metal was new, and the boat hadn't been seaworthy for some time. This odd-shaped ring probably wasn't a link to anything. Why couldn't she just find a box marked Leroy Fiske or Don't Show This to Mel? Ending up with more questions than answers, Melanie dropped the chain inside the box and pushed it to the back of the shelf to pull the next one forward.

Pulling the flashlight from beneath her chin, she shined the light into the space vacated by the box. "What is that?"

Gauging the length of time she'd been up in the attic by the perspiration trickling into the cleft between her breasts, Melanie decided to risk a few more minutes of explore time. She twisted her hair into a rope and tucked it inside the collar of her T-shirt. It wasn't the box or the empty space that had snagged her curiosity, but what lay behind it.

A door.

A locked door, to be precise.

She pulled a couple of boxes to the floor to lighten the weight of the shelf, then lifted one corner slightly and angled it away from the wall. She froze for a second at the screech of metal across the wood floor. But there was no thunder of running feet at the noise, no shouts of alarm from below. With only the sound of her own excited breathing to keep her company, she continued her search. Melanie sidled behind the shelf to inspect the door that was barely as tall as she. She ran her fingers across the shiny steel hasp and padlock that sealed the door shut, wondering at the purpose of a new lock on an old door and who held the key to open it.

"What are you hiding in here?" And who was hiding it?

She tugged on the padlock, just in case the old door frame was brittle enough to break away, but the wood held fast. She needed a pry bar or a pair of bolt cutters to get inside.

Or a chain.

The fear of discovery hurried her feet around the shelves. She opened the box of Abby's souvenirs and grabbed the broken bridle chain. With a little seesawing, the links were narrow enough that she could slip the chain behind the hasp just where the door and frame met. She scratched some of the wood pulling it through. But if she could get a long enough length on either side, she could wind the ends around both hands and pull, hopefully forcing the screws to pop. Just a little…

A board creaked in the shadows behind her.

Melanie spun around. She was still alone up here, right?

Then she heard another creak. And another.

"Oh, damn." Someone was coming up the attic steps.

She tugged the chain from behind the hasp and hurriedly lifted and shoved the metal shelves back into place. There was no way to mask the noise, so she didn't bother shutting off the lights and hiding. But if she was quick, she wouldn't really have to lie about what she was doing up here. She thrust one box onto the shelf and picked up the other.

She froze a second time when a beam of light hit her back, silhouetting her head and shoulders against the box she hadn't quite slid back into its place.

"What are you doing up here, girl?" Henry's voice sounded more curious than perturbed. But all that would change if he suspected she'd been snooping around the door that someone had gone to a great deal of trouble to camouflage to keep inquisitive people like her away.

And then she realized she still held the chain in her hand. There was no way she could return it to the proper box without giving away that she had taken it. Pulling up the hem of her T-shirt, she stuffed it into the front of her jeans as quietly as she could before turning away from the box and praying she'd pushed it far enough onto the shelf so that it wouldn't crash to the floor behind her.

Melanie pointed her flashlight back at Henry, blinding him a bit to the mess she'd left behind her. "Aunt Abby asked me to get the boxes of decorations for Saturday's barn dance."

Henry dropped the beam of his flashlight to the boxes she'd set at the top of the steps. "Looks like you got 'em all right here."

"I didn't remember how many there were. I wanted to make sure." Melanie used the moment out of the spotlight to take several steps across the attic before Henry captured her in the beam of his light again. She pasted a smile on her face and shrugged. "It's hotter than blazes up here and I don't want to have to make another trip."

His brown eyes were unreadable orbs in the attic's dim light. "You sure you weren't pokin' your nose into things that don't belong to you?"

"This used to be my home, too." Melanie moved her arm over the bulging coil of chain tucked beneath her clothes. Hopefully, there were enough shadows in the room to mask the bulge of the contraband she'd been forced to take. "Anyway, could you blame me? I miss Dad. I miss the way things used to be when I was little and he and I were a family. I even miss the two of you being silly together—fishing together for hours and telling stories." She glanced around the rafters and walls, carefully avoiding the shelves and hidden door behind her. "You've saved things from Deanna's life and Abby's and yours—but not Dad's. Or mine."

Melanie curled her toes into her boots, forcing herself to stand fast as her uncle closed the distance between them.

"I miss Leroy, too. I don't have much left of him besides memories—and you. Once you could walk, you almost always tagged along with us." He surprised her by squeezing her shoulder. She couldn't help a tiny flinch, but she refused to give away the depth of her suspicions by running from him. "I'll never forgive myself for not standing up to the great-aunts and cousins who helped themselves to the baby quilt our mother made for you before she died. They took Grandpa's rolltop desk and all of Leroy's fishing lures he tied, and who knows what else that should have gone to you. I guess they sold them as collectibles and antiques. Your daddy left the land to me, and I've provided well for you, I think—but the rest of it should have gone to you. I'm sorry I can't change the past."

"So am I."

Henry pulled away to hook his thumb into the strap of his overalls, no doubt hearing the cynicism coloring her tone. "I was a grieving man. I had a baby of my own and a new little girl thrown into my lap who kept askin' for her daddy. If it wasn't for Abby and her strength, I don't know how I would have gotten through that time."

Melanie turned her head and blinked, hating the unshed tears that made her eyes gritty. She wanted to feel anger, not sadness. Crying wouldn't answer any questions about her father's death. "Maybe because his body was never recovered, I feel like I have nothing of his except that old wreck of a boat."

"Tell you what, I'll make some calls—see if any of those surviving relatives still have something of Leroy's. If they aren't willing to share, I'll offer to buy it for you." Didn't he look pleased with himself? Almost like he cared about her. "I'll make it an early birthday present."

But what kind of man lied to his niece, the woman he'd supposedly raised as his own daughter, and smiled about it? It was a lot easier to feel the anger now.

"What about Dad's pocket watch?" The heavy gold circle burned against her skin inside her pocket. "I remember him carrying it every day—showing it to me nearly every night. I'd love to have that back."

Henry scratched at one of his sideburns, frowning as if she'd spoken gibberish. "You asked me about that before. I told you it's probably at the bottom of the lake with him."

Liar!

Instead of giving her anger a voice or daring him to lie about the hidden door, as well, Melanie opted for escape. She returned her flashlight to its shelf and picked up a box. "I'd better get these down to Abby."

"I'll give you a hand."

Did she imagine he hesitated at the top of the stairs? She could hardly turn back to see if he was shining his light around the attic, checking to see if she'd found anything she shouldn't have.

Depositing the box in the kitchen where Deanna and Abby were working, she answered her aunt's thanks with a muttered "Sure."

"Melanie." She paused in the doorway at her aunt's voice and smelled the spice of her perfume coming closer. "Deanna tells me you need to go into town to shop for a dress for the dance." Great. Abby and Deanna had been making plans for her love life again. But as Melanie faced her aunt, the bridle chain shifted inside her jeans and started to slide down her pant leg. "We'll be going into Falls City on Thursday. You're welcome to come with us."

Melanie angled her hips to one side and hooked one ankle behind the other to keep the chain from sliding out onto the floor. If her hidden treasure was discovered, explaining why she had the weird souvenir would be awkward at best. At worst, it would make access to the attic to get a look behind that locked door impossible. So, instead of grabbing her pants and running, she stood there in a silly pose and hoped this conversation would end quickly. "I really have to go to this dance?"

"It would be an insult to Henry if you didn't. He's paying for everything. The festival is our last big celebration before harvest. I won't let you wear boots and an old T-shirt to a party." Melanie pressed her hand against her thigh as Abby moved closer to pull Mel's hair out of her T-shirt. "Maybe we can do something with this mess while we're in town, too."

Melanie nodded, backing toward the hallway. She backed right into Henry and nearly knocked the two boxes he carried from his hands. "Sorry."

"Why are you in such a rush?" he asked. "Did our conversation upstairs upset you?"

"What conversation is that?" Abby asked.

A quick escape was no longer an option.

Henry set the boxes on the kitchen table. "She asked me about Leroy again, where some of his things might have gotten to over the years."

"Is that so?" Abby's dark eyes were suddenly a lot less indulgent. "I told you that's a sore subject for your uncle."

"And it's not for me?" Melanie snapped. "I have a right to ask questions. He was my father. I want to know how he died. I want to know *why* he died."

"It happened fourteen years ago," Henry reminded her.

She swung around to vent her frustration on him, too. "And I still don't know anything about that night. Why would he go out so late? Was he meeting somebody? If strange things are happening around this place now, why couldn't they have happened fourteen years ago, too?"

"Strange things?" Abby took a step toward her. "What strange things are you talking about?"

Henry put up his hand, silencing his wife. "Leroy used to tell me all his plans. How he was going to turn the lake into a recreational area and give guided fishing tours to city folks who wanted to enjoy a bit of country living on the weekends. I saw the plans for the new house he'd wanted to build for Edwina, but after her death, he decided to stay in this house that Grandpa built. He told me a lot of things over the years. But not where he was going the night he died." Henry wasn't a tall man, but he was tall enough to force Melanie to tilt her chin to hold his gaze when he moved closer. "This is *my* home now. I built this farm and business and everything you see into the success we all enjoy. I gave you your own place. I sent you to school. I did everything a father would do for his child."

"You're not my father."

"I will not be talked to like this, like you think I know something about your daddy's death, like there was something unnatural about it, in my own home."

Melanie's pulse hammered in her ears as the rage swelled inside her.

Abby could probably read the heat crawling up Melanie's neck. "Maybe you'd better go back to your cottage, Mel, until your temper cools off."

"Maybe I'd better." And then she was pushing past Henry and hurrying out the front door…where she came face-to-face with Silas. Or rather, face-to-chest—with the strap of a rifle that hung across his back. And the man was wearing black leather gloves. In this heat wave? Talk about strange things. "Where have you been all day?" she snapped. "The rest of us emptied and loaded that entire truck without you. I thought a good man was supposed to lead by example."

Silas gripped the strap in one gloved hand and a thick manila envelope in the other down by his side. He didn't budge. He didn't have the courtesy to speak directly to her, either. "What's eatin' her?" he asked her uncle.

Melanie was summarily dismissed, without any answers, without any kind words.

She felt Henry's heat at her back. But he wasn't there to defend her or offer any explanation for her red-faced exit. "Is that the package I asked for?"

"Yes, sir." Silas held up the envelope. "Should I go ahead and give it to Mrs. Fiske?"

"She may be in charge of the books, but I'm the boss." Henry reached around Melanie for the envelope. "You go on in the house and have a glass of lemonade in the kitchen while I take care of some business in my office."

"Be happy to, sir."

Melanie had to step aside for Silas to enter. She kept right on moving, across the porch and down the stairs. Grabbing the snakelike chain winding its way down her pant leg, she ran across the yard, across the gravel road, up the sidewalk and into her house, slamming the door behind her.

Her steps carried her all the way to her kitchen table, where she braced her fists against the top and let out a feral groan of pure, pent-up emotion.

The rawness of tears and frustration burned her throat when the door opened and closed behind her again. A deep voice asked, "What's wrong?"

Chapter Seven

Melanie spun around and charged at Tom Maynard. "Get out of here! This is my home. There should be at least one place on this farm where I can have some privacy."

He caught her wrists when she tried to push him toward the door. "Hey. I'm not the enemy here."

"Let go!" She tried one of those crazy extrication moves he'd taught her, twisting within his grasp.

But he countered with a move he hadn't taught her, and the next thing she knew, he'd cupped her jaw between his hands and tilted her face to catch her tear-blurred gaze. "Talk to me, Doc. You bolted across that compound. What happened?"

She blinked until she saw concern and maybe the hint of anger in the hard line of his eyes.

"Melanie?" The soft growl of her name was her undoing. Fisting her hands into the damp cotton of his shirt, she walked into his chest, tucking her head beneath his chin and burrowing against his strength and heat. His arms went around her, anchoring her to him. He slipped his palm along the nape of her neck, lifting the weight of her hair off her back as he dipped his lips against her ear. "Did Silas threaten you again? You need to talk to me. At least tell me you're not hurt."

"I'm not hurt," she whispered between sobs. She flattened her palms against his chest and made a token effort to smooth out the wrinkles she'd put in his black T-shirt. But she couldn't quite bring herself to put any distance between them. "I'm sorry. I know I didn't ask…"

"You hold on as hard as you need to."

Melanie debated for all of three seconds before sliding her arms around Tom's waist. His shoulders folded around her like a shield. Hold on, she did. She dug her fingertips into the corded muscles of his back, and all those months of suspicion and lies and confronting the past on her own came pouring out with an embarrassing outburst of tears. She turned her ear to the strong beat of Tom's heart, focused her thoughts on the tender stroke of his hands on her neck and back, absorbed the heat of his body into the chilly isolation of her life.

The man had no qualms about touching and butting into her business, and right now she needed someone who wasn't afraid to crash through the protective walls she'd erected around her heart. Melanie couldn't remember the last time she'd been held like this, the last time she'd felt safe enough to cry. She couldn't remember the murmur of soothing little nonsense words or leaning against someone else's strength. She couldn't remember someone caring.

They stood like that for several minutes. Tom didn't budge, didn't retreat, didn't let go until the worst of the flood had passed and she sagged against him.

"You okay, Doc?"

Gradually, she became aware of the musky spice

of his skin. She realized those tree-trunk thighs and solid chest created an enticing friction against her softer curves. She freely admitted—to herself—that she was far more attracted to her new friend than any mere friend should be. But Melanie didn't want to risk alienating the one man she was beginning to trust. She'd already bawled her eyes out in front of him and left a damp spot on the front of his shirt. Telling him that the prickly, plain-Jane virgin of the Fiske Family Farm was developing feelings for him would probably send him running for cover, and she'd be alone again. In control of her thoughts now, she sniffled into his shirt and eased her death grip on him. "I'm okay now. But if you tell anyone I was crying..."

He leaned back against her arms still anchored at his waist but made no other effort to disengage from the embrace she'd forced upon him. He seemed oddly content to brush the long red waves away from her face, gently coming back to catch the strands that stuck to her moist cheeks. A crooked grin cut through the stubble that shaded his jaw. "I thought you didn't like secrets, Doc."

"Tom..." She started to protest the nickname she hadn't earned, but he wouldn't hear it.

"This secret's safe with me." He finally broke the contact between them and crossed his finger over his heart. "I promise. You are smart, funny and do not cry if anyone asks me."

"I'll hold you to that." Smiling with him eased the embarrassment of shaking her left leg and finally allowing the bridle chain to tumble out of her jeans into a pile on the floor. She didn't care how odd it must look. She picked up the chain and twisted it into a coil before setting it on the denim place mat at her kitchen table. Thirsty and hot after that crying jag, she headed to the sink to run herself a glass of water. She drank half of it and poured the rest of it over her hands to splash against her face and neck. "I'm not normally a crying type of woman. Hope I didn't embarrass you."

"I never mind the opportunity to put my hands on you," he teased.

Melanie felt her skin coloring with heat, but this blush was a pleasant sort of warmth compared to the feelings that had overwhelmed her a few minutes earlier. "You're relentless."

"I am," he admitted in a tone that was as refreshingly honest as it was unapologetically masculine. Tom crossed to the table to pick up the chain and identify it. "Did you steal this from Henry's house?"

"Didn't mean to." She dried her hands and dabbed her face with a towel. "But I didn't have a chance to put it back without being seen. Henry caught me snooping... Wait. Were you spying on me?"

"Were you worried about getting caught?" he questioned without answering her query. "Is that why you were running like death was chasing you?"

Melanie shivered at his particular choice of words. "That's a creepy analogy to make."

"I call things as I see them." He dropped the chain back onto the table. "I thought I sensed a look of distress when you were on the porch with Deanna. When we were done with the truck I wanted to catch up with you and see what was going on. What did the Barbie doll say that upset you?"

Melanie shook her head, unwilling to admit how her cousin's interest in Tom had gotten under her skin.

"Deanna thinks you're hot. She's hoping you'll ask her to the dance on Saturday."

"And that upset you enough to steal a piece of horse tack from your uncle's house?" He came over to the sink where she stood and leaned his hip against the counter beside her. "Should I be flattered?"

. This time, she couldn't help but smile at his teasing. "All right. So maybe I was a little jealous. Can't I have at least one friend here? Does she really need to have every man on the place drooling after her?"

"One, I don't drool for any woman. Two, I'm not interested in someone who doesn't get my jokes. And three…" He reached out and palmed the side of her hip, drawing her half a step closer. "I like some curves I can get my hands on."

"You like…?" The sensation of his firm grip branding her through her jeans stole her breath. Her blood raced with unexpected anticipation to the naughty parts of her, and she found herself hoping he'd do something more to excite, er, ease the heavy feeling in her breasts and the needy constriction of muscles between her thighs. She just needed a friend to talk to right now. She shouldn't be wishing he'd pull her even closer, right? She pushed away and put some space between them before her brain completely short-circuited. "That's not why I was running. I can deal with Deanna. Henry and Abby and Silas—they all upset me."

"Should I tell you that you're blushing again?"

"No." The heat crawling up her neck intensified.

"Well, I will tell you that I *am* flattered to hear you were a little jealous. I have no interest in your cousin, and I don't like the idea of anyone upsetting you." His amusement ended with his fingers sifting through the hair at her temple, tucking the waves behind her ear and smoothing the length of it behind her shoulder. "Now tell me what happened."

She explained her suspicions about her father's so-called accident. She told him about the door she'd found in the attic and her father's watch. With big, bad Tom Maynard staring down at her, his arms folded across his chest and his probing green eyes watching the nuances of her expression, Melanie told him everything that had happened fourteen years ago and the mysterious things that seemed to be happening around the farm now.

"And you think Henry, Abby and Silas know more about what happened to your father than they're letting on?"

"Yes. But they won't talk about it so I have to snoop around my own family to find answers for myself. Do you know there's no sheriff's report on Dad's drowning? At least nothing in Sheriff Cobb's files." When she didn't think she could stand that green-eyed scrutiny anymore, Melanie opened the refrigerator door. "You want something cold to drink?"

"I'll take one of those beers."

She opened two and carried them to the table. "I probably shouldn't be telling you any of this. I don't know who to trust anymore. They insult me or lie to me or just tick me off."

"Now who's the antisocial one?" Tom clinked the neck of his beer bottle to hers.

Melanie took a swallow of the bitter brew, savoring the chill running down her throat. "The more I push for answers, the more I get stonewalled. It's not like I can go to the authorities with my suspicions. Sterling

Cobb is Henry's best friend. And the sheriff before him was as corrupt as—"

"Wait." Tom glanced over his shoulder.

"—they come. Supposedly, all his records disappeared before Sterling was elected."

"Melanie—"

"Who knows if he even investigated Dad's death as anything other than…" Before she understood either his warning or his intent, he'd slipped his hand behind her waist and pulled her hips into his. "What are you—"

Tom dipped his head and pressed his lips against hers, stopping up her words with a kiss. Her lips parted with a surprised gasp and he angled his mouth to capture her bottom lip between his and then tease the top lip with the raspy stroke of his tongue. When the startled moment passed, her hand came up to caress the rough angle of his jaw and guide his warm mouth back to the tentative foray of her own lips. She heard a low-pitched groan from deep in his throat that triggered an answering need inside her. His tongue darted into her mouth to dance against hers, giving her a taste of hops and heat that was more intoxicating than the beer itself.

Part of her was aware of his free hand sliding something into his pocket, but even that thought vanished when that hand cupped her bottom and lifted her onto her toes. As Tom's mouth moved over hers, Melanie slid her fingers around his neck, learning and loving the tickle of beard stubble against her palm. The tips of her breasts pinched with excitement at the friction of his harder chest rubbing against hers.

She heard the front door close with a firm click. "Am I interrupting?"

The room spun around her as Melanie dropped onto

her heels and pushed away at Abby's teasing tone. But
Tom's grip tightened around her waist, preventing her
escape. What an idiot she was, giving in to a few com-
pliments and this embarrassing visceral attraction she
felt. But when she tipped her chin up to tell him exactly
what she thought of a man who would play on her loneliness and inexperience, she discovered narrowed green
eyes boring down into hers, warning her to do what?
Hide her confusion? Not feel hurt? Play along?

Play along with what?

She'd been so caught up in the need to share her frus-
trations and fears with a willing ear that she'd missed
the soft rapping at her front door. Now her aunt was
waltzing into Mel's kitchen with a sympathetic smile
and a basket of something that smelled fresh from the
oven. "I knocked, but no one answered. I was worried
about you, dear. I brought you some cookies Phyllis
just baked."

The bridle chain!

Realizing her fingers were still clutched in the front
of Tom's shirt, Melanie released her grip and scrambled
away from him, scanning the tabletop in a panic. But
the chain she'd taken from her aunt's souvenir box was
nowhere to be seen.

Then she saw Tom pat the front pocket of his jeans.
She glanced up to a barely discernible nod. He'd hid-
den it for her so her snooping wouldn't be discovered.
But why the kiss?

Suspicion warred with gratitude inside her, but she
couldn't very well confront him about his motives with
Abby in the room. So she turned to her aunt. "They
smell yummy," Melanie conceded, although right now
she had no appetite. "Chocolate chip?"

"I know they're your favorite." Abby smiled at her. "Think of them as a peace offering. I'm sorry if our conversation upset you."

"Conversation?" Abby considered that argument and cold dismissal a mere conversation? One that could be forgotten with a bribe of sugar and chocolate?

But with Tom's gaze tracking her every move, Melanie opted for a reply as sincere as she suspected her aunt's apology might be. "I'll get over it."

"Of course, you will." Abby set the basket on the table and unwrapped the red napkin inside to display the treats. "I see you've already found your own comfort. You two should share these." Abby stroked her fingers along Tom's forearm and winked. "Good work, Mr. Maynard. Our Melanie is a tough nut to crack. I'll see you both tomorrow."

Melanie nodded as her aunt sashayed out the door. It took her brain a few moments to switch gears from the surprise of Abby's visit to the surprise of Tom's kiss. She locked the door before she turned and leaned against it. "Good work? Pretending you're interested in me is *good work*?"

"If you don't want someone to know your secrets, then you need to stop talking. I heard her lurking outside and thought someone might be listening. That's not why I kissed you." When he made a move toward her, she crossed to the coffee table to retrieve the book she'd been reading. "It's not the only reason I kissed you."

"Save the sweet talk, *Duff*." She hugged the book to her chest, sending a clear message to keep his distance as she carried the book to the table. "And you wonder why I don't trust men coming on to me. I thought it was okay for me to..."

"I was very okay with it."

Despite the husky approval in his tone, she plopped the book down in front of her as her humiliation bubbled up into a temper. "I must be really entertaining for you to play with. You're no better than Silas. I'm just a means to an end. For whatever it is you're up to."

"Don't you dare lump me in with that jackass." Tom splayed his fingers at his waist, creating a formidable profile. "Yes, I kissed you because I didn't think you wanted anyone to hear the chat we were having. I was looking out for you."

"You couldn't tell me to shut up?"

"And have you argue with me?" He pulled the chain from his pocket and dropped it link by link onto the table. "How did you want to explain this to your aunt?"

"Fine. So I appreciate the save." Melanie gestured toward the door where her aunt had exited. "But now she thinks you and I are a thing."

"Is that so bad?" He shrugged, still trying to sell her on his sincerity. "Look, maybe you're blind, or maybe you're just ignoring it, but we've got some chemistry here. I'm not afraid to have your aunt sharing the news that we've got something going on. A rumor like that will help Silas keep his hands off you. It'll teach Deanna that not every man is into skinny, spoiled children. And it'll show these rubes around here that you've got backup."

Discouraging Silas from targeting her as a potential mate did have its appeal. And the notion of physical chemistry went a long way to explain these feelings she thought she had for Tom. But there had to be something in this for him. Plus, the fact that he, of all people—after she'd poured out her hurts and suspicions to him—was keeping secrets from her, too, grated against every nerve in her body. She picked up her beer and swallowed a cooling drink. "You think I need backup?"

"Everybody needs someone watching their back. Especially stubborn redheads who keep poking at mysteries no one wants to talk about." He circled the table, reaching out as if he wanted to touch her. "You've officially got me."

Melanie palmed the center of his chest and kept him at arm's length. "I suppose you expect me to have your back now, too?"

"I expect you to keep being my friend." He leaned into her hand, dropping his voice to a drowsy timbre. "But make no mistake, Melanie Fiske—I will be kissing you again. Things were just getting interesting when your aunt walked in."

Anticipation skittered through her veins at his matter-of-fact promise. Her fingertips curled into the soft cotton of his T-shirt. "Friends don't kiss each other like that."

"You don't want me to kiss you again?"

Her blush betrayed her before she could voice the proper protest. "You know I can't hide that I like you. Maybe because you're not one of them." She looked toward the door and the main house beyond. "Or maybe because you really talk to me and say what you think and..." She snatched away the fingers that were still clinging to the firm muscles of his chest and turned a pleading gaze up to him. "Just don't lie to me, okay? I want to be able to trust you."

"You can." Tom stepped back, his shoulders expanding with a deep breath. He crossed his arm over his chest and trailed his fingers over his healing shoulder.

The hesitancy of the man who was normally confident made her think he was reconsidering that assurance. "Look, Doc, there's something I need to—"

"My name isn't Doc. I may never be a doctor, so you need to stop calling me that." She cut him off before he could feed her any more bunk that would make her regret this shaky alliance they were forming. She pulled out a chair to sit. "Let's just finish our beers."

"And our conversation." He pulled out the chair opposite her, swinging it around to straddle it. "You think your father was murdered and the previous sheriff wrote it off as an accident?"

"Maybe. If he even reported it." Melanie picked up a napkin to wipe away the condensation beading on the outside of her beer bottle, wishing she could clean up this mystery just as easily. "If there's nothing to hide, why won't anyone talk about it?"

"Would somebody around here have a motive to kill him?"

"Henry. Most of this land was left to Dad, with a smaller parcel for Henry to farm. When Dad passed, Henry got all of it."

Tom braced his elbows on the back of the chair and leaned forward, his eyes narrowing in that questioning gaze of his. "Your father didn't leave the farm to you? Or at least name a trustee until you reached a certain age?"

"There wasn't any will. There weren't any papers. None that Henry could find—or so he says. I had some greedy relatives who took everything of value. I didn't think I was ever going to have anything that was my father's until I found this." She pulled the watch from her pocket and handed it to Tom.

He read the engraving before opening the watch and looking inside. "This was your father's?"

"I found it in a box in Henry and Abby's attic. I know it's Dad's because of the engraving. The picture is my mother. You can't really tell anymore."

He studied the smeared portrait before snapping it shut and returning it to her. "Did you ask Henry about it?"

"Not directly. But I've asked him more than once if he had anything that belonged to Dad."

"And?"

"He denied it." Melanie rubbed her thumb across the engraving with loving reverence before sliding it back into her pocket.

"You think Henry knows where the will is? Or was? If someone is hiding a secret, it's probably been destroyed by now."

"Maybe it's hidden inside that closet."

He nodded at the possibility. "Anybody else with a motive to kill your dad?"

"Dad was a pretty quiet guy, but I think he was well liked. From an eleven-year-old's perspective, I thought he was perfect." She remembered the loss she and Tom shared and felt her heart squeeze with compassion. "You probably felt the same way about your mom. When you lose someone you love too soon, it's hard to remember any faults they might have had."

Tom nodded. "Mom was a beautiful, strong-willed woman. She had to be to raise all of us and be married to a cop. I suppose she could have rubbed somebody's feathers the wrong way. Broken another soldier's heart over in the UK before she married Dad and emigrated to the US. But you're right. Everybody I knew loved her."

"Your father is a cop?" He'd told her that the Kansas City police had arrested the men responsible for his mother's murder, but he'd never mentioned his father worked for KCPD. "Did he help with the investigation? He probably wasn't allowed to, I suppose. The son of a cop, hmm? I suppose that's why you're so good at asking all these questions."

Tom picked up his bottle, shifting in his seat before downing almost half of his beer. "Have you ever seen anything illegal go on around here?"

Another question. Maybe it was his way of deflecting any topic that got too close to that pain deep inside him. Melanie took another drink, trying not to think about tasting the beer on Tom's tongue when he'd kissed her. Answering his question seemed a lot easier than forgetting that kiss or ignoring the urge to comfort him.

"Firsthand? Fights like that one you got into that first day. No one ever presses charges. We have an occasional shoplifter. If the person returns the item, they let him go. If not, that's one crime Sheriff Cobb is willing to handle." She added, "We get the occasional hunter or fisherman who's on the property without a permit. But Silas turns them over to the Conservation Department."

"I don't mind the odd jobs I do around here. But patrolling the grounds around the farm and lake every night feels an awful lot like I'm part of a private security firm. Only, instead of working in a war zone, we're protecting citizens in our own backyard."

Melanie couldn't argue with that assessment. "Things are different than they were fourteen years ago. Having so many people around that no one seems to care when one of them goes missing? Not to begrudge you your job, but who hires ex-military for farmwork and tourism? Sometimes I think Henry's running some kind of militia group and he keeps me around because he's planning a war and he'll need a medic."

"A lot of money goes through this place," Tom suggested. "The Fiske Family Farm is more like Fiske City. Houses, cross streets, businesses, boat ramps and fishing docks? About the only thing you don't have here is a motel for guests."

Melanie pushed aside the basket of cookies and pulled the bridle chain closer to her. She pulled the watch and mysterious black ring out of her pocket, too, and made a small pile of clues that made no sense. "I'd leave tomorrow if I could. But I'm afraid I'll never find out the truth if I do."

Tom set his beer on the place mat in front of him and reached clear across the table to pick up the black metal ring. "What are you doing with a gas block?"

Melanie watched him turn the object over in his hand. "You know what that is?"

"It's part of a gun. Looks like a .750 ml gas block. For an AR-15 or some type of automatic rifle. It channels the gas from discharging the weapon back into the barrel of the gun to power the loading mechanism." He held it up between his thumb and forefinger and looked at her through the center hole. "Where's the rest of the rifle?"

Melanie snatched it from his fingers, preferring her speculation that it was a link from a chain to his certainty that it had come off a rifle. "I found it. Just this."

"Where? Can you show me?"

Soldier Tom was back, the intensity of his reaction to the object frightening her just a bit. "Why do you care?"

"If I'm going to do a decent job with security, I need to know who all owns a gun on this farm. I need to know who has the skills to take one apart and put it back together. I especially need to know if there's somebody out there in the woods running around with a customized assault rifle."

"Customized assault rifle?" Now he was really scaring her. Silas had been wearing a gun like that when she'd seen him at the main house an hour ago. "It was on the *Edwina*. In a storage well. I didn't find any gun with it. Although…"

"What?" He was on his feet, striding around the table.

"Someone repaired the storage wells. The rest of the boat is falling apart, but the seals were watertight. Like someone was using them."

He pulled her to her feet. "I want to see that boat."

His suspicion blended with hers. "I can take you there tomorrow."

"Make it later tonight, when I head out for my security rounds." He brushed her hair off her forehead and tucked it behind her ear, easing the order into a request. "If you don't mind a late-night walk through the woods."

"I'll show you a shortcut," she offered. "Do you think it has something to do with my father?"

He shook his head. "That gas block is brand-new. It's the rest of the rifle that worries me, not knowing where it is or who owns it. I don't like surprises. It makes me think that I'm not the only thing out there in those woods at night who could kill someone."

Chapter Eight

Duff snapped the last picture of the *Edwina*'s storage wells with his phone. Since he was out of cell range here by Lake Hanover's northern shore, he'd transfer the photos over to his handler, Missouri Bureau of Investigation agent Matt Benton, when he met with him at the edge of the property later tonight.

The flash might have given away his location to anyone passing by, but that was the beauty of volunteering for Silas's night patrol. There were no passersby. Everyone on the farm had either turned in for the evening, or they'd gone into Falls City to spend their paycheck at one of the two bars in town.

A ripple of awareness pricked the short hairs at the nape of his neck. He *was* alone, right? He checked the tree line twenty yards away, and the wind-whipped surface of the lake beyond the weathered dock, to ensure no one was watching this detour from his usual route around the perimeter of the property. Judging by the fast-moving clouds blocking the moon overhead, a squall line was moving in—and any evidence he might be able to retrieve from the wreck Melanie had shown him last night would be washed away.

The electricity he felt must be a by-product of the

coming storm. Still, it wouldn't do him any good to stop here longer than was necessary. Dismissing that sense of being watched, Duff pulled out a handful of swabs and plastic bags he'd filched from Melanie's infirmary and wiped the interior of each storage well. The chances of picking up trace amounts of gunpowder, metal fragments or packing residue that could prove weapons had once been stashed here were remote. But if there was any chance he could prove guns had been here, he was going to take it.

What other reason could there be to upgrade the storage bins on the beached boat? The dock wasn't one used by tourists coming in to fish, so there'd be little or no traffic in the area, making the *Edwina* a perfect place to hide the guns until it came time to ship them. The old gravel road leading to the lake was rutted and overgrown, but a truck with four-wheel drive—or an ATV like the one he was riding tonight—could get through to haul contraband. Maybe he'd just missed a delivery.

Or maybe Melanie's interest in her father's death had prompted Henry or Silas to move their stash before she discovered it. That meant locating other places to hide the weapons—like behind the locked door in the attic that Melanie had mentioned. Since he hadn't wormed his way into Fiske's inner circle yet, getting a look inside the main house would be a challenge. Maybe Melanie could get him in. Or maybe she'd be willing to go back up into the attic and get a picture of whatever was behind that door for him.

If he could bring himself to risk both her safety and revealing his identity.

As Duff sealed the swabs in plastic, his thoughts strayed to the farm's resident medic. It hadn't been an

easy task to seduce Melanie over to his side. But he'd
been more intrigued by the challenge of getting to know
her than he'd been interested in any woman for a long
time. She had a sense of humor he appreciated, a sharp
brain inside her head, that amazing red hair and sweet,
soft lips that seemed eager to be tutored by the right
man.

He wanted to be that man. His body was warming up
right now in anticipation of taking up where that kiss
had left off, and the temperature had nothing to do with
the heat brewing that storm overhead.

But that woman had a burr in her britches. She didn't
trust anyone, and that stuck in his craw because he was
the kind of guy a woman *should* believe in. She had that
whole hang-up about men lying to her, and the fact he
was in the middle of a colossal lie with this undercover
assignment meant that whatever trust she was beginning to feel would fly out the window if she found out
he was really Tom Watson, KCPD detective, and not
Duff Maynard, ex-army sergeant.

That was the problem he should be stewing about,
not whether or not he could make an opportunity to
teach her a few more lessons in intimacy and seduction.
She'd turned the tables on him last night, transforming
a kiss meant to silence her into a real gut kick of desire. Audience or not, he'd wanted to pull her against
him and plunder her willing mouth beneath his. For a
few seconds, he'd forgotten that his interest in her was
supposed to be an act. Hell, he'd damn near confessed
that he was a cop when she'd made not lying part of
the deal to keep her talking about everything she'd observed over the past few months. Melanie had been
hurting, and he'd hurt for her. He understood her re-

lentless need to find closure for her father's death—be it confirmation that it was an unfortunate accident or proof of something more sinister.

He wanted to do something to help her. Launch an official investigation. Hold her if she needed another cry. Stand between her and anyone who dared to upset her. He wanted to strip off the emotional armor she wore like a Kevlar vest and show her just how brave and beautiful she really was.

A gust of wind reminded him that he was here to do a job, not to do Melanie Fiske. As much as his gut was telling him the woman needed help in her quest to expose the truth about her father's death, he had to ignore this unexpected attraction and ease his conscience by reminding himself that she'd needed someone to listen to her last night, and he had. He couldn't risk another mistake like the one he'd made with Shayla by moving this relationship into something real. Listening would have to be enough.

Duff jumped off the boat before glancing up at the lightning flashing through the clouds. Why did he feel Mother Nature was trying to warn him about something? He packed the swabs inside the saddlebag on the back of the ATV and paused for one more look around. He even took a couple of steps out onto the dock that rocked on the murky waves to make sure there wasn't someone on a boat in the cove.

Duff strode back to the ATV and climbed on. If there was someone out there watching him, he could explain his detour with the excuse that he'd heard or seen something and wanted to check it out. But spending too much time in any one place when he had miles to patrol would be harder to justify. The first drop of rain hit his cheek as he started the engine. He paused long enough to pull the green camo poncho from his saddlebag on over his head, checked to make sure he still had easy access to his gun beneath the poncho, then shifted into gear and rode into the woods, trying to beat the storm.

It was pouring by the time Duff reached the rendezvous point.

A black pickup was parked with its lights off on the overgrown service road by the fire tower that had been abandoned in the era of satellite technology. It wasn't noticeable unless someone knew to look for it. Duff shut off his ATV several yards back before approaching on foot.

The canopy of leaves and branches added another layer of shadows and secrecy to the site where he'd met Matt Benton four times in the past twelve days. Agent Benton's eyes must have adjusted to the darkness, because the truck door opened and he was pulling a black MBI ball cap on over his wheat-colored hair before Duff reached him.

The agent extended his hand to greet Duff. "Watson. You sure picked a hell of a night to hand over evidence for the lab. Everything all right?"

Duff nodded. Red-haired distractions aside, he was making progress on his investigation. "I confirmed that four handguns went out with a furniture shipment on Tuesday. All Glock 19s with the serial numbers sanded off. I marked one of them with an acid stain so we can track it. Nothing came in on the truck, though. Have you picked up any chatter from the bug I planted in Fiske's office?"

"The conversations are coming through loud and

clear at our listening post, although we haven't heard of any deals being made. Unless Fiske is talking in code."

Duff had considered that possibility, too. "He mentioned tourists chartering boats for guided fishing tours. Any chance those could be when the handoffs are being made?"

"Those shipments hit KC and St. Louis about once every other month. I'm guessing a new shipment will arrive shortly for distribution if it's not already here on the property."

Duff blinked away the moisture gathering on his eyelashes. "You got any other intel for me?"

Benton tucked the plastic bags Duff gave him inside the jacket he wore, and pulled out his phone in the same fluid motion. "I've got info on the names you gave me. Bernie Jackson's trucking business consists of two trucks—one driven by him, one by his brother-in-law. Everything looks legit, although it's Jackson's fifth try at starting his own company. Seems he's always hurting for money."

"Money troubles could be motive for helping Fiske and Danvers move the merchandise into the city."

"Maybe he's just a patsy and doesn't know what he's hauling for Fiske. We've got a forensic accountant looking into his records. I didn't want to raise a red flag, though, until we've got more from your end."

"My guess is they use multiple routes and storage areas, not just Jackson." Duff dried his fingers on his damp jeans before texting the pictures he'd taken of the *Edwina* to Benton's phone. "Did you find anything on that missing guy I texted you about?"

"Richard Lloyd?" Benton scrolled through the images on his phone to show Duff a couple of mug shots.

"He's in the system for the drunk-and-disorderly arrests you mentioned, but no felonies. He hasn't popped up on legal warrants or traffic stops anywhere." Benton shook off the water dripping from the bill of his cap and showed Duff an image of a newspaper photo. "I thought this was interesting, though. From the *Falls City Weekly* a year ago. Could be coincidence. But it's not the kind I like."

The mix of thunder, wind and rain forced Duff to lean in so he could hear everything Matt was saying. He looked at the picture of Richard Lloyd, decked out in head to toe camouflage gear, sitting on a tree stump holding up the antlers of the elk he'd shot. It wasn't the hunting prize that caught his attention, but the long wood stock of the Mauser rifle linked through the elbow of Lloyd's arm. Duff's blood boiled with the same anger he'd felt the day his grandfather had been shot. "The shooter at my sister's wedding used a Mauser." Did the fact that SueAnn's brother had gone missing have anything to do with the gun smuggling or the assault on the Watson family? "Can you blow up this picture and get a serial number off that rifle?"

Benton took his phone and returned it to his jacket. "The lab's working on it. If we can confirm it's an illegal firearm, and we can tie Lloyd to the Fiske Farm—"

"Then all I have to do is find him." SueAnn wouldn't be thrilled to learn her brother might be involved in the farm's illegal activities. But maybe it was time to talk to her and Daryl again to see what they could tell him about where Richard had gotten that rifle.

"You two done chatting about your investigation?" The passenger door opened on the truck and Duff's body tensed at the unexpected addition to their meeting. But his wariness rushed out with a smile as a tall, lanky man with dark brown hair climbed out, pushing his glasses up onto the bridge of his nose. "I assume time is of the essence here?"

"Niall?" Duff reached out to shake his brother's hand before pulling his middle brother in for a back-slapping hug. "What are you doing here?"

"Agent Benton said you asked for a doctor. I volunteered. Which arm is it?"

"The task force physician checked me out a week ago—gave me a shot of antibiotics." Although he pulled up the edge of the poncho, Duff couldn't resist poking fun at his ME brother. "I don't know if I like the idea of someone who dissects dead bodies working on me."

As usual, his brainiac brother refused to take the bait. Niall pulled a penlight from his crime-lab jacket and lifted the bandage covering Duff's wound. He prodded the tender skin for all of ten seconds before covering the cut again. "No signs of infection. Whoever put the stitches in did good work. They're ready to come out, though."

Duff experienced a rush of pride at the compliment to her work that Melanie would never hear. "How are the wedding plans coming with you and Lucy? You haven't scared her off yet, have you?"

"We're still on track for September, and we'll be adopting Tommy right after. I'm assuming you'll be done with this case by then? Every Watson is involved in the ceremony now." There was no denying the smile that relaxed Niall's stern countenance whenever he mentioned the spunky little brunette and the baby who had captured his heart. "Dad agreed to walk Lucy down the aisle. I'm counting on you to be the best man."

"I'll be there." Duff understood that, despite all their precautions, the longer the three of them were together, the greater chance they had of being discovered. But he was anxious to hear about his family. "How's Grandpa? I expect that's the real reason you're here."

"He's worried about you. Undercover is always a dangerous assignment. And once he heard you'd been in a knife fight…" Niall wiped the rain from his glasses before continuing. "I promised Dad and Grandpa I'd check on you personally. I'll give them a good report."

Duff had asked his brothers, sister and father, all members of KCPD in one aspect or another, to help as couriers while he was on this assignment—keeping him posted on Seamus Watson's recovery. "Is Grandpa getting any stronger?"

"His speech is showing a little improvement—Keir's fiancée, Kenna, has been working with him on that. But he's still not mobile like he used to be. Jane won't let Grandpa go anywhere without his walker." Jane was the live-in nurse their father had hired to take care of Seamus. "She doesn't want to risk him falling and rein-juring the muscles that are starting to regain strength. I know that's making him a little crazy."

"I imagine…"

Duff spun around at the soft squeak of waterlogged boots.

"We've got company." Matt Benton was reaching for his gun.

But Duff had already spotted the red hair behind the scrub cedars on the far side of the fire tower. He put his hand on the agent's arm, warning him to keep his weapon holstered, and turned to head off Melanie as she emerged from the trees. "Doc? What the hell are you doing here?"

"Why are they calling you Watson? This man's your brother and he's an agent? What's going on here?" She marched at them, her eyes shooting daggers with every streak of lightning that flashed through the sky. Her voice was a blend of hurt and accusation that cut straight through him. "I thought you wanted to be the only thing in these woods who could kill someone. Both those men are armed. You lied to me, Mr. *Watson*. That's the one thing I asked you not to do."

Duff turned to Matt and Niall before she reached them. "Go. I'll handle this."

Niall was reluctant to retreat. "Did we just blow your cover?"

He appreciated the show of support as much as he cursed his brother's refusal to do as he'd ordered. He pushed Niall toward the truck. "Go. Now. If she's out here, somebody else might be, too."

"Nobody followed me."

He ignored Melanie's reassurance. "Give my love to Grandpa. Tell him I'm gonna get the guy who hurt him." Matt Benton had already reached the truck. "Get me the answers I need."

Matt started the engine. "You're good?"

"I'm good." Duff turned to Melanie, assessing how much she'd seen and heard by the temper coloring her neck. Plenty, it seemed. He had to do some serious damage control or this case would go sideways fast. He was peripherally aware of Matt turning the truck around and driving off into the night. "We need to talk."

"Now you want to be straight with me?"

"We can't stay here." He peered into the shadows

around them, wondering if anyone had followed Melanie as stealthily as she'd tracked him. "Are you alone?"

"Of course, I'm alone. I'm always alone."

Duff got the accusation. She'd let him into her life, had formed a tenuous relationship with him, and now she felt betrayed. This alliance was going down the tubes fast. "I never meant to hurt you. If you weren't so damn curious—"

"This is my fault? You're the liar." She crossed her arms in front of her. "I'm not moving until you tell me the truth."

"I have my reasons…" None of them seemed good enough to justify the pain that darkened her eyes. Her baby-oil scent was intensified by the rain that drenched her hair and clothes and left nothing to his imagination where it hugged her shoulders and breasts. "You're soaked to the skin." Duff pulled his poncho off over his head and tried to wrap it around her.

But she smacked the plastic to the ground. "I don't need a raincoat. Who were those men?"

"My brother, Niall, and Missouri Bureau of Investigation agent Matt Benton."

"Who are you?"

He wasn't lying his way out of this one. He wasn't about to walk away from this assignment because another woman had blown his cover, either. "Are you on foot?"

"I need a name. Not that I'm going to believe you."

Melanie was ready to verbally duke it out with him, but the argument couldn't happen here. He clamped his hand over her arm and walked her into the woods toward the ATV, tightening his grip when she tried to squiggle out of his grasp.

"Let go of me."

"We have to get out of here. I can't have this location compromised."

"Fine." She climbed onto the back of the ATV's wet seat, hugging her arms around her middle. Was that for warmth? Or a wall she was determined to resurrect between them? "Let's go someplace where we can have a private conversation. I think it's time you told me the truth."

Chapter Nine

"Be practical, Doc. I'm not the enemy here." The rain soaked through the shoulders of Duff's T-shirt, cooling his skin. Given her soggy state, Melanie had to be chilled to the bone. She fought him when he tried to give her his poncho a second time, but since he outweighed her by a good fifty pounds, he forced it over her head, anyway. "It's not much, but it'll warm you up."

"You're stalling, Mr. Maynard or Watson or whoever you are." She tugged her hair free of the hood. Its wet, heavy weight slapped against the back of the plastic poncho. "Let's go."

Duff climbed on in front of her and started the engine. "You'll have to hold on to me." She muttered something that wasn't very ladylike before her fingers curled around the sides of his waist. Her grip tightened when the ATV lurched forward, but he could feel the rain hitting his back as she held her body stiffly away from his. After traveling about half a mile to slightly smoother terrain, he slowed the four-wheeler and glanced back over his shoulder. He raised his voice over the noise of the engine. "You were at the lake, weren't you? How long have you been following me?"

"I saw you sneak away from the compound. I thought

we could talk some more. About us." He felt a punch of guilt right in his gut. "There is no *us* happening, is there?" She sounded a little less angry, but the resignation he heard in her tone worried him. He'd never intended to hurt her. He'd never intended to care about hurting her. "Instead, I find you investigating Dad's boat without me and meeting with two men I've never seen before. You were using me to get closer to Henry."

"I don't care about your uncle right now. And I wasn't sneaking. I leave every night for my security patrol." He turned onto the path leading down to the old dock. "I've covered over five miles tonight. How did you find me?"

"I know all the shortcuts and hidey-holes around these hills. That fallen tree at the edge of the woods is hollow. I crawled into it while you were looking at the boat. Then I tracked the sound of the ATV. Once I knew you were heading north, I followed the creek bed. It's a straighter shot than the path you took." A streak of lightning lit up the sky, and he felt her jump at the answering clap of thunder. When she scooted a little closer, squeezing her thighs around his hips, he didn't mind. The physical connection between them seemed to be about the only way he could reach her. "Henry knows all the shortcuts, too, by the way."

That didn't bode well for maintaining his invisibility in these woods. "Does Silas?"

"Some. But I've known these hills years longer than he has. Plus, he's lazy. If he can't drive or ride his way to his destination, he sends someone else. He's not willing to cross Falls Creek, especially when it rains like this. Henry can barely get him onto the dock when they're loading or unloading the fishing boats."

"Sounds like he can't swim."

"Sounds like you're avoiding my questions." They hit a tree root that threw her against him, but she quickly scooted back to keep those few inches of distance between them. "Are you working for Henry? Buying off another cop like Sterling Cobb to cover up his secrets?"

Duff swiped the moisture off his face before steering the ATV toward the lake's edge. "I'm one of the good guys, Doc, even though, technically, I am a liar."

"At least you admit it."

"I'm part of a task force investigating the smuggling of illegal guns into Kansas City. We believe someone on your uncle's farm, if not Henry himself, is behind the gun trafficking."

She was silent long enough that he wondered if she'd heard him over the growl of the engine. But then she asked, "Guns? That's why you asked about the rifle part I found."

"That's why I was taking pictures of your dad's boat. Those refitted storage wells are a perfect hiding place to stash weapons until they can be shipped out."

"You think the guns are coming through here?"

"I know they are. I loaded a box of handguns onto Bernie Jackson's truck. The box was sealed, but I'm nosy that way."

Instead of defending her uncle or the place where she'd grown up, he felt a heavy sigh against the back of his neck. "That would explain a lot. I thought the secrets all had to do with Dad. But if Henry's doing something illegal… No wonder he's paranoid about keeping people he can control here." Duff pulled up beside the *Edwina*. He killed the engine and climbed off so he could face her.

"So you believe me?"

Lightning illuminated the clouds, followed by a thunderclap. Melanie huddled inside the poncho and snapped her gaze up into the sky. "You do know a clearing where there's water is probably the last place we should be in this storm?"

"The fiberglass hull won't conduct electricity. Right, Nature Girl?"

"Really? Another nickname?" But she nodded. "Only in salt water. Dad said it's the salt clinging to the hull that's actually conducting the electricity. This is a freshwater lake. We should be safe."

"I knew you'd have the answer. Come on. I'm tired of getting wet." He held out a hand he hoped she would take. He could tell by the tilt of her eyes that she was deciding whether or not to accept the amends he was trying to make. The next clap of thunder hastened her decision. She linked her hand with his and he led her to the upturned boat to take shelter beneath the gunwale. They weren't completely out of the elements, but the fiberglass frame protected them from the wind and the worst of the deluge. With his back against what was once the bottom of the boat, he sat on the edge of the storage well and pulled her onto his lap. "I need you to listen to me."

"I get it. You're some kind of spy. That's why you wanted to be my friend. You need me to get close to Henry or you think I know something about those guns. I don't." She leaned back against his chest, draping the poncho over both of them. "I understand the need to lie when you're working undercover. But friendship wasn't enough? Why did you pretend you were interested in something more?"

"Because I *am* interested in something more." Duff's

arms snuck around her waist before he realized she was snuggling closer out of practicality, not because she'd forgiven him. With that sweet baby scent of her wet hair filling up his nose, he had to close his eyes against the desire to nuzzle the shell of her ear. "I'm not a spy. I'm a Kansas City cop. You can't tell anyone who I really am or why I'm here." The irony of what he was about to ask wasn't lost on him. "Can I trust you to keep my secret?"

"Can I trust you not to lie to me again?"

Lightning forked from the sky, striking a distant tree. When Melanie jerked against him, he tightened his hold on her. "You got a thing about storms?"

"My father died on a night like this."

He felt her relax and adjust herself to a more comfortable position. He stifled a groan as her bottom nestled against his groin. She was seeking honesty and comfort, not the passion she sparked inside him.

"The violence reminds me of that night. Thunder woke me and I went to Dad's room. He wasn't there. I never saw him again."

He could imagine the little girl's terror had doubled when the one person she counted on wasn't there for her. Melanie kindled something far more potent than passion inside him. He hurt for that little girl who'd never gotten the answers she needed to understand why her daddy wasn't coming home. "I'm sorry."

Hugging her tight against his chest, Duff gave in to the need to taste her. He nosed aside her hair and pressed a kiss to the cool skin at the nape of her neck. Her answering shiver moved through him, stirring needs and desires.

When she tilted her head to give him access to more of that creamy expanse, Duff obliged by lapping up each droplet of water clinging to her skin, and lingering on the warm pulse beating underneath. "This is where I feel closest to Dad," she murmured, giving him the smooth line of her jaw to explore. "Life here was a part of who he was. We spent so many wonderful days on or beside the water." She tipped her head forward, pulling her hair over her shoulder and wringing it out beside her. "That probably sounds childish."

He was far too aware of his forearm caught beneath the weight of her breasts, and how badly he wanted to fill his hands with them. But this embrace was about rebuilding trust, and maybe even earning her forgiveness. So he pressed a chaste kiss to the base of her neck, cooling his jets. "Makes sense to me."

He watched the charcoal-gray water and whitecaps slapping against the bobbing dock as the lake churned with the storm's fury. Even as his body warmed with the woman sitting on his lap, his thoughts strayed back to the city and to memories that were equally turbulent. His grandfather's unconscious, bleeding body. A shooter disappearing into the snow.

He let his thoughts drift farther back in time to that fateful night when he'd seen his father crying for the first time. He wasn't entirely aware of his arms tightening around Melanie, but he was aware of when she shifted in his lap so that she could see his face. "What is it?"

He thought he smiled, but it was probably more of a scowl as those long-buried emotions surged inside him. "The night at the hospital when Dad told me Mom had been shot—she never even made it into surgery. I remember being so angry. I didn't believe him. I jumped in my car and drove like the crazy teenager I was to the convenience store to see the crime scene and police cars and blood for myself."

A hand on his shoulder allowed him to continue.

"I thought I could find Mom there—that Dad and the other cops just hadn't looked hard enough. That the woman in the ER was someone else." He pulled his gaze from the lake and his thoughts from the past to look into whiskey-brown eyes that glistened with tears. Duff caught one tear with his thumb before it joined the raindrops beading on her cheek. "I drove by that store nearly every day for years, always with some irrational thought that one day she'd be there." He caught the next tear, too, and found the pain of his past easing with Melanie's empathy. "Even though the place has been torn down and built into a drugstore, I drive by that corner every now and then. So, yeah, I get why this place means so much to you."

And then Melanie Fiske, the woman who was one surprise after another, framed her hands around his jaw and sealed her lips against his. Her kiss was as tender as it was bold. He didn't need to teach her a damn thing about what turned him on, about what touched his heart. The woman might be inexperienced, but she was a natural talent and Duff needed everything she was willing to give him.

He tunneled his fingers into her hair, tilted her head back and opened his mouth over hers, sliding his tongue between her lips to claim her heat. She slipped her arms around his neck and lifted herself into the kiss. Her breasts pillowed against his chest, their lush shape imprinting his skin through the wet clothes between them. His hands fisted in her hair as his body caught fire with the need to consume her caring and passion. Each foray of her lips, each skim of her hands against his neck and hair, each husky moan deep in her throat was like tinder to the desire burning through him.

He spread his thighs, giving the response she triggered in him room to swell behind his zipper. She dragged her hand between them, he thought to push him away because he was moving way too fast for her. But she brushed her fingers over the taut button of his nipple in a curious caress, and he groaned as his skin jumped. Perhaps startled by his eager response, she turned her mouth from his. "I'm sorry. I didn't mean to pinch—"

"It's all good. That reaction means I like what you're doing." He pulled her fingers back to his chest. "I *really* like what you're doing."

"If you're lying to me—"

He reclaimed her mouth, telling her as succinctly as he could that this was no act. She made the pain of his past go away. She made him believe he could trust a woman again, that he could allow himself to need her. She must have gotten the message. Because her hand slipped lower, and when she tugged his shirt from his belt to slide her hand against bare skin, he thought he might explode.

Duff moved his lips to the point of her chin, to her eyelids and the tip of her nose before coming back to claim that sensuous mouth. He battled with the bulky poncho to get his hands inside her clothes to explore her the way she was learning his body. Her cool skin heated beneath his touch, and she stretched to give him access to each delectable curve. He flicked his thumb over the straining tip of her breast through the satiny material covering it and felt her jump in response, just as he had.

"It feels good, doesn't it," he murmured against her mouth. She nodded, burying her face against the side of his neck. "How about this?"

He palmed her breast, lifting its bountiful weight in his hand. He skimmed the backs of his fingers beneath the stretchy material of her bra, capturing the pearled flesh between his fingertips and palm. Melanie gasped his name, tilting her passion-glazed eyes up to his.

"Say it again," he whispered, lowering his head.

"Tom." She pushed herself into his hand.

"Again."

"Tom—"

He reclaimed her mouth, savoring the rush of her response. *Incendiary* was the only word that flashed in his mind when he thought of the two of them together. Melanie didn't need to be experienced—she just needed to be his.

He'd just found his way to the clasp of her bra when he heard the snap of a twig.

Swearing against her lips, he pulled his hands from her clothes, shifted her against his side in a one-armed hug and reached for his gun.

Chapter Ten

A swath of dripping brunette hair swung into view before Deanna Fiske came face-to-face with the barrel of Duff's Glock. "Whoa!"

She backpedaled a step, colliding with Roy Cassmeyer when he came around the edge of the boat. "Now what?" Roy saw the gun, grabbed Deanna and reached for his own weapon.

"I wouldn't do that, son," Duff warned. The wary alertness pounding through Duff's veins didn't want to dissipate.

"No, sir." Roy put up both hands, leaving the gun strapped at his waist. "We didn't mean to startle you." He glanced over at Melanie as she straightened her clothes. "Or interrupt."

"You two alone?" Duff asked.

"Yes, sir." Roy must have realized his hands were still up in surrender because he pulled them down to his side. "Sorry, Mel. I never figured you... We were looking for a place to get out of this rain."

Duff grabbed Melanie before she bolted like a skittish colt and anchored her to his thigh as he lowered his weapon. "You know better than to sneak up on a man, Roy." He slipped the gun back into its holster and prayed that Melanie wouldn't say or do anything—either accidentally or intentionally—that would give away his real identity and purpose for being here. He inclined his head, inviting the two twentysomethings to duck under the rusted overhang of the old boat's windshield. "What are you two doing out in this mess?"

Deanna giggled as she squeezed in beside Roy. "Same thing you are. Mom will never believe me, Mel, when I tell her you're here, making out with Duff. And there I was, offering you pointers. You're always about books and work and 'I miss my daddy.' I'd never have guessed that you knew how to give a man a little sugar."

Duff thought he'd choke on the treacly sweet barbs Deanna was dishing out.

Before he could shut her up, Melanie pointed to the gun Roy was wearing. "Do you always carry a gun on a date? Is my cousin really that much trouble?"

Direct hit. Duff couldn't help but grin. Give him a woman with a brain and a backbone any day. He was already falling a little bit in love with Melanie's unique blend of fire and innocence, with her commitment and compassion. But he was proving to be a total sucker for that wicked sense of humor.

Deanna arched a dark eyebrow, maybe miffed that Melanie hadn't folded at her taunt. "Duff has a gun. Doesn't it make you feel safe to be with an armed man?"

"I'm on security detail," Duff reminded the skinny little flirt who needed to watch her mouth, especially those not-so-sly digs at Melanie.

"Uh-huh." Now that was a brilliant comeback.

Melanie straightened the hair he'd tangled in his hands, then splayed her fingers at the center of his chest. Was she taking over the charade of two lovers who weren't very happy to be discovered? "Is there a reason I shouldn't feel safe out here?"

"No, ma'am," Roy answered. "The security around the farm is really tight. Silas makes sure of that."

And yet the young man was still packing a gun. Did Henry think his daughter needed protection from something out here in the woods? From someone? Why wouldn't Duff have been informed of any particular threat to look out for, unless Henry and Silas didn't want him to know about whatever Roy was up to? "Where have you been?"

"Boat dock."

"Nowhere."

"You two want to get your answers straight?"

Roy draped his arm around Deanna's shoulders, glaring down at her. But, apparently, she couldn't take a hint. "I surprised Roy at the boat dock. He was out on the water. Barely made it in before the storm hit. I thought we could warm each other up, but he insisted we leave—"

"Shut up, Deanna."

"Don't tell me to—"

"There's a storage shed at the boat dock," Melanie pointed out. "You could have used that for shelter."

"That's what I said," Deanna pointed out, poking Roy in the stomach.

Roy straightened, about to spew some well-rehearsed line. "I wanted to get Deanna home. You know how spotty cell reception is out here. I didn't want Henry and Abby to worry."

"There's a landline in the storage shed," Melanie reminded him.

Roy's cheeks colored like bricks. "I forgot."

Duff needed to check that dock and the boat Roy had been on. He liked the kid, and would hate to discover he was part of the smuggling operation. But, whether Roy was innocent or not, retracing his activities tonight, before Silas or Henry knew Duff was onto them, meant squaring things with Melanie and getting the two lovebirds out of the way. "The storm's letting up." He pointed to the hills to the west. "Home and dry clothes are that way. You'll still get wet, but it should be safe to travel."

Roy assessed the sky, as well, before nodding. "We'll leave you two alone."

He reached for Deanna's hand. But she pulled against him. "I don't want to go home. I snuck out to see you, and you've been in a snit ever since I got here."

"I told you not to come see me tonight." Deanna stumbled when Roy tugged her to his side. "How am I going to explain to your daddy that you missed curfew?"

"They don't have to know what we were doing."

"We weren't doing anything."

"Whose fault is that?"

Duff stood, snagging Melanie's hand to balance her as he dumped her from his lap. "I've got a flashlight on the ATV. Take it—if you two don't mind walking. We'll use the headlight to find our way back."

"You won't tell Mom and Dad you saw me, will you, Mel?" Deanna asked. "Of course not. You snuck out to see a guy, too. I won't tell, either."

"Maybe you should get going," Melanie urged her cousin.

"Ooh, they want to be alone. Take your time. I know we will." Deanna giggled until Roy shushed her.

"Thanks, Duff." Roy grabbed the flashlight and pulled Deanna into the tree line with him. "You're embarrassing me. Now come on."

"Embarrassing you? You know, Roy, I know a dozen men who would love to—"

"Seriously. Can't you be quiet for two seconds?"

Once the bickering young couple was out of earshot, Duff turned to Melanie. "I'm sorry about what Deanna said. You don't need pointers from anybody."

Melanie pulled her hand from his, hunching her shoulders against the weather as she headed toward the ATV. "She wasn't lying about my lack of experience. You were hurting. I wanted to comfort you. I didn't really know what I was doing. It's okay, Duff."

He caught her hand and pulled her back to face him. "Uh-uh. Duff's a nickname I've had since I was a kid. I want you to call me Tom. Just like you have been. It's my real name." He moved his hands to clasp her shoulders and waited for her to tilt those pretty brown eyes up to his. "Thomas Watson Jr. I'm a KCPD cop, just like my father and grandfather before me. Only one other person ever called me Tom. But I'm getting used to hearing it from you. I like it."

The thunder had ebbed to a soft rumble. "We'd better get back to the farm, too. The last thing we need is someone sending out a search party for us," Melanie said.

Duff tightened his grip on her arms. "This isn't a part-time thing that you turn on and off when we have an audience. You never know when someone will be watching. If we're going to do this, then we have to work like a team. You have to commit to this mission twenty-four/seven."

"I get it. Didn't I cover for you all right just now?"

"You did great, Doc." Duff watched the rain hitting her freckles as she waited for him to choose his next words. "But I feel like you're pulling away from me. That something your twit of a cousin said is making you doubt me. What happened here wasn't any kind of training session or test run. I know other men have taken advantage of your connection to Henry—put the moves on you without meaning it. But other than the fact I lied about my last name and why I'm here, there's not a thing that's happened between us that hasn't been real. Think about the chemistry between us instead of the charade—"

"You don't have to sell me. I understand what team-work is." She pushed at the middle of his chest, and this time he let her move away. "I can do this. I *will* do this."

"It could be dangerous. If I'm found out, your uncle—"

"I know. He'll sic Silas on us. Or something worse."

He had a pretty good idea of what *worse* could mean. His stomach churned at the idea of anyone hurting Melanie that way. If it wasn't for that curiosity of hers, he'd never have put her in this position of becoming an undercover operative with him.

She needed to understand the consequences the same way he did. "Whether anything comes of you and me, I need your word that you'll protect my identity and the real reason I'm here, or I'm going to walk away right now and you'll never see me again." He caught a cord of her auburn hair between his thumb and forefinger and toyed with the curly wet silk before cupping the side of her neck. "I don't know how much more honest I can be. My life is in your hands."

After several long moments when he wasn't sure what she was going to say or do, she turned her cheek into his palm, sending a rush of reassurance up his arm to nestle close to his heart before she pulled away. "I'll keep your secret. I won't tell anyone about your meeting place by the old fire tower. I'll help you get the information you're looking for. If you're ever unaccounted for and someone asks where you've been, I'll cover for you." And then she broke the contact between them and backed away. "But you have to do something for me."

"You want me to help investigate your father's death." He nodded, already planning to do at least that much for her. He followed her to the ATV. "If anything on my case leads to information about your father, I'll share it."

"Can you get your doctor brother back here to take a look at SueAnn?"

"He's not that kind of doctor. Niall is with the crime lab." When she started to protest, he put his hand up to stop her. "Okay. Maybe Niall knows enough to help her."

"And you'll take me to Kansas City with you when you leave. Once I find out about Dad, I'll have no reason to stay here."

"You're already compromising my mission just by knowing—"

"Escape to KC or no deal."

The woman struck a hard bargain. Still, he needed her to maintain his cover and help him find the weapons. "All right. It might mean a hasty exit if things go south—as in drop everything and run when I tell you to—but I promise to get you out of this place when my mission's over. Deal?"

"Deal." She extended her hand to shake his.

But Duff wasn't ready to go back to being just friends after what they'd shared a few minutes earlier. Hell, he was still half-hard with need, and that soft, smushy place around his heart didn't seem to be toughening up any when it came to the stubborn redhead. So he took hold of her hand and helped her climb on to the ATV seat behind him. "Want to check out the boat dock with me? Roy might have been running an errand for Henry—setting up for a drop-off, making a delivery."

"With Deanna there? Henry wouldn't risk her safety."

"It sounds as though their meeting wasn't planned. Maybe Roy wasn't expecting to find Deanna there."

"Or she wasn't expecting to find him and covered with her usual sexy shtick. Is she smart enough to be a part of this?" Maybe Melanie's armor wasn't completely back in place, either, because, instead of clinging to the sides of his belt the way she had on the ride here, she wrapped her arms around his waist.

Duff allowed himself a few seconds to relish the gesture of trust before he started the engine and headed toward the gravel road. "You think that bimbo routine is an act?"

"I wouldn't have thought so, but so many things have changed around here lately, I can't be certain."

"Wouldn't be the first time someone used an innocent to help mask his crimes, either. Look at meth labs in suburban family homes or children used as suicide bombers."

"There really *is* something awful happening here."

"Something awful enough that innocent people in my city are being hurt because of it. People in my family are being hurt."

"Your family?"

"KCPD believes a gun smuggled through here was used to shoot my grandfather." The rain had filled the ruts with water, forcing Duff to slow his speed so they wouldn't slide into a ditch. "Grandpa was enjoying my sister's wedding the day he got shot. His spirit's tough, but his body is fragile. He may never be the same."

"He survived?"

Pain, anger and a burning need for retribution filled his soul, just like the rain soaking the earth. "Barely."

"I'm sorry." Melanie's arms squeezed around his waist, and that dark desperation inside him seemed to dissolve along with the storm. "I'll show you a way to the boat dock without taking the main road."

"Thank you."

"For showing you a shortcut?"

"For keeping my secret."

He turned in the direction she'd indicated, ducking his head to dodge the low-hanging branches that masked the path beside the lake. Other than telling him where to turn, Melanie was silent for another quarter mile before she spoke again. "Who called you Tom?"

"My mom."

Her grip around him loosened and she sat back. "Then maybe I shouldn't."

Duff grasped her hands to keep them linked together. "I never asked anyone else to."

"Tom, I—"

"Yeah. Just like that." Hearing his name in that husky tone was pretty heady stuff for a man who'd sworn off relationships. He stopped the ATV and let the engine idle while he turned halfway around on the seat. "Maybe you've been right all along about the nickname thing. When you say *Tom* it sounds like you're not as mad at me as you thought you were."

"I'm not mad. I just… I wanted you to be real."

"Trust me, Doc, what I'm feeling for you is real. I thought I had this place all figured out—that you were all part of some country-bumpkin mafia. I never figured on someone like you being here. You're a distraction I wasn't planning on."

"I'm no kind of distraction." She laughed, but it was a self-deprecating sound that made him a little ticked off at Deanna and the people who had made her feel that way.

"Don't sell yourself short, Doc, er, Melanie."

"It's okay. I'm getting used to hearing you call me that, too."

"You will be a doctor one day. If anyone can come from where you've been and earn all those degrees, you can. I'd bet money on it." He loved seeing her blush at the compliment. He'd never known a woman so responsive to a word or touch. He prayed to God he was putting his faith in the right woman this time.

He bent his head to capture her wet lips in a kiss. When she reached up to cup his cheek and return the kiss, Duff's eyes drifted shut, and he drank in her sweet scent and eager mouth, knowing he was falling harder and faster than a smart undercover cop should. There was confusion in her big, brown eyes that matched the emotions roiling inside him when he pulled away. But there was a sound of satisfaction in her sigh that echoed through him, calming his doubts…for the moment. He released her and repositioned himself on the seat before shifting the engine into gear. "You got my back on this?"

"I've got your back." She rested her cheek between his shoulder blades and held on tight as they sped around the lake.

MELANIE WAS RIGHT about the shortcut. In a matter of minutes, they popped out of the trees onto a man-made beach and approached the modern aluminum boat dock along the edge of the water. After parking the ATV, Duff pulled out his cell phone and switched it into flashlight mode. He followed Melanie up the rocky embankment and slipped beneath the metal railing to reach the stairs that led up to the parking lot and storage shed or down to the boathouse and covered dock where two power boats bobbed up and down in the slips where they'd been tied.

Duff took the lead and headed down the stairs. "Do you know which boat Roy would have been on?"

"Probably the *August Moon*. We usually rent the *Ozark Dreamer* out to tourists."

Unlike the quiet cove where the *Edwina* was beached, this place was all about modern amenities. There were four slips in total, one rigged for docking power skis. There were canoes stacked on racks inside, too, along with equipment cabinets and life vests. Melanie opened a toolbox sitting on one of the shelves and pulled out a flashlight.

"I think this is where Deanna was waiting for Roy." She knelt beside a wadded blanket and an overturned cooler and pulled out a can of soda pop, indicating the contents before setting it upright and closing it again. "Looks like they left in a hurry. I understand wanting to get away from the water with the lightning—but why not grab their stuff and go up to the storage shed to wait out the storm?"

"It seemed to me like Roy was a lot more anxious to leave than she was."

"What are we looking for?" Melanie asked, poking around inside the canoes and equipment.

Duff walked out along the gangway and peered inside the *August Moon*. "Guns, ammo and cash would be the obvious thing, but that's probably too easy. Anything that looks out of place. Storage compartments that look like they've been recently disturbed." Duff spotted a trio of scratch marks on the aft fishing deck of the *August Moon*, and climbed on board for a closer look. "Tracks along the shore, in case Roy hauled something off the boat."

They explored the area for several minutes. Duff snapped pictures of the scratch marks and a smear of some gelatinous goo on the gunwale that hadn't been washed away by the rain or the waves. Fish guts? He found a deeper gash on the fishing deck itself, as if someone had tried to butcher a fish or cut something loose.

He heard a soft gasp before Melanie called out to him. "Tom? I found something."

Duff vaulted over the side of the boat and hurried to the last slip on the dock. He swore like the man's man he was when he saw the decomposing dead body caught halfway beneath the dock, bobbing among the cattails.

He reached for Melanie, palming the back of her head and turning her into his arms, away from the nibbled-on bones and bloated, peeling skin wrapped in a long black coat. "Ah, hell, Doc. I never wanted you to see something like this."

The leather belt binding the arms to the body, and the shreds of rope tied to the wrists and ankles, indicated that this was no accidental drowning. Although Duff and the task force had suspected that the people involved in the gun smuggling were capable of murder, he hadn't expected a dead body to be the type of evidence he'd find.

Melanie's fingers clung tightly to the front of Duff's soggy T-shirt, but short of wrestling her to the ground, she was determined to look at the distorted body. "He's been dead awhile, hasn't he?"

"I'm no forensics expert like Niall, but I'm guessing the body has been submerged for a couple of months, give or take." He wondered at the marks he'd seen on the back of Henry's boat. Had Roy discovered the body, too, and tried to hide it from Deanna? Or were those cut marks and the fraying ropes indicators that Roy had been trying to dispose of the body? "The storm must have stirred it up from the bottom of the lake."

Melanie's grip on him eased and she turned her light back to the boat he'd been inspecting. "Or it got caught on the *Moon*'s propeller." As the dock bobbed with the waves, the boat and lift rose above the water, giving him a glimpse of frayed rope caught in the propeller blades.

"Hold that light steady if you can." If she was willing to play detective with him, and it kept her focus off the dead body, Duff was going to put her to work. While she held the light, he got down on his stomach and took several pictures before plucking a few rope strands free and stuffing them into one of the plastic bags left in his pocket. Maybe Roy had accidentally snagged the body and had tried to cut it free. "The rope looks like a match."

"You should take pictures of the body, too. Before he floats away—" she cringed "—or falls apart."

"Wait for me in the boathouse while I get it up on-shore." With her father's drowning, this was probably the last crime scene she needed to be around.

But either that endless curiosity or red-haired stubbornness had kicked in. "Don't be such a tough guy. I can help."

"It's not a tough-guy thing. I'm trying to look out for you."

"There'll be cadavers in med school."

Not like this one, he'd wager.

Maybe speed was the kindest thing he could do for her at this point—get this awful task out of the way so that she could move on to something less gruesome. He pointed to the poncho she was still wearing. "We'll use that."

While she stripped off the poncho and spread it on the ground near the dock, Duff waded into the water and carried the body to the shore. He set it on the poncho and pulled one corner over the poor guy's ravaged face so Melanie wouldn't have to look at it. While he checked pockets for a billfold and identification he suspected he wouldn't find, she pointed to a hole in the chest of the long, black duster that was holding the main part of the body together. "That's a bullet hole, isn't it? Right through his heart."

"Looks like it."

She pointed to the belt that had been tied, not buckled, around his torso and arms. "If this is his belt…" Before he could stop her, she touched the two ends of the swollen leather square knot. "This hasn't been chewed on. It's been cut. Where's his belt buckle?"

A really bad feeling washed over Duff, rocking him back on his heels. His brother Keir had identified their grandfather's masked shooter by a one-of-a-kind fancy belt buckle in pictures he'd taken during the ambush at the church. And the man Duff had chased across the roof had worn a long black duster. If the gun had come from the Fiske farm… If this man was the killer hired to destroy his family…

"Tom?" He snapped his gaze over to Melanie, startled from his thoughts by that sweet husky voice. "We have to report this," she said.

He needed to talk to his family. Pronto. This could be the connection they'd been looking for. Duff raised his phone up to the moonlight peeking through the lingering clouds, hoping to see bars of connectivity here. "One of us will have to stay with the body while the other gets to a phone."

"There's one in the shed."

"I'd prefer to use a secure line that won't show up on your uncle's phone bill."

"You can't call Agent Benton. That'd give you—us— away if he and a crime scene team showed up here."

"I don't want to give anyone a chance to move it. We're still out of cell range. I need to get back to the fire tower or find a private spot in one of the main buildings to notify my team." He pushed to his feet, climbing a few steps up the embankment. "I need you to call Sheriff Cobb. You can use the shed phone for that."

"What if he's part of the smuggling operation? What if Cobb already knows there's a dead body in the lake and hadn't planned to do anything about it?"

"I'll get word to the task force. They can keep an eye on Cobb and whatever he does or doesn't do."

But Melanie wasn't listening. "It's hard to be sure, but this coat looks familiar."

"You know this guy?" Duff pocketed his phone and jumped down to the shoreline behind her. There wasn't enough of a face to identify, and the fingerprints would be long gone. Maybe Melanie had spotted something he hadn't.

"SueAnn's brother had a coat like this. It would have been cold enough to wear one when he went missing. You don't suppose…" Now that he was done taking pictures, Melanie pulled the edges of the poncho over the dead man's body. "This will kill SueAnn. With her blood pressure, I don't know if she could handle the stress of finding out Richard's dead."

"If it *is* him. Let's not jump to conclusions. We have to identify him first." Duff watched her rise to her feet and stumble back to the edge of the dock. Her normally telegraphic skin was as pale as the moonlight. Forgetting the potential link to his grandfather's case, his task-force mission and the urgency of getting word to his family, Duff knelt beside her to peer into her eyes. "Doc? What's wrong?"

She dragged her gaze from the corpse back to Duff. "Is this what happened to my father, too?"

Chapter Eleven

Everyone Melanie knew from the farm and Falls City seemed to be gathered near the fishing dock as the sun came up. Everyone except for Tom, who'd left to place a call to Agent Benton, and SueAnn, who was dealing with a lack of sleep and explicit instructions from Melanie not to be disturbed.

Although she was praying that the dead body down on the shore wasn't Richard Lloyd, Melanie had a bad feeling that Mother Nature had uncovered one secret that the farm had been hiding. Yet, with one revealed, a dozen more seemed to hover in the air around her.

Roy and Deanna sat in his pickup at the top of the embankment, looking as miserable as Melanie felt. Her own jeans and shirt were still damp, and sticky now that the sun was warming the air. Apparently, Roy had admitted to snagging the body on the boat. That explained why he'd been so anxious to get Deanna away from the fishing dock. But why hadn't he reported it? And why had he been out on the lake so late in the first place? And if this did prove to be murder, would Henry or whoever was responsible make Roy the fall guy for the crime?

Henry was on the dock with Silas and Sterling Cobb.

Silas seemed more concerned about the dock bobbing beneath him than with the hushed conversation. His fist was wrapped in a haphazard bandage that was stained with dried blood. The rifle she'd seen him wearing at the house was missing from his shoulder, as were the gun and knife that were usually strapped to his waist. Had she ever seen the bald man unarmed before? Did his weapons have anything to do with the bullet hole in the dead man's chest, or the ropes and belt binding the corpse's limbs? And would the sheriff appreciate her pointing out that he'd been wearing leather gloves in July, possibly hiding that injury to his hand the night before last? She had a strong feeling that Silas wouldn't.

And what about the bespectacled paramedic who'd shown up with the coroner's van and was helping a deputy and another paramedic zip up the body and load it onto a gurney? Although it had been dark and rainy last night at the old fire tower, she was certain that the dark-haired man with a ball cap pulled down low over his forehead was Tom's brother. She didn't think she should strike up a conversation with him, but as she glanced around the crowd of onlookers standing behind the yellow crime-scene tape, she wondered if Tom knew his brother was here—if there'd be a surprised recognition between them that would be hard to hide from Henry, Silas or the sheriff.

And where was Tom, anyway? Clearly, he'd had time enough to contact his task-force handler and his brother. She'd told the sheriff that she and Tom had been at the dock looking for shelter and privacy when she'd discovered the body and called it in, and had let Sterling Cobb fill in the blanks about why they'd been together and what they'd needed privacy for.

How far would that kiss-and-grope session at her father's boat have gone if Roy and Deanna hadn't interrupted them? Had she ever let down her guard like that with a man before? Had she ever felt that crazy sort of hunger, that connection to another person's soul?

She'd wanted to stay mad at him for lying to her. But he'd touched her heart, instead, sharing the story about coping with his mother's death, truly understanding her pain. She'd meant her kiss to console him, to promise she'd never betray to anyone those painful emotions they shared. But that chemistry he mentioned had flared between them, instead, and getting closer—learning his body, absorbing his strength, feeling his caring surrounding her—suddenly felt like the only way she could ever feel normal or safe again. She'd been ready to straddle Tom's lap and give him access to whatever he wanted from her, so long as he never let her go.

Until Roy and Deanna's arrival had reminded her of the reality at hand. Storms and secrets. Lies and danger. Falling in love with Tom Watson had no place in her world.

Melanie shivered. *Falling in love?* Is that what was happening to her?

Tom had comforted her, argued with her, made her laugh and gotten so far inside her thoughts that she was having a hard time reconstructing the defensive barriers that had sustained her these past several months. She hadn't needed anyone for a long time. But she needed him.

But was his tender concern for her really about *her* and not a fear that she'd reveal he was working undercover?

Despite her confused feelings, she wanted Tom to

be here. Except for the undercover medical examiner, whom she didn't think she should talk to, she felt alone right now. And ever since Tom had barged into her life, become her friend and forced her into an alliance that could get them both killed, the one thing she hadn't felt was alone.

"Melanie, dear?" She startled at the arm around her shoulder. Aunt Abby's hug lasted about as long as it took Melanie to identify the older woman. "My goodness, your clothes are still wet." Abby rested the back of her knuckles against Melanie's cheek in a display of maternal concern. "You'd better come back to the main house with me so you can change out of these things before you catch cold."

She probably did look like a drowned rat with her soggy clothes and hair that kinked and expanded as it dried in the humid air. But a shower and dry clothes and her aunt's momentary compassion weren't going to make the unsettling fact that there'd been a murder in their little utopia go away. "I have to stay. I found the body. The sheriff said he may have more questions for me."

"Sterling will wait if your uncle asks him to."

No doubt. "I'd rather get it over with."

"I understand you were out here last night with Duff. Awfully late, from what I hear." Melanie couldn't help but slide her gaze up to the parking lot where Roy and Deanna were parked. One or both of them had tattled. Probably to divert attention from their own late-night return. "Where's your new boyfriend this morning? I'm sure Sterling will want to interview him, too."

"Boy—" Melanie clamped her mouth shut to stifle her protest. A couple? Lovers? Was that the story Tom

expected her to tell to anyone who asked? The dock
rocking beneath her feet wasn't the only thing throwing her a little off-kilter this morning. "I'm a grown-
up. I don't have to account for where I spend my time.
Or who I spend it with."

"Being a grown-up and understanding what a man
wants from a woman are two different things."

Melanie bristled at what sounded like the beginning
of a birds-and-the-bees lecture. "I understand Tom well
enough. He likes being out in nature. And I like being
with him." That wasn't a lie. She *could* do this. "He en-
joys the quiet of the night."

"Last night was anything but quiet."

In more ways than one. Melanie swayed as the wake
from a Conservation Department powerboat searching
the area rolled to the shore beneath them. "We couldn't
exactly plan the weather, now, could we?"

"That explains why you were at the lake last night."
Abby squeezed Melanie's forearm, practically tutting
her tongue against her teeth in an expression of pity
and concern. "But where has Duff gotten off to now?
Leaving you to deal with this unfortunate mess all on
your own. If he really cared about you, he'd be here to
support you."

So the sheriff's questions could wait, but not her
aunt's? Melanie took a couple of steps toward the edge
of the dock to watch Tom's brother and the deputy carry
the body bag up the stairs to the parking lot. "Look at
all these people. He hates crowds."

But Abby wouldn't let her subtle accusations against
Tom drop. "You don't find it strange that he ducked out
on you like this? Do you know where he is right now?
How do you know he didn't kill that man?"

She whirled around on her aunt. "Because *that man* has been dead a lot longer than the time Tom, er, Duff, has been here."

"You don't have to defend me, sweetheart. I'm right here." The deep, growly voice behind her was like music to her ears. Tom wrapped a big flannel shirt around her and briefly clasped his hands over her shoulders. "I couldn't find a jacket so I grabbed this out of my bag. Hope it doesn't make you too hot."

"Thanks." Fighting the urge to fall back against his chest and let him deal with her aunt's sniping, Melanie summoned the remnants of her own strength. Although flannel wouldn't have been her first choice for something dry to cover up with, she was pleased that he'd thought of her discomfort. Or maybe coming back with one of his big shirts was just the excuse he was using to cover his absence. She discovered the motive didn't matter. After rolling up the long sleeves, she snuggled into the oversize shirt. The brushed cotton smelled like Tom, and she found its warmth and scent as reassuring as the brush of his hands on her shoulders had been. Masquerade or not, she breathed a tiny sigh of relief, knowing she was no longer alone with a gathering full of potential enemies.

When she turned to truly thank him, she realized he was wearing a different T-shirt. His jeans were dry, too. "You changed."

"The clothes I had on when I fished John Doe out of the lake were pretty gross. I talked to one of the guys with the coroner's van and gave the stuff to him." His brother, Niall, she assumed. So part of the delay in returning to her had been about him being a cop doing his job. "I thought they'd want to bag it since there might be some evidence from the corpse on it, too."

"Bag it? Gross? Corpse?" Abby hugged her arms around her waist. "You two may have hearts of stone, but I can't deal with this. Especially if he turns out to be Richard. Whatever will we tell SueAnn?" She turned to the three men still conversing on the dock beside the boat. "Henry, dear, could you drive me back to the house?"

"I'll do it, sir," Silas volunteered. He pushed past the sheriff, touching his injured hand to Abby's elbow, no doubt anxious to get as far from the water as he could.

"I'll take care of my wife, Silas," Henry declared, motioning the big man to stay put. He handed the sheriff a paper evidence bag that a civilian probably shouldn't have been holding in the first place and moved between Silas and Abby. "You and Sterling make all this go away. Understand? Dead bodies are bad for business."

"Yes, sir."

Henry's gaze bounced off Melanie and centered on the top of the hill. He leaned back and snapped another order at Silas. "Tell Roy to report to my office as soon as the sheriff is done with him. And make sure my daughter gets safely home."

"We'll take Deanna home with us," Abby announced.

Resigned to being their messenger boy for the time being, Silas latched on to the nearest post as the dock shifted with Henry and Abby's departure. But Melanie was less amused by his anxiety as she focused in on the plastic window in the bag Sheriff Cobb was holding. She could see the stiff, mutilated belt that had been tied around the victim's body. She wondered if he'd given any thought to the odd piece of evidence.

"Sheriff, did you look at that belt?" She pointed to the distorted leather than had been sawed through. "Don't you find it strange that the body was tied up with it?"

Sheriff Cobb shrugged. "Tool of opportunity, I imagine."

"But why remove the buckle?"

"Maybe this is a robbery gone bad. I remember that shiny silver thing Richard used to wear."

"So you think it's Richard, too." She found her courage enhanced by Tom's presence behind her. "We don't know that yet, do we?"

Silas muttered something under his breath. "Maybe the buckle just got in the killer's way. It's probably down at the bottom of Lake Hanover."

"What did the buckle look like?" Tom asked.

"Why do you want to know? Are you investigating this case?"

Tom shrugged, refusing to be baited. "I want to know so I can keep a lookout for it on my patrols. In case it washes up somewhere. Maybe there'll be fingerprints on it that could tell you who killed him, Sheriff."

"I appreciate having another set of eyes out here." Sterling Cobb seemed unaware of the tension between the two men. "Richard wore a unique belt buckle. So maybe you're right, Mr. Maynard. It could help identify that this is him. If we can match it to the belt." The sheriff rested his elbow on the butt of his gun as he sorted through his memories. "That buckle was silver. Had some gold or brass on it. Made him look like he was some kind of rodeo cowboy."

Melanie turned to the sound of footsteps hurrying across the dock behind her. Daryl Renick wasn't smiling as he joined them. He pointed to the carved silver buckle with a brass spur emblazoned on it at his own waist. "It looked just like this. Minus the notches for each of his kills."

"Kills?" Tom and Melanie echoed together.

"He had a list of animals he wanted to hunt. Every time he bagged one on his list, he carved an *X* on his buckle."

Sheriff Cobb chuckled. "That boy always was a cocky son of a gun, wasn't he?"

"Could I take a picture of that, Daryl?" Tom pulled out his phone, and Melanie's concern flared for an instant. Would Silas or Sheriff Cobb see the dozens of pictures Tom had been taking around the lake and farm?

"I don't care, but make it fast." Daryl's dark eyes barely acknowledged the click of Tom's phone as he turned to the sheriff. "I want a look at that body. Word is it's Richard. I want to see him for myself."

"You're not going to be able to identify him by looking at him. He was in the water a long time," the sheriff warned.

"I knew him better than anybody here. I know what clothes he was wearing when he disappeared. If there's anything in his pockets, I could identify it. Please." Daryl's scruffy face was lined with worry, and Melanie reached over to squeeze his hand. He said, "My wife can't take much more of not knowing what happened to her brother. Even if the news is bad, if I can tell her that Richard's been found…"

"Is SueAnn all right?" Melanie asked.

"She woke up having those fake contractions again. They stopped. But this…" Daryl's fingers pumped around hers. "Maybe you'd better come check on her when you get done here."

"I will. As soon as I can."

Sheriff Cobb seemed to understand the urgency of the situation. "We'd best get up the hill and talk to the coroner before he leaves, then. They want to take the body to Kansas City 'cause we don't have the proper facilities here. I don't mind them takin' a dead body off my hands. But if you want to see it... Silas." He nodded to the farm's security chief before tipping his hat to Melanie. "Miss Fiske. I'll call if I need anything else from you."

Daryl hurried up the steps to the parking lot, and Sheriff Cobb followed more slowly after him. Melanie's concern shifted from SueAnn to Tom. The lines beside his eyes had narrowed into a frown. He stared at the image on his phone as if he'd seen a ghost.

Before she could ask what was wrong, though, Silas's mocking voice reminded her Baldy was still there. "Something eatin' at you, Sergeant?"

"Tom?" He had gone quiet. Too quiet. Had he just pieced together something about his case? No matter what, she wasn't about to let Silas goad him into revealing something he shouldn't. She could buy Tom a few seconds of distraction while he cleared his thoughts and remembered he wasn't supposed to look as though he was playing detective. Since she was already in medic mode, she turned to Silas and nodded toward his injured hand. "Do you want me to take a look at that cut? Looks like the bandage hasn't been changed for a while."

"I'm fine." Silas pulled his hand away from the post, flexing his fingers. "You didn't answer my question, Sergeant Loser."

She, on the other hand, had been playing detective for months now, and felt right at home pointing out suspicious details. "How did you cut yourself? Is that why you had gloves on the other day? To hide that wound?"

Silas blinked, and when he opened his dark eyes again, they were focused squarely on her. "A working man wears gloves to protect his hands." No farmer she'd met wore black leather driving gloves to toss a hay bale or fix a barn roof. Not that she'd ever seen Silas do either of those jobs. Before she could challenge him on evading the question, he snagged her by the wrist with that same bandaged hand. "I'll pick you up tonight for the dance."

"I told you I'm not—"

"No, you won't." Tom was back with her. His phone was back in his pocket as he pried Silas's hand off her. While Silas shook the feeling back into his hand, Tom slid his arm around her shoulders. "She's going with me."

Silas grinned. "You've got patrol duty tonight."

"Not until ten o'clock. She's with me until then. Afterward, too, if she wants." When Silas opened his mouth to argue, Tom poked his finger into the middle of the bald man's chest. "And if you put your hand on her like that again, I'll break it."

Chapter Twelve

Melanie curled her toes into an eyelet-trimmed pillow, stretching herself awake on the love seat where she'd dozed off. She blinked the bent page of her book into focus in the dim light seeping through the curtains and frowned.

After a rain-soaked night without sleep, she'd been anxious to get into a hot shower and fall into bed for a long nap. But finding a dead body, imagining her father suffering a similar fate, and discovering just how much she wanted Detective Thomas Watson Jr. to be more than a friend and coinvestigator, had all crept into her head, haunting her dreams and forcing her out of bed to find a story she knew had a happy ending. Not that it helped much. Asleep or awake, those images and worries and wishes were still with her.

"Melanie?" A sharp knock on her door startled her and she leaped to her feet, realizing an earlier knock had wakened her in the first place.

Smoothing the crumpled page of *Jane Eyre* back into place, she closed the book and hurried to the door. "What's the emergency—"

The door swung open before she could reach it, and she jumped back at the sight of Tom filling her doorway. "Damn it, woman, why don't you answer...? Are you okay?"

Melanie nodded, retreating a step as he closed the door behind him.

The anger that had narrowed his eyes dissipated at her unblinking stare. This wasn't soldier Tom or loner Tom or sexy Tom... Well, okay, to her way of thinking he was always *sexy* Tom. But this was a new version of the man she was getting to know. He'd shaved, revealing all kinds of interesting angles along his carved cheeks and rugged jawline. And he'd put on a white button-down shirt that hugged his shoulders and arms as nicely as a T-shirt. Plus, he'd removed the shoulder holster he always wore. This was date-night Tom.

Date-night Tom?

"Aren't you ready?"

Melanie snapped her gaping mouth shut. "You were serious about going to the dance?"

"As a heart attack." He plucked the book from her hands and set it on the table beside the lamp. "This shindig started five minutes ago. Now throw on something pretty and let's go."

She stumbled along in front of him as he scooted her toward her bedroom. "I thought you said that to put Silas off about hounding me to go with him. I thought we were going to do some investigating while everyone was out at the barn."

"You're right on both counts." He grabbed her hand and pulled her into the bedroom when she apparently wasn't moving fast enough. The momentary shock of having a grown, sexy, date-night man in her bedroom for the first time heated her skin with excitement. But she didn't get much time to blush. For one thing, he was still wearing his gun, although he'd tucked it into a holster at the back of his waist, reminding her of their undercover charade. Secondly, Tom released her and walked straight to her closet and opened it. He thumbed through the meager selection of blouses and jeans, looking for a fancy dress that didn't exist. Maybe she shouldn't have begged out of that shopping expedition with her aunt and Deanna. "We can't sneak out of a social event unless we put in an appearance first. And if we don't show at all, your aunt or uncle will send someone to look for us. That's the last thing we want." He pulled out the sleeveless turquoise cotton dress that she'd worn for her graduation from Metropolitan College four years earlier. "Here. Do this one."

He was no more a fashionista than she was. But Melanie understood the pressure of time. She snatched the hanger from his hand, pushed him out the door and changed. She slipped on a pair of flip-flops and hurried into the bathroom next door, frowning at the smashed bed-head look she'd accomplished when she'd fallen asleep on the couch with wet hair. After running a brush through it without much success, she braided the curls into a long plait.

She was dabbing on some lip gloss when she realized Tall, Dark and Date-Night was watching her work. Tom leaned his shoulder against the door frame while his gaze took a leisurely stroll from the top of her head down to her toes and back. "You've got legs, Doc."

She capped the lip gloss and dropped it back into a drawer, facing him with a wry smile. "Two of them, as a matter of fact."

Even as he laughed, he reached out to capture the end of her braid between his fingers and tugged her toward him.

She stopped herself from tripping by bracing her hands against his chest. She marveled at his masculine shape, then moved her fingers across the crisp cotton covering his sturdy muscles and warm skin. He trembled when she flicked her fingertips over his taut nipple. Or maybe she trembled at the knowledge she could induce that helpless reaction from him. His voice dropped to that growly rumble she loved. "You are built like nobody's business."

"That's good?"

"That is *so* good." When his mouth touched hers, her lips were already parting, hungry for his kiss. She might not have a long track record with this kind of thing, but he was an excellent teacher, and she'd always been an eager student. He nipped at her bottom lip, then eased the excited nerve endings with the raspy stroke of his tongue. She mimicked the same nibble and stroke on his firm mouth and he groaned. "I'm the one who said we had to make an appearance, right?"

She never got a chance to answer.

When his tongue slid into her mouth, hers darted forward to meet his. His hands left her hair to pull her arms around his neck, and then he was sliding his hands down her back, moving closer. He palmed her butt and pulled her onto her toes, bringing her body into the hard heat of his as his mouth opened possessively over hers.

Just as she thought she was getting the hang of all the touches and tastes that triggered that husky growl in his throat, he tore his mouth away and moved his hands to frame her on either side of the doorway. His chest heaved with a mighty breath, rubbing against her breasts, making her whimper as a jolt of electricity shot through the tips and cascaded through her like stars falling straight into the needy heart of her. Tom captured her mouth in one more chaste kiss before pulling her fingers from the collar of his shirt and grasping her hand. "We need to go now, or we never will."

MELANIE WAS BREATHLESS by the time they finished the two-step and applauded the band, which was stopping for a short break. After sharing several dances, she was beginning to think of tonight as a real date. Feeling Tom's body move against hers, knowing how secure the grip of his hand was around her own, hearing him laugh and talk about everything—from how he'd learned line dancing from his grandpa in an attempt to impress a girl in college to speculating about who had given Roy a black eye—made Melanie feel as if they'd known each other much longer than a couple of weeks.

Although she was still anxious to leave the Fiske Farm behind her and do more with her life once the ghost of her father was laid to rest, she was rethinking the idea of independent spinsterhood. She simply hadn't met the right man until Tom had barged into her life. Tom 'Duff Maynard' Watson made her happy. He made her hope. And even if he was just a good guy who lusted after her a little and cared about her like the good friend he'd become, she knew she'd never regret falling in love with him.

Melanie stumbled over her own bare toes as the truth hit her.

Before she could glance up to see if she was broadcasting her feelings with a telltale blush, Tom tugged on her hand, pulling her past the punch bowl where Silas was doctoring his lemonade with a shot from his flask. Tom scooped up a cup of the untainted drink, taking a sip before handing it to her. Silas scowled in their direction, but she realized the condemning look wasn't aimed at them, but at Abby and Deanna Fiske, who were chatting with the band's bass player and lead singer. Henry joined them, wrapping an arm around each woman's waist and saying something that made them all laugh.

My, what a show her aunt and uncle were putting on for the tenants and staff who worked here. Maybe they were eager to take everyone's minds off the news of the dead body. Maybe they were showing off their wealth and success. Either way, they seemed oblivious to Silas's grumpy mood and to Roy lurking in the shadows near the door like a dog who'd been banished from the house for the night.

Melanie didn't have time to ask Tom if he'd observed what she had. Instead, he picked up her flip-flops from beneath their table and pushed them into her hands. He dipped his mouth beside her ear. "Giggle."

"What?" She held on to his arm for balance as she slipped the sandals onto her feet.

"Laugh like I said something clever and you can't resist me."

"Tom…"

"That'll do." He grinned a split second before moving his mouth over hers in a quick, hard kiss. "I don't know why that's such a turn-on. Time to make our escape."

"You want me to pretend like I can't wait to be alone with you?" Catching on to the subterfuge, she did her best imitation of Deanna's flirtatious giggle.

Tom made a face at the silly, high-pitched sound. "Never do that again."

Melanie laughed out loud, grabbed her phone off the table and followed him out of the barn.

Tom traded a nod with Roy before taking a circuitous

route across the compound to avoid anyone's notice. Once assured that the main house was empty, she and Tom entered off the back deck and made a beeline for the stairs. He hurried her up to the second floor, keeping watch while she lowered the attic steps. The stuffiness of the room nearly stole the air from her lungs. She pointed to the window in the back wall. "You want me to open that?"

He stopped her hand when she reached for the overhead light. He picked up the two flashlights on the shelf near the top of the steps and handed one to her. "The light and an open window might draw someone's attention. We can sweat for five minutes. I figure that's about how long we've got before we need to be seen somewhere else. Let's make this fast."

Nodding her understanding, Melanie set her phone on the shelf and switched on her flashlight to lead him across the room to the metal shelves. She shined her light on the box of her aunt's rodeo queen memorabilia and frowned. "Someone else has been up here since my last visit." Everything had been stacked in neat rows on the shelves again, blocking the wall behind them. "What if they cleared out the room because I was snooping around? I hope I didn't mess up your investigation."

He squeezed her shoulder. "We find what we find. But only if we look."

Melanie nodded. "The door's behind there."

Tom lifted the shelves, contents and all, creating a space big enough for him to slide behind. "Light," he ordered. Hurrying to do his bidding, she joined him and shined her light on the padlock as he knelt in front of it. He had a special tool in his back pocket that made quick work of the lock. He stuffed the padlock and tool into his pocket and opened the door. "Son of a bitch."

Melanie couldn't squeeze between the shelves and door fast enough to see inside the room that was no bigger than a walk-in closet. "Oh, my God."

She swung her light around, counting the heavy black bags stacked two deep against one side of the tiny room. On the wall opposite the door stood a set of shelves that held boxes of ammunition, cell phones still in their packages and what looked like several bundles of cash, stacked and wrapped like cubes in sheets of clear plastic. The last wall had several broken-down shipping boxes labeled with an innocuous Lake Hanover Freight stamp leaning against it.

Tom pulled a rifle from one of the bags. He pointed to the small black ring anchored to the middle of the barrel. A gas block. Just like the one she'd found on her father's boat. Melanie felt sick to her stomach. This was happening, right here, in the house where she'd grown up. "Children live on this farm. Thousands of innocent people come through here all summer long. How can there be so many guns? How can this be safe?"

"It's not."

Leaving Tom to snap pictures as he emptied first one bag, then another, Melanie moved over to the shelves to study the items there. "There must be thousands of dollars here."

"Tens of thousands. Maybe more." He opened the next bag and laid the guns on the floor. "I'll call Benton. I can text him these images from here. Go back to the opening and keep an eye out for visitors. I need to document the serial numbers on these weapons to confirm that they're stolen or unregistered before they get sanded off. This may take longer than five minutes."

Her eyes widened when he pulled a roll of adhesive

tape out of the pocket of his dark-wash jeans. "You come prepared for anything, don't you?"

"Borrowed it from Henry's office." He tore off a length of tape and pressed it to the trigger assembly of one of the handguns. "I'm no CSI, but if I can pick up any kind of prints—"

"Then you can prove who's smuggling them."

"You said you saw Silas wearing black leather gloves the other day?"

"Yeah. Then he had a bandage on his hand this morning."

Tom snapped a photograph before pulling something from inside the bag of weapons. "Did it look like this?"

He held up a leather glove, shining his light on it. She knelt beside him, studying it. "That's blood."

"The leather's been sliced through, too."

"Somebody was using a knife on the *August Moon*. Cutting ropes to tie up that body? Removing the belt buckle that could identify Richard? You don't think Silas had something to do with that dead body, do you?"

"I do." He dropped the glove into a plastic bag and stuffed it into his pocket. She wondered when he'd raided her infirmary for supplies again. But then, she supposed there were some mysteries about this man she would never fully understand. "Whether he was cleaning up someone else's mess—or he was responsible for the murder itself, I can't say."

"Someone else's mess? Like Roy's? Do you think *he* was trying to dispose of the body? Maybe Deanna surprised him before he could get it on or off the boat. He didn't seem too happy to see her last night."

"That could explain the black eye. Either he screwed up his job, he wasn't supposed to find that body, or whoever he reports to—Silas or Henry—punished him for letting Deanna anywhere near it."

Bracing her hand against Tom's sturdy thigh, Melanie pushed to her feet. The cubes of money were as fascinating as they were disturbing. On closer inspection, she discovered they, too, had labels printed on them. They each had dates and initials—KC, SL, DC—money from Kansas City? St. Louis? Denver, Colorado? Or being paid out to…whom? Silas Lou Danvers? Deanna Christine Fiske? Could her self-absorbed cousin really be involved in something like this? Her curious thoughts took a sideways turn when she read a label that had no initials. "Isn't a Gin Rickey a drink?"

"What did you say?"

Surprised to feel Tom's heat beside her, she pointed to the dusty label on the cube of money. *Gin Rickey.* She heard an audible gasp as his shoulder sagged against hers. "Tom, what's wrong? You know what this means, don't you?"

"It's the code name for a hired killer."

"A hired…? Someone here…?"

"My brother Keir—he's a detective, too—was looking into another case and discovered the code name for a hit man. One of the contact numbers led to this part of the state." He swiped his palm over his jaw, scratching at the smooth skin as though searching for that perennial beard stubble that was usually there. A fist squeezed around Melanie's heart. That was pain, not anger, she saw in his expression. "The man who shot my grandfather. The man we could only identify by—"

"A belt buckle like Daryl's." She reached up to cup the tight line of Tom's jaw. "The body in the lake…

You think he shot your grandfather. You think some-one hired Richard Lloyd to shoot your grandfather."

"Rickey? Richard?"

Unfortunately, it made sense to her, too. Richard's disappearance. His hunting expertise. The odd jobs Henry would send him on. All this cash. "This money was used to pay Richard to kill...?"

Tom pressed a kiss into the palm of her hand before going back to work. "We need the crime lab to ID that body. Not that it does me much good. Lloyd had no reason to come after my family. I never met any of you before I came here."

"It's not like you can ask who hired him. And why kill him? Who shot Richard? The person who hired him?"

"The best way to cover your tracks is to eliminate them." Tom shrugged. "Either that, or he screwed up the job. Maybe Grandpa was supposed to die. Or one of us was. Or we all were."

Melanie's stomach tightened with fear. "Could some-one here know you're a cop? That you're from a fam-ily of cops?"

Tom went utterly still for a few moments before re-suming his work. "I haven't seen indications that any-one suspects me. Except you. You were the only one curious enough to find out. More likely your uncle or Silas just sold Richard's services."

"For all this money." She shook her head. Tom had once joked that he was looking for some country-bump-kin mafia. Apparently, she was living right in the mid-dle of it. Silas and Roy were relatively new hires. But Richard would have been a child like her fourteen years ago when her father died. How long had these criminal activities been going on at the Fiske Family Farm? Had

Leroy uncovered the same secrets she and Tom were discovering now? Had Henry silenced his own brother to protect those secrets?

Melanie was about to share her suspicions with Tom when she heard the smack of the screen door slamming below their feet. Dashing to the top of the steps, she trained her ear to the stomps and mutters she could hear from the first floor. "Someone just came in."

Tom was right beside her, exchanging his phone for his gun.

She heard another door, followed by the clink of glass against glass. "Whoever it is went into Henry's office."

There was a slur of angry words— —and then a second clink. Someone was pouring a drink. Or two. "Think you're too good for me." That wasn't her uncle's voice. A board creaked beneath Melanie's flip-flop and she froze. "Somebody there?"

Not her uncle. Something much worse.

She turned to Tom, dodging his hands as he tried to pull her away from the opening. "How much longer do you need?"

"No." He was answering a question she hadn't asked.

"How long to finish cataloguing all that evidence and get it to your friends?"

Tom was shaking his head, reaching for her as she backed away. "It's not worth—"

"We might not get a second chance."

"Doc—"

"Do your job." She descended the attic steps and pulled on the rope, closing the door into the ceiling. "Do it fast."

She tiptoed down the stairs.

Chapter Thirteen

Melanie was nearly to the bottom step in the main hallway when Silas lurched out of Henry's office. He was twisting the lid onto his flask as if he'd just refilled it at her uncle's liquor cabinet. When his rheumy gaze landed on her, she offered him a polite smile and hurried past him to the front door.

He grabbed her arm, stopping an easy escape. "What are you doing here, girl?" He stuffed the flask into his hip pocket and eyed her like a tipsy vulture. "Sergeant Loser dump you?"

She couldn't help but glance up the stairs, relieved to see no sign of Tom. He'd face much worse than the lecture she'd received if he was caught in the attic. Quickly averting her gaze, she tugged against Silas's grip. "No, I was just—"

"Headin' back for the comfort of your old room? Need a shoulder to cry on?" Silas's fingers tightened painfully around her upper arm and he pulled her to him. She thrust her hand against the center of his chest to wedge some space between them. But even half-toasted, his strength easily overpowered hers. She squeezed her eyes and mouth shut as he pushed her face into his shoulder. "I knew there was something wrong about that guy. He ain't one of us."

She didn't want to be one of them, either. And she certainly didn't want or need any comfort from this bully. Melanie mentally ran through all of the release moves Tom had shown her at their morning defense lessons to end this embrace. Going limp and bending her knees, she sank out of Silas's arms before he could tighten his grip. But, again, her freedom was short-lived. He clutched her by both arms this time.

Her attempt to stomp on his instep merely tripped him and they crashed into the wall together. Maybe she could talk her way out of this. "Would you still like to dance with me tonight? I hear the music starting up again at the barn. We should go."

"I'm tired of dancin' to your tune, Deanna, darlin'." His breath reeked as he nuzzled the side of her neck. The hand at her waist slid over her hip to pull up the hem of her dress. "Leadin' me on like a trained dog."

Melanie slapped his hand away and twisted out of his grasp. "You're drunk. I'm not Deanna."

Clarity didn't help. He slammed his hand against the wall, blocking her path. "Maybe taming you would make things interesting, after all. Where is that boyfriend of yours, anyway? Couldn't he get the job done?"

"Silas..." The fear that colored her voice at his crude suggestion morphed into a whole different type of fear when she heard a scraping sound two floors above them. Silas tilted his face up the stairs. He'd heard it, too. She needed to cover for Tom. She'd promised to have his back. He needed to be safe. Swallowing her disgust, Melanie touched Silas's cheek and turned his bald head her direction again. *Run, Tom.* "Um… Maybe I do need a shoulder to cry on. Could you just hold me?"

"Sure thing." He forgot the noise with a lascivious grin. Instead of a hug, Silas grabbed her and pushed her against the wall. Melanie knew she was in trouble when she couldn't get the behemoth to budge. "You got that sensible underwear on tonight, Mel?" Bile churned in her stomach as Silas's hands ran over her. She couldn't find any comfort in knowing he was no longer confusing her with another woman. "Doesn't matter. Naked's the way I like my women. I'll make you forget all about him."

Melanie panicked at the assault, blanking on every trick Tom had taught her. She was helpless to do more than scream in her mouth as Silas ground his lips over hers, filling her mouth with the taste of stale whiskey. He thrust other parts of his body against places she'd never wanted him to touch.

For a brief moment, she knew that if she mentioned Tom was in the house, she could get away. Silas would leave her to confront the intruder. She could save herself if she sacrificed Tom. But she'd seen all those guns upstairs. She'd seen Roy's black eye. She'd seen a decomposing body. If Silas found out Tom was a cop and he'd found evidence to link him to those crimes, she'd be finding Tom's body floating in the lake with a bullet hole in his chest.

That couldn't happen. She couldn't let the man she loved be hurt by these people.

But she couldn't stand one more second of Silas pawing at her, either. She'd find another way to get away *and* help Tom escape. She wrenched her mouth away from Silas's. "Let go of me!" She scratched her fingers over his scalp, startling him into drawing back. She shoved the butt of her hand up against his nose and heard a pop.

He grabbed his face and tumbled backward. "You bitch!" Anger and pain must have cleared his foggy brain enough to see her running down the hall. After just a few steps, his hand clamped over her wrist, jerking her back into the hard slap of his hand across her cheek. Melanie's knees buckled as white dots swam across her vision, blurring her senses to a banging sound and a shouting voice. Silas shoved her up against the wall. "You uppity, teasing—"

A massive forearm closed around Silas's neck and dragged him away from her. Suddenly free, Melanie collapsed against the wall. Silas kicked his feet and clawed at the bulging muscles that were choking him. Blood dripped from his nose onto the rolled-up white sleeve. She blinked her eyes clear to see Tom's furious expression as he strangled his prey.

"Tom! Tom, stop!"

Silas's bloody face turned red, then purple. His struggles became little more than flailing hands. Then his arms dropped to his sides, his eyes closed and he went limp like a rag doll. Silas's bulky frame bobbed up and down as Tom heaved several deep breaths. Melanie looked up into Tom's narrowed green eyes and found them burning through her. "You okay?"

She pushed herself up straighter and nodded. "Is he dead?"

"No. But he'll be out for a few minutes." He glanced up and down the shadowed hallway. Had any of them screamed or cursed loudly enough for someone to hear them? "You up to helping me?"

Again, she could do little more than nod.

"Grab his feet."

Melanie pushed away from the wall and lifted Silas's heavy boots after Tom shifted his grip beneath the big man's arms to haul him into Henry's office. Adrenaline was still pumping so hard through her system that it was hard to concentrate. "What are we doing?"

"Creating a plausible reason for him to be passed out here." Tom dumped the unconscious body onto her uncle's leather couch. She positioned his feet while Tom pushed him onto his side to retrieve the flask from Silas's back pocket.

"When Silas comes to he'll tell Henry about us. You should get out of here. You should get in your truck and just leave."

"I'm not going anywhere. And he won't talk." Tom opened the flask and poured the amber contents all over Silas's shirt and the couch. "Getting drunk on the boss's whiskey and passing out in his office isn't going to earn him any brownie points. If he wakes up before he's discovered, he'll leave to cover his tracks. If he's discovered here, he's got too big of an ego to admit he lost a fight." He tossed the flask onto Silas's sleeping body. Tom's fingers curled into a tight fist at his side. "I'm sorry I didn't get here sooner. I could hear what was happening and… I'm sorry." He reached over to lift the braid of her hair off her shoulder and Melanie flinched. "You're not okay."

The adrenaline must be wearing off now because she was suddenly so chilled she was shaking.

It was the second time Duff had seen Melanie charge across the compound into her cottage, desperate to escape the toxic hell of her family and so-called friends. Although she'd avoided his touch, at least she didn't slam the door on him this time, shutting him out of her pain and anger.

To think that that bastard had hurt her...to realize she'd put herself in that position to protect him... The rage at seeing Silas strike her was still coursing through him. But Melanie didn't need rage right now. She needed... Well, hell, he wasn't sure what she needed, but he wasn't about to walk away and let her deal with Fiske family crap on her own. He didn't plan to leave her alone again until they were miles away from this place. And, even then, he didn't think he ever wanted to be far from her.

Still, when she marched straight to the sink and turned on the water to soap up her hands and arms, he quietly closed the door and waited for her to vent. She didn't. She dried off her hands, then turned on the water again to wash her face. "How did you get past Silas?"

"Didn't have to. I climbed out the attic window and dropped onto the roof of the back porch. Shimmied down that oak tree shading the porch from there." When she started rinsing out her mouth, as well, Duff had to go to her. He picked up the towel she'd tossed onto the counter and handed it to her.

She dabbed at her face. "And then you circled around the house to come in the front door. That's good thinking. No one will suspect we were in the attic."

When she put the towel down, Duff saw the red handprint on the side of her face and cursed. Her brown eyes widened with surprise, but instead of apologizing for startling her, he reached for her hand and led her into the infirmary. When she protested his caveman need to protect his woman, he grabbed her by the waist and lifted her onto the examination table, warning her to stay put while he searched for an ice pack. "Damn it, Doc. I feel like I'm always on the wrong side of saving you."

"What are you talking about?"

He fumbled with the ice he pulled from the minifridge but, eventually, forced several pieces into a towel before folding it into a rudimentary packet. "When Silas puts his hands on you or Deanna insults you or I know your brain is making comparisons to dead bodies that have to be breaking your heart —I want to protect you from all that."

"It could have been worse. You taught me how to fight him."

"It wasn't enough."

"I'll be okay."

"I know. Because you're brave and resourceful and stubborn to a fault. You're so used to saving yourself..." He gently pressed the ice pack to her bruised cheek. "But can you blame a guy for wanting to keep someone he cares about safe?"

"You couldn't have stepped in to stop Silas any sooner—not without giving away why you're here. We both heard you moving the shelf in the attic, although I think he was too drunk to know what it meant." She reached up to cover his hand with hers, holding the ice pack in place, cooling the protective rage inside him, too. "I need you to succeed. I need you to put these people away. Forget about Dad. You have to stop the guns and the violence."

Uh-uh. He slipped his fingers into the hair behind her ears, tilting her turbulent brown eyes up to his. "I'm not forgetting anybody. Once we get the players into custody, they'll be willing to talk. I'm not giving up on your father. We'll get these guys—as soon as the lab gets back to us, the task force should be able to obtain warrants. I'll put them away in prison and then I'll take you away from this place. I promise."

She nudged him back a step and this time he let her hop down off the table. "Did you find what you needed to solve your case?"

"Yes." He followed her through the cottage to her bedroom, where she opened the top drawer of her dresser and pulled out her father's watch. "We'll have to play this game out another day or two. We can't let anyone know what we're up to until my team is ready to move in. Otherwise, Henry and Silas will move the guns again, and we need to catch them with the evidence. Can you handle that?"

She nodded, but he didn't quite believe her. "What's next? Another rendezvous at the old fire tower?" She ran her palms over the hips of her dress, searching for a spot to put the watch. "I should put on a pair of jeans."

Instead of changing, she scurried around him into the bathroom. Duff put the watch in his own pocket to carry it for her. She dumped the ice into the sink, inspecting the mark on her face before dabbing at her face and lips with the towel. She turned her back to him and pointed to her zipper. "Can you undo me? I want to shower."

Instead of undressing her, he wrapped his arms around the top of her chest and pulled her to him, hugging her from behind. "You're okay, Doc."

She struggled only momentarily before sagging against him. "I know. I mean, in my head, I know I'm okay." She reached up to hold on to his arms. "But I got really scared tonight."

"I know, babe. I'm so sorry." He pressed his lips to the crown of her hair. "You want to get out of here?"

"Kansas City?"

Duff tightened his hug. "Not yet. But I've got an idea. My truck is parked out in the parking lot. Trust me?"

A few minutes later they were bouncing over the gravel road that led to the old dock. The moon was bright enough that any time they cleared the canopy of leaves and branches, he got a glimpse of Melanie's face. To his relief, the farther they got from the compound, the more color he detected on her freckled skin. She rolled down the window to breathe in the fresh night air. "This was an excellent idea. I'm feeling better."

If she was strong enough to listen, he had something he needed to say. "You could have told Silas I was upstairs. You could have told him I'm a cop and what I'm doing here. He'd have come after me instead of you."

"I thought about it," she admitted. "But I wouldn't have had your back very well, then, would I?"

Duff knew right then and there he was in love with this woman. He reached over to capture her hand in his. "Yeah, Doc. You had my back."

They drove in bumpy silence several more minutes until they reached the old dock and the wreck of the *Edwina*. After parking the truck, he untied his work boots and toed them off, tossing them into the back of the truck, along with his socks and belt. He locked his gun, wallet and phone in the gear box and untucked his shirt. Catching on to his intent, Melanie tossed her flip-flops into the bed of the truck and grabbed the old blanket he kept rolled up behind the seat. Then they walked hand in hand out to the edge of the dock, spread the blanket out to protect them from splinters and sat, dangling their feet in the water that was still warm from the afternoon sun.

The moonlight bathed Melanie's skin with an angelic glow and reflected off the lake, but the trees surrounding the cove still provided a feeling of privacy. The water lapped quietly in the grasses on either side of them, and splashed up to their ankles and calves with every gentle sway of the dock. A symphony of cicadas and frogs serenaded them.

"It's like an IV for you out here, isn't it?" He loved watching her flex her legs and splash her toes in the water. "Feeling better?"

"This has always been a special place." She leaned closer and rested her cheek against his shoulder. "I like it even better that you're sharing it with me."

"Just trying to have your back." Her wet toes came out of the water to slide beneath the rolled-up hem of his jeans to tickle his leg. His entire body warmed at the brush of her skin against his. Yep, he was totally gone on this woman. "I wish I'd been able to get to you sooner tonight. When I said I needed your help, I never meant for you to have to…" He muttered a choice word, then kissed her hair, apologizing for bringing anything harsh into this peaceful place. "I want to bust that jackass's face again for touching you."

"*I* want to bust his face. You know, you never did show me how to do a good old-fashioned uppercut." She studied her fist in front of her for several seconds before she drew her hand back to her heart. "It was different than when you touch me."

"I hope like hell it was." Duff pulled his right leg out

of the water, stretching it out on the blanket behind her so he could face her. He cupped her face between his hands and leaned in to kiss her.

He'd meant it to be a gentle reassurance. But when she fisted her hands in the front of his shirt and pulled herself up into the kiss, parting her lips and sneaking her tongue out to meet his, he forgot about gentle. Her husky groan ignited his own hunger, and he slipped his hands down, trying to pull her into his lap, closer to the male part of him that always responded to her passion. But the angle was awkward and the dock was rocking and he needed her to understand the difference between his touch and Silas's.

With a groan of his own, he tore his mouth from her lips and rested his forehead against hers. He ran his hands up and down her arms. "I can't keep my hands off you because you excite me. You challenge me and frustrate me and make me laugh and make me crazy. You make me want to talk about things I never talk about." Her warm, whiskey-colored eyes looked up into his, and she looked so gorgeous that he couldn't help kissing her again, taking his leisurely fill of her mouth, then touching his forehead to hers again. He needed her to understand. He needed her to believe his words. "There's a difference between control and desire. Between respect and using. You need to know how special you are. How beautiful. And if any man doesn't make you feel that, he doesn't deserve you."

She flattened her palms against the sandpapery new stubble that was itching his jawline again. Her lips curled into a bemused smile as she rubbed her hands over his cheeks before sliding them around his neck to caress his short hair. Duff's blood heated with anticipation, even as he held himself still beneath each provocative touch. He idly wondered if she knew what she was doing to him, if she could hear his heart thump faster in his chest or feel the quickening rhythm of his breath stirring her hair. She drew her fingers tenderly over his shoulder to rest beside the healing wound there. "I love the way you kiss me. And I like…" His eyes narrowed, waiting expectantly as her wicked hands danced across his chest. "I like exploring how you feel under my hands. You're all different textures and hard planes and vulnerable places and…" Her blush intensified. "I love how your hands make me feel, too, and…I want you to show me what it's like when a man cares. If you're interested."

Oh, he was interested. Very. More than he should be. But he needed her to be sure of what she was asking of him. He touched a fingertip to the blush climbing up her neck. "Am I your first?"

Melanie nodded. "First kiss. First date. First time." That blush intensified, just like the emotions burning inside him. "I'm twenty-five years old. Does that make me a freak?"

Duff caught her chin in his hand and tilted her face to his when embarrassment made her look away. "It makes you special. I can't tell you how honored—and how scared—it makes me to be your first."

"Scared? Of having sex with me?"

"Of making love to you," he clarified. "I want it to be a good memory for you. I'm scared I'm not up to the task." He tugged her braid between them and pulled the rubber band from the end before slowly unwinding her hair. "Anything you don't like…anything that frightens you...you tell me. I'll make it right. Or I'll stop. Whatever you need."

"I wouldn't trust anyone else with the job."

Her husky vow was as much of a turn-on as it was a reassurance. "Yeah?"

"Yeah." He fanned her hair around her shoulders and sifted his fingers into the thick, sexy waves. "I need you to kiss me now."

He needed that, too. Once their lips met, conscious thought flew out of his brain and instinct took over. She wound her arms around his neck and crawled up his body, pushing her breasts against his chest. They pebbled and poked him and his hands were there in an instant, squeezing their weight and rolling the tips between his thumb and hand until she was panting "more" against his mouth.

The woman had rock-solid instincts, too. She tugged at the buttons of his shirt and pushed the wrinkled cotton off his shoulders. He was groaning for more when she palmed his pectoral muscles and started playing with his responsive flesh. He unzipped her dress and wriggled it off over her head, hating that he lost contact with her lips but consoling himself by pressing a kiss to her abdomen and the underside of her breast and the fine line of her collarbone as every inch of her was slowly revealed to his hungry gaze.

The dress joined his shirt somewhere on the dock and then they were skin to skin. Melanie crawled into his lap, straddling him. Her fingers brushed against his stomach muscles and trailed lower, tugging at the snap of his jeans. Her thighs squeezed around his hips and he rocked himself helplessly against her feminine heat. This was going too fast. She might think she was prepared for this, but he couldn't simply strip her naked and bury himself inside her without making sure she was ready for him.

"Trust me?" he whispered against her mouth, chasing her lips as they grazed along the column of his neck, eliciting tiny little shocks of electricity that threatened his resolve.

With her nod, he wound his arms tightly around her and leaned over the edge of the dock, pulling her into the water with him. There was no startled gasp, no cold shock, only the tightening of her arms and legs around him. The warm water sluiced in between them, and for a few seconds Duff simply held her, treading water and enjoying the rocking motion of the waves around them, tempering the desire pounding through him. He moved his hands along her arms and back and around the thighs that wrapped his waist, gently bathing her, washing away any memory of Silas's hands on her.

Once the frantic energy radiating off her dissipated, they swam around for a few minutes, splashing each other, sneaking kisses in unexpected places, laughing and playing tag and kissing again. Melanie was like a water nymph, with her long hair floating in the water around her, hiding the best bits from his appreciative gaze until she moved and he caught a glimpse of a breast or bottom as she darted from his touch.

A breathless Melanie grinned as she reached behind her to unclasp her bra. "I've never been skinny-dipping with someone else before. Aren't we supposed to be naked?"

So much for cooling his jets. The weight of his wet jeans pulled his feet down to the solid bottom, but he was standing on shaky ground as she bared her beautiful breasts to him and the moonlight. Suddenly, Duff was hungry and impatient. The water couldn't temper his need any longer. When she made a token effort to swim away, he caught her by the ankle and pulled her hard against him, lifting her breast to his mouth and capturing the tip in a needy suckle. She moaned, splaying her fingers at the back of his head, holding his mouth against her.

"Tom..."

"That's the magic word." He carried her to the ladder at the edge of the dock and climbed up after her. He snatched up their discarded clothes and pushed them into her arms to cover herself. Then he grabbed the blanket and her hand and hurried back to his truck.

The time it took to spread the blanket in the bed of his truck, form a makeshift pillow from their dry clothes and peel off their wet ones was far too long to be apart from this woman who'd gotten so far into his head and under his skin that the only way he could feel right again was to let her into his heart. Once he'd rolled on a condom and she was reaching for him, Duff settled between her knees and pushed himself inside her. He hesitated when he reached her tight barrier. But this sexy, brave woman was having none of that. She dug her fingers into his spine, angled her hips and urged him to fill her. She winced and buried her face against the juncture of his neck and shoulder as she stretched to accommodate him. Stars dotted the inside of his eyelids as her body gripped him. He was dangerously close to losing himself inside her.

But Duff held his breath, held her. "You okay?"

"I think I'm more okay than I've been in a long time. I've never felt this close to anyone before. This feels...

right. But…" Was it possible for a woman's entire body to blush?

"But what?" His arms shook with restraint as he propped himself above her. "You know you can tell me anything."

"Aren't there supposed to be bells and whistles?"

Duff's laugh echoed through the clear night air. "Yeah. Very definitely." Her eyes drifted shut as he reclaimed her lips and moved inside her. "Bells and…" Together they found a rhythm that rocked them as sweetly as the waves on the lake. And when the whispers of his name turned into silent, needy gasps, he pressed himself against that sensitive bundle of nerves and felt her detonate around him. "And whistles."

He swallowed up her husky cry with a kiss. And with the waves of her pleasure convulsing around him, the combustion hit him, too.

Afterward, he collapsed atop the blanket and pulled her into his arms beside him.

Melanie snuggled close, tangling her legs with his and pushing her hair out of her eyes. The dampness from the lake and their loving cooled his skin as their heavy, stuttered breaths synced and slowed. She settled her cheek against the pillow of his shoulder and whispered, "Wow. I liked the bells and whistles. A lot."

"Me, too, Doc."

He pulled the edges of the blanket over them and hugged her close. The peal of imaginary bells rang in his thoughts as Melanie drifted off to sleep, while Duff watched real stars dot the night sky above them.

Chapter Fourteen

Melanie couldn't decide which she liked better—the powerful, beautiful and cherished feelings from Tom's lovemaking, or the quiet, intimate talks they shared in between. She loved that he was a snuggler as much as he was a fighter, and that he could touch her heart with his growly words as well as he could kiss her and make her body feel things that, well, she'd only read about in books.

She was slightly winded from her second lesson in seduction, and feeling the grooves of the plastic truck bed liner digging into her hip, but she wasn't going anywhere. Not as long as the night was clear and Tom wanted to hold her. Toasty warm against his side, she traced figure eights through the crisp curls of brown hair that dusted his deep chest and smiled. "So that's the deep, dark secret about your nickname? A bike wreck when you were ten?"

His assent rumbled through his chest. "I kept trying to tell everybody in the hospital how 'tough' I was after breaking my nose and getting my front teeth knocked out after going stuntman off that rock wall behind our old house. But with my injuries, I couldn't say the *T* sound, so it came out 'Duff.' Since I was prone to taking a risk or two, the name stuck."

"A risk or two?"

"I've been to the ER more times than my brothers, sister and father combined."

Melanie's fingers stilled above his heart. "I don't think I like those statistics."

He captured her hand against his chest. "It's okay. I'm tough." He chuckled. "Or, I should say, I'm *Duff*."

She smiled at the story from his childhood. "I don't think you're as 'duff' as you claim. I saw how you felt when you talked about your mother. You light up when you mention your family. Seamus, especially. I bet you're a lot like him."

"Light up? Uh-uh. Next you'll be saying I'm sweet and sentimental. I have a reputation to maintain, woman. I make a living being a tough guy." He gave her bottom a swat, then splayed his fingers there, massaging the spot as if the teasing tap might have stung. It hadn't. But there was something else on his mind. "You should think seriously about going back to school to become a doctor. I imagine I could use one."

Because he wanted her to stick around and be a part of his life for at least the six years it would take to complete her degrees? Instead of laughing at the self-deprecating joke as she was meant to, she shivered. There were no guarantees she'd have anything more than this night with Tom. Silas Danvers, Uncle Henry and a stash of illegal guns and blood money were waiting for them back at the compound. Tom had a job to do. He was already an hour into his night security shift. And though he'd called in on the walkie-talkie in his truck to say that he was on duty, eventually, they'd run into someone and he'd have to resume his Duff Maynard persona.

And she'd have to pretend that she didn't know about the guns or *Gin Rickey* or the way she longed for a new life with the real Detective Watson away from the farm.

"Hey." He tucked his fingers beneath her chin, turning her face up to his. "You doze off on me again? I fed you a great straight line I can't believe you're passing up."

Although her heart wasn't in it, she summoned a smart-aleck comeback about how no school in the world could teach her enough to keep him out of trouble. But before the words left her lips, Tom's entire body tensed beside her and his fingers moved up to cover her mouth.

Obeying the universal *shush* sign, Melanie reached for her clothes as Tom quickly tugged on his shorts and jeans, and pulled his gun from its holster. Now she could hear it, too—footsteps moving through the trees.

He motioned for her to stay down as he silently vaulted over the side of the truck and crept into the shadows.

She was dressed except for the zipper and flip-flops by the time she heard terse voices approaching. "There was no call, no text. You know it's policy to get eyes on an operative when he misses a check-in."

She crouched in her hiding place until she recognized Tom's growly tone. "Something came up that needed to be dealt with. And turn those stupid flashlights off before somebody sees you."

Melanie peeked above the side of the truck to see Tom and two other men approaching. She recognized the blond MBI agent from the rainy night at the fire tower before their lights were quickly snuffed. Her eyes readjusted to the moonlight, but she still didn't recognize the second man, who wore a dark gray suit jacket and slacks, along with the gun strapped at his hip. Although he'd taken off his tie, he looked out of place in the casual world in which she lived. Another member of the task force?

As she scooted off the back of the pickup, Agent Benton eyed the rumpled blanket and her hastily dressed appearance. "Yeah, I see how you're dealing with it. This is how you handle someone blowing your cover?"

"Back off, Benton. Melanie's been an invaluable resource." Neither apologizing for nor explaining away what had just happened between them in the back of his truck, Tom swept her damp hair over the front of her shoulder and zipped up her dress. "I trust her to keep my identity and your operation a secret."

The dark-haired man she didn't know seemed vaguely familiar as he circled the truck, surveying the landscape, assessing the shadows. "You're sure, Duff? I remember Shayla Ortiz." When he got close enough for her to see his chiseled features above his open shirt collar, she realized he was a shorter, more polished version of Tom. He flashed her a smile as he extended his hand to her. "We haven't met yet. I'm Keir Watson."

"Watson?"

He held her hand as she tilted her questioning gaze up to Tom.

"Yep, he belongs to me." Tom smacked the younger man on the back of the head, urging him to release her. "Melanie Fiske, this is my brother, Keir. He's KCPD, too."

She remembered the tall, lanky doctor with the glasses. "How many brothers do you have?"

"Two. This pip-squeak is the youngest." Tom sat on the tailgate to pull on his socks and boots.

"And the handsomest. Nice to meet you." The *pip-squeak* looked fully grown, fully armed and completely dangerous despite his obvious charm. "This big doofus giving you any trouble? I'd be happy to rescue you."

"Really? Back off, little bro. You've already got a woman."

Keir answered with a soft laugh. "That I do. Kenna sends her regards."

"Regards?" Matt Benton swore under his breath. "I'll do a 360 to make sure there aren't eyes on us while you two share tea and crumpets. You Watsons have five minutes."

When the agent left to survey the surrounding area, Keir propped his hands at his hips beneath his jacket. "Is Benton always this uptight?"

"Pretty much." Tom shrugged. "But he's good with paperwork and hoop jumping, so we make a good team. Everything all right at home? Grandpa? Dad?"

"They're good. Millie's worried that you're not eating enough. So not much has changed. Niall said you started the first day with a knife fight." He turned his startling blue eyes to Melanie. "Didn't know there was a woman in the picture, but then, Duff thinks grunts and curse words are the same thing as communication."

"Who's Shayla Ortiz?" Melanie asked, sinking onto the tailgate beside Tom, ignoring the innuendo in his brother's teasing.

"A mistake." He palmed the back of her neck and pulled her in for a quick, hard kiss. Melanie felt the responding heat creeping up her neck. "Go sit up in the cab of the truck. We won't be long. I need to chase these guys out of here before someone sees them." But Melanie was reluctant to move. There had to be a pressing reason for Tom's brother and handler to risk coming this far onto Fiske land. And that worried her. She could see Tom thinking about repeating the order, but he ended up shaking his head. "Or you could just stay here to get the task-force report and save me the trouble of repeating it." Soldier Tom with the clipped words and wary posture was back as he walked around to the gear box. He tossed his white shirt to Keir and pulled out a dark colored T-shirt to shrug into. "There's a sample of Silas Danvers's blood there. Benton will need it to confirm a match to the blood I found with the guns."

"Got it."

"If Benton says we've got five minutes, he'll be back in four and a half. So talk."

Despite the brotherly repartee they'd shared, Keir wasted no time telling him that Niall had done the autopsy on the body she'd found in Lake Hanover himself. "It's Richard Lloyd. Dental records match. Death by gunshot wound to the chest, close range. The lake was just the disposal site. Niall says he's been down there two months."

Tom paused in the middle of adjusting his shoulder holster across his back to squeeze Melanie's hand. Even though she'd halfway suspected the truth, they were talking about an old friend of hers, and the details weren't pretty. "Benton could have told me that. Why are you here?"

But Melanie wanted information, not sympathy. "Tom suspected there was a connection between Richard and your grandfather's shooting at your sister's wedding. Did you find evidence to support that?"

"Tom?" Keir seemed more surprised by the name than the fact she knew so many details about their family and Richard's death. But a glare from big brother sent Keir back into cop mode. "The coat he was wearing, his size and weight—he's a match for the guy who shot Grandpa. And that belt buckle you described is exactly what I saw on the guy. It's been identified in court records as belonging to a suspect involved with other shootings. Richard Lloyd is our hit man."

"Poor SueAnn." Melanie thought of her friend and how confirmation of her brother being murdered—of being a *murderer*--could worsen her precarious health. And then she wondered how Tom was handling this news. "I'm sorry the people I know had anything to do with hurting your family."

He responded with little more than a curt nod. The time for the emotional connection they'd shared tonight had passed. "We found cash confirming *Gin Rickey* is someone—or the code name for multiple someones—who lives here on the farm. Fiske or Danvers must have hired Lloyd out to do jobs."

"Any idea who hired him to come after us?" Keir asked.

Tom shook his head. "There might be something in the computer records I sent. They'll take a while to go through."

Melanie remembered her earlier encounter with Silas at the main house, when he'd worn the leather gloves. "Silas had a big envelope of some kind he handed to Henry. Could that have been a report—or record of whatever you're looking for?"

"Danvers doesn't strike me as someone who's into

filing reports," Tom pointed out. "Did he say what was in the envelope?"

"Uncle Henry just called it 'the package,'" she answered. "Silas had been gone a long time. He could have driven into Falls City. Or even Kansas City. Maybe there was cash in that envelope. I never saw inside it."

"All right, you two." Matt Benton reemerged from the trees. "Family fun time is over. The coast is clear for now, but can we get back to the business at hand?" He patted the pocket of his jacket. "I've got warrants. The judge thought those pictures you sent were enough to okay storming the compound and taking in Fiske, Danvers and anyone else with access to those guns. We'll seize the boats and vehicles, too, to let the CSIs go over them for trace evidence. The judge didn't want to wait and give them time to move the merchandise again."

Tom nodded. "I've confirmed they have multiple venues to bring the guns in and out of the area—"

"And multiple hiding places on the property," Melanie added. "There's a lot of acreage we haven't explored yet."

"We?" Agent Benton angled the brim of his ball cap and studied her as if he'd temporarily forgotten her existence. "Ma'am, if you've done anything to compromise this investigation—"

"You wouldn't have those warrants if it wasn't for her," Tom warned. He pocketed two spare magazines of bullets before closing the gear box. "What's our timeline look like?"

Agent Benton's threatening expression eased into simply unfriendly. "We're already blocking off the county highway and access roads, and any decent deputy is bound to report it. Apparently, Sheriff Cobb has been known to tip off Fiske whenever there's anything suspicious around the farm, so one of my men is keeping Cobb occupied in town going over the autopsy report. We'll be ready to move in sixty minutes."

Tom closed the tailgate and glanced down at Melanie before looking back at Keir and Benton. "Get her out of here. I don't want Mel anywhere near the raid. Make sure your men are well armed and wearing vests. I've already got Danvers on multiple counts of assault, and the key players are armed like a military unit. I have a feeling Fiske and his men won't go quietly. I'll go keep eyes on the compound to direct where to send in the troops."

They didn't have sixty minutes.

The walkie-talkie on Tom's front seat crackled with static. Instead of parting ways, the three men joined Melanie at the open driver's window to listen. The static cleared to the sound of a man's frantic voice. "Duff? Duff—it's Daryl. What's your twenty? Come back."

"They're looking for you." Keir's eyes narrowed with the same suspicion Tom's often did. "Could Cobb have already tipped them off?"

Agent Benton swore under his breath. "Could be a setup."

There was more static before the line cleared to some muttered reassurances. "Duff, this is Daryl. Is Mel with you? I need a medic."

Melanie opened the door and picked up the radio before anyone could stop her. She pressed the call button. "I'm here, Daryl. What's the problem? Over."

"Mel?" He exhaled an audible sigh of relief. "I'm at the infirmary with SueAnn. Her water broke. She's in labor."

"PUT HER IN my truck and let's go."

"Go where? Henry and Silas aren't going to let us drive off down the highway. If they don't stop us, they'll at least follow us to make sure we're going to the hospital, and then they'll see your roadblock. She certainly can't hike out through the hills in her condition." Melanie unwrapped the blood-pressure cuff and jotted down SueAnn's vitals. They weren't good. The baby's heartbeat was strong, but if SueAnn couldn't start recovering her own pulse and heart rate between contractions, there was no way she'd be able to deliver the baby vaginally before they both suffered irreparable damage or died.

She felt a firm hand on her shoulder and looked up into Tom's stony expression. "Doc, we can't stay. My team is en route. I can't guarantee anyone's safety here."

SueAnn had collapsed against the pillow and closed her eyes. Daryl turned to Melanie. "It's not good, is it?"

She knew he was referring to his wife's condition, not Tom's cryptic warning. She wasn't even sure Daryl had realized how well armed the man standing over them was, or if he understood the covert warnings about the imminent danger. Melanie shook her head. "She's not strong enough to deliver the baby here. She needs a real doctor."

Daryl pushed to his feet. "Screw Henry and his rules. Tell me what to do to get one here. I've already lost my best friend. I'm not going to lose her and my son or daughter."

"We're not bringing anyone else onto this compound." Tom pushed aside the eyelet curtains and scanned outside, his body on full alert. "The dance is breaking up. People are on the move."

She crossed to him and rested a hand on his arm, willing him to look at her. "Tom."

He glanced down into her eyes and shook his head. "That's not fair, babe."

"There's another way off this farm."

He shook his head again, understanding what she was asking. "Can she make that trek?"

"*We* can."

"Get her prepped." He pulled out his cell and punched in a number. "Keir. I've got an emergency medical evac. A woman's in labor and she's having complications. We'll bring her to your location at the fire tower. Have an ambulance meet us there."

Like Tom, Melanie moved into action. There might be bullets flying soon. There would certainly be chaos once a team of law-enforcement agents arrived. With roads closing, the help SueAnn needed might not get here in time if they waited. Risking a jarring ride had to be better than the nothing she could do here. She stood beside Daryl and pointed to the corners of the blanket where SueAnn lay. "We'll use this as a make-shift stretcher and carry her."

"Let me do that." Tom nudged her aside and pushed the phone into her hands. "Give Keir whatever medical info he needs and he'll relay it to the paramedics." There was a nagging little memory dancing at the corner of her mind when she took the phone, but there was no time to make sense of it before Tom ordered her to move. "My truck leaves in sixty seconds."

While Tom and Daryl carried SueAnn out the front door, she stuffed SueAnn's file into her paramedic's backpack, grabbed an extra blanket and pillow and hurried outside, giving Keir an approximate ETA before ending the call. Earlier, she'd spared a few precious minutes to change into her jeans and hiking boots, so it was easy for her to hop into the bed of the truck beside her patient. She tapped the roof of the truck cab, indicating they were as ready as they were going to get, and Tom shifted into gear. He kept his headlights off for as long as possible before the gravel road reached the tree line to mask their escape. Encouraging Daryl to talk in soothing tones to keep SueAnn as calm as possible, she stuffed the pillow under SueAnn's knees and covered her with the warm blanket.

"I guess we kind of broke up the dance." Daryl held tightly to his wife's hand. "Abby said I should take her straight to the infirmary. Folks were askin' where you and Duff had got off to. I tried callin' your phone, but there was no answer. Lots of folks tried. You're gonna have a bunch of messages when you check your voice mail." He sort of laughed, though it sounded more like a squashed-up sob. "Silas was the one who said he saw you headin' off to the lake with Duff."

"Silas saw us?" So much for shaming him into silence.

"Yeah. That's why I called you on the radio."

"Where's Silas now?"

Daryl shrugged. "Last I knew, Abby was brewin' him a pot of coffee at the main house to sober him up. He was pretty pissed that Deanna snuck out of the dance with Roy before it was over."

That wasn't why he was pissed.

"How many people called my phone?" Melanie's stomach sank as they bounced over the next rut.

"I don't know. Five or six. Maybe more."

She hadn't gotten any of those messages because she'd left her phone in Henry and Abby's attic.

MELANIE HEARD THE rumble of ATV motors cutting through the sticky night air as soon as Tom skidded to a stop on the muddy gravel near the *Edwina*.

"Why did you tell me to stop?" Tom hurried around the truck. From the angle of his gaze, she knew he'd heard the ATVs approaching, too. "Is SueAnn all right?"

"This is my fault. I'm so sorry." Melanie jumped out of the truck bed as soon as Tom lowered the tailgate. She pointed to the distant engine noises echoing throughout the hills. "We only have a couple of minutes before they'll be here."

"Sorry about what? We need to keep moving."

"Silas might not have reported seeing you and me in the main house. But a ringing telephone would certainly have sent someone upstairs to look." She pulled out the pocket linings of her jeans to show him the problem. "I left my phone in the attic. Everyone's been calling me. They'll know we were there. Even if they don't figure out you're a cop, they'll know you're a traitor. They'll know *I'm* a traitor."

Instead of placing blame, Tom grasped her on either side of her waist and lifted her back into the truck. "They're probably moving the guns right now."

"Or following us." She jumped back to the ground and Tom cursed. "With those small vehicles, they're going to be more maneuverable on the terrain between here and the fire tower, and they'll catch us in no time. We need to split up."

"No. When Silas and whoever's with him get here, it's not going to be an argument. They eliminate people who know their secret and won't keep it. Get in the damn truck."

When he reached for her again, she twisted out of his grasp. "You know I'm right. You need to get to a spot where you can notify your team to move in now, before all the evidence is gone. And I sure don't want SueAnn in the line of fire if they catch us."

The engines were getting louder.

"I don't want anyone in the line of fire. This is my job, Melanie. This isn't your fight."

"The hell it isn't." She held out her hand, hearing the noise of the approaching ATVs like grasping hands clawing over her skin. "Give me the keys to your truck. I can lead them away from the fire tower and your friends. They won't expect you to be on foot, and the two of you can make better time than if I'm carrying her."

He pulled his keys from his pocket, but held them tight in his fist. "You go to the rendezvous. Keir will be there to meet you. I'll play decoy."

"No. Get SueAnn out of here. It takes two people to handle that stretcher and I can't carry her that far. Not fast enough."

"Doc—"

She snatched the keys from his hand and dashed to the front of the truck. "Stop arguing with me! Save her. Get the bad guys. You promised."

Tom was there at the door when she started the engine. "I'll keep that promise. *Everything* I promised." He pulled something else from his pocket and handed it to her through the open window. It was her father's pocket watch. "Your good luck charm."

"Thanks." She stuffed it into her pocket. "You're not going to arrest me for driving without a license, are you?" When he didn't laugh, she turned away to start the engine. She couldn't look at that tight clench of his jaw and know how much he wanted to save her. "I'll be fine. I'll ditch the truck somewhere and hide until they're gone. I've been hiding in these hills for years now."

His big hand reached through the open window to palm the back of her neck. He kissed her, all that emotion on his face branding her with a hard, possessive stamp on her lips. She touched her fingers to his jaw, answering back with the same raw promise before he broke away. "I'm coming back for you. You are not alone in this fight." He caught a lock of her hair between his fingers as he stepped back. "I'll be back for you."

"Tom…"

He squeezed his eyes shut and shook his head as if he didn't want to hear his real name. Then those green eyes popped open. "I love you."

She summoned a croaky whisper that was a stunned mixture of joy, fear and piss-poor timing. "I love you, too."

But Tom and Daryl were already at the back of the truck, lifting SueAnn on the homemade stretcher. He slammed the tailgate as if he'd spanked her bottom, spurring her into action. "Go!"

With the two men moving in a quick march, hauling SueAnn on the blanket between them, Melanie stomped on the accelerator. The truck fishtailed, spitting up twigs and mud until the tires found traction and she sped off around the lake.

FORTY MINUTES LATER, Melanie's thighs ached from maintaining her crouched position up on a wide limb of an ancient pin oak where she'd often come to read as a little girl. The noise of the ATV engines had stopped, and the crackle of walkie-talkie static and men's voices had faded into the distance. Since she hadn't heard any mention of Duff Maynard or Sergeant Loser or some other stupid nickname referring to Tom on the radio, she prayed that meant he'd gotten SueAnn to his brother and a waiting ambulance.

She perched in her hiding spot until the only noise she could hear was the breeze moving through the leaves. Hoping it was safe to make her way back to the fire tower and let Tom know he didn't have to worry about her, she climbed down. It would be a long hike, but she still had a couple of hours of night sky and shadows to hide in before the sun came up. That should give her plenty of time to skirt the compound and avoid company before she ran into the backup Tom had promised.

She hoped Tom was safe. She hoped he loved her enough to take her home to Kansas City to meet the rest of his family. And though in some ways it felt as though she'd be leaving her father behind her, she hoped with every cell of her being that she never had to come back to this beautiful prison of a life.

She allowed herself to finally inhale a deep breath.

And then she heard the unmistakable sound of a gun being cocked behind her. Melanie stopped at the harsh metallic rasp, her hopes washing away with the lake beside her. She slipped her fingers into her pocket to touch her father's watch, reminding herself she wasn't alone.

Henry Fiske was smiling when she turned to face the barrel of his gun. "You've always been trouble, haven't you, girl?"

Chapter Fifteen

Melanie wondered if her father had taken a similar boat ride on board the *Edwina* the night he'd died.

Her uncle steered the *August Moon* over waves that got choppy as they neared the dam. Boating at night without any lights was dangerous, but as she swayed on her seat above the fishing deck, she knew safety wasn't Henry's concern.

She'd forgotten her uncle had grown up in these hills, just like she had. She should have stayed hidden longer. But she had a feeling it would have only been a matter of time before Henry tracked her down and made her pay for her defiance. One thing she hadn't forgotten about her uncle was how much he hated anyone who didn't follow his rules and blindly go along with his plans. But she was past the point of pretending she didn't hate him and what he'd done to control her life. She was only glad that Tom wasn't here, that he'd gotten away, that he would live to destroy the three people on the boat with her.

The two-way radio in the cockpit flared to life with static and the sound of Roy Cassmeyer's voice. "Mr. Fiske? This is Roy. Do you read me? Over." There were a few more seconds of static. "Sir? We've got a situation at the compound. What should I—?"

"Turn that thing off," Abby groused from her seat across from Melanie.

Henry severed the connection and shut off the radio.

Tom and his task force must be the *situation* Roy was dealing with.

Silas jerked the rope he was tying around her wrists. "What are you smilin' about?"

She wouldn't give him the satisfaction of yelping at the pinch of pain. She wouldn't argue against the gun her aunt trained on her while Silas tossed two of the heavy bags of guns overboard. They floated on the surface for a few seconds, but started sinking before the boat left them in its silvery wake and they disappeared into the darkness. That's what was in store for her, too. "Did you kill my father like this?"

Abby reached into a third bag at her feet. "You don't know when to let a thing drop, do you? You're just as stubborn as Leroy was. He wouldn't do what he was told, either." She pulled out Melanie's cell phone and waved it in front of her before tossing it overboard. Melanie heard a splash, but couldn't see much beyond the *Moon*'s shiny white bulwarks. "You went snooping again. And I asked you not to." She kicked the heavy bag toward Silas and ordered him to tie it to Melanie's waist. "Now I have to throw all this merchandise away. Our buyers will be disappointed. But it's better than being put out of business."

If only she knew.

Silas's bruised face hovered in front of her. There was no pretense of politeness when he dragged her to her feet and looped a length of rope behind her, pulling her against him. "Where is your boyfriend? Is he a cop? How long have you been helping him spy on us? We're gonna kill him, too, you know."

"Take your filthy hands off me." Bound, but not defenseless, Melanie sank her teeth into his arm. With a bellowing curse, he drew back to strike her. But she rammed her shoulder into his gut, knocking him off balance. They crashed into the side railing, rocking the boat when they hit. Water splashed over the side, soaking the front of his shirt.

Seeing Silas's stunned look, she thought she'd found her chance to escape. She pulled herself up to the railing. Swimming would be difficult with her limbs tied, but impossible once they tied the heavy weight of the gun bag to her body.

A hard, cold piece of steel pressed into the back of her skull, stopping her. "Sit."

Obeying Abby's gun, Melanie crawled to the stern, finding a place to sit more easily than Silas was finding a way to stand again. While a part of her reveled in his discomfort and the knowledge they hadn't found Tom yet, another part still wanted answers. She looked beyond her aunt and the white-knuckled Silas to Henry. "You said you loved your brother. Did you kill him? Is that why talking about him upsets you?"

Abby sat, keeping the gun trained on her. "*I* killed your father. We wanted to include him in our plans to turn this place into a gold mine. But he was all about living off the land and not wanting anything dangerous to happen around his little girl. We had our own daughter to provide for, and I wasn't about to raise Deanna as some poor, backwater hillbilly." Melanie thought that simple life had been pretty special. "How did Leroy think we were going to get the money to transform this place into what it's become? Selling a few doughnuts and handmade tables? We offered to buy his half, but he refused. When he threatened to report us for having such forward-thinking ideas, he and Henry got into a fight. I had to save my husband's life. I hit him with this very gun." She leaned back, perhaps thinking Melanie would turn submissive with shock or grief and shut up. "With the storm that night, it was easy enough to stage an accident with the *Edwina*."

Coldhearted bitch. For a few seconds, Melanie wondered how well her aunt could swim. "Why spare me? Once I was old enough to understand such things, I could have contested your claim to the land."

"Couldn't kill a child. And why make a fuss? You were happy with us, weren't you?" Until she wasn't anymore. That's why they'd tightened their control of her life. No wonder they'd pressured her to find a man and stay on the farm.

"Your guns kill children." She was beyond feeling pain or regret. "You hired Richard out to kill people. That's what all those disposable phones in the attic were for. Call *Gin Rickey* if you need a job done. Did you kill him, too?"

"Richard got himself into trouble all on his own. When the last client who hired him wasn't satisfied, we agreed to help dispose of the body to assure customer satisfaction, and so he couldn't be traced back to us. We like our privacy here."

"You weren't expecting Roy to snag him with the propeller, were you?" She imagined that discovery had set a whole lot of scrambling to save the family business into motion. "Who hired him?"

"A lot of people. They didn't volunteer the information. Once they paid the fee, I wasn't all that interested in exchanging names."

Silas stumbled to her seat at the back of the boat. He secured her ankles to the bags that would drag her to the bottom of the lake. But Melanie had one last question she needed answered first. "Did any of them hire Richard to shoot up a wedding at a church in Kansas City?"

"Always so many questions. It really is quite tedious, dear. Not a trait that men like."

Henry finally joined the conversation. "I know I'm bored with it." He stopped the engine and let the boat glide to a stop. "We should be in deep-enough water here. Even if you did call the cops on us, girl, they won't find anything. No guns. No witness."

"I guess you're going to die an old maid, after all." Abby nodded to Silas.

Still looking a little queasy, he picked up Melanie and set her on the aft fishing deck.

Once her aunt stopped talking, Melanie heard a different sound. The growl of an engine. Something much bigger than any ATV.

Hope surged through her. She wasn't alone, after all.

"Now!" Henry ordered. "We need to clear this boat."

Silas set the bags on the deck beside her. But when Melanie refused to take that fatal step herself, he pulled his knife. When he thrust it at her, she grabbed his belt and pulled him into the water with her.

Blood filled the water around her as Silas dragged her down into the darkness.

DUFF LOOKED AT the infant sleeping in a blue knit cap in the Saint Luke's Hospital nursery, hoping the fatigue,

fear and coffee churning in his stomach didn't reach his
face and scare the kid. Or the grandparents sliding him
wary looks. Or the nurse he'd snapped at when she'd
asked him to return to the surgical ICU waiting area.
He'd already worn a path in the carpet there, waiting
to hear if Melanie would be downgraded from criti-
cal to stable condition after surgery to repair the lung
Silas Danvers had cut open, trying to save himself from
drowning. He barely remembered the one-sided fire-
fight between Matt Benton and the Fiskes before they'd
surrendered and he'd dived into the lake to save her.

He nodded his acquiescence when a woman in pink
scrubs approached him. "I know. I'll leave."

Duff replayed the words the medics had told him
when he'd finally gotten Melanie on a boat and medeva-
ced her on a helicopter waiting at the Fiske compound.
There were worries about infection from the lake water
that had gotten inside her body, layers of muscle and
skin to repair. A whole lot of blood loss.

He got on the elevator and rode down to the second floor, remembering other things, too. Melanie had
talked a lot at first when he'd pulled her on board the
Ozark Dreamer. She'd tried to tell him how to stanch the
wound, how to relieve the pressure around her collapsed
lung. She'd told him what she'd learned from Henry and
Abby, despite him telling her to shut up and save her
strength. But then she'd stopped talking. His love and
his prayers hadn't been enough to keep her with him.

Keir had driven him to Saint Luke's while Mel was
in surgery. His dad had brought him a change of clothes.
Sleep wasn't really an option until he knew Melanie was
going to wake up and talk to him again.

The elevator opened to the sound of a squealing baby,

and for a split second, he wondered if he'd remembered to push the elevator button. But then he saw the plump, silver-haired woman holding the happy infant, Duff's future nephew, as an eighty-year-old retired cop, standing with the aid of a walker, tickled the infant's tummy.

"Grandpa."

Seamus greeted him with a slurred tone of concern. "Son. How ah you?"

"How are you, old man?" he tried to tease.

"Ah'll hang in there if you will."

Millie Leighter's blue eyes were shiny with tears when she tipped her face up for Duff to kiss her cheek. "We're so worried about you. We're keeping you and Melanie in our prayers."

"Thanks. Any news?"

She shook her head before pressing her cheek to Seamus's shoulder. Seamus patted her arm in comfort. Millie might not be blood, but she was definitely family.

Stopping at the coffee machine to consider another cup, Duff was greeted by Niall's fiancée, Lucy McKane. The petite brunette slipped her arms around his waist and squeezed him in a hug. Her eyes were a little misty, too, when she pulled away. "We're all anxious to meet Melanie. I know we're going to love her as much as you do." She held up the baby bottle in her hand. "I'd better go feed Tommy."

He shouldn't have been surprised to see the rest of his family when he entered the waiting room. Keir and his fiancée, Kenna Parker, were there, sharing a conversation with his grandfather's nurse, Jane Boyle. His sister, Liv, jumped up from her chair and dashed across the room to give him a hug, followed more slowly by her husband, Gabe Knight, with a handshake.

"You know they have the best doctors here," Gabe offered.

"I know."

Liv brushed her short brown bangs off her forehead. "Niall went to the front desk to see if he could talk to the doctor who performed the surgery and give us a report." She squeezed his arm. "Maybe you should try to get some rest?"

With a noncommittal nod, Duff walked on past them to the man he was proud to be a carbon copy of in so many ways. Green eyes, brown hair, stocky build, a badge. He sank into the chair beside his father. Thomas Watson Sr. was a solid, steady presence who thankfully didn't ask him how he was feeling or offer any platitudes. Thomas put his hand on Duff's shoulder and simply sat in silence with him for several minutes.

While he had no doubt of his family's love and support, Duff couldn't help but remember a similar gathering the night his mother had died. They'd rushed her to the hospital, but she'd never had a chance. Duff braced his elbows on his knees and leaned forward. "How did you do it, Dad? How did you survive when the woman you love is… And you can't save her…and…?"

Thomas squeezed his shoulder and nodded to the rest of the room. "I had my family."

Niall strode into the room, with Seamus and Millie and all the others gathering behind him as he crossed to Duff. "Melanie's awake. She came through surgery just fine. She'll be sore for a while, but she's breathing on her own. They've moved her to a private room. You can go see her."

Duff was already on his way.

His only hesitation came when he first pushed open

the door and saw her lying on the hospital bed. With beeping machines, and tubes and needles hooked into her arm, this was a much more modern version of the infirmary she'd built back in her cottage. Tears stung his eyes. She looked so pale except for her rich, beautiful hair, fanned across the pillow like an auburn halo. He was supposed to be so damn tough, the man who could handle whatever was necessary to get a job done. But he was about to stand here and cry like a baby until Melanie blinked her eyes open and smiled.

"I finally made it to Kansas City."

Tom laughed and hurried to her side. He leaned over to kiss her lightly on the forehead, not wanting to do anything that might hurt her. He pulled up a stool to sit as close to her as he dared and captured her hand in both of his. He nodded to the big basket that had been delivered to the table on the opposite side of the bed. "I didn't know what kind of flowers you like, so I got you books. Bought a copy of everything they had down in the hospital gift shop."

Turning her head, she reached over with her taped-up hand to finger the spine of one of the paperbacks. "I love them. I'm going to need a new bookshelf."

"I'll get you one. Whatever it takes to convince you to stay with me."

"To stay…?" He didn't have an engagement ring, but he reached into his pocket for something he thought she'd like better. He pressed her father's watch into her hand. She carried it to her lips before setting it beside her and linking her fingers with his again. "Thank you."

"That was smart to leave it at the boat dock so I knew where to find you. Your dad would have been proud of you."

"Sorry I couldn't find out who hired Richard to shoot your grandfather."

"We'll get him. We're a lot closer to the truth now, thanks to you." He brushed aside a lock of hair that wasn't really out of place. "In the meantime, I'll settle for getting a lot of illegal guns off the street and making my city a little bit safer."

"Silas?"

"Dead. He ran into his knife multiple times. I helped him." He recalled the short fight in the lake vividly. Stopping Danvers for good had been the only way he could get past him to reach Melanie and pull her to safety.

"Henry and Abby?"

"Arrested. Along with Roy, Sterling Cobb and a few others."

"SueAnn?"

Tom grinned. "Boy. Daryl Jr. The doctor delivered him by C-section, so they're staying here a few days longer for observation. But they're both going to be fine."

"You? You look tired."

"Nothing seeing your pretty brown eyes can't fix."

He leaned in to kiss her again, but the door swung open and a parade of well-wishers filed in. Watsons, soon-to-be Watsons, four generations of Watsons—bringing flowers, sharing embarrassing stories about how Tom was on a first-name basis with the ER doctors at Saint Luke's, thanking her for helping with his investigation, inviting her to dinner, inviting her to Niall and Lucy's wedding, wishing her well.

Then, in a flurry of waves and handshakes, Jane Boyle donned her nurse persona, said Melanie needed her rest and shooed them out. The room seemed conspicuously quiet after they'd gone, but his father was right—they'd left a lot of love and support in their wake.

"As you can see, you probably won't ever be alone again if you hang out with me here in KC."

Melanie was smiling right along with him. "Did you mean what you said before? I can stay with you?"

"Didn't I prove I was a man of my word?"

"I never should have doubted you."

"Well, I did lie to you. In the beginning."

"And I was headstrong and independent and refused to use your nickname. I don't know why you ever picked me to help with your mission."

"I picked you because you were headstrong and independent and refused to use my nickname." Tom paused and grinned. "And the red hair." He caught a silky lock between his fingers. "Love the red hair."

Melanie laughed. She instantly grabbed her stomach and grimaced. "That hurts."

Tom shot to his feet. "I'll get a nurse."

She grabbed his hand, stopping him. "I love you, Tom."

He lowered his hip to the edge of her bed. "I love you."

She stroked her fingers across his jaw before cupping his cheek. He knew he needed a shave, but she was smiling. "I like this look even better than date-night Tom."

"What does that mean?"

"I'll explain later. After you kiss me. Lips this time. Like you mean it."

He did.

Epilogue

The unhappy man watched one Watson after another file out of the redhead's hospital room. They were happy, chatting excitedly, sharing relief, making plans.

He'd had a plan, too. One that each of those Watson boys had screwed up in one way or another. He knew they'd suffered. He'd *made* them suffer. And still they hugged and laughed, held hands and smiled. It wasn't fair. The woman he loved couldn't laugh or smile anymore. He couldn't hold her ever again, and it was their fault. It was Thomas Watson's fault.

He waited for them to gather their things and get on the elevator—two elevators since there were so many of them. His pool of contracted help had vanished with the dustup at the Fiske Farm. There was no *Gin Rickey* for him to call anymore. Not that that moron had been able to complete the job the way he'd wanted. He would have to take care of business himself.

While the second group of Watsons waited for the next elevator, he watched the pretty nurse in the blue scrubs separate herself from the others to pull her cell phone from her pocket. She'd been living with them for months now, taking care of the old man, bossing everybody around. He didn't think they liked her much, judging by the arguments that seemed to flare up when she was around, but she must be good at her job if they were keeping her...

Hold on. The woman pressed her hand against her forehead, the conversational tone of her call changing to heated whispers.

And then he saw Thomas's reaction to her distress. That stolen look of concern. That deep breath before he left the group at the elevator to join her.

The man watching would have laughed if he'd been willing to reveal his presence.

Watson was making this too easy. The big papa bear had the hots for the live-in nurse. As he watched Thomas walk over to comfort Ms. Boyle, he knew there was an even better way to make Detective Lieutenant Thomas Watson Sr. pay for his crime. His efforts to destroy the Watson family hadn't worked. But he could still make Thomas pay.

He could hurt the woman he loved...

* * * * *

Look for the thrilling conclusion to
USA TODAY *bestselling author*
Julie Miller's suspenseful series
THE PRECINCT: BACHELORS IN BLUE.

Coming Soon.
Only from Mills & Boon Intrigue.

Join Britain's BIGGEST Romance Book Club

50% OFF your first parcel

- **EXCLUSIVE offers** every month

- **FREE delivery direct** to your door

- **NEVER MISS a title**

- **EARN Bonus Book** points

Call Customer Services

0844 844 1358*

or visit

nillsandboon.co.uk/subscriptions

* This call will cost you 7 pence per minute plus your phone company's price per minute access charge.

MILLS & BOON®
are delighted to support
World Book Night